S0-ARH-207

IF THE WATERGATE COVER-UP HAD SUCCEEDED, WE MAY HAVE HAD...

THE LAST PRESIDENT

SPECIAL
$1.99

by Michael Kurland & S. W. Barton

A CRITIC'S CHOICE PAPERBACK • 1-55547-248-6 • $3.95 (CANADA $4.50)

THE LAST PRESIDENT

Books by Michael Kurland

The Infernal Device

Pluribus

Books by S. W. Barton writing as Bart Whaley

Codeword BARBAROSSA

THE LAST PRESIDENT

by Michael Kurland & S. W. Barton

A BERNARD GEIS ASSOCIATES BOOK

A Critic's Choice paperback
from Lorevan Publishing, Inc.
New York, New York

"You ought to be jailed for speaking against the government!" cried Miss Cannon. "We're living in a democracy!"

—JOHN DICKSON CARR
Below Suspicion

• PROLOGUE
Friday, June 16, 1972

EDWARD ST. YVES put down his binoculars and picked up the phone. He dialed a very private number.

"Yes?" a guarded voice answered.

"This is Barkley," St. Yves said.

"Yes?"

"I'm calling you from the Howard Johnson's motel across the street from the Watergate complex."

"I understand."

"Our men have just come into contact with the local people," St. Yves said.

"Yes? How serious?"

"I don't know. I'm going to clean up here and see what I can do," St. Yves said. "Be prepared for a phone call."

"Me?"

"It may come to that. This must be stopped now. You understand? I'm calling the Company, but they may want someone at the top to verify."

"Okay. Do what you have to. The big man is here. I'll tell him."

"He'll be delighted," St. Yves said, and hung up.

• CHAPTER ONE

THERE IS AN odor unique to police stations. Compounded of sweat, soap, cheap toilet water, machine oil, dried vomitus, stale urine, and the smell of fear, under a thin mask of ammonia cleanser, it is most noticeable early in the morning. At four o'clock this Saturday morning in the Second District Police Station at 2301 L Street, Washington, D.C., it was particularly strong.

Christopher Young carefully adjusted the knot of his black knit tie before pushing through the station's heavy wooden door. As junior officer of the Central Intelligence Agency's Washington domestic operations station, he found himself with erratic regularity in one of the District police stations on Company business. The assignment required a delicate hand, since he had no official status with the police at all. If a couple of Company men were apprehended rifling the safe of some embassy undersecretary, he was to try to get them out. But if a couple of thieves thought it would be useful to tell the arresting officers that they were CIA agents, Kit would be unable to deny the allegation.

Kit walked up to the desk sergeant and laid down his open identification case. "I got a call," he said, stifling a

15

yawn and trying to sound more alert than he felt.

"Right," the desk sergeant said with disinterest. "Five John Does, apprehended at the Watergate complex. They won't say word one about anything. But we got a phone call said you people would be interested." The sergeant reached under his desk and brought out a couple of bulging oversized manila envelopes. "Here's what they had on them," he said, undoing the flaps and letting the contents spill out onto the desk.

Kit stared down at the assortment of burglary tools and photographic and electronic gear. Some of it looked familiar. "They said they were Agency?" he asked.

"They're deaf and dumb," the sergeant said. "We got this phone call said you'd be coming down."

"I wonder who called us?" Kit said. "I'd better talk to them."

The sergeant called upstairs and a man in a cut-off sweat shirt and denims came trotting down to take Kit to the holding tank. "Hi," the man said, sticking out a hand. "I'm Veber, one of the arresting officers."

Kit grabbed the hand and shook it firmly. "Where'd you find them?"

"In the Watergate. Inside the DNC headquarters, as a matter of fact. Night watchman noticed something funny and called in."

"The DNC?"

"Yeah. The Democratic National Committee. What the hell are you people doing in the Democratic Committee?"

"You got me," Kit said. "We don't know yet that they're our people. What did they say when you arrested them?"

Veber shrugged. "Not much. One of them turned around, nice and calm and polite, and said 'Are you gentlemen with the Metropolitan Police?' Didn't seem very excited."

"I can see why he wondered," Kit said.

Veber looked puzzled for a second. "Oh, my hippie

clothes? We're on a special detail. At least we don't have to put dresses on, like those cops in New York. Come on, they're up here."

The holding pen was up one flight of stairs. It held five unruffled, ordinary-looking men in business suits. One of them stood up as Kit approached with Veber. "Hello," he said. "Are you Company?"

Kit looked him over. A short, stocky man with an air of control and competence, he could have been a successful lawyer or a congressional aide, or an FBI special agent or a Company man. Or, for that matter, a clever thief.

"More to the point," Kit said, "who are you?"

"Let me see some ID first," the stocky man said. "I hate repeating myself."

Kit smiled. "Do I look like a cop to you?"

"Do I look like a burglar to you?" the man said without emotion. "Show me a card."

"Give me a name," Kit said.

"Chandler," the man said, naming the Deputy Chief of Station for Washington, and Kit's immediate superior.

Kit pulled out his ID card. "Here."

The man gave it a cursory glance. "Talk to me," he said. "Alone."

Veber shook his head. "Don't mind me."

The stocky man fixed him with a stare. "You don't walk down to the end of the corridor, I don't talk."

"Give me a minute with him," Kit told Veber.

"I guess," Veber said, unconvinced. He retreated to the end of the corridor and turned his back on them, staring out the window at the early morning drizzle.

Kit turned back to the stocky man. "Well?"

The man paused for a minute to select his words. "I'm George Warren," he said. "We are not, at least at this time, with the Company. Not directly."

"What the hell does that mean?" Kit demanded. "Not

17

directly? What the hell did you get me down here for? Who called the Company?"

"I want you to make a phone call for me," Warren said. "That will explain everything."

Kit took a step back away from the cell bars. "You've got to be kidding. Why the hell should I make a phone call for you?"

"Listen to me," Warren said patiently. "Does the number three nine five, three thousand mean anything to you?"

"Three nine—"

"Keep your voice down!" Warren demanded. "Do you know that number?"

"No."

"It's the phone number of the Executive Office of the President in the White House. It's a listed number, you can look it up."

"So?"

"Call it. Ask for extension four nine four. They should be expecting your call by now."

"It's four thirty in the morning," Kit objected.

"Our government is awake twenty-four hours a day," Warren said. "You're here, aren't you?"

"Yeah, okay. I'll call, but this better be straight. What do I tell them?"

"They'll tell you," Warren said. "This is a national security matter, so don't open up to the locals." He indicated Veber with a jerk of his head.

Kit nodded his head slowly. "I'll be back." He walked down the corridor to join Veber.

"Have an exciting talk?" Veber asked, pulling his gaze away from the murk outside.

"It had its points," Kit said. "Where's your phone?"

Veber took him to an office down the hall and, reluctantly, left him. "Yell if you need anything. I'll be just across the way."

"You bet," Kit said, closing the door behind him. He found a District of Columbia Section white pages in the metal cabinet in one corner of the office and turned to UNITED STATES GOVERNMENT. There was an entry for EXECUTIVE OFFICE OF THE PRESIDENT with twelve listings. One of them read: At Night, Saturdays, Sundays & Holidays Call ------395-3000.

He picked up the phone and did just that. It was picked up on the second ring. "Three thousand," a female voice answered.

"Extension four nine four, please," he said.

"One second. It's ringing."

"Hello?" A gruff male voice.

"I'm calling from the Second District Police Station," Kit said carefully. "There is a gentleman in one of the holding cells that suggested I call you."

"I see," the voice at the other end said. "On whose behalf are you making his call?"

"He calls himself Warren," Kit said. "George Warren."

"Yes," the voice said. "What I meant was, do you represent the Metropolitan Police?"

"No."

"Then—who do you represent?"

"To whom am I speaking?" Kit asked. He could see that there was going to be a continuing identification problem.

"I'm an official of the executive branch," the voice said. "I represent the President."

Kit made a quick decision. "I'm an officer of the Central Intelligence Agency, and I'm going to have to know to whom I'm speaking before we proceed."

"Oh," the voice said. "Thank God. We certainly don't want the local police in on this. Now listen, you're speaking to Charles Ober. You know who I am?"

"Yes, sir," Kit said. Everybody in the United States had heard of Uriah "Billy" Vandermeer, the President's Chief

19

of Staff, and Charles Ober, the President's Chief Domestic Affairs Adviser. *The New Yorker* called them the Teutonic Bobbsey Twins, and *Time* referred to them as the Prussian Household Guard. This was inaccurate if not unfair, since Vandermeer's father was Dutch, and Ober was a native American for at least the last four generations. But the wisdom of Washington had it that nobody, not even cabinet officers, got to see the President without first clearing with Billy or Charlie.

"Okay," Ober said. "Now, have these men been, what do they call it, booked? Under what names? Have any of them talked—that is, have they said anything at all?"

"They've all been booked, sir," Kit said. "No names given. Right now they are five John Does. None of them have made any kind of statement to the police."

"Okay. Now, what's the scenario? What happens next?"

"Well," Kit thought for a minute. "Later this morning, they'll be taken to the Fifth Street Courthouse for a preliminary hearing for the purpose of setting bond. The judge probably won't set bond on them unless he has valid names."

"Okay," Ober said. "Well, that's the thing we want to turn off. How do you get them out of that?"

It was not a question Kit had expected to hear. "I can't do that," he said, the abrupt answer pushed out by the surprise of the question. "I mean, I can't just tell the police to let them go."

"Shit!" Ober said. "Look, supposing they were your boys: CIA, Agency, like that. What would you do then?"

"Well," Kit said, "even that's kind of hairy. I can't do anything officially. If the Metropolitan Police want to book anyone at all, for any crime, for whatever reason they have, there's nothing I can do about it. Nothing at all."

"What do you do then?" Ober asked. "What the fuck do we pay you for?" There was a tension in his voice that hadn't been there before; the question was almost a petulant whine.

20

"I work on a sort of unofficial understanding," Kit told him. "Officially I can't admit that any people who are picked up are our people." Kit switched the phone mouthpiece to his other hand. "I suggest to the duty sergeant that the guys in his holding tank are really upright citizens and it would be a shame to charge them. He informally checks with the captain, who agrees that there wouldn't be enough evidence to obtain a conviction, so there's really no point in keeping them, and the charges are informally dropped.

"But what I'm really telling them, and what they're trusting my word on, is that there's some national security consideration in the case."

"I understand that," Ober said. He was back in control again and his voice was smooth. "What did you say your name was?"

"My name is Young," Kit said, refraining from adding that he hadn't said.

"Well, Mr. Young, you've put your finger on it exactly. National security is the issue. The men in that cell are members—I trust in your complete discretion—of a special White House national security unit which undertakes special, highly sensitive problems."

"Like bugging the Democratic National Committee?"

"Exactly!" Ober said, sounding pleased that Kit had brought it up. "Who would you have do that? The FBI? Your people? No—you must stay above anything that could in any way be construed as political. But when we received word that the DNC was, unknowingly, being influenced by money and agents of the People's Republic of Cuba, that had to be checked. Now, I can assure you that it would be in the best interest of your country if the investigation of the break-in were to end here. This is not an attempt to get these men off—any of them would gladly serve prison time in the interest of his country—but we cannot allow the ongoing investigation to be compromised."

Kit slowly shook his head. "There's nothing I can do. Look, Mr. Ober, I'm sure that what you're telling me is true, but I have no authority to take action on behalf of these men. You get hold of my superior and have him call me and authorize this action, and I'll use my best influence and see what I can do."

"Your superior! How the hell— Wait a minute! Will you hold?" Without waiting for Kit's assurance, Ober put the phone on hold, leaving Kit listening to that curious hollow sound of miles of phone wire connected only to itself.

Kit leaned back in the chair with the phone cradled against his shoulder and put his feet up on the desk. For a few minutes he stared at the ceiling, trying to make some sense of the great Rorschach of cracked and blotched green paint. Then, realizing that this was slowly putting him to sleep, he turned to read the notices on the bulletin board.

"Hello?"

Kit sat up, almost dropping the phone. He grabbed for it with both hands and restored it to his ear. This was someone new. "Hello."

"You recognize my voice?"

It wasn't Ober, and it wasn't Chandler. "No," Kit said.

"This is the President speaking," the voice said.

"Yes, sir." Kit took his feet down from the desk. "I wasn't expecting—"

"You recognize my voice?" A flat, emotionless question.

"Yes, sir." Kit did, now.

"I am your Commander in Chief," the President said.

"Yes, sir." Not technically accurate, since the CIA wasn't part of the military, but the President was certainly Kit's ultimate boss.

"I give you my personal assurance, as President, that what Charles Ober has told you in regard to these five men is accurate, and that it is a matter of national security to get them the hell out of that jail. You got that?"

"Yes, sir."

"Yeah. And as President, as your Commander in Chief, I give you a direct order to see that those five men are released. And for God's sake, don't let any of those media bastards hear anything about this. Right?"

"Right. Yes, sir."

"Now, you've got the ball—run with it! Your President's depending on you." There was a click and the phone went dead.

Kit spent a minute staring into space. He had no option except to believe Ober's—and the President's—word that national security was involved. If only it weren't the Democratic National Committee. If word of this did get out, and it was discovered that CIA had claimed the burglars as their own, it would be embarrassing for the Company. And Kit's superiors would see that all the embarrassment came down onto his own shoulders.

Clearly, if Kit was going to do this at all, he'd better do it right. He'd have to speak to everyone involved: the arresting officers, the duty sergeant, and anyone else who had dealt with the five John Does, and impress on them the value of having a short memory.

Veber came into the office. "You look thoughtful," he said.

Kit nodded. "I just spoke to my boss."

• • •

THE OVAL OFFICE, June 18, 1972 (5:24–6:17 P.M.)

MEETING: The President, Vandermeer, and Ober.

AUTHORIZED TRANSCRIPTION FROM THE EXECUTIVE ARCHIVES

Following a discussion of election campaign strategy, Billy Vandermeer raises the matter of the flap at the Watergate complex.

V. It is late but I hope, sir, we can turn briefly to that little problem area that came up yesterday. The matter that Charlie had to wake you up for.

P. Yeah. Must have been four in the morning. But I have no complaints. You handled it fine, Charlie.

O. Thank you, sir.

V. Ed St. Yves, too. He has a good head on his shoulders. He got it all buttoned up and under control right away. This could have been damn serious.

P. We put it on the line, didn't we? I mean, with me on the phone. We let it all hang out. A great defensive play. Blam, right on the receiver with no yardage gained. But we sold it, didn't we?

O. Yes. The five were released with nobody taking a second look. And that CIA liaison guy came through for us. The kid could have kicked this whole thing right up to his bosses at Langley. Instead, he accepted your direct authority as Commander in Chief.

P. Right. Good guy.

V. But you know damn well that he's going to cover his ass. He's probably typing his report out right now—in triplicate.

O. Billy, we always knew that it's only a matter of time before the Director gets wise to the SIU.* Hell, he's already got it roughed out.

V. Sure, but a botched bag job like yesterday is just the ammo he needs to move to eliminate SIU.

V. Yeah. Well, we don't want to give the Director a handle. And we might want a dependable pipeline into the Agency. So I suggest we use what we're given.

P. Okay. What's the game plan?

V. We transfer Christopher Young to the White House Staff—immediately. He's proved his loyalty to the presidency. We reward him now. Make him White House Liaison to the Intelligence Community: CIA, Defense Intelligence, like that. That way he's rewarded and CIA's signaled off. Besides, Young is

---

* Special Investigations Unit.

the perfect tripwire if—or maybe I should say when—CIA takes to snooping around the White House.

P. Great! Don't you agree, Charlie?

O. That might play.

* * *

The clock by Kit's bed said four fifteen when he woke up. For a second he had that curious sense of disorientation that attacks people with erratic sleep schedules: he didn't know whether it was four fifteen in the morning or afternoon. Lifting his blinds, he stared out at the gray Washington sky. Afternoon. That made it Sunday. That meant he hadn't slept through his date with Miriam. He had a full fifteen minutes to pick her up at her apartment in Georgetown. Cursing the selective deafness that enabled him to sleep through every alarm in every clock ever made, he rolled out of bed and staggered into the shower.

He was only half an hour late. Miriam was on the steps of her red brick building waiting for him, trying not to look annoyed, the wind playing games with her long brown hair.

"The traffic—" he said.

"Bullshit!" she replied, not looking at him.

"Okay, I overslept. It just feels so damn silly saying 'I overslept' at five in the evening." He pulled her toward him to kiss her. After a moment's stubborn resistance, she yielded and returned the kiss with sudden warmth.

"I *am* very fond of you, you know. If you'd grow your hair longer, I'd run my fingers through it. And if you'd get a normal job and work normal hours, you'd be able to keep your social engagements."

"I like my job," he told her. "Excitement, danger, romance, far-off places, angry women . . . Are we going to Aaron's?"

"Right," she said. "My car or yours, as the actress said to the bishop?"

"Yours," Kit said. He gave Miriam a last hug and they

25

started, hand in hand, for her parking space. "And you drive. It's not fit work for a man. I almost killed myself twice getting over here."

"Sleep-driving is a special skill," Miriam agreed, unlocking the passenger-side door of her Volkswagen and starting around. Kit watched Miriam as she climbed in beside him, and once again he wondered at the providence that had brought her into his life. They had met at one of Aaron B. Adams' small dinner parties three years before. Professor Adams had seated his newest assistant professor, Ms. Miriam Kassel, campus liberal, next to Christopher Young, Jr., CIA, apolitical conservative, and then sat back to watch. They disagreed on just about everything political, and somehow they were unable to talk about anything but politics. Kit's worst moment had come when, in exasperation, he had admitted that actually he just didn't care much one way or the other about politics. Miriam had exploded and told him that not caring was a worse moral crime than being wrong.

But somehow Kit and Miriam had found, without discussing it, that there was something pulling them together that made all the arguments about politics worthwhile, that made the times when they didn't argue sweeter and fuller and more beautiful than either of them had known before.

"That strange buzzing in your ears," Miriam said sweetly, "won't stop unless you buckle your seat belt. Not that I'm trying to influence your actions."

"Oh. Sorry." Kit buckled the belt. "You know, actually, I have a very good job. It keeps me here near you. I could have been assigned to Saigon or Pnom Penh or one of those other resort areas where the natives spend their spare time taking potshots at American civilians."

"They only acquired the habit because American soldiers spend so much time shooting at them," Miriam said.

"Oops," Kit said. "I'm sorry; I shouldn't have mentioned it. I just wish you wouldn't take your gripes against the

26

policies of this administration out on me. I'm merely a minor bureaucrat. My job is to report facts, not to decide what's done with them. I just work for the government."

"The CIA," Miriam said.

"Intelligence-gathering is not a more intrinsically evil profession than college teaching."

"If the CIA's only activity were intelligence gathering, I wouldn't say a word. "But both you and I know that isn't so. You must know it far better than I."

"Please get that pedantic tone out of your voice," Kit said. "I'm sorry I can't discuss the inner policy-making of the Agency with you, but I'm far too junior for anyone to ever discuss it with me. Technically I'm not even supposed to admit to you that I'm CIA."

"Come on," Miriam said. "When Aaron first introduced us he told me you were CIA. It must be a very open secret."

"Professor Adams is part of what we call the old-boy network. He was in OSS with a lot of people very high up in the Agency now, including my present boss. But since he's retired from the, ah, government service, he's assumed the right to discuss many things that we GS types aren't supposed to talk about—including my work."

"What's your point?" Miriam asked.

"My only point is that, since I'm not allowed to discuss my work, it isn't fair for you to take potshots at it—or me."

"Bang," Miriam said. "A potshot's better than a bullet any day."

"Listen, I agree with you," Kit said. "I think the war is a mess and it's being handled all wrong."

"Yes, but you also think they ought to go over there and beat the shit out of those nasty North Vietnamese," Miriam said. "Bomb 'em back to the stone age."

"Damn right," Kit said as a way of ending the discussion. And it did. Miriam sulked the rest of the way over to Professor Adams' Chevy Chase estate.

* * *

Professor Aaron B. Adams did not maintain his three-story stone house with swimming pool and guest cottage, along with its two acres of very subdividable land, on the salary of a tenured professor in Georgetown University's department of government and political science. Not even when that was added to his retirement pay from the various secret branches of the government he had served in. Had it not been for an obscure Adams ancestor somewhere—*after* the two who had been impecunious but honorable Presidents—who had gone into business in Boston importing Japanese habutae silk and had later expanded into mother-of-pearl buttons, Professor Adams could not even have afforded the guest cottage.

Of course, as Professor Adams himself liked to say, his fondness for money was such that, had he not inherited it, he probably would have occupied himself with making it. In which case the United States would have lost a brilliant intelligence officer and Aaron B. Adams would have led a much duller life.

Miriam parked behind the four other cars in the driveway, groped in the back seat for a large straw tote bag, and preceded Kit into the house. Neither residents nor guests were in evidence as they crossed through the huge living room and through the open French windows to the cabaña area next to the pool, which was one of the most imposing features of the Adams house.

Even compared to the house and grounds surrounding it, the pool was large. The previous owner of the house had been told by a mystic that his son was going to be an Olympic swimmer, so he built a full Olympic pool for him to practice in. This was in 1932 when labor was cheap and Sonny was five years old. Thirteen years later, after paying a lot of money to get his son cleared of charges of draft evasion, the father closed the house and moved back to Iowa.

For nine years, the house and the pool lay vacant. Then Adams bought it at auction and moved in, lock, stock, and unwritten memoirs. After two years of starting his memoirs, Adams decided he was too young for such nonsense and took a part-time teaching position at Georgetown. "You understand this is only temporary," they told him. "Suits me," he said.

In his spare time he taught a couple of courses for the newly formed CIA, at the behest of some of his old OSS buddies. He tried to give a sense of historical perspective to the business of espionage, and found himself fighting a growing trend to rely less upon men and more upon gadgets. Gradually his job at the university grew into a full-time position. Then he was offered a full professorship with tenure, and discovered that he had become an academic.

Adams was pushing himself out of the pool as they approached. A short, compact man, he looked in very good shape for his fifty-plus years. "Welcome," he said, shielding his eyes against the sun to stare up at them. "What's up? Have you got suits, or do you need loaners?"

Miriam held up the straw tote bag. "Still in here from the last time," she said. "As a matter of fact, I forgot to take them out."

"Probably mildewed," Kit said, "and we'll come down with some exotic form of crotch rot. But we'll make do."

Adams nodded thoughtfully. "Togetherness, even in vulgarity. This here modern generation shows promise, as Plato once said. Pick a cabaña and change. Gerald is inside somewhere decanting for the other guests"—he indicated an assortment of the usual academic and government types scattered about the pool area with a wave of his hand—"and if you'll indicate a preference, I'll have him deal you in."

Gerald was a middle-aged war orphan whom Adams had picked up in one of his trips to occupied Europe during "the Big One," World War II. It was believed that Gerald could not speak; it was certain that he did not. He could, however, understand in almost every language. He served Adams as a sort of majordomo and secretary.

"Coffee," Kit said.

"If you could have him mix me a Bloody Mary," Miriam said, "I'd appreciate it."

"Whatever you appreciate," Adams said, "I arrange." He did his best to affect a lecherous leer.

"If you weren't the head of my department, I'd tell you what you look like when you do that. And to hell with your togetherness!" And she turned around and strode toward a cabaña.

"An abrupt mood change," Adams commented, pushing himself to his feet and heading toward the poolside intercom.

"Women," Kit said, shaking his head sadly in an exaggerated gesture of compassion. "Unstable."

"I understand they make the best mothers," Adams said. "I myself have attempted to make an occasional mother, with varying degrees of success."

"How'd you like to have a talk with me for a few minutes?" Kit asked. "After I change into my suit, so it doesn't attract attention poolside."

"We can wander off and look at my petunias," Adams said. "By the way, when you encounter Miriam in the cabaña, see if you can find out what she thinks I look like when I do that," he added, once more composing his face into a leer.

"Fair enough," Kit said, and headed off to change and talk to Miriam.

"Groucho Marx," he said when he returned in his navy-blue swim trunks.

"Exactly the effect I was trying for," Adams said. "The two heroes of my youth were Groucho Marx and Krazy Kat.

30

I've given up trying to look like Krazy Kat. Are you and Miriam having a fight?"

"Not about anything important," Kit said. "Only about my job and politics."

"That's good," Adams said. "I was afraid it was over food or sex or something important. I like you both, and I'd hate having to see you on alternate weeks. You'd never have stood a chance with Miriam in the first place if I hadn't thought it destructive of departmental morale to make passes at assistant professors."

"I know," Kit said, "and I appreciate that."

They walked over to what Adams referred to as the "more or less formal garden" on the east side of the house, and stood staring at the carefully sculptured rows of varicolored blooms.

"It's about the job," Kit said.

"I assumed," Adams told him. "Who else can you talk to about the Company but an old lag like me?"

"A strange thing happened to me yesterday," Kit said. "And it doesn't exactly involve the Company."

"Tell me about it," Adams said, looking interested.

Kit described the trip to the police station in the early morning, the events leading up to the phone call, and the call itself.

"So you got them off," Adams said.

"Yes. I don't know whether I was right or wrong, but I couldn't see that I had any choice." He picked up a twig and broke it between his fingers. "What do you think?"

"There are several interesting possibilities that present themselves," Adams said. He ticked them off on his fingers. "One: it may not have been the President, or even the White House, you spoke to."

"What?" Kit looked startled. "I hadn't thought of that! How—"

31

"Easy," Adams said. "According to prearranged plan, in case they get caught they tell the police to call you, and then they tell you to call the White House. Meanwhile, under the street by the police station, a henchman is splicing the phone wire and practicing his imitation of that famous presidential voice."

"Son of a bitch!" Kit said.

"Two," Adams said, "it *was* Ober and the President, and everything they told you was completely true."

"I vote for two," Kit said.

"Three," Adams said, "it was Ober and the President, but the whole story was a complete fabrication. Which would imply that a group of common criminals have something so serious on the White House that they can make the President and his chief domestic adviser lie for them.

"Four: The President of the United States, for purely political motives, had his agents burglarizing and bugging the offices of the Democratic National Committee.

"Five: Ober was doing it without the President's knowledge or consent, but was able to get him to agree to cover it up."

"I don't like any of those but two," Kit said. "I've been mulling over variants of three, four, and five all day while I typed out my report."

"Your response was completely correct in any of those scenarios except one," Adams said. "And if the President tells you to do something that's proper to do, then it's your job to do it. I agree that option one isn't very likely."

"You think it's proper of me to help get off his men if what they were doing was actually a burglary for political motives?"

"If you knew that for sure," Adams said, "then no."

"What you're saying is that the President's motives are none of my concern, is that right?"

"Not at all. What I'm saying is that it is not your privilege to guess at the President's motives. It is, however, your job to make a full report of this to your superiors and let them evaluate the President's motives and what to do about them."

"I'm doing that. But I'd really like to figure this out, for my own sake. None of it really makes sense. Cubans infiltrating the Democrats?"

"I doubt that," Adams said. "But I'm quite willing to believe that the President of the United States *thinks* there are Communist agents secretly supporting the party that's trying to oust him—implacable enemy of communism that he is. The man doesn't seem to trust anyone."

"Don't you think it could have been just a political move?"

Adams shrugged. "Sure," he said. "But that's the most stupid of the possibilities. Any professional intelligence officer would have assessed the gain against the possible damage and dropped the idea. If you get caught you could blow the whole campaign, and if you don't get caught, what can you learn? Where the next pep rally is going to be held? No, if I had to vote, I'd go with the President's paranoia."

"But you think I did right in going along with it?"

"I'm not going to give you right or wrong," Adams said, "but you did what you had to do. You had no acceptable choice."

Kit nodded. "But it's nice to hear someone else say it."

Adams looked up at the gathering clouds for a moment, "I'll tell you something else."

"What's that?"

"Be prepared for a sudden job offer from the White House."

"What kind?"

"I don't know, but it will either be in the Executive Office Building or in Antarctica. And listen—either way, keep in touch."

PRESIDENT REELECTED
LANDSLIDE 61% MAJORITY
CARRIES EVERY STATE BUT MASSACHUSETTS:
FAILS TO CARRY DISTRICT OF COLUMBIA

—*Washington Post*,
November 8, 1972

• CHAPTER TWO

CHARLIE OBER ran his staff meetings like a Prussian officer. When he was at UCLA he'd taken a course in European History in the Nineteenth Century, and *The Prussian General Staff* had been required reading. The description of the orderly, Spartan existence of the Prussian officer had touched Ober somewhere deep in his soul. He joined ROTC, but found them too namby-pamby and disorganized, so he dropped out six months later.

The advertising agency he'd worked for after graduation had frowned on Prussian tactics in the office, but these government types almost seemed to expect it. They lined up docilely in the rows of seats in front of his desk, waited quietly for him to come in, stood as he entered, and otherwise behaved as subordinates should. It was very gratifying to see how effective his methods of office management were.

They watched without expression as he marched across to his desk, his broad but trim frame held in military fashion, his dark, thinning hair slicked back against his skull. It never occurred to Charlie Ober that his childish tantrums when thwarted, along with his absolute power over his subordinates' jobs, might have something to do with their attitude.

"The President wants to start this term with a clean slate," Ober told the mass of faces of the assembled executive staff staring up at him like pink raisins in a pudding. And a token black raisin. "So he wants us all to hand in our resignations."

There was a murmur of surprised protest from the raisins.

"Now, if we've done good jobs, and I'm sure all of us have, then this will just be *pro forma*. The President will spend a week or two going over all the resignations, and refusing to accept those of persons he's happy with. He'd appreciate a short paper with your resignation telling him why you should have your job back. You know—what you've done while in the office, why the office itself shouldn't be abolished."

A young staffer stood up. Ober didn't remember his name. "You mean we work our asses off getting the President reelected, and for the next two weeks we won't know whether we get to keep our jobs? That doesn't seem fair. Why doesn't he just ask for the resignations of those he's not satisfied with? Why make the whole staff go through this?"

Ober leaned forward, his palms down on the desk, and memorized the young man's face. "It's not just the executive staff," he told them. "Everyone in an appointive office anywhere in the country is being asked the same as we are. It's to show the voters that they're going to get a new beginning. 'A new beginning' is the phrase we've picked for the first year of this term. We might even get a couple of extra bills through the Democrat Congress on the strength of that phrase alone. But we have to do something to make it look like more than hollow words. This is part of that something. Do you understand?"

36

Ober looked around, seeing dismay on some faces, dogged acceptance on others. His foot tapped a disjointed rhythm behind the desk, in an unseen but habitual accompaniment to the thoughts on his mind. There was Coles, whose resignation would be accepted with little regret: a man who didn't know the meaning of the word loyalty. Bender, in the corner, would be left to sweat it out for an extra week and ponder the significance of Ober's words.

"Those of you who have been loyal to the President," Ober said, "have nothing to fear. But loyalty must come first, even before our jobs. If it was in the President's best interest for me to quit my job, I'd resign tomorrow."

Teaseman stood up now, at Ober's nod. "I've prepared a model resignation form we can all follow," the stout man from Press Relations said. "Of course, for your job description and accomplishments in office you're, heh heh, on your own." He sat back down.

"Any questions?" Ober asked.

"Whose bright idea was this?" That was Barry Coles, puffing on his unlighted pipe.

Ober drew his tight lips apart in a smile. "We may all give suggestions and ideas to the President," he said, "but the decisions are his alone." *And I'm going to enjoy putting it to you, you insubordinate son of a bitch!*

Sten Craig, Ober's aide, raised his hand, and Ober nodded to him. "What are the legal implications of this, jobwise?" Craig asked. "Like, what happens to seniority and benefits if you put in your resignation?"

A perfect question, perfectly timed. That should get their minds off the moral aspects of this thing. Hit 'em in the job if you want to get their attention. Ober had been proud of the question from the moment he thought it up two hours earlier. "The resignation will not affect job benefits," he said. "Unless, of course, it's accepted. And I'm sure none of us in here have to worry about that."

The thin smile came on his face again. "Let's have them in to the Oval Office by Monday morning, okay, fellows?"

It was early Thursday afternoon when Kit got back to his office in the Executive Office Building, having spent the morning at a CIA briefing.

Barry Coles had the next office. A thin, ascetic Columbia economics professor who had been brought into the administration as a token Eastern intellectual, he spent most of his time puffing on his pipe, reading airmail editions of British magazines, and preparing position papers that disappeared, unread, into the files.

Now he was methodically packing up the belongings in his desk. "I hate to part with the electric stapler," he said, waving the device at Kit as he paused in the door. "I feel as though it's grown to be a part of me, and I part of it."

"You could claim it followed you home," Kit said. "What happened, you finally quit?"

"I hand in my papers with the rest of the herd," Coles said, "fully expecting to be—I think the expression is 'culled.'"

"What papers?"

"You don't know? Where've you been this morning? We've all been requested to hand in our resignations. Part of the President's 'New Broom—Clean Sweep' program. They will not, of course, be accepted. Except in a few cases—like mine."

"You think this is all one of Charlie Ober's machinations?"

"It has all his earmarks, doesn't it? Little sneaky move that looks good till you get up close to it. You want to see my resignation?" He pulled a paper off his desk.

"Sure."

"Here. They gave us a form to follow, but it was a

puling, mealymouthed sort of resignation, not the direct ballsy resignation that the public has a right to expect from their servants." He handed it to Kit, who read it with amused interest.

From: Barry Coles, Ph.D.
             Adviser on Economic Affairs, Foreign
               Department of International Trade
             The Executive Office Building
To: President, the United States
Subject: Resignation

    I resign.
    Sincerely yours,

                        Barry Coles, Ph.D.

ACCOMPLISHMENTS WHILE IN OFFICE:
Papers produced: 37
Papers acted on by executive branch: None
Papers read by executive branch: None
Score: 0 for 37

"I think I'll follow the standard form," Kit said, handing the documents back. "One gets the feeling you haven't been completely happy here."

"It's been invaluable for me," Barry told him. "But I can't say I see what they've gotten out of it."

"What was its value to you?"

"It's impossible to really know about government until you are one," Barry said. "Even ignored as I am in this little office, I'm closer to the center of power than I will ever be again. There's a certain exhilaration in being on the inside. Don't you ever feel it?"

Kit shook his head. "Not me. I'm nothing but a highly paid messenger boy. It was much more exciting over at the Agency before I accepted the President's shilling."

"You mean the Department of Agriculture, don't you?" Coles asked, smiling.

"Sure do," Kit said. "You know, there's nothing stranger looking in this government than a document with a cover sheet stamped 'Department of Agriculture—Top Secret.' Are you going to be happy back at Columbia? Where all you can do is teach about government instead of being one?"

"Home, as a wise man once said, is where they have to take you in. At Columbia I've got tenure. Here, all I've got is heartache. I understand that in previous administrations the Presidents used to listen to the people they hired to give them advice. They wouldn't often do anything about it, but at least they *listened*."

"It does seem as though many of us are here more for show than substance."

"Why are you here?" Barry asked.

"I ask myself," Kit said. "They offered me the job because I did them a favor, but why I took it . . . I suppose it was something of the feeling of getting closer to the center of power. And a feeling that it might be good for my career. When I go back to the Agency, I may skip a few grades."

"Well, be careful of this president," Barry Coles said. "You have no control over his actions, but the same brush can give you a good coat of tar. If these advisers of his take him too far down the wrong path, don't get dragged along."

"You've been soured," Kit told him.

"I," Coles said, "am naturally sour. What I've been is sobered. Come look me up in New York."

"You have my word."

The phone in Kit's office buzzed, so Kit gave Coles a quick handshake and dashed over to pick it up.

"Mr. Young?" the operator's nasal voice asked.

"That's right."

"There's a Mr. Schuster down here to see you. Shall I send him up?"

"Mr. Schuster?"

"That's right. He's with the *Washington Post*."

"Oh." What the hell could the *Post* want with him? "Sure, send him up." He couldn't talk about his job—not that there was anything to talk about—but refusing to see the *Post* man would give the appearance of having something to hide. Not telling him anything would merely make Kit seem like a normal bureaucrat.

After a few minutes, a slight young man with a prominent nose appeared at Kit's door. He had on a raincoat at least two sizes too big for him and a fedora that must have been his father's. A cigarette dangled from his lips. "Mr. Young?"

"That's right," Kit said, getting up. "Mr. Schuster?"

"Right. I'm a reporter for the *Washington Post*. Do you mind if I ask you a few questions?"

"Have you any identification?" Kit asked. The question was reflex.

"Right. Here." The young man pulled cards from his wallet that showed him to be Ralph Schuster, 28, of the *Washington Post* city desk. He had a District of Columbia Police press pass and a congressional press pass to go along with his D.C. driver's license. The three photographs on the documents showed that he varied between sporting a beard and going clean-shaven. At the moment he was clean of face.

"Okay," Kit said, handing the cards back. He waved Schuster to a chair and flopped back into his own. "You can ask whatever you like. You understand that I reserve the right not to answer."

"Of course," Schuster said. "Is it true that you're the

White House Liaison for Intelligence Matters?"

"That's what it says on the organizational charts."

"Is it true that you moved into this job on the nineteenth of June?"

"I think that's also a matter of public record," Kit said. "Why?"

"Mr. Young, I want you to help me. Anything you can say will be of help, either on or off the record. Your confidentiality will be completely respected."

Kit leaned back. "What are we talking about?"

"Let me lay my cards on the table," Schuster said. "Here's what I've got: On the night of the sixteenth of June the offices of the Democratic National Committee in the Watergate Towers were burglarized by five men. They were arrested in the offices by plainclothes officers of the Metropolitan Police. A camera was left behind when they were removed. The film in that camera had not yet been exposed. The men were released at the request of the CIA, and the operation was hushed up to the extent that the boys of the DNC didn't even find out that the men had been arrested. DNC was told that they were apprehended in the building but released at that time for lack of evidence, whereas actually they were taken to the station house and booked before they were released.

"I traced the camera back by its serial number. It was one of several purchased by the Fleming Importing Company, which a cursory check showed to be a CIA front operation.

"You were the CIA man on duty at the Washington DOD desk that night. You were called to the police station. You met with the men. You made a mysterious phone call. The men were then released. Two days later you suddenly take a job with the White House."

Schuster paused and lit a fresh cigarette from the stub of his last. Then he crushed the stub out in the glass ashtray on Kit's desk. "That's what I've got," he said.

Kit stared at him. "That was five months ago," he said finally. "Isn't that a long time to be following up a minor burglary?"

"That's the trouble," Schuster said. "I've been doing this pretty much on my own time. The city editor thinks it's a minor story, too. I don't. I smell something big in it. I'm learning to trust my nose, and, Mr. Young, this story smells. What do you think, Mr. Young? Was it a minor burglary? Who were the five John Does, Mr. Young? What were they after in the DNC headquarters?"

"You put me in a difficult position, Mr. Schuster," Kit said. "As you must know, I can neither confirm nor deny any part of your story. I do have a job in the Executive Office. So do about two thousand other people. I did come from another branch of government; so did most of them. I did come to work on a certain date, two days after an event you claim happened. I'm sure that most of the other people here come to work within a day or two of something significant happening somewhere."

"You could deny my story, Mr. Young," Schuster said. "If you wanted to, you could deny it. If it wasn't true. If any part of it isn't true, you could deny that part. Supposing I go over it again, point by point, and if there's any part of it you'd like to deny, stop me when I reach that point. Okay?"

Kit laughed. "I can't do that. I'm sorry, Mr. Schuster, but I have nothing to say on that subject."

"Right," Schuster said. He stood up and pulled a card case out of his jacket pocket. "Here's my card," he said, extracting one from the case. He scribbled on it with a ballpoint. "That's my home phone, if you want to get me direct for any reason. You can leave messages at the *Post* number anytime—twenty-four hours. Thank you for talking to me." He flipped the card onto the desk.

"I wish I could help you," Kit said.

"I can wait," Schuster said. "Five months already, like you said." He left the office and strode down the hall, his oversized raincoat flapping almost to his ankles.

• CHAPTER
  THREE

RALPH SCHUSTER didn't approve, and the expression on his face showed it. Here he was standing in the middle of the third level of a parking garage in downtown Washington at three o'clock in the morning feeling like a jackass—and probably looking like a sneak thief if the security man should happen to drive by. And whoever he was supposed to meet was nowhere in sight.

Mysterious phone calls from husky-voiced women might lead to clandestine meetings—indeed, should lead to clandestine meetings—but not in the middle of a for-Christ's-sake parking garage.

A pencil flashlight blinked briefly at him from inside one of the three cars on the floor: a late-model gray Chevy. He walked over to it and peered in through the windshield. There was a woman in a gray coat behind the wheel, and she motioned him into the passenger's seat.

Schuster climbed into the seat and closed the door. He noticed that the interior light didn't go on when the door was open. The woman immediately reached over him and pushed down the locking button.

"What's this all about?" Schuster said. "Why the melodrama?" There wasn't enough light for him to get a good look at the woman. He had an impression of a thin, angular face of indeterminate middle age.

"This isn't a joke, Mr. Schuster," she said in a husky whisper. She turned to look at him. "I'm neither melodramatic nor paranoid. You must believe that if you wish to ever see me again."

"You haven't told me yet why I want to see you at all," he said.

"First the ground rules," she said. "You're not taping this, are you?"

"No."

"Good. Rule one: Don't ever tape our meetings. And don't ever take notes until you get home."

"No notes?"

"That's right."

"Lady, I'm a reporter. It's my job to take notes."

"And you have to swear to me that you'll never reveal your source to anyone, from your girl friend to your city editor. *Anyone.*"

"Why all the secrecy?" he asked. "What are we talking about?"

"Do you agree?"

He thought about it for a moment. "Of course," he said. "Yes. If it's worthwhile. Otherwise I'll just forget I ever saw you."

"You will never forget," she said.

"Okay," he said. "What are we talking about?"

"We're talking about malfeasance in high places," she said. "We're talking about first-degree felonies, including burglary, arson, wiretap, bribery, and conspiracy to commit kidnapping and extortion. All conducted out of the Executive Office Building at the direct order of the President of the United States."

Schuster stretched his feet out and leaned back. "Go on," he said.

PRESIDENT ANNOUNCES NEW
3-MAN SUPERCABINET

OBER—VANDERMEER—GILDRUSS

Friday, January 5, 1973, special to the Washington Post
In a surprise news conference in the Oval Office this morning, the President announced the appointments of Charles Ober, Uriah Vandermeer, and Dr. Peter Gildruss as the three chief officers in a new "Supercabinet" to oversee the executive branch of the government.

"The reorganization," the President said, "will be along the guidelines set up in a report by the President's Advisory Council on Executive Organization, a group that has been working on the problem for the past four years.

"In general terms," the President added, "the three offices will be chairman of the Domestic Council, who will have charge of the formation and implementing of domestic policy, the chief of the Office of Management and the Budget, who will, among other things, oversee Congress's attempts to spend the taxpayers' money, and the head of the newly formed Foreign Advisory Council."

The President named Uriah Vandermeer, his chief aide, to head the Domestic Council, Charles Ober to oversee the OMB, and Dr. Peter Gildruss to head the Foreign Advisory Council.

WATERGATE CAMERA TRACED TO WHITE
HOUSE; POLICE SOURCE REVEALS CIA
INVOLVEMENT
BY RALPH SCHUSTER

Washington, Friday, January 5—A Leica camera left behind by five burglars who entered the Democratic National Committee headquarters in the Watergate complex last June 16 has been traced to a staff member of the White House Executive Department, a highly placed government source revealed today.

The camera's serial number has been traced back to the Flem-

47

ing Importing Company, reportedly a Central Intelligence Agency front organization in New York. According to a confidential source, CIA records show that the camera was borrowed, along with other equipment, by a member of the White House staff two days before the robbery.

The five burglars were actually arrested while still inside the Watergate Complex, but they were subsequently released and their booking record was destroyed. An official of the Metropolitan Police confirms that pressure was brought on the arresting officers by the CIA to effect the release of the five men.

The burglars were apparently interrupted before they could accomplish their goal, still undetermined. A roll of film found in the camera had not been exposed.

A White House spokesman, when questioned about the alleged connection, denied any knowledge or involvement of the White House in this "second-rate burglary attempt." The Central Intelligence Agency declined comment.

• CHAPTER FOUR

EDWARD ST. YVES' appearance revealed nothing about the inner man. Not that he was nondescript. He was, if anything, too descript. His light-brown hair was kept closely and meticulously cropped, and massaged several times a day with a pair of military brushes. His angular face was well tanned except for the thin white line of an ancient scar running under his right eye. His mustache was neat and thin, and looked as though each hair had been carefully ironed into place. From a distance he gave the illusion of being quite tall, although he was of average height.

He seemed to have complete run of the White House and the Executive Office Building, although few people in the EOB knew precisely what he did. He was liable to show up at any office at any time and make some strange request of its occupant. If the requests were checked, they were always found to have been approved from on high, although he never cited higher authority but merely demanded what he demanded as though it were the most natural thing in the world.

It was Kit's first day back at the job after a two-week trip to Maine with Miriam, where they had holed up in her parents' summer cabin. St. Yves appeared at the door to Kit's office on the second floor of the EOB shortly after ten o'clock. "You Kit Young?" he asked.

"That's right," Kit said.

"I'm St. Yves. You free for lunch?" He barked out the question and stared intently at Kit, waiting for the answer.

"Yes," Kit said.

"Good. We'll eat together. I'll buy. Things to talk about. Pick me up at my office at twelve thirty. Room sixteen."

"I know."

"Course you do. Twelve thirty." And with a curt nod, he strode off down the corridor.

Which left Kit with a shade over two hours to catch up with all the scut work that no one else had bothered to do in his absence, and wonder what the hell St. Yves wanted to see him about. Room sixteen, the Special Intelligence Unit, was popularly known within the Executive Branch as "the Plumbers," or the Dirty Tricks Unit, and St. Yves was reputed to be in charge.

Kit took the logbook for classified documents that was his responsibility and spent the next hour and a half wandering from office to office, verifying that the last person signing for each document was, in fact, currently in possession of it. Then he went to the interoffice loan vault, where documents on loan to the White House from the various intelligence agencies were stored. There he spent the next half hour checking red-and-gray-covered documents against the list, and was pleased to find that they were all there. Nothing was less fun than searching the corners of the White House and the Executive Office Building for a document that some executive assistant borrowed from some assistant secretary and then shoved in the back of a desk drawer and forgot about.

At twelve thirty sharp Kit showed up at the door to room sixteen. A thin, hawk-faced woman met him at the door. "You're Kit Young," she said, holding out a slender, well-manicured hand. "I'm Dianna Holroyd. That's with two *n*'s. I'm executive secretary and den mother for this group. Mr. St. Yves asked me to tell you he'll be a few moments."

"What's happening?" Kit asked, gesturing into the office, where workmen were moving filing cabinets and ripping telephones from the wall with chaotic efficiency.

"We're expanding," Dianna told him. "Part of our operation is moving across town, and the rest is taking over most of this hallway."

"What's happening to the Vice-President's press office?" Kit asked, amused at the constant game of musical chairs that went on in the EOB.

"That's moving into the President's Counsel's office. The President's Counsel is moving across the street into the White House. I don't know whose office he's getting."

"Fascinating," Kit said sincerely.

"It's like dominoes," Dianna agreed, smiling. She was very pretty when she smiled.

"Greetings!" St. Yves said, appearing from behind a moving file cabinet. "We got our marching orders this morning, and so we march. Into bigger digs. The SIU takes on new functions, grows with the times. You hungry?"

Kit admitted to hunger, and St. Yves shepherded him upstairs and out onto Seventeenth Street. As they walked over to the nearby restaurant, St. Yves kept up a steady stream of small talk. He had led an adventurous life, traveled all over the world, and spoke with equal facility of Katmandu and of Paris. His stories were sprinkled with the names of heads of state, movie stars, authors, rich men, wise men, beautiful women, traitors, spies, and assassins, all of whom he knew well or had been closely associated with.

Kit learned two things from the conversation: first, that St. Yves was at least ten years older than he looked, and, second, that St. Yves wanted something from him. What it could be, he had no idea, but he was sure that before the meal was over St. Yves would let him know.

The Sans Souci was the in place for those few in official Washington that knew, or cared about, good food. Since Dr. Gildruss, the President's Adviser for International Affairs, was such good copy, the Sans Souci had been mentioned several times in various newspaper columns and news magazines. Now it was becoming the in place for those who wanted to be seen eating in the in place. This had not, as of yet, St. Yves assured Kit as he ushered him through the doors, affected the food.

"And," St. Yves said, "it's a good place to talk, because it's so fucking public nobody pays any attention to you."

The maître d' placed them at a table along the far wall and St. Yves talked Kit through the menu: "The *coquilles St. Jacques* isn't bad; a little rich, perhaps. Keep away from the *tournedos*. The chef makes béarnaise as though he were dueling with the saucepan. Do you like veal? The veal is superb. I'm going to have the sweetbreads myself. This is the only place west of the Avenue Georges Cinque where they really know how to handle sweetbreads."

Kit, whose idea of lunch was a cheeseburger, no fries, and a vanilla malted, studied the menu intently while St. Yves continued his guided tour of the entrées. When the waiter came over, Kit, in a spirit of rebellion, ordered a small steak, medium rare.

"The *ris de veau à la maréchale*, Charles," St. Yves ordered, closing his menu and tapping it thoughtfully on the table. "With a small *salade maison* to begin—not on the side, you understand, but before—and perhaps a bottle of the Haut Brion sixty-seven."

Charles nodded, extracted the menus, and went off. St. Yves leaned forward, elbows on the table, and stared at Kit. "We don't know much about you," he said.

"Who's we?" Kit asked. "And what do you want to

know?" He suddenly felt very much on the defensive. St. Yves had that effect on people.

"Oh, we know all the usual stuff," St. Yves said, picking up a fork and revolving it over and over between his hands. "Your birth date, your schooling, college grades, extracurricular activities, the first girl you ever laid, all that stuff. You're a patriotic, loyal American. But of course with your background you're not old enough to be anything else. The closest thing to a subversive in your family is your uncle Harry."

"Uncle Harry?" Kit asked.

"Right. Your mother's older brother. He joined the Young People's Socialist League in nineteen thirty-two. Didn't you know?"

"No. The subject never came up." Kit now had no idea of what was going on. What could St. Yves want to know that wasn't already in his file?

St. Yves focused his attention on Kit. "What we want to know are your political beliefs," he said, lacing his long, slender fingers together under his chin. "Your concept of where this country is headed, what its goals should be, and what you feel you should do about it. What I'm asking you, I suppose, is what you think it means to be an American. If this sounds too patriotic, or any bullshit like that, I'm sorry."

"I don't think patriotism is bullshit," Kit said. "I think sometimes it's misplaced, and goes over into chauvinism."

St. Yves looked warily at Kit. "Who'd you vote for in November?" he asked. "You don't have to tell me, of course."

"I will tell you," Kit said. "I didn't vote."

"Is that straight?" St. Yves said, sounding surprised. "You live in the most political town in the world, work for the President, and you didn't vote?"

"That's right. I feel I have to remain completely non-political. I have to do my job honestly and fairly, no matter what party's in power and no matter who's elected president. So I don't want to get involved with the process to the point that it would matter to me."

St. Yves put his hands on the table, palms down, and leaned back. "That's probably the most naïve political philosophy I've heard espoused since I left the third grade."

"You asked me and I told you," Kit said, the annoyance showing in his voice. "I guess the basic fact is that I'm not that interested in the political process. Most politicians, as far as I can tell, are either idiots or crooks, and yet they keep getting voted back into office. And there doesn't seem to be anything I can do about it either way."

"Don't get pissed," St. Yves said. "I didn't mean to sound disapproving. I just wanted to find out whether you're for us or against us."

"Us?"

"The President."

"I think he's a good man, and I think he has guts. Going to China took guts."

"Right," St. Yves said. "He's a gutsy guy. Ah!" The conversation died out while they paused to watch the maître d' compose a *salade* and place it in front of St. Yves. "A *chef d'oeuvre* as always, Charles, thank you."

Charles smiled and left, to be replaced a few seconds later by a tall man with a blond crew cut who paused in front of the table. "Edward! How are you?"

St. Yves looked up from the salad which was commanding all of his attention. "Mr. Vandermeer." He pushed back his chair.

"No, no," Vandermeer said, "don't get up. Tell you what, I'll sit down for a minute." And, pulling a chair out from the next table, he turned it the wrong way and straddled it, leaning forward across the bentwood back. "You must be Kit Young," he said, staring at Kit through his steel-rimmed glasses. "Billy Vandermeer." He stuck out his hand to be shaken.

Kit took Vandermeer's hand and received a firm, no-nonsense handshake. "A pleasure," Kit said. "I've been looking forward to meeting you." Uriah "Billy" Vandermeer was the mystery man of the administration. When the President had taken office, Vandermeer's position had seemed no more important than that of an appointment clerk. But now, with the second term about to begin, and Vandermeer the chairman of the newly created Domestic Council, even Cabinet officers had to check with Billy to get in to see the President. And instructions from Billy were the closest most staffers got to orders from the President. A shadowy figure, often ignored by the press, he was the man who got things done. He and Charlie Ober, head of OMB, more than any other men, held the reins of power in the White House.

"As it happens," Vandermeer said, "I've been looking forward to meeting you. I've been meaning to thank you personally for the help you gave us over at the Second District Police Station over that business at the Watergate."

"I was just doing my job." It was the first thing that came to mind, and even as he said it Kit realized it sounded inane.

Vandermeer leaned forward, pushing the chair over until the back was resting against the table. "That may be, and it says a lot about you that you feel that way, but you did that job very well. All cleaned up, and without a ripple. And now you're going to be working for us, and I'm glad to have you aboard."

Obviously it hadn't sounded as inane to Vandermeer as it did to Kit. And *now* he was going to be working for *them?* For whom had he been working for the past six months?

"Excuse me," Vandermeer said, and he jumped up, almost upsetting the chair, and waved at a slim blond girl who had just appeared in the entrance and was looking around. "My daughter," he explained. She waved back and started toward them, maneuvering between the crowded tables with the unconscious grace of a Borzoi. Her long blond hair cascaded off her shoulders and down the back of the tan shirtwaist dress that clearly had not been bought within a thousand miles of Washington, D.C.

"Hi, Dad," she said, reaching the table and giving her head a shake to settle her hair back into place.

"Hi, love," Vandermeer said. "Gentlemen, may I present my daughter, Kathy. Kathy, this is Edward St. Yves and Christopher Young."

Kathy gave St. Yves her hand. "Mr. St. Yves," she said, her eyes opening wide, "my father has told me a lot about you."

St. Yves laughed. "If the things he's said about me are only half as nice as the things he's told me about you, then 'One may not doubt that somehow, good shall come of water and of mud.'"

Kathy's face lit up with a bright, wide smile. "'Somewhere, beyond space and time,'" she said, "'is wetter water, slimier slime!'"

"I've always thought so," St. Yves agreed, deadpan.

Vandermeer looked from St. Yves to his daughter. "What are you two babbling about?" he demanded.

"Oh, Dad," Kathy said. "It's only Rupert Brooke. Only one of the greatest poets who ever wrote in English."

"I'm glad you recognized the poem," St. Yves said, "since he's one of my favorites, too. Which makes it a special pleasure to meet you. Your father never mentioned that you were coming to Washington."

"He didn't know," Kathy said.

"Complete surprise to me," Vandermeer said. "I thought she'd be starting college in September. But instead she applied for this Senate Junior Aide program—where they let teenagers work their young, ah, fingers off for next to no pay for some senator so they can learn about government. She got an appointment with Senator Jensen, and I didn't know a thing about it. Starting with the January session. All on her own." He shook his head. "Won it in a competitive examination in her school system. They didn't even know who she was; she uses her mother's name, you know."

"It must sound horribly silly to you gentlemen," Kathy said. "But believe me, it's the most exciting thing that's ever happened to a girl from Grand Rapids."

"She's going to live in a dormitory with the other junior aides," Vandermeer said. "But she's promised to come have dinner with me at least twice a week. And what more can you ask of a daughter? And, speaking of food, we must get to our own table."

Kathy raised her hand in farewell. "'Immense, of fishy form and mind,'" she said. "'Squamous, omnipotent and kind.' I hope to see you again. You too," she added to Kit. Then she dashed off behind her father.

"Youthful enthusiasm," St. Yves said, staring at her retreating form. "Lovely girl. Vandermeer must be very proud of her."

"He and his wife are separated?" Kit asked.

"Divorced," St. Yves said.

"Ahem," said the waiter, appearing at the table. "I didn't wish to interrupt. Shall I serve?"

"Yes, bring on the food. My young friend here must be starved."

The waiter brought their lunch, and they ate in silence until St. Yves placed his knife and fork neatly together on his empty plate. "As you may have gathered," he told Kit, "we'd like you to work with us."

"You mean you people in room sixteen? What would you like me to do?"

"Officially you'll stay in your present job, and keep your present job title," St. Yves said. "But you'll have an assistant to do all the rote work that keeps you busy now. We want you to be liaison for plans and procurement between our group and CIA and Defense. Are you interested?"

Kit shrugged and nodded. "Sure. If that's what the President wants me to do. I'm getting tired of checking the locks on safe doors anyway."

"It was never intended that you should stay in that job," St. Yves said. "But the reelection was everybody's first concern, and we had to get that done and out of the way before some of our other plans could go into operation."

TRANSCRIPT: AMERICA WANTS TO KNOW (excerpt)

Sunday, January 21, 1973
A live telecast from our nation's capital interviewing the news-makers—and the decisionmakers—of the day. Today's interview is with Nelson H. Greener, president of the newly formed Institute for an Informed America.

Interviewers:
   Daniel Gores of the *Baltimore Sun*.
   Susanne Witclair of the Hearst syndicate.
   Ian Faulkes of the British MacPherson News Syndicate.
Moderated by George Brownworthy.
BROWNWORTHY: Welcome to *America Wants to Know*, Dr. Greener. Could you start by giving us a little of the background of the Institute for an Informed America?
GREENER: Well, Mr. Brownworthy, strictly speaking, of course, there is no background on the institute. We are a brand-new organization. Our history, as the saying goes, lies ahead of us.
BROWNWORTHY: Yes, but what are the roots of the institute? How was it formed, and what will its function and, ah, purpose be?
GREENER: The Institute for an Informed America was formed because a group of concerned citizens felt that the opinions and attitudes of the great majority of Americans—what our presi-

dent has called the Silent Majority—was not being given proper weight in the halls of government.

The institute will function as a research facility and information outlet for those of conservative views in the government and outside, much as the Brookings Institute serves the liberal establishment.

BROWNWORTHY: Miss Witclair.

WITCLAIR: What sort of activities is the institute going to engage in, Dr. Greener? Will you only be working for the government?

GREENER: Our goal is to assure that Americans have access to all sides of significant issues. We will work for the administration, we will work for private individuals, and, if we see an area that would be desirable to explore, we will be free to initiate the research on our own. We plan to prepare reports on subjects of vital interest to the citizens of this country. We will sponsor debates and seminars, and maintain a speakers' bureau of experts on issues of interest to conservatives. We will always endeavor to represent the average citizen—the great Silent Majority out there in America's heartland, and not merely the bunch of effete intellectual snobs that make up the East Coast establishment.

BROWNWORTHY: Mr. Faulkes.

FAULKES: Does that mean you'll be mainly a propaganda outlet, pushing the conservative viewpoint as the answer to all problems?

GREENER: Now, I don't think that's a fair question, Mr. Faulkes. The institute staff will bring their intellectual resources to bear on our problems in the spirit of open, fair scientific enquiry, with no preconceived formula or solution.

BROWNWORTHY: Mr. Faulkes.

FAULKES: Then the institute will stick mainly to the intellectual approach to problems, preparing studies and position papers, that sort of thing?

GREENER: By no means. Besides the research facilities, our organization will include film crews for documentary work, public-relations people, media people, psychologists, and experts in such diverse fields as drug abuse, agriculture, prison reform, education, city planning, and oceanography. All of whom will be working in these areas on a day-to-day basis. No, the Institute for an Informed America will get into areas that would astound you.

• CHAPTER FIVE

CALVIN MIDDLER was his name. He was a little over six feet tall, slender, and he moved with an almost feline grace. He was twenty-eight years old but passed for twenty-two. Which was a good thing, because in his circle twenty-eight was a suspect age, too close to thirty to be completely trustworthy. Too many years to be warped by Middle-American materialism before the New Values had taken hold. He was known as a college dropout, which was true. It wasn't his fault if his associates believed that he had dropped out a lot more recently than 1965. He was also known as a Special Forces veteran, just back from 'Nam, who had joined the antiwar movement after seeing his buddies blown to bits in support of American imperialism. Which wasn't true. He had spent his two years in the Army as a cook's helper in Fort Dix, New Jersey.

It was eleven thirty, and he'd been waiting in the Why Not? for over an hour. The crowds on Bleecker Street were beginning to thin out as the Saturday-night tourists made their way back to the subways to leave Greenwich Village to the hippies, yippies, teenie-boppers and aging beatniks who called it home. Calvin was beginning to wonder if maybe she wasn't going to show, the girl with the sweet voice who wanted the machine guns, when there was a tap on his shoulder. "Don't turn around," the sweet voice said in his ear.

"Okay," Calvin agreed. He lifted his cup and took a sip of cold coffee. "Why not?" He spoke softly and kept his eyes facing forward.

"We don't want you to know who we are," the girl said. "It should be obvious."

"Fine," Calvin said. "Then stop wasting my time. I'll close my eyes and you walk out of here and we'll both forget the whole thing."

"What's that?" the girl said. "What do you mean?"

"Look, I'm not going to do business with a voice I hear over the phone and then behind my back, no matter how pretty the voice is. I've got to protect myself—you can see that."

"You can call me Cash," the girl said. "Two hundred a weapon, I believe was the price."

"No prices were mentioned over the phone," he said.

"You quoted that to a friend of ours once," she said softly, into his ear.

Calvin was developing a very strong urge to find out what this girl looked like. "Go away," he told her, "and tell whoever you work for that either I deal face to face and only with principals, or I don't deal."

She thought that over. "You've got the merchandise?"

"Yes."

"Why do you care who deals?"

"I got high ethical standards," he told her. "You want these beautiful pieces of machinery for revolutionary activities, that's one thing. You want to start a gang war or go shooting up the proletariat, that's something else."

She got up and walked around the table, sitting in the chair opposite Calvin. She had short, fluffy blond hair and a round face, and might have been as old as twenty, maybe.

The dungarees and pea jacket didn't go with the hair, which looked as though it had seen the inside of a beauty parlor in the recent past. Then Calvin caught on: it was a blond wig—and she had shaved her eyebrows off.

"Okay," he said, "we deal. What's your name?"

"Zonya. How many pieces can you get?"

"How many can you pay for?"

"We can take five now," she said. "What about ammunition?"

"I can get you a little."

"A little isn't good enough. Our people have to have practice."

"Hell, they use standard forty-five caliber ammo," he told her. "Any gun store in the country outside of New York will sell it to you."

"Oh," she said. 'That's okay then. Five pieces and whatever ammo you have for a thousand dollars. Are they near here?"

"I can put my hands on them," he said. "But the price has gone up since you overheard that conversation."

She pushed her chair back. "Listen, mister," she said, her voice a hard squeak, "don't try to rip us off."

Calvin put his hands palms up on the table. "Look, Zonya, machine guns don't grow on trees. You want to wait awhile, I can probably get you some cheaper guns—but these ain't them. Besides, whatever you think you need machine guns for, shotguns will probably do just as well, and them you don't need me for."

"We want machine guns," she said stubbornly, not willing to discuss it.

"Fourteen hundred dollars," Calvin said.

"Twelve," she said.

"I don't bargain," Calvin told her. "Whoever told you about me should've told you that."

"He said you were interested in helping revolutionary

movements," she said. She was gradually working her way up into a rage, her hands opening and closing in her lap.

"Cool it!" Calvin said. "Keep your cool!"

Zonya sat there for a minute, staring at him as though she were trying to read his face, and then she said, "I guess I'm not very good, am I?"

"Nope," Calvin said immediately. "You came here to score weapons, not to get insulted by what I say. You haven't been at this very long."

"I'll learn," she said. "We've got to get as tough as iron, resilient as earth, and relentless as rain. Mao said that."

"What's the name of your group?" Calvin asked.

"We're the People's Revolutionary Brigade," she told him.

"I've never heard of you."

"We're new."

The waitress brought over the refill and took his soiled cup away. Calvin watched her leave—she had a nice ass— and turned back to Zonya. "You have friends in any other groups, one I might've heard of maybe, who can vouch for you?"

She thought about it for a minute and came out with a name.

"Never heard of him," Calvin said.

"He's in the Weatherpeople," she said. "At least that's what he told me."

"Well, *I* never heard of him. But then I don't know all the Weatherpeople."

After a little more thought, Zonya came up with a name that Calvin allowed he had heard of. "Okay," he said. "Twelve hundred it is. I'll even throw in a couple of free lessons; you shouldn't waste too much ammo."

"Good," she said. "Very good."

"Is tomorrow soon enough?" he asked. "Meet me here about ten, we'll arrange a trade."

"I can manage that," she said.

"You leave now," he told her. "And don't wait around to see where I go."

"I wouldn't do that," she said. "We have to trust each other."

"Right." Calvin waited until she was out the door, then he put a bill down on the table to pay for the coffee and hurried out to a pay phone on Bleecker Street. He dialed a number he had memorized. "Made contact," he told the man who answered. "A young female calling herself Zonya. Set up a meet for tomorrow."

"Very good," the phone voice said.

"I need five Thompsons."

"What are they planning to do, rob the Mint?" the voice asked. "What the fuck do they need five Thompsons for?"

"I didn't ask," Calvin said. "Do I get them?"

"Sure thing," the voice told him. "We'll send them to your apartment. Don't lose them. Join their group."

"It's all arranged," Calvin said. "I'm teaching them how to use the damn things."

"Very good."

"Send along a manual, will you?"

"Sure thing." The voice hung up.

• CHAPTER SIX

On the first and third Thursday of each month TEPACS met in Professor Adams' study. Starting in 1965 as a bi-weekly poker game, the gatherings had quickly attained the mock formality of the Thursday Evening Poker and Conversation Society. From there, given the bureaucratic orientation of most of the members, the acronymic TEPACS became inevitable.

As TEPACS had evolved over the years, Aaron Adams had chosen men who were personally and professionally interesting to him. After all, it was his house. Now the group was a good cross section of the decision-making level of Washington bureaucracy, articulate, intelligent men who played damn good poker.

Early in the afternoon, Adams' silent myrmidon, Gerald, turned the felt side of the gaming table up, set out the chips, set up the wet bar for heavy use and filled the ice bucket. Adams padded in from the pool and performed the ritual of placing TEPACS' framed constitution on the wall over the table. Calligraphed on parchment by a former member of the group who was now Chairman of the Joint Chiefs of Staff, the constitution was to hang only at meetings. Its presence was as important to the games as the ritualistic opening of two new decks of cards. Tradition, after all, is tradition.

THE CONSTITUTION OF THE THURSDAY EVENING POKER AND CONVERSATION SOCIETY

ONE

TEPACS shall exist to further the art of good poker, and otherwise benefit mankind.

TWO

TEPACS shall meet on the first and third Thursday of each month. Play shall begin promptly at 2000 hours and end precisely at 0200 hours.

THREE

Poker shall be defined as five-card draw, five- or seven-card stud ONLY. Within these limits, the dealer may choose.

FOUR

The office of Secretary shall rotate from session to session. The Secretary shall supply the cards.

Adams went upstairs to shower and dress and then came down to eat the *omelette aux herbes fines* that Gerald had prepared for dinner. When they were alone, Adams ate in the kitchen with Gerald. When there was any third person in the house, Gerald would not permit it.

Obie Porfritt was, as usual, the first to arrive. And, as usual, his first words on coming through the door were, "Evening, Aaron. Where is everybody?"

"You're a shade early, Obie," Adams said. "Make yourself a drink." He nodded to Gerald, who put the scotch on the bar, looked at Adams and tapped his nose twice with his ring finger, and left the room.

"Boy!" Obie said, staring after Gerald. "What I'd give for a couple of aides who couldn't talk." He took a tall glass, filled it halfway with scotch, and then stuck in two ice cubes and two inches of Seven-Up. "Had a hard day," he said, "entertaining constituents. Least, they damn well better have been entertained."

Obie was Representative Obediah Porfritt (R., Neb.), a hardworking, intelligent, capable representative of the citizens of central Nebraska. He put as much time as he could into personal contact with his Nebraskan constituents, as he knew himself to be a boring public speaker who came across badly on television. His great fear was that someday the Democrats would find some farmer with charisma to run against him in his district.

"What sort of entertainment do constituents go in for these days?" Adams asked.

"Not much in the way of song or dance," Obie told him. "They actually came to see the President, congratulate him on his reelection, let him know they support him, in case he was wondering. I only escorted them to the Oval Office."

"Did they come away with pens?" Adams asked.

"Tie pins and cufflinks. And a group photograph and autographed presidential photos. How can a poor congressman compete with the presidential seal?" Obie slumped down into an armchair and stared into his scotch. "Do you have any idea of how much the government spends a year on cufflinks? I hear he wanted to put his picture in the middle of them, right in the center of the presidential seal, but Vandermeer wouldn't let him."

"Obie!" Adams said in mock horror. "And you a Republican. Do you mean that the fair citizens of Nebraska weren't interested in talking to you at all?"

"Oh, sure," Obie said. "I sat them down and told them an amusing story about my plan for getting the Army Corps of Engineers to inspect the Middle Loup River with an eye toward inserting a dam. That got their interest. Very amusing."

"They were amused?"

"They were delighted. I was amused." Obie took a long gulp of whiskey. "Over Wilbur Mills' dead body do I get a dam on the Middle Loup."

"You mean you can't deliver?"

"Sure I can deliver. All I told them was that the Corps would inspect. And inspect they will. The Corps loves to inspect. No problem there."

"Ah."

Colonel Francis Baker entered the study and skimmed his hat onto the couch. "I'm early," he said, "but I may make up for that by leaving early. Fair warning." He took a wide glass, plumped two ice cubes in it, and surrounded them with bourbon. A tall man with silver-white hair who looked trim and youthful in his uniform, Colonel Baker had begun his Army career by being drafted during the Korean War. To his surprise he liked the Army; it was dirty, muddy and dangerous, its regulations were mostly stupid, and entirely too many officers were incompetent, but for the first time in his life he felt that he was doing something worth doing. Something that mattered. And he did it well.

He had gone to OCS after Korea and slowly worked his way up the chain of command. Now, back from a field command in Vietnam, he was holding down a staff job in the Pentagon and waiting for his first star.

Adams nodded at him. "Sit down, Colonel," he said. "Leaving early should be no problem. If you've lost enough, I'm sure nobody would object."

Colonel Baker snorted. "That's a precedent I don't think I'll set." He was known as an ultraconservative player, who seldom lost.

Ian Faulkes and Grier Laporte were the next to arrive. Ian, a Londoner who had been living in the United States for the past six years, was employed by the MacPherson

69

News Syndicate to report and comment to the British on their American cousins. A slender, handsome man in his early forties, he dressed with the faultless arrogance found only in upper-class Englishmen.

Grier, a fifty-year-old Texan with a pot belly, had a wide handlebar mustache and was bald as a marshmallow. His suit looked as though he had borrowed it from a larger friend who slept in his clothes. As always, he had on a string tie with an American flag tie clasp. One of the founders and owners of a commercial freight airline called Globeair, he served the company as their Washington lobbyist.

Grier fixed himself a bourbon and Saratoga. "Time," he said. "Let's get down to the serious business at hand, gentlemen."

Ian took a chilled ginger beer from the small bar refrigerator and poured it into a sloping glass. "Thank the Lord that's over," he said. "I think I'll put in for a well-deserved vacation."

"Thank the Lord what's over?" Baker asked.

"That special I was doing on your presidential election," Ian said. "You can't conceive what it's like to attempt to explain the American presidential process to the great British public."

"Say," Obie said, settling down into his playing chair. "What's the matter with our elections?"

"You've got no complaints, Obie," Grier said. "You picked up the biggest majority yet in this last one, didn't you?"

"Goddamn right. My constituents know when they've got a good thing going. That's my motto: 'You've got a good thing going in Obie Porfritt.' "

The last three current members of TEPACS entered during this conversation. They were Rear Admiral David Bush, son of Admiral David "Pigboat" Bush of World War I fame and currently Deputy Chief of the Office of Naval

Intelligence in the Pentagon; George Masters, Director of Training Aides for the FBI; and Sanderman Jones, who did this and that for the State Department. They fixed themselves drinks and then got down to the serious business of cutting for deal.

Grier Laporte won the deal with a three of clubs. "A little stud, gentlemen," he said, taking off his jacket and rolling up his sleeves.

"What was that about the election?" Sanderman asked Ian. "Your viewers don't understand the process, or the result. Or what?"

"Not particularly the last election," Ian said. "But American presidential elections in general. In their wisdom, the electorate choose a majority from your Democratic party. Then they turn around and, by an overwhelming landslide, elect a president from your Republican party so he can veto all the laws your Democratic legislators enact. And thus does government come to a standstill while two of the coequal branches fight it out. Fortuitously, one of the branches is more equal than the other, so progress is made."

"You gonna play cards or lecture us on democratic institutions?" Grier demanded. "Come on, ante up!"

They played in silence for a while, except for an occasional obligatory poker comment. Then Colonel Baker turned to Sanderman Jones. "Much reshuffling going on in State? Is it going to affect you?"

Jones shook his head. "Not me," he said. "There's a lot of head-rolling going on, but it's mostly in the more visible sections of the department. Intelligence hasn't yet felt the ax."

"I heard about that," Faulkes said. "It's That Man, isn't it? What does he think he's doing? First the resignations, now this."

"He knows just what he's doing," George Masters said. "Our President is a man who demands complete loyalty to himself. Not to the country, or the job, but to himself personally. Some of the people in the Bureau who've crossed him in the last four years are getting the word now. It's either early retirement or field work out in the boonies."

"Crossed him how?" Faulkes asked.

Masters shook his head. "Sorry," he said.

"It is rumored," Adams told Faulkes, "that the President asked his investigative and intelligence agencies to provide him with information regarding his domestic political enemies—among others. For the most part, that information was provided. Some, however, resisted this politicizing of the process of government. Those people are gradually being surgically excised."

"Is that right?" Faulkes asked Masters. "Have you any comment? Did anything like that happen at the Bureau? Has anything changed since Hoover died?"

"No comment," Masters said, "but I'll tell you this: A lot of people have been throwing shit at J. Edgar Hoover for the past thirty years for the way he ran the Bureau, but if the facts ever come out they're going to eat their words. That man bowed to no political pressure. Everything he did was for what he considered the good of the country. And nobody, in any office, ever used him or the Bureau. And nobody tried more than once."

"Are you saying the FBI is being subverted?" Faulkes asked.

"I'm not saying anything," Masters said.

"Could we shut up and play cards?" Obie Porfritt demanded.

• CHAPTER SEVEN

KIT PARKED his car in the alley behind the building, but the back door was locked, so he had to walk around to the front. The plaque on the door, a two-foot brass square that jutted out about six inches, said:

INSTITUTE FOR AN

INFORMED AMERICA

founded 1973

Kit rang the bell and after a while a woman came to answer it and let him in. It was Dianna Holroyd, whom he had first met in room sixteen. "Welcome," she said. "Mr. St. Yves said you'd be coming over. We close at six, but I waited to let you in."

Kit checked his watch. It was ten after six. "Sorry I'm late," he said.

"No problem," she said. "Actually I have to stay until you people leave and close up after you. Woman's work is never done. They're upstairs, first door on your right."

Kit climbed the stairs and found St. Yves waiting for him on the landing. "Glad you're here," St. Yves greeted him.

"Sorry to pull you into this at the last moment, but Mercer got an attack of—would you believe?—appendicitis, and is now lying in a bed in Doctor's Hospital while they decide whether or not to cut him open. Come in and meet the crew."

The room was small and furnished with no more than a few folding chairs and a bridge table. Kit shook hands with the four men as St. Yves introduced them: Curtis, short and competent-looking; Peterson, blond and tall, with the fingers of a craftsman; Lowesson, who had the distinctive look of an ex-cop; and Berkey, small and skinny, with the equally distinctive look of an ex-con.

Since his lunch meeting with St. Yves six months before, Kit had been blessed with an assistant and a larger office at the EOB. His title was the same, but most of the job was now done by the assistant, except for the morning ritual of carrying the bound Daily Intelligence Summary over to the White House and putting it on the President's desk in the Oval Office. His primary job now was liaison between the traditional intelligence services and the "Plumbers," as St. Yves called the covert group which was responsible, as Vandermeer put it, for "plugging the leaks." The SIU had just moved this section into the Institute for an Informed America, which St. Yves was still gloating over as being the perfect cover. St. Yves and the planning staff stayed on at room sixteen, to keep immediate access to the President and Billy Vandermeer.

"Okay, everybody," St. Yves said, "just sit down and relax. Here's the drill: It's a surreptitious entry for the purpose of information-gathering in an apartment over on Twelfth and T."

"Great neighborhood," Berkey commented.

"Yours not to reason why," St. Yves told him, "yours merely to drive the getaway car. Now, here's the way I've worked out the division of labor. We've set up an OP in an

74

apartment across the street on the second floor. Young and I will work out of there and establish surveillance. The subject should be going out shortly after we get there. When he does I'll give Curtis the word on the walkie-talkie, and Curtis will stay on his tail. If for any reason he heads back early—"

"You know where he's going?" Peterson interrupted.

"Fellow's going to a party," St. Yves said. "If he heads back early, Curtis jumps to the nearest pay phone and gives the word, giving you, Peterson, and you, Lowesson, plenty of time to get out. Make sure you keep everything neat and don't leave a mess. And you, Curtis, make sure you've got a dime. You're the lock-and-key man, Peterson, in case you hadn't guessed. Lowesson will help you search the place, and Berkey, you drive. Clear?"

"What are we looking for?" Peterson asked.

"Ah, that's the question!" St. Yves said. "The subject seems to have an informant inside the White House, and the Chief wants to find out who the tattletale is. Anything that relates to the White House, or the government, we want copies of. Anything you don't understand, we want copies of. Also, we want a phone bug and a couple of wall mikes planted. I already have the listening apparatus installed in the OP."

St. Yves distributed the small walkie-talkies to his crew, sticking three in a canvas bowling bag for himself. Then they all went through the routine of emptying their pockets and piling all identifying wallets and papers onto the bridge table.

"If you want to keep the stakeout happy," Peterson said, "you'll put in a refrigerator and a hot plate."

They went downstairs and left by the back door. "Three cars," St. Yves said. "I'll go with Young. Twelve forty-seven T Street, top floor. Name on the mailbox is Ralph Schuster."

Ralph Schuster tried for the third time to get the knot

to his tie adjusted. For the third time he ripped it out again and started over. He tried a fourth and fifth time, before giving up and leaving it as it was. After all, he was a reporter for the *Washington Post*, not a fashion plate. He pulled on the jacket of his blue suit and then remembered that one of the buttons was off the left sleeve.

But at least Suzanne couldn't complain about the overcoat, since she had helped him pick it out. It was camel's hair, which was quite nice, shorter than he would have liked, and a hundred dollars more than he wanted to spend. And he really didn't understand what was wrong with his old trench coat with the zip-in lining. But whatever Suzanne wanted, Ralph was eager to supply. Not that Suzanne wanted much. For the first few months he had seen her, he hadn't been aware that she wanted anything. It was only gradually that Ralph learned to interpret her look of amused tolerance and ask her what was wrong.

"Oh, it's not *wrong*," she would say. "I wouldn't change you for the world."

"But if I wanted to change it myself," he would insist, "what should I change?"

And she would shrug her amused shrug and smile her tolerant smile and mention the ratty raincoat, or the skinny black tie. When she saw that he didn't mind she even started bringing him things, like the wide blue tie with the narrow red and white stripes that he had just given up knotting.

He shrugged into the camel's-hair overcoat, picked up the blue card inviting him to the French Embassy reception, and left his apartment, carefully locking the door behind him. He would be early, he noted, looking at his watch. It was just after nine. The reception started at nine, and no guests would really be expected until around ten. But everyone expected reporters to be gauche. And he wanted to be there when Suzanne arrived. She would be with her husband, but perhaps they could slip away for a while.

76

Two men who were parking a car across the street looked startled when Schuster came out of his apartment house, but he didn't notice. As he walked down the block to his car one of the men ran out in the street to stop another car that was going by. He spoke earnestly to the driver, gesturing toward Ralph. Whereupon the driver nodded and did a hasty and illegal U-turn. When Ralph started his car and drove off, the other driver was on his tail.

"Son of a bitch!" St. Yves said. "That was close. Another five minutes and we would have spent the evening watching an empty apartment, waiting for him to come out." Pulling his small canvas bag full of walkie-talkies out of the rear seat of Kit's car, he led the way into the apartment across the street from Schuster's. "You ready, Red Bear?" he called into one of the three walkie-talkies that he pulled from the bag.

"*Right,*" came Peterson's voice.

"The den is empty. You may commence hibernation."

"*Right.*"

St. Yves went to the window and turned the venetian blind slats so that he could look through them. "Here they come," he said.

Kit sat down on the ancient red couch that lined one wall of the furnished apartment. His job didn't seem exactly essential to the success of the operation, but he thought he had figured out what he was doing there—why he had been called. Having Kit share in the extralegal operation served several purposes from St. Yves' point of view. It "blooded" Kit, and made him one of the brotherhood by participation. It helped ensure his loyalty. It tested his ability to perform under stress, since even the relatively safe job of standing lookout in an illegal operation can be trying to the faint-hearted.

"How'd you know he was going out tonight?" Kit asked.

"That's the preparation that goes into a well-planned job, my boy," St. Yves said, beaming with self-satisfaction. "I've been scouting this job for several days. Got this apartment, set it up. Ran a check on Schuster's hours. Then, day before yesterday, I happened to be standing there when the mailman came by. A blue envelope with the crest of the French Embassy was dropped into Schuster's box."

"So?"

"So"—St. Yves fished into his coat pocket and pulled out a blue card—"it was a reasonable assumption that one of these was inside."

Kit examined the invitation. "Clever," he said. "But why didn't you go? You could have kept a close eye on Schuster."

St. Yves turned his head enough to stare coldly at Kit. "I'm not in the slightest interested in Mr. Schuster," he said. "I'm interested only in the name of his confidential White House source. And when I find out, there's going to be one less White House employee. He'll be lucky if the Chief doesn't file charges."

Kit shrugged. "Come on, official sources are leaking information all the time, from all branches of government; it's the great Washington game."

"When you work for someone," St. Yves said, "you owe that person a certain amount of loyalty. And when the person you work for is the President of the United States, why then, by the nature of the job you owe him your complete loyalty. You don't have to agree with him, you don't even have to like him, but you have to be loyal. It's one of the things he gets in return for the burden he assumes when he takes office." Kit had never heard St. Yves speak so intently nor so seriously. He was stating his credo, and a man's religion is not to be argued with lightly.

"*Blue Bear.*" Peterson's voice sounded.

St. Yves grabbed the nearest walkie-talkie. "Right."

"*In.*"

"Right." St. Yves turned to Kit. "Come over here and keep an eye on the door," he said. "I'm going to set up the scope."

"Right," Kit said. It seemed to be contagious. He got off the couch and pulled a straight-back metal-and-plastic chair over to the window. He stared through the blinds at the deserted street while St. Yves retrieved a small battered suitcase from the far end of the couch. The suitcase was lined with thick foam plastic that acted as a shock packing for its contents. Resting on the foam was a complex-looking set of tubes and lenses which St. Yves began to expertly screw together. When he was finished with the optical erector set, he had produced a small tripod-mounted telescope with a 35-millimeter camera mounted at the eyepiece end. The camera was a single-lens reflex with a ground-glass top, so by looking down at the ground glass you could see whatever the scope saw.

"You look like you're preparing for a long watch," Kit said, as St. Yves adjusted the scope and sighted it in on the doorway across the street.

"I doubt if the son of a bitch is stupid enough to leave the information lying around," St. Yves said. "We might have to be watching and listening to him for a while before we get through him to Mr. Rat."

"Schuster—Schuster," Kit said. "Skinny guy with a big nose? I met him once."

"That right?" St. Yves said calmly, peering into the ground glass.

"I forgot till just now. He came up to my office to question me about the Watergate business."

"What'd you tell him?" St. Yves asked.

Kit shook his head. "Not a damn thing. What could I tell him?"

"That's right," St. Yves said, his head still down over the scope. "Some of the things he found out, you didn't know."

Kit stared out at the empty street and saw his face reflected back at him in the window glass. Did St. Yves suspect him? Was this a double test to see if Kit would react in some way to the possibility that the name Christopher Young might be found on some slip of paper in Schuster's desk drawer? St. Yves had clearly known that Schuster had met with Kit even before Kit had placed the name. He must have gone through the name register at the entrance to the Executive Office Building. When Schuster had asked for Kit, both names had been recorded. Had St. Yves invited Kit along to see if he suddenly remembered the name? Did that make him more suspicious—or less? Was St. Yves playing cat-and-mouse with him? Did that explain the lecture on loyalty? Or was this whole thing just making him paranoid? Wheels within wheels. Kit shook his head and decided to ignore the whole business. Schuster was the one with a problem, not him.

Schuster turned off Massachusetts Avenue onto Belmont Road and began looking for a place to park. The French Embassy was on the next block. There would almost certainly be valet parking, but that meant tipping the valet and Schuster was constitutionally unable to pay someone else to park his car or pull out his chair at a restaurant. He believed in tipping for service, but not when the service was created merely to get the tip.

He found a place almost directly across from the Embassy and parked and locked the car, then hurried across the street. Waving his invitation at the uniformed doorman, he allowed it and his coat to be taken from him as he was ushered into the building.

Outside, the man called Curtis pulled his car up at a

convenient fire hydrant where he could see both Schuster's car and the French Embassy's front door. He turned off the engine and lit a cigarette, prepared for long wait.

Inside Schuster's apartment Peterson finished screwing together the phone in the living room and picked up his walkie-talkie. "Blue Bear," he said.

"Right."

"Phone check," he said.

"Right."

Peterson put the walkie-talkie down and dialed a number on the phone. It rang five times.

"Suicide Prevention Center?"

"What took you so long?" Peterson said.

"Excuse me?"

"It rang five times."

"I'm sorry," the voice said. It sounded like a young woman.

"Talk to me," Peterson said.

"Of course," the voice said. *"Whatever I can do to help. What is your problem? Do you want to talk about it?"*

"I need someone to talk to me," Peterson said, his voice flat, emotionless.

"Yes, yes," the woman said. *"What shall we talk about?"*

"Whatever you like," Peterson said.

"Yes, well. Let's talk about your problem," the woman said. *"Maybe I can help. We're trained, you know, to help."*

"My problem is, I need to talk to someone. On the phone."

"Yes, well, what about?" the woman asked. *"Where are you calling from?"*

"I don't think that's relevant."

"Are you feeling depressed?" the woman asked.

"No."

"You must be honest with me if you expect me to help

you," the woman said. "*And I do want to help you, you must believe that.*"

The walkie-talkie made a churping sound, as of suppressed laughter. Then came St. Yves' voice: "*Phone check okay.*"

"I have to hang up now," Peterson said into the phone.

"*Let me help you!*" the woman said. "*You mustn't give up!*"

"Good-bye," Peterson said in his flat voice. "Thank you for trying." And he hung up the phone.

Schuster walked through the Embassy mansion and out into the greenhouse. She was sitting there waiting for him. Her hands, folded demurely in her lap, were covered by long white gloves that made her arms look too slender to be real, too slender for the remembered strength of passion. The blue dress with its almost conservative neckline in this day of daring wives made her prim and proper and gave little hint of the exciting body it sheathed. She was in earnest conversation with the undersecretary of something or other when he came out, but her eyes caught his and did not let them go.

He walked past the two of them, and stood with his back to her, admiring flowers he wasn't sure were there, waiting for her to come.

Then her hand was on his arm. "Ralph."

"Hello."

"Just 'hello'? That's not very friendly."

He turned to look down at her. "Hello, my love," he said. "If I get more friendly I'll screw you here in the greenhouse, and your husband will challenge me to a duel."

"Can't you take me away and screw me somewhere else?" she said, her gray eyes staring intently up into his brown eyes, just the hint of a smile on her face.

"Say the word," he said.

"My husband couldn't come," she said. "He'll be here at one to have a drink with the French Ambassador and let me drive him home. Can we be back at one?"

"That," Schuster said, taking her arm, "is the word."

"We mustn't leave together," she said. "Go out the side door and walk toward the Circle. My car's in back. I'll pick you up."

"I hate this!" Schuster said. "Couldn't we—"

"Later," she told him. "Right now, this. Later, your more direct approach, perhaps."

"All right," he said. "We can't talk about it here. Besides, that's just one of the things we can't do here. Pick me up. I'll be the man with the chattering teeth and the blue thumb."

Curtis glanced up as a man came out of the side entrance to the Embassy, but he headed off in the wrong direction, and he wasn't wearing a camel's-hair overcoat. A minute later an old MG, driven by a woman with a light-blue scarf around her head, came from around the building and headed after the man, who was already out of sight. Curtis sank further down into his seat and turned on the engine again to blow some warm air into the car.

"That man is crazy," St. Yves said, taking off his earphones. "But the phone tap works fine." He rewound the tape on the voice-activated recorder.

Kit had his chair up against the window and was leaning forward, resting his forehead against the frame and peering out at the building across the street. "How's that?" he asked.

"He called up the Suicide Prevention Center for the phone check."

"Maybe he knows something we don't," Kit commented.

"Damn, the batteries on this tape recorder are low. I don't know if I have replacements."

"Plug it in."

"It doesn't plug in. Yes, here. No, damn, they're the wrong size."

Kit watched the empty street while St. Yves struggled with the equipment. In the Company, he reflected, they checked out equipment before they used it, but he decided it would be more politic not to mention it. "Say," Kit said, "there's a sports car pulling up in front of the building. Parking by the red line at the curb."

"Diplomat," St. Yves said, uninterested. "Those bastards park on the sidewalk when they want to. Why diplomatic immunity should extend to parking tickets is something—"

"That's him!" Kit said. "Getting out of the car—that's Schuster!"

"You sure?" St. Yves shouldered Kit aside and pulled two venetian-blind slats apart. "Son of a bitch!!" He grabbed for one of the walkie-talkies, then realized that he had pulled the batteries to see if they fit in the tape recorder. Dropping it, he ran across the room to his little canvas case and pulled out another. "Red Bear, Red Bear—quick!"

"Yes?"

"Get the fuck out of there. Hibernation is over—repeat, over. Head for roof. Subject is going in front door now, repeat now."

"Right."

St. Yves put the instrument down. "Now, how the hell did that happen?"

"Your man is somewhere right now, guarding an empty car," Kit said. "What now?"

"Go get the license number of that MG," St. Yves said.

"Okay." Kit went outside and strolled over to the car, then strolled back.

"They made it out okay," St. Yves said. "Let them stay on the roof for a couple of minutes, then we'll bring them down and split. Peterson thinks Schuster won't notice anything disturbed, but he's not sure. At least he retrieved all the equipment. Wouldn't do to give Schuster another camera to find. What about the car?"

"License number DPL one four five three."

"Good!" St. Yves grabbed for the phone. "If it was a regular plate, we'd have to wait for DMV to open in the morning, but I think we have a list of DPL plates somewhere in the office." He talked on the phone earnestly for about five minutes, and when he hung up there was a gleam in his eyes. "The car is registered to the wife of a Canadian cultural attaché," he said. "Cultural attaché. How nice. 'Chaste to her husband, frank to all beside, A teeming mistress, but a barren bride.'

"Mr. Schuster doesn't know it now, in the position he's in, or will shortly be in, but I think we have him by the short hairs. By the very short hairs, indeed. Come on, get those people off the roof. Let's get the fuck out of here."

• CHAPTER EIGHT

THE OVAL OFFICE, Tuesday, June 26, 1973 (10:15–11:05 A.M.)

MEETING: The President, Vandermeer, Ober, and St. Yves.

AUTHORIZED TRANSCRIPTION FROM THE EXECUTIVE ARCHIVES

Following a discussion about new staff appointments with Vandermeer. Ober and St. Yves enter.

P. Hi, Charlie, Ed. (unintelligible) are you?

O. Yes, sir.

P. I saw the press coverage on the opening of the institute.

O. Right, sir. The Institute for an Informed America is on line, and going ahead.

P. I don't think we got enough mileage out of that. Put a couple of our Jew-intellectual writers on it—get articles out to the great silent majority out there. Something about how the Democrats will ruin the country if we can't get a majority in Congress in '74. You know, how the Democrats put people on Welfare instead of creating jobs for them. A projection, with dates and all.

O. Great idea, sir.

P. How's it coming with your boys, Ed? The institute working for you?

St. Y. Great cover, sir. Gets most of the operations out of the White House. We've still got our office in the basement of the EOB, of course, but—

P. It sure simplifies the money thing. No more Mexican banks, or any of that crap. We put the word out that anyone wants to help us, he donates a little bread directly to the institute.

V. What about that leak? You got a handle on that?

St. Y. I think so. This reporter, Schuster, we've been running a security check on him. He has a, um, contact that might prove helpful to us. That is, we may be able to hold it against him.

P. Contact? You mean (unintelligible) friends? Like Cubans or Communists? The *Washington Post* has a Commie reporter?

St. Y. No, sir. Not that sort of contact. This is a lady.

V. So he's not a fag, so what?

St. Y. We're having a psychological profile done on Schuster. But I think, if my experience is any good for judgment, that Schuster cares about his lady friend. She's the wife of the Canadian cultural attaché.

P. We've got him, huh? Between a rock and a hard place? What's the game plan?

St. Y. At the right time we're going to switch from passive to hot surveillance.

V. Hot?

St. Y. Let him know we're following him around. Then, when he's good and nervous about that, confront him with what we have. We should shock the name of the informer out of him. With a little luck, we might even double him. He'd be our man at the *Post*.

P. Good play.

O. How's Young working out?

St. Y. Fine, fine. We blooded him last night. He sat watch with us, was in on the entry operation. Cool head.

P. That the Agency guy we brought over? Good guy. See him every morning. Puts the Daily Intelligence Summary on my desk.

(inaudible)

V. . . . but we're not making any headway on the Hoover thing, that right?

O. It's all a shot in the dark anyway.

St. Y. No, I think the President's thinking is sound. We know Hoover had a set of blackmail files.

P. Son of a bitch used to tell me stories out of them.

St. Y. Well, these files are supposed to have been destroyed, but I think we're getting close to one partial set.

P. Good, good. Can't think of anything more useful as a handle on some of those Democrat senators. Work on that, Ed.

St. Y. It's top priority. Well, thank you for your time, Mr. President.

P. Always good talking to you, Ed.

    (St. Yves exits)

    (Inaudible conversation)

V. That other thing is moving ahead, but our document man needs a bit more time. That telegram thing.

P. That Kennedy thing? Good. Take your time. It needs a delicate touch. Those media bastards are going to love this one. Full text on page seventeen of the *New York Times*. They'll have no choice. Sure they can't spot the forgery?

V. Expert says that maybe they could if they could get the originals, so we'll see they get only copies.

P. Great work. I think I'm finally getting the kind of staff around me I can trust.

St. Yves, his highly polished shoes up on the desk, was on the telephone. "The son of a bitch doesn't seem amenable to any of the more standard forms of persuasion," he said. "But the Big Man says we have to get him. Now." He took a small silver pocket knife out of his jacket pocket and, flipping the blade open, began cleaning under his already immaculate nails. "We must demonstrate to him the error of his ways. In an immediate and forceful manner. You have any ideas?"

St. Yves listened for a minute. Then he chuckled, a sound that welled up from somewhere deep inside him. "Warren, you're a genius. What the hell would I ever do without you? You have a slimy mind. It should work. You have anyone for the job? . . . Okay. Go ahead. But stay out of it your-self, understand? There's no way we can let this be traced back to the Office. Call me when it's done."

St. Yves hung up and stared at the phone for a minute. Then he broke out laughing again.

Dianna Holroyd walked into the office to find St. Yves leaning back in his swivel chair and gasping for breath. "Here's the weekly action report," she said, carefully setting a folder on her boss's desk. "What's so funny?"

St. Yves sat up and looked at her through tear-washed eyes. "Warren's going to get Schuster," he said.

"Oh. How?"

"You don't want to hear," St. Yves told her. Then, laugh-ing again, he waved her out of his office.

When the doorbell rang, Suzanne Chartre was washing her hair and thinking about Ralph Schuster. He was a rough diamond, her Ralph, but well worth polishing. And such a passionate man! Not that her husband wasn't passionate, or that she didn't love him. But Charles' lovemaking had grown more and more perfunctory.

The doorbell rang again, and Suzanne realized that there was nobody else home to answer it. She wrapped a terry cloth towel around her waist-length hair and put on the red satin robe that Charles had bought her before his passion had waned, adjusting it carefully to be properly modest for Washington, D.C.

"Yes, what is it?" she asked the short, well-dressed man on the porch. Obviously not a tradesman. But not quite Embassy Row. American government official of some sort, probably. Come to see her husband. But why out here? And why Sunday?

"Mrs. Chartre?"

"Yes?" Not for her husband. It was a beautiful warm day outside, she noticed. She'd have to get dressed and get

89

out. Perhaps do some shopping. What *did* this man want?

"Mr. Schuster sent me."

"Excuse me?" Ralph? Sent him? What for? Perhaps he was hurt!

"You're alone?"

"Why, yes." What a strange question.

"I thought you would be. Ralph said so." The man pushed his way by her, and was in the hallway.

She turned and followed him in. "Now, wait a minute!"

The door slammed behind her as a second man, tall, rough-looking, wearing an Army fatigue jacket and a green knitted cap, entered the house.

"What is this?" Suzanne said, trying to stay calm, but feeling the fear rising in her throat.

"We've come to see you, Mrs. Chartre," the tall one said, his voice like gravel falling on a bass drum. "Ralphie says as how you're good. Very good, he says. Are you good, Mrs. Chartre?"

"Get out!" Suzanne gasped the words. She knew she was trembling, but couldn't control it. Where had these men come from?

"Aw, that's no way to talk, Mrs. Chartre," the short one said, grabbing her by the upper forearm and pulling her toward the stairs. "Ralphie says you like it. He says you like it a lot. So we're going to give it to you."

She tried to scream, but the small man clamped his hand over her mouth. Then something was being stuffed in her mouth, and she realized it was the satin belt to her robe. The small man took her shoulders and the tall man took her legs and they hustled her upstairs and into the bedroom.

Five hours later when Charles Chartre, cultural attaché to the Canadian Embassy, came home, he found his wife naked, lying on their bed, staring at the ceiling. Her eyes were puffy and black, and blood from her mouth and her genitals was drying on the pink pastel sheet. There were bruises over much of her body. She did not hear him when he called out. Her eyes did not focus on him when he leaned over her. He called his doctor and then the police. Then he returned to the side of the bed. "Darling," he said.

This time her eyes almost focused. "Ralph," she whispered. "Why?"

• CHAPTER NINE

THE FRONT DOORBELL in Aaron Adams' house played the first eight bars of "Yankee Doodle." He'd always meant to change it to something less strident, like the "Ode to Joy" or the *Internationale*, but deed had not yet followed thought and it still played "Yankee Doodle."

This evening, when the call to arms sounded, Adams was settled comfortably in his study reading. He laid the book aside, stretched, and went to the door. It was a little past ten, and he was expecting nobody.

He looked through the peephole and saw an Army uniform with three rows of ribbons. Four stars twinkled on the right shoulder loop. Adams pulled the bolt and released the lock. "Tank!" he said, opening the door. "What the hell are you doing here?"

General Hiram "Tank" MacGregor stalked past him and into the house. "That's a fine way to greet an old friend who's traveled miles to see you," he said. "How are you, Aaron—how the hell are you?"

Adams closed the door and led the way into the study. "Well, it's been a while, hasn't it?" he said. "What about a drink? I'll tell you: what about an Irish coffee?"

"Wonderful, Aaron, if it isn't too much trouble. Go easy on the cream, though. This inactive staff life is hard on a man's waistline."

"You settle down, Tank. Let me go out in the kitchen for a second; there should be a pot of coffee set up in there ready for me to perk. To what do I owe the honor of this visit? Why didn't you call first? Not that I mind your dropping in, but you might still be standing out there pushing the bell. About half the time I don't bother answering."

"Maggie has a sister who lives a couple of blocks down, over on Rosedale," MacGregor said, settling down into one of Adams' leather chairs and calling after Adams as he headed for the kitchen. "Can't stand the sister, so I came here while Maggie went there."

Adams brought the electric percolator in and plugged it in at the bar. "Five minutes," he said. "Ain't modern science wonderful?"

MacGregor rubbed his hands together thoughtfully and stared into the flame that flickered in the fireplace. "It's come, Aaron," he said. "The President is appointing me Chief of Staff."

Aaron carefully poured a measured amount of whipping cream into the blender. "Congratulations," he said. "I'm not surprised. Who better?"

"Yes," General MacGregor said. "It's a fine way to end a military career. The short but violent life of the professional soldier. The President is hoping I'll turn it down, of course. Maggie is, too, for that matter."

Adams thought this over while the blender whipped the cream, drowning out any chance for conversation. "I can understand Maggie's wanting you to turn down the job," he said when he turned the blender off, "but why should the President care? The senior officers of the services traditionally pick the Chiefs of Staff and tell the President who to appoint. Now, the Chairman of the Joint Chiefs is another matter; that has been known to be a political appointment."

"This President," MacGregor said, "seems to have a preference for men who owe him personal loyalty. He would have men about him who are his, even down to the lowest level. If he wasn't afraid of the reaction, he'd like nothing better than to appoint some loyal brigadier general to the chairmanship, skipping him over the heads of a couple of hundred senior officers."

"It's a damn good way of engendering personal loyalty in even the most objective of men," Adams agreed. "If you know that you owe your job to the incumbent, and you're out when he's out, the tendency to support his decisions must be almost overwhelming."

MacGregor kept his gaze on the fire and accepted the Irish coffee silently when Adams handed it to him. He was obviously deeply troubled.

Adams settled into his own chair and sipped at his coffee, allowing the soothing combination of caffeine and alcohol to settle in his stomach and work its way into his bloodstream. He was remembering the time, almost thirty years ago, when he had first met Tank MacGregor.

It was somewhere in eastern France and MacGregor, three years out of West Point, was commanding a company of war-beaten Sherman tanks. Adams was called forward to interrogate some high-ranking Wehrmacht officers who had been captured by MacGregor's men. "How did you capture them?" he asked the twenty-three-year-old captain.

MacGregor grinned and shrugged. "They didn't expect to see me where I was."

"Where was that?"

"At the German fuel depot. We were running low on diesel."

Adams stared at him. "The German fuel depot?"

"That's right. We ran down the road single file at about

four in the morning until we came to the depot. Then we filled our tanks and blew the thing up. In the ensuing confusion we managed to pick up a few prisoners."

"How did you know where the Germans kept their fuel depot?"

"I stared at a map and figured out where I would have put it if I were a German supply officer."

By the time the war ended in Europe, Tank MacGregor was a lieutenant colonel, and well on his way to becoming a legend. In Korea, MacGregor got his eagle and developed ways to use the helicopter that turned it into a weapon of war. After Korea, MacGregor returned to Europe as Deputy Chief of Staff at SHAPE, and discovered organizational and administrative talents that brought him his first star. He also discovered the usefulness of his strong personal charisma and began self-consciously to develop those traits of character and appearance that built the charisma. Not that he yearned for personal power or glory, but being Tank Mac-Gregor helped him do his job. The units under his command felt that they had something to live up to, and someone who would listen to their gripes, which made them better soldiers.

So MacGregor kept unchanged the oversized wire-rim glasses, and the cork-tipped stogie that he chewed on but never lit. And the legend grew, and he got his third star and his fourth, and he began appearing on *Face the Nation* and discussing defense policy and the war and the draft.

"What's your problem?" Adams asked MacGregor. "You don't want to be appointed Chief of Staff? Or you don't just want him to appoint you, you want him to love you, too?"

"No, nothing like that, Aaron," MacGregor said. He suddenly realized he still had his hat on, and he took it off and skimmed it across to the couch. Adams was shocked to see how gray his friend's hair had become.

MacGregor shook his head. "I don't know, Aaron. I don't

know what I'm saying. Last year, when I finished the tour in 'Nam, I was all set to retire. Just slowly and gracefully fade away. I've done enough, Aaron. God knows, I've done enough."

"But?"

"But something's happening I don't understand. I can't turn down Chief of Staff, Aaron, but I'm afraid that, after I've got it, I won't be able to do it."

"Why not?"

"The President's taking over the Army. And we're going to bump heads. And you know me, Aaron: old inflexible Tank. I can't bend, so I'll probably break. I just wish to hell I could figure out what that man thinks he's doing. And why he's doing it."

"What is he doing?"

"All the sort of shit that screws up the chain of command and keeps people wondering who's spying on who. He's starting to take the title 'Commander in Chief' very seriously." MacGregor took the cigar out of his mouth. "And the hell of it is, Aaron, that I voted for him."

Adams took his ancient clay pipe from the table by his chair and cleaned the dottle from it with his penknife. "It's not just the Army," he said.

"What's that?"

"It's not just the Army that the President is concerning himself about. He's replaced most of the senior staff at CIA below the Director, and Lord only knows how much longer Dan Bohr will last. And just about the whole top level of the FBI is his now." Adams pushed a plug of Balkan Sobranie tobacco firmly into the clay bowl of his pipe.

MacGregor leaned back in his chair and stuck the cigar back firmly between his teeth. "What's he up to? I thought he just liked to play soldier."

"I'm not sure," Adams said. "There are a lot of little

pieces, and only someone high up in the Executive Office would be able to get a good look at the pattern. But there are a few, ah, disquieting signs."

"Like what?"

"The IRS has set up something they call the Special Intelligence Unit to examine selected tax returns. The President's men do the selecting and send the lists down. Columnists who've written articles against the administration, owners of newspapers that didn't support the President, movie stars who actively opposed the President's policies, even congressmen who voted the wrong way.

"The Post Office is setting up a special unit to open mail at the President's request. That's first-class mail, you understand, and without any sort of legal formality like a warrant."

MacGregor shook his head. "Hell, Aaron, you fellows used to do that over in CIA. Probably still do. Not that I think it's right."

"I'm not discussing morality," Adams said. "You bend the law a little bit if you think it's for the country's good; maybe that's acceptable. At least it's debatable. But we did it against foreign agents, not Democrats."

"Just what is it you think is happening?"

"As I said, I'm not sure," Adams said. He paused to light his pipe with his vintage Zippo. "The President's built this three-man wall around himself. Ober, Gildruss, and Vandermeer are the untouchables, and nobody can get to the President except through them." He pointed a finger at MacGregor. "Think about this: The chain of command in the Army goes through the Chief of Staff—you—to the Chairman of the Joint Chiefs to the Secretary of the Army to the Secretary of Defense to Dr. Peter Gildruss, Supersecretary, and then to the President."

"So?"

"So everyone on the chain from you to the Secretary of Defense is accountable to both the President and to Congress. But the Supersecretary, Dr. Gildruss, is not a constitutional position. He's accountable to no one but the President. And he's empowered by the President to give orders to anyone in the chain under him, which is to say everyone in the Defense Department and the State Department. The man could trigger a war, and he's not as accountable as the Secretary of Commerce. Every general officer has to be approved by Congress, but the guy in charge of the whole military and intelligence establishment is appointed by the President."

Tank MacGregor nodded thoughtfully. "I noticed that as it went by," he said. "With all the newspapers talking about how it would consolidate the government and make decision-making easier and maybe even save us some money in the long run, nobody seemed to notice that in the interest of efficiency he was stealing the reins of the government from the Congress."

"Strange talk for the Army Chief of Staff," Adams commented.

"The word, Aaron, is treason," MacGregor said. "That's what kept running through my mind when I first had these thoughts. And that's what the court-martial would say, maybe. But then I realized something." MacGregor paused and sipped at his drink.

"I swore an oath, Aaron, many years ago at the Point when they pinned those little gold bars to my shoulders. It's almost the same oath that the President swears: to support and defend the Constitution of the United States against all enemies, foreign and domestic, and to bear true faith and allegiance to the same.

"I took that oath very seriously back then, and I guess I still do. I hope it never comes to choosing between the

President and the Constitution. But that phrase keeps coming back to me—'all enemies, foreign . . . and domestic.'" MacGregor shook his head. "Let's talk about something else," he said. "You still running that poker game?"

● CHAPTER TEN

Sunday, September 2, 1973

OF INTEREST TO THE GENERAL PUBLIC. THESE CONVENTIONS, "WORLDCONS" THEY ARE CALLED, ALTHOUGH MOST OF THEM HAVE BEEN HELD IN THE UNITED STATES, HAVE BEEN YEARLY EVENTS SINCE 1943. THE LAST ONE, HELD IN LOS

A

BUST

84MPS

URGENT
WASHINGTON, 12:20 (MPS)—FIRST LEAD PRESIDENT NEWS CONFERENCE
AT AN UNSCHEDULED PRESS CONFERENCE CALLED THIS MORNING IN THE OVAL OFFICE OF THE WHITE HOUSE THE PRESIDENT ANNOUNCED THE APPOINTMENT OF DANIEL BOHR, THE DIRECTOR OF THE CIA, TO THE POST OF AMBASSADOR TO IRAN. HE SAID THAT HE WAS PLEASED TO HAVE A MAN OF BOHR'S INTELLIGENCE AND EXPERIENCE AVAILABLE FOR A POST THAT WAS GROWING INCREASINGLY MORE IMPORTANT IN THE FOREIGN RELATIONS OF THE UNITED STATES.

BOHR, WHO WAS WITH THE PRESIDENT, SAID HE WAS GLAD TO SERVE WHEREVER HIS COUNTRY NEEDED HIM.

BOHR'S DISTINGUISHED CAREER AS A PUBLIC SERVANT BEGAN IN F.D.R.'S SECOND TERM, AND HE HAS SERVED ABLY IN A VARIETY OF POSTS IN THE DEPARTMENTS OF STATE, DEFENSE, THE INTERIOR, AND FOR THE PAST SIX YEARS IN THE CENTRAL INTELLIGENCE AGENCY.

AS THE NEW DIRECTOR OF THE CIA, THE PRESIDENT HAS NAMED RALPH CARMICHAEL, WHO IS CURRENTLY SERVING AS ASSISTANT ATTORNEY GENERAL. CARMICHAEL HAS SERVED WITH THE PRESIDENT IN VARIOUS CAPACITIES SINCE THE PRESIDENT FIRST CAME TO WASHINGTON AS A CONGRESSMAN IN 1948.

IT IS NOT ANTICIPATED THAT EITHER BOHR OR CARMICHAEL WILL HAVE ANY DIFFICULTY IN THEIR SENATE CONFIRMATIONS. (MORE)

EDITORS: BOHR AND CARMICHAEL BIOS FOLLOW.
CONTINUED

83MPS
ANGELES OVER LABOR DAY WEEKEND LAST YEAR WAS ATTENDED BY OVER THREE THOUSAND PERSONS. THE THREE DAYS OF SCI-FI REVELRY INCLUDED SUCH HAPPENINGS AS BUST IT
      BUST IT
                     BUST IT

85MPS
   B U L L E T I N
FIRST LEAD RALPH SCHUSTER
WASHINGTON, 12:30 (MPS)—RALPH SCHUSTER, A REPORTER FOR THE WASHINGTON POST, WAS FOUND DEAD IN HIS APARTMENT THIS MORNING. SCHUSTER APPARENTLY COMMITTED SUICIDE BY PUTTING THE BARREL OF A SMALL CALIBER REVOLVER IN HIS MOUTH AND PULLING THE TRIGGER. A NEIGHBOR HEARD THE SHOT AND TELEPHONED THE POLICE,

WHO WERE THERE IN MINUTES. THEY FORCED THEIR WAY
INTO THE APARTMENT AND FOUND SCHUSTER'S BODY ON
THE LIVING ROOM COUCH. HE LEFT A NOTE, THE TEXT OF
WHICH HAS NOT BEEN RELEASED AT THIS TIME, BUT IT
IS BELIEVED TO STATE THAT HE WAS DRIVEN TO HIS ACT BY
"THE PRESIDENT'S MEN." WHAT HE MEANT BY THIS IS
NOT KNOWN.

SCHUSTER WAS ON THE CITY DESK OF THE POST,
WHERE HE HAD BEEN FOR THE PAST THREE YEARS.

(MORE)

Kit Young groaned and rolled over in his sleep, throwing what was left of the bedclothes onto the floor. *An unappetizing sort of man*, thought Miriam, looking down at his twisted form, *half child and half ape. I can't for the life of me figure out why I'm so fond of him.* She prodded him with her index finger. "Wake up, my love," she said softly, "the bird is on the wing!"

Kit opened one eye and stared fuzzily up at her. "He'll freeze his ass off," he said. "It's cold out there." He groped around for a minute, his hand encountering nothing but rumpled sheet, then he sat up and opened his other eye. "What have you done with the blankets?" he demanded.

"They're on the floor where you threw them."

"Did no such thing," he said. "What time is it?"

"Almost one. Want some orange juice?"

"That's what I like about you," Kit said, swinging his legs over the side of the bed. "You're always ready with a kind word and a glass of orange juice. I don't know how anyone can be so damn cheery in the morning."

"How would you know what I'm like in the morning?" Miriam said sweetly. "You've never been awake in the morning."

Kit considered this. "I'll take a shower. When my blood sugar gets high enough I'll join in this repartee." He stood

102

up and staggered into the bathroom. "Any clean towels?" he called out as he closed the door.

"On the rack," she yelled through the door.

"Um!" he called back. Then the water went on. Miriam went out into her kitchen and busied herself preparing brunch: Nova Scotia salmon, bagels, cream cheese, thin slices of Bermuda onion. She broke five eggs into a bowl and whipped them up, then set her French enameled frying pan on a low fire and hoped the butter wouldn't burn before Kit got out of the shower.

Miriam found that she enjoyed the mornings when Kit stayed over with her for themselves, and not just as echoes of the night before. She would get up before Kit—no great problem—and prepare an elaborate breakfast. On days when he wasn't working and slept until early afternoon, she would prepare an even more elaborate lunch. Perhaps she was finally developing the nesting instinct, and any day now she'd start going all soft inside at the thought of tiny feet and wet diapers and 4 A.M. feedings. Well, she certainly hoped not. She and Kit had a very good thing going: they enjoyed each other's company, they respected each other, they turned each other on, they were good in bed together, and they never argued about money. It would sure be a shame to spoil all that by getting married.

Now that Kit had left CIA and gone to work directly for the President, their one great source of argument was gone. Not that Miriam had changed her views, but now Kit flatly refused to discuss politics or the administration in any way. Miriam didn't agree with his position, but he was immovable.

So she suppressed her feelings and, since politics was the only thing they had ever argued about, they never fought anymore. But it was still there between them. Kit was looking increasingly depressed when she saw him, and he admitted that it was about the job but refused to discuss it. He had several times snorted and left the room in the middle of a news broadcast, usually when something Miriam thought quite innocuous was being discussed. He still didn't seem overly concerned about the continuing social unrest or any of the other issues that Miriam held close to her heart, but even little unimportant changes in government or things like the interview with the director of the new Institute for an Informed America would get him upset. She had urged him to discuss it, if not with her, then with Aaron, but he was adamant about keeping his mouth closed. "Maybe someday I'll write one hell of a memoir," he said.

So they had peace, and Kit had problems that he couldn't share with her. And she was happy for the peace, and unhappy for what Kit couldn't share, and still it was better than fighting.

Kit came out of the bedroom buttoning his shirt-sleeves and stood in front of the big living room mirror to knot his tie. "What's the tie for?" Miriam asked, knowing she was fighting a losing fight. "Where are we going?"

"A man is either dressed or undressed," Kit said, "and if he's dressed, he has a tie."

Miriam shrugged expressively. "I refuse to argue with a man's religion," she said.

"I had a great-uncle who went insane," Kit told her. "Spent his declining years in a home for the bewildered up in Massachusetts. Walked around all day stark naked except for a string tie and a top hat." He paused. "Aren't you going to ask me why?"

"I know better," she told him.

"When I graduated from college I went up to see my great-uncle," Kit continued. "Must have been in his eighties then. I asked him. 'Uncle Jebedah, why don't you have any clothes on?' 'Why should I?' he asked me. 'It's hot as the other place in here, and nobody ever comes to see me anyway.' 'But Uncle,' I objected, 'what about the hat and tie?' He looked at me like I was the one who was crazy. 'Somebody *might* come,' he said. I have never forgotten those words of wisdom."

"I'll scramble the eggs," Miriam said.

After brunch, Kit shared the couch with the bulky Sunday editions of the *New York Times* and the *Washington Post*. Miriam sat at her window desk editing the galleys of her latest article for *Polity*. It was almost 3 P.M. when the phone rang.

"It's for you," Miriam said. "How does anyone know to call you here?"

"I always leave this number when I'm staying over," Kit said absently, taking the phone. "They don't call unless it's urgent."

He took the phone and listened, with only an occasional "Yes," or "I see," to break long stretches of silence. Miriam turned in her chair and stared at him, finding herself getting angrier and angrier. How *dare* he leave her number when he spent the night with her. What did he do, post it on the office bulletin board? This was too much. Why didn't he just write it on a few phone booth walls while he was at it?

Kit hung up and looked at her. There was a strange vacant expression on his face.

"What do you mean leaving my number with your office?" Miriam demanded. "You've a hell of a nerve."

"They don't know it's your number," Kit said, focusing on her. "It's just a number. They couldn't care less where I spend my nights. I'm on the right side."

There was something wrong. By now it had come through Miriam's fog of anger that Kit wasn't responding to her emotion. Something he had heard on the phone had preempted his response. "What do you mean?" she asked softly. "What do you mean, 'on the right side'?"

Miriam sat down on the couch next to Kit. "A guy named Schuster. Reporter for the *Post*. I knew him. They just told me."

"What? What did they just tell you?"

"They found him this morning. The police. Vandermeer wants me to follow the case. There'll be an official announcement."

"What case?" Miriam asked, taking his hand. "What are you talking about?"

"He killed himself," Kit said. "In his apartment."

"Oh," Miriam said. There was a strange, stretched quality in Kit's voice that she had never heard before, and she reached for understanding. "You knew him? I don't think you've ever mentioned him. Was he a friend?"

"No. Not a friend. I met him once. I—saw—him a few more times. I think it's safe to say I wasn't his friend."

"What does Vandermeer want you to follow? If he committed suicide, what more is there? And why should Vandermeer care, anyway?"

"He left a note," Kit said.

"A note? Explaining why he—whatever he did?"

"Shot himself. Through the head. The note doesn't explain why. It's very short."

"What does it say?"

"It says, 'Fuck all the President's men.' It was in his typewriter. That's all it says."

"Oh," Miriam said. "How strange."

"Yes," Kit agreed.

That afternoon Edward St. Yves met Billy Vandermeer in the latter's White House office. "Glad you could take a few minutes to see me," St. Yves said. "Sorry it had to be on such short notice, but I've got something I think will interest you."

"I have a well-developed faith in your judgment, Ed,"

Vandermeer said. "If you ever have something you think will interest me, scoot it on over here right away. It's about the Schuster business?"

St. Yves shook his head. "That little son of a bitch," he said. "Who would have thought?" He sat down in one of the metal-frame red chairs surrounding the desk. "I really thought we had him. I really did."

"How's that girl of his? The Canadian, ah, lady?"

"She's been out of the hospital a month. Must have been hysterical. She wasn't hurt that bad."

"Some people are sensitive," Vandermeer said. The sun glanced off Vandermeer's horn-rimmed glasses, making it impossible to read his expression. Looking at his blond visage, St. Yves was suddenly reminded of Vandermeer's daughter, Kathy, and felt himself on tenuous ground.

"I don't like to figure wrong," St. Yves continued more cautiously, "and I sure figured this one wrong. We haven't had any contact with him for the past three weeks. Give him a chance to get with that girl again. Think about it some. Then Warren gave him a call a couple of days ago. Put it to him. Something would happen to the girl again."

"That wasn't very subtle."

"All he suggested was she might be *persona non grata*-ed as an undesirable. But I'm sure he got the drift. Said he'd think it over. That was Thursday. Then—blam! How can you predict such a thing?"

"It was, um, an accident?" Vandermeer asked.

St. Yves stared at Vandermeer, his blue eyes glinting. "It was suicide," he said.

"Yes, um, of course. What I meant was, there was no —to your knowledge—there was no external force that might have, um, prompted such an act? That is, beyond the pressures we've just been discussing."

"To the best of my knowledge," St. Yves said, "the son of a bitch just up and shot himself."

"Right," Vandermeer said. "Well, enough about that. It's a, um, dead issue."

"You making a statement?"

"Have to," Vandermeer said. "We express regrets. Assign a man to cooperate with the D.C. Police. We picked Kit Young."

"Very good," St. Yves said. "He'll know which problem areas to steer clear of."

"Any prospect of plugging the leak with Schuster gone?" Vandermeer asked. "The President is very concerned about the leak. He feels keenly about disloyalty."

St. Yves shook his head. "I don't recruit men like that for room sixteen," he said. "My men are loyal to the President and to me; they don't give a shit about the Constitution or the Washington Monument or the United States Code. They're loyal to the country through the President and the President through me."

"What about the leak?" Vandermeer asked.

"We'll keep checking," St. Yves said. "With his contact gone, the source is probably going to have to establish a new one before he can continue. One thing you should consider: it's distinctly possible that the leak comes straight out of CIA. Those people may be trying to discredit us. It would be useful if the President passed the word to the new Director to check on that."

"I'll mention it," Vandermeer said.

"Now," St. Yves said, putting his briefcase on one corner of the desk and snapping it open. "Here's what our document boys have come up with for you." He took a file out of a zippered compartment and passed it over.

Vandermeer took it gingerly, as though afraid that it might blister his fingers. The file cover had the printed seal of the Department of State on it, and was stamped TOP SECRET in red block letters. A typed label on the file's tab read: "Saigon Embassy Cables / Nov. 1963."

"This is it?" Vandermeer asked, his voice almost a whisper.

St. Yves nodded. "All the documentation," he said. "And done right. Original typewriter, original carbon, the right paper. We got some help from the Technical Services Division of the Agency; the new director's a big improvement."

"It'll pass?" Vandermeer asked. "Everything?" St. Yves looked at him peculiarly, and he realized that he was still whispering.

"It should," St. Yves said. "But to make sure, like I said before, we make sure they only get their hands on Xerox copies of these. Can't let these leave the files, after all. You check them over and give me your okay, and Operation Counterfoil is launched."

Vandermeer opened the folder and glanced at a few of the telegrams inside, then closed it and pushed it over to St. Yves by the edge. "I don't want to read it," he said. "Better if it comes as a surprise to me when the media boys come waving it at me. You sure you got the tone right?"

"As right as a forgery can ever be," St. Yves said. "There's always a certain stiffness in forged documents because the forger is unwilling to be original—to use any phrases that weren't in the real copy."

"You certainly know your craft," Vandermeer said.

"Yes," St. Yves agreed. "Do we go with Counterfoil?"

"Okay," Vandermeer said. "I'll pass it upstairs."

"Right," St. Yves said. "You shouldn't have any trouble with the Democrats for a while after this comes out."

"Speaking of Democrats, what about the special operations for the election? How are they coming?"

"They're well under way. We've picked our primary targets from the list of men the President wants out. We've got some very good men on special operations. A few opposition congressmen seem to have sex problems of one sort or another. It'll take a while to get them pegged, but we've got a good lead time here. You want a list of the operations?"

Vandermeer shook his head. "No," he said. "I don't think so. Not at this point in time."

• CHAPTER ELEVEN

MALCOLM CHAYMBER got out of the cab at the corner of Third Avenue and Fifty-fourth Street, Manhattan. He looked around cautiously as the cab pulled away, haunted as always at moments like this by the conviction that someone he knew would walk around the corner and recognize him.

His heart pounding with fear and excitement, as it invariably did at the start of one of his adventures, Chaymber walked the two blocks to the bar called Peters and went in. Of course, Chaymber admitted to himself, the fear was part of it. It was cathartic. Without the excitement, the danger, and the fear, the whole thing would seem like a sordid little meaningless affair of the flesh each time; and despite his body's hunger, he probably wouldn't be able to go through with it. So the very factors that made it so unwise—that it was illegal and dangerous, and could ruin his career—in a strange way were what made it possible.

Peters was, as usual, crowded to overflow. Account executives with forced laughs and hungry eyes jammed at the bar. Pretty boys with tight jeans and lean, muscular bodies

111

posed against the far wall and nursed their drinks to make them last. Couples at the tables leaned over in close conversation, earnestly lying to each other. The tacky tinsel Christmas decorations looked worn out already, and it was still a week before Christmas.

Chaymber wedged himself into a spot at the bar, ordered a scotch, and looked around at the scene. *And we call ourselves gay,* he thought. As he always thought. He would stand there, speaking to no one, and have three or four drinks. And one of the young men across the way would begin to look appealing to him, would suddenly attain attributes of truth, beauty, wisdom, and grace that would astound even his own mother, and he would think of some clever line to approach the youth with: a line that would enable them both to preserve some measure of self-respect as they both pretended they believed it.

"You are quiet and pensive," a voice on his left said.

"What?" Chaymber turned. A young man with brown hair and frank eyes was staring at him.

"Pensive," the young man said. "And quiet. And a little morose. You're eyeing the meat rack over there as though you contemplate a painful duty."

"Not painful, no," Chaymber said.

"Then what?"

"I don't know if there's a word," Chaymber said.

"If there were, what would it mean?"

"I think 'doomed to disappointment' would approach it."

The young man put his hand to his head and twisted it as though turning a key. "Nope," he said after a moment, "my mental thesaurus has no single word that means 'doomed to disappointment.' The closest it can come is 'life,' but that's the closest it can come to a lot of things." He brushed some dust off the sleeve of his suede jacket. "My name is Sandy, by the way."

"Richard," Chaymber said. "Richard Hatch." He held out his hand and Sandy shook it firmly.

"No last name," Sandy said. "I had one once, but I lost it in the dust of a previous journey."

"It must have been quite a trip," Chaymber said.

"Oh, it was," Sandy agreed. "I traveled from there"—he nodded over at the meat rack—"to here, but on a very circuitous path."

"You hardly look old enough to have a past," Chaymber said, mentally digesting the fact that Sandy had once been a hustler.

"The past is only yesterday," Sandy said, and then he grinned. "And that's either very profound or very, very stupid."

"I'm hungry," Chaymber said, suddenly realizing it was so. "Come have dinner with me."

"Glad to," Sandy agreed. "But, you understand, I'll buy my own."

"I wouldn't have it any other way," Chaymber said.

They went to dinner and they talked. Malcolm Chaymber talked about the world and Sandy talked about himself. Chaymber was unprepared to talk about himself, so it was a fair exchange. They enjoyed each other's company and, for the first time in one of these relationships, Chaymber didn't feel lied to or manipulated.

Sandy told Chaymber what it was like being a male hustler: the insecurities, frustrations, self-denials; and how he had left the meat rack. "I met a father figure," Sandy said. "Not a sugar daddy, you know, but a real surrogate father. And, believe me, incest can be beautiful. He was a novelist. You'd know his name, but there's no point in my using it except to impress you, which it wouldn't; you're not the sort to be impressed by names. But anyway, we traveled together and I met all his friends. And he never in-

113

troduced me as his 'son' or his 'nephew' or any of that bullcrap, but always as his friend. It lasted for two years and then we parted—friends—and he laid some money on me, and here I am."

"I have a wife," Chaymber told Sandy over coffee, "and two children."

"Does she know about—you?"

"Yes."

"I've never been close to any woman since I left home when I was fourteen," Sandy said. "I mean, when I was a hustler I went through the usual macho trip of pretending that I only did it for the money, and I really preferred girls in the sack. So I took a few to the sack and I grunted and groaned, but I was never able to get it off with them."

"When I started coming to New York," Chaymber told Sandy, "my wife threw a tremendous scene. She thought I had a girl here."

"What did you tell her?"

"I finally told her the truth. I was afraid she'd go through the roof, maybe get a divorce, but it was just the opposite. At first she didn't believe me. Then she started laughing. Then she got very sympathetic and told me we'd work it out."

"Did you?"

"We worked out a very important part of it; we stopped lying to each other. We also stopped having sex."

Sandy had a loft on Houston Street, and they went there after dinner. "Careful where you step!" Sandy warned, switching on the overhead lights. The loft was done in a severe modern style, all chrome and bent plastic and stretched canvas like a harsh parody of the Bauhaus forty years later. The various work and sleep areas were formed by heavy drapery hangings suspended by wires several feet below the fourteen-foot ceiling.

"Welll!" Chaymber said. "I'm impressed. The place is huge."

"That's why I didn't put up full partitions," Sandy said. "I get privacy and keep spaciousness at the same time."

Sandy pulled Chaymber through the various "rooms" to the rear of the loft. In the center of the large clear space, there rose a creation of welded bronze and steel rod, tube, and sheet. "My latest," he said proudly.

"You didn't tell me you did anything like that," Chaymber said, obviously impressed. "What do you call it?"

"Right now I call it *Chaos*," Sandy said. "*Chaos* by Sandy. But I don't know what I'll call it when it's done. I have such fun doing them that I don't have time to think about what they are. And then people come and pay me to take them away and make room for the next. It's like being paid to make love."

"Which you were," Chaymber said.

"No," Sandy corrected him. "I was paid to screw, but never to make love. Come with me—I'll show you the difference."

They stayed in the loft together until the next evening, when they went to Pietro's for dinner, then went to see *The Sunshine Boys* at the Broadhurst Theater. Then they went back to the loft and stayed together until eight the next morning, when Chaymber left to catch the shuttle back to Washington.

Sandy went back to sleep, and slept till noon; then he rose and showered and had a cup of coffee and picked up the phone to dial a number. "St. Yves," he said. "Tell him it's Sandy."

"Hi. It's me, Sandy. I got him. . . .

"Of course I'm sure. He called himself Richard Hatch, but it was him. I got a look in his wallet. Senator Malcolm Chaymber. No question. . . .

"Okay. I'm seeing him again next week. I'll keep him on

115

the string—no sweat. But listen, go easy on the guy, will you? I kind of like him."

George Warren drove his light-green Camarro north on the Garden State Parkway, keeping to the posted sixty-mile speed limit. The day was crystal-clear and the woods, covered with fresh snow, gleamed with peculiarly three-dimensional purity. Neither of which facts Warren noticed. For him, weather was an annoyance that made him add or subtract layers of clothing, and scenery was no more than an incidental backdrop.

What concerned Warren was people and how to manipulate them. He considered himself something of an expert in this, and performed his expertise with cold-blooded efficiency. After ten minutes with a girl he could tell how many times he'd have to say "I love you" before she would spread her legs. After ten minutes with a man he would know whether threats of extortion or physical torture were more likely to cause him to become talkative.

Warren turned off the Parkway and headed west. When the odometer had clocked ten and a half miles, he pulled over to the edge of the two-lane blacktop and shut off the engine.

The manila envelope that St. Yves had given him was behind the sun visor. He pulled it out and examined the two photographs it contained. The first, a tall, skinny, blond Caucasian in his mid-twenties, was his contact, CALVIN MIDDLER. The second, a candid shot of a short, round-faced, blond Caucasian female in her early twenties, side view, was ZONYA (BELIEVED ALIAS, PRINTS NOT ON FILE). After staring at the two photographs for a few minutes, he slowly tore them into small pieces, which he wadded up and put in a lump on the dirt shoulder of the road. Then, with a heavy Zippo lighter, he set fire to the lump. When it burned out he ground the ashes into the dirt.

Warren checked his watch as he climbed back into the car. It was eleven twenty in the morning, ten minutes before rendezvous, and just time to get there. He started the car and drove slowly ahead, looking for a side road on the left. A few hundred yards on, he came to it and turned.

About a quarter mile in, the road turned to dirt. Well-worn tractor ruts made the going more difficult, pitching the car about like a small boat in a choppy sea. Warren was forced to slow down to a crawl, and shortly he gave up altogether. He slowly maneuvered the car around so that it was facing back out, then he got out and locked it. By the odometer he had less than half a mile to go anyway. He opened the trunk and took out a knapsack, pulling the straps through his arms and adjusting it to ride high on his back. Then he closed the trunk and started off down the road.

Ten minutes later he came to a clearing where two Army-surplus command tents had been pitched. There were nine or ten people of indeterminate sex, dressed in various versions of woodsman-hippie, gathered in a wide circle in front of the far tent. In the middle of the circle, neatly stacked, were six machine guns and two Army ammo boxes. The boxes were open, and two of the group were kneeling by them and filling clips for the machine guns with the loose bullets. The rest of them were watching intently, while passing two small hash pipes around the circle.

The circle broke apart as Warren approached, and one of the hash pipes hastily disappeared. The girl holding the other pipe kept it between her lips as she turned toward Warren, jauntily thrusting it out like F.D.R.'s cigarette holder. It was Zonya—the girl in the photograph—but now her hair was long, thin, and brunette.

Warren spotted Calvin Middler as one of the two men loading clips. Since they were supposed to already know each other, Warren waved casually. "Hi, Middler," he said.

Calvin jumped to his feet. "This is the man I been tell-

117

ing you about," he told the group.

"I don't know," the young man who had hidden the hash pipe said, "He looks pretty straight to me."

George Warren slowly and calmly looked the youth over. The others, silent and hostile, waited for him to speak. "I don't look straight to you, boy," he said finally, "I look neat. You look sloppy and undisciplined—all of you." He walked over to Middler and tapped him on the chest with his right forefinger. "You called me here to meet these infants?" he demanded. "In the jungles of Bolivia I worked with starving peasants—illiterate, disease-ridden, filthy, malnourished, hopeless men—and we turned them into an army. But these upper-middle-class infants who think that to be sloppy is to be free, and that smoking dope is an act of rebellion against authority—" Warren turned to the group. "They chewed coca leaves in the jungle. Not to turn themselves on, but to stop them from feeling the hunger pangs and let them keep drilling and working. And we won in Cuba, and we'll win in South America. But the United States?" He thrust his finger in the face of the youth who had called him straight. "You people call yourselves the People's Revolutionary Brigade. Why? What people? What revolution? You people are so stupid you don't even know enough to post perimeter guards. What the fuck do you think you're doing out here?"

"Now, calm down, Carlos," Middler said, raising his arms in the air in a cross between pacification and benediction. "These people are new to all this. But they've got guts. You read about that bank robbery in Brooklyn last week?"

"You mean the one where four masked men with machine guns held up a row of young girl tellers and a sixty-four-year-old bank guard and got away with eight thousand? I read about it."

"It was our first operation," Zonya said.

"Zonya!" the young man yelped. "Shut up!"

118

"What for, Jay-boy?" Zonya asked. "You think he's a nark?"

"Look" Warren said. "Whatever your friend Jay thinks, I'm not a nark. What I am is a contact man for goodies: goodies that explode, goodies that shoot, all goodies that bother the capitalist pigs. You want to see?"

"Sure," one of the group spoke.

"I'll show you what I've got. You make good use of them, I get you more. But you people better get more professional if you want to do any good. The FBI and the CIA aren't staffed with amateurs." With a shrug of his shoulders, Warren dropped the backpack, catching it with his right hand as it fell. He undid the flaps and distributed the contents in a line on the ground in front of him.

"These are bombs," he said. "They're professionally made, and can be depended on to do what they're supposed to."

"Which is what?" Zonya asked.

"Blow up things," Warren said. He picked up one of the objects and held it in the air in front of him. It was the general size and shape of a cigar box with a brown drafting-paper finish. On the side of the box were two small spring clips for wires to be attached. "You pass a six-volt current through these clips, you blow up a car, a room, a locker, a bank, a few people, whatever. You want to use a couple of lantern batteries if you can, be sure you've got enough amperage. One six-volt lantern battery will probably do. A transistor radio battery or four flashlight batteries in series probably won't.

"A cheap wristwatch makes a good timer." He pulled one out of his pocket. "You remove the plastic crystal, then pull off the second and minute hands. Drill a hole in the plastic at the center, and one at twelve o'clock. Stick a couple of wires through the holes. You've got a twelve-hour

119

timer. Up to twelve hours. Set it for the delay you want. Accurate to within a minute or two. Carry a short-tester with you to test the watch right before you hook it into the circuit. Anybody know any electronics?"

"I do," a small young man with a large mustache volunteered.

"Good, come with me." The two of them crossed the field to where a tall tree, about as thick around as a large man's circling arms, grew by itself. Warren placed the charge on a low branch next to the trunk and fastened the watch-and-battery timing circuit to the two clips, after checking with his pocket short-tester. Then they came back to the group. "Let's get back in that gully," Warren said. "And bring the guns and the other charges." They all scrambled down the side of a stream bank behind the tents.

The whole group huddled together, staring out between the two tents at the tree. "I set about a five-minute delay," Warren said, "the shortest I feel safe with. Any time now."

Then it blew. A sharp, clear sound, loud enough to cause brief pain, and followed promptly by the lesser echoes, as the wave reverberated off the snowy hills. The air was suddenly filled with snow and mist. The tree wavered. And then it fell straight down on itself, as though collapsing inward. And then it stopped. And then it slowly, slowly tilted against the sky. The tilting grew faster and the tree fell to earth with a shuddering crash.

"That's it," Warren said, as the group climbed back up the bank and brushed themselves off. There was a hole in one of the tents where a fireplace-sized log had burst through on its way to ground. "It's not a toy."

Zonya hefted one of the cigar boxes with respectful care. "We could sure off a few pigs with one of these," she said.

"That's just what we don't want to do," Middler said. "Not now. Not yet."

"Why not?" Zonya demanded.

"Because we're trying to build public support, not destroy it. We've got to use the bombs to destroy the countinghouses and guardhouses of the capitalist system—not to kill people. Not until stage three. And we're not even in stage two yet."

"He's right," Warren said. "I'll leave you with these three explosive devices. If you want more, you're going to have to show me more. I want the PRB to develop a bomb doctrine—and a command and priority doctrine, for that matter—and I and my people will support you. But you've go to be more military. And that includes such mundane details as posting guards on an operation."

"Who are your people?" Jay demanded in a voice that fought hard not to sound surly.

"I am Carlos," Warren said, "and you are all my people. Wherever I am needed, I will be. Come, walk with me, Middler." He picked up the empty knapsack and started back the way he had come.

"I'll be right back," Middler called, and ran to catch up with Warren.

When they were out of earshot of the People's Revolutionary Brigade, Middler said, "Well, what do you think?"

"See if you can take over—or at least become group planner."

"No sweat," Middler said. "Zonya's holding the group together. And we're, ah, getting very close."

"Good luck," Warren said. "Tell her how smart she is; that's what she wants to hear."

"Did you talk to your boss?"

"Yes."

"And?"

"He agreed," Warren said. "As of now, you're not just an informant, you're on the payroll."

"Of the CIA? I'm a CIA agent?"

"That's right."

"Do I get to go to the CIA school?"

"Probably. After this assignment." There was certainly no reason to tell Midler that he was really working for the SIU.

"I'd better get back."

"Right. I'll be in touch."

Bill Heym got up from his desk in the *Washington Post*'s newsroom and crossed the bullpen to the glass-enclosed cubicle with NATIONAL EDITOR in black on the frosted-glass door. Pushing the door open, he stuck his head in and said, "I've got something for you, Gerry."

Gerry Poole, the national editor, wadded the yellow paper he was staring at and tossed it in the wastebasket by the door before looking up. "Knock," he said. "After twelve years you could have at least learned one thing: Knock. Please. Supposing I had a young lady in here?"

"She'd be a reporter," Heym said, "and you'd be assigning a story."

"All the more reason," Poole said.

"I've got something for you," Heym repeated. "Something hot."

"How hot is hot?"

"It's so hot I don't want to think about it, that's what."

"Spill."

"There's a guy sitting at my desk. It's his piece. If it's true, it's the hottest story of the year, and I hope to hell it's not true. How do you like that?"

Poole nodded and took the remaining stack of yellow copy and put it aside. "Bring him in."

Heym waved across the large room. "Hey, Coles!" he yelled. The thin man in the tweed jacket rose from the chair by Heym's desk and came over. Heym ushered him into the office. "This is Gerry Poole, our national editor. I'd like you to start over for him. He'll want it first hand from you. Gerry, this is Dr. Barry Coles, a professor of economics at Columbia University."

Poole got up and shook hands with the intense not-quite-young man who was examining him with lively interest through large horn-rimmed glasses. "Coles," he said. "Barry Coles. I know the name. Wait a second"—he pointed a finger at Coles and shook it—"I know! You did an article for *Foreign Affairs*. Something about land management in the two halves of Vietnam."

"I'm impressed," Coles said. "That was two years ago."

"Yeah. And then you went to work for the White House, and you were one of the ones kicked out after the last election." Poole tapped the side of his head. "I've got that kind of a memory, I can't help it."

"This is something new," Heym said. He carefully closed the office door and sat Coles down in the chair facing Poole across the desk, then sat himself in a corner. "Okay, Professor," he said, "the floor is yours."

"I've been doing research in the State Department files," Coles said.

"I thought you went back to Columbia," said Poole.

"I did. But it was between semesters and I was at loose ends. Then Dr. Greener of the Institute for an Informed America offered me a six-month grant, and I accepted."

"What was the subject of the grant?"

"The Economic Influence of American Policy Intent and Reality in South Vietnam, nineteen-sixty to nineteen-seventy. I was to work with the actual documents. My clearance was still good for that."

"Isn't the IIA a little right-wing for you, Dr. Coles?"

"The paper is for general release, under the imprint of the IIA, and they'll print what I give them," Coles said.

"There were no prior restrictions on the, ah, slant of my findings. I made that perfectly clear, and Dr. Greener had no quibble."

"Fine," Poole said. "So, what happened?"

"So—this is one of the files." Coles opened his worn leather briefcase and extracted a thick manila folder. "In here is a Xerox of the Washington–Saigon State Department cable traffic for the month of November 1963. You'd better read it yourself. The effect is cumulative."

Poole took the folder and started rapidly reading through the Xeroxed flimsies. When he neared the middle, he slowed. A couple of the sheets he read through twice. He didn't say anything until he finished the entire folder. Then he closed it and put it down on his desk. "Son of a bitch!" he said.

"What do you think, Gerry?" Bill Heym asked.

"There's not much question. None of the cables comes right out and says it, but if you put a couple of them together—well, there's not much question. We'll have to see the originals, of course."

"There's no way I can take them out of the building," Coles said. "The Xeroxes are the best I can do."

Gerry Poole leaned back in his chair and laced his hands under his chin. "Now look, Dr. Coles," he said. "You come in here and hand us what purports to be a cable file that proves—that strongly suggests—that John Kennedy ordered the assassination of President Diem. Now my personal inclination would be to burn the file and forget that I ever saw it; but I can't do that. First of all, I'm a newspaperman, and this is what my friend Mr. Heym here would call a hot story. And second of all, you'd only take it somewhere else. But it has to be authenticated. Neither this paper nor any other reputable news medium will touch this story until it's been authenticated to hell and back."

"We can do some work on the Xeroxes," Heym suggested. "We could have Dr. What's-his-name—White—go over them."

"We'd need some others for comparison," Poole said.

"I can get you more," Coles told him.

"That's no good. We need an independent source," Poole said. "Can you get someone else in with you?"

"Probably," Coles said. "I've never tried, but probably."

"Okay. You figure a way to take Gerry in with you—as your assistant or something, and let him make some Xeroxes. Then we'll have Dr. White, our document man, see if he can authenticate them."

Barry Coles stood up. "It's a hell of a thing," he said. "I don't know whether I hope he can or I hope he can't."

• CHAPTER
TWELVE

DIANNA HOLROYD, the executive secretary of SIU, was a tall, vital woman who ran room sixteen with calm efficiency. She looked barely forty, but her personnel file said fifty on her next birthday.

Kit Young was at her desk going over the CIA inventory file—the list of CIA material on loan to SIU—when she suggested that they have a drink together after work, "if you're not afraid to be seen with an older woman." She arched her eyebrows suggestively as she said it.

"Delighted," Kit said. Rumor had it that Miss Holroyd liked younger men, but in any event, there was no better possible source of information about the inner world of SIU than its executive secretary.

"I'll drive," she said, meeting him in the west entrance lobby. "It relaxes me. I'll drop you at your car later."

And it did seem to relax her. The tense lines in her face eased as she pulled on her cotton-and-leather driving gloves and steered her big XK-150 coupe out of the underground garage. Once on the street, she swung west onto Pennsylvania Avenue and guided the heavy open car through the tight traffic with experienced skill and evident delight. She concentrated on driving the ancient Jaguar with an intensity that precluded conversation.

Turning onto the Whitehurst Freeway, she crossed the Francis Scott Key Bridge and headed north on the George Washington Memorial Parkway. It seemed quite a way to go for a drink, but Kit asked no questions.

She drove for about twenty minutes, and then took an exit and a twisting side road that ended on a cliff overlooking the Potomac. "There," she said, turning the engine off. It was her first word since starting the car.

"You drive well," Kit said.

She looked at him. "Just that?" she asked. "It's usually 'You drive well for a woman.'"

"You drive well for a woman," Kit amended. "Or for a man, or for a trained seal."

She smiled. "There's a leather case behind your seat," she said. "Can you reach it?"

"Sure," Kit said. He reached behind and pulled the case out.

"That drink I promised you is in it," she said, opening it carefully to reveal three bottles, four glasses, and a plastic ice bucket. "Scotch or vodka?"

"Scotch," Kit said.

"Over? Water? I'm sorry, no soda in the case."

"Over is fine."

Dianna maneuvered ice into two glasses and jiggered scotch into one and vodka into the other. Then she closed the case and put it by her side. "Mud," she said, passing Kit his glass and raising hers.

Kit sipped his drink and watched the reflection of the setting sun break into a thousand golden ripples in the Potomac in front of the car. "Okay," he said. "What's it all about?" He turned to look at her and found her staring through the windshield. She was a striking woman in profile, with the sort of late-maturing beauty that softens and deepens as the years pass. Twenty-five years ago she had probably been skinny, gaunt, and awkward, but the lines that age put in her face were lines of wisdom and trust and a certain feminine compassion.

"We haven't talked much, you and I," she said.

"That's true," Kit agreed.

"What makes you think this is 'about' anything? Maybe I just want to get to know you. We should work closely, you and I, we should know each other."

"I would like," Kit said, "to know you better." He smiled. "As the real power behind SIU, you're an important person to be friendly with. But"—he stared into his glass—"for some reason I don't think you brought me here out of sudden admiration for my deep masculine voice or my triceps."

Dianna leaned back and laughed from somewhere deep in her throat. "You're right," she said. "You're very perceptive. But, you know, that's what most of them are going to think."

"Most of whom?"

"My fellow Plumbers. They think I've entered the menopausal age of lust. I chase young boys around to lure them into my bed. I can't keep away from anything in pants."

Kit said, "They think that."

Dianna nodded. "And with good cause," she added. "I—let us say I discovered sex late in life. I enjoy it, every messy minute of it. And you'd be surprised how many young men like older women. They want to be mothered, I suppose. And if what I'm doing is mothering, then I enjoy that, too. Older men don't want to be mothered, they want to be married."

She paused and stared at him. "And now you wonder why I'm telling you all this."

"You believe in frank honesty as a, um, seductive technique?" Kit asked.

"Not at all," Dianna said. "Although I do believe in brutal honesty, whenever possible. I don't need seductive techniques. I don't chase, despite what my associates think. I seem to attract this sort of young man without effort. Thank God. I'd be no good whatever at chasing. Besides, I know all about you and your Miriam."

Kit stared at her. "You know what?" he demanded.

She shrugged. "It's in your file."

"They ran a check on me?"

"Of course," she said. "You don't think the SIU is going to trust CIA if it doesn't have to, do you? We got your CIA backgrounder and then carried on from there."

"I should have guessed," Kit said. "I don't even know why I'm either surprised or annoyed, but I am—both."

Dianna nodded. "So I'm not here to seduce you," she said. "But my known proclivity in that direction gives this meeting what you might call a natural cover."

"Cover," Kit said. "For what?"

"I'd like to ask you a few questions, Mr. Young. Just between the two of us."

Kit considered for a moment. "Fair enough," he said.

Dianna shifted in her seat so she could look at him better, one arm wrapped around the steering wheel and one leg drawn under her Harris tweed skirt. "It's getting cold," she said. "We'd better put the top up."

They got out of the car and Kit helped Dianna assemble and button down the frame and canvas top. Then they got back inside the Jag, and Dianna pushed the starter and slowly guided the car down the side road parallel to the river. "I want to talk to you," she said, "about your investigation of the death of Ralph Schuster."

Kit nodded. "Okay. What about it?"

"How did he die?"

"Just like you read in the papers," Kit said. "Suicide."

"You're sure?"

"Come on, Dianna," Kit said. "You must have read the reports I turned in."

"I read them," she said. "What I want to know is what you didn't put in them."

"Like what?"

She pulled the car off the road again and turned the engine off. "Like Suzanne," she said.

"Schuster's girl friend," Kit said. "There was no reason to put her in the report. You know how damn hard it is to keep anything secret. Think of all the reasons why I shouldn't mention her, and then tell me one why I should."

"She was raped."

"Yes, I know, about a month before Schuster committed suicide," Kit said, wondering how Dianna knew anything about her. "I asked Schuster's psychiatrist—you know he was a depressive? That he was seeing a shrink?"

"Yes."

"Yes, well. I asked his shrink whether Mrs. Chartre's experience could have caused Schuster enough stress to push him over the edge. The doctor didn't think so."

"He hadn't seen Ralph for about six weeks," Dianna said. "Since before the rape."

"That's right," Kit said. This conversation was heading somewhere and Kit wasn't leading. All sorts of interesting questions came to mind, but he suppressed them and waited.

Dianna took off her driving gloves and put her right hand on his shoulder. "I have a sense about people," she said. "And, over the years, I've learned to trust it. And my sixth sense tells me you're not one of *them*. I need to believe that. I need to tell you something. And then I need you to tell me something."

"Not one of whom?" Kit asked.

She considered him. And then she reached behind her

130

seat for her glass and poured it full of vodka. Without ice. She drank about half of it down in a gulp and stared at the wood-paneled dashboard. "The bastards," she said. "The bastards that are all around us and won't let us live."

Kit nodded, wondering precisely who she meant.

"Suzanne was beat up pretty bad during the rape," Dianna said. "She was put in the hospital. Naturally Ralph couldn't go visit her, and it drove him crazy. I sat up with him for the better part of three nights while he ranted about what animals men are."

"You knew him?"

"I was his source," Dianna said. "It was my idea. There was—is—crap going on here that I can't stomach. Not silently, anyway. Surely you figured that out by now?"

"I was approaching that conclusion," Kit said.

"Going to turn me in?"

Kit paused for a second. "No," he said.

"We started with a purely business relationship," she said. "I'd sneak away in an unassigned motor-pool car and meet him after midnight in some parking lot."

"Very dramatic," Kit said.

"Very paranoid," Dianna amended. "Paranoia has become endemic in the Executive Branch. Everyone is treading on eggs, with the vague feeling that they're doing something illegal and are going to get caught. So someone who decides to snitch, like me, becomes doubly paranoid."

"You passed information to Schuster? On what?"

"The various nasty and illegal things SIU was doing in the name of National Security, or Executive Privilege, or Power to the President, or whatever. Schuster was slowly building a story, documenting what I gave him where he could and printing just enough to keep his editors happy until he could get it all together."

"And meanwhile the Plumbers are going crazy tapping

131

each other's phones and trying to trace the leak," Kit said. "And you can avoid it all because all the orders go across your desk."

Dianna shrugged. "Wrong. If they tapped my phone, the order wouldn't cross my desk. So I had to assume they were. Schuster and I found a safe house and spent hours going over details. Gradually we became good friends. More. Partners in a love affair. Except that instead of loving each other, we both loved some sort of abstract goal we were aiming for. The idea that your President shouldn't lie to you, that the Constitution is the supreme law of the land, and not Executive Whim."

"Dangerous radical doctrine," Kit said, "in these days of the Silent Majority."

Dianna laughed. "Have you ever met the 'Silent Majority'?" she asked.

"What do you mean?"

"Thirty girls in a room in the White House basement. They call it 'Plans and Schedules,' I think. All day long they type letters in support of the President on some subject or other. About a thousand letters a day, shipped out to the Midwest on Air Force planes for mailing."

"Son of a bitch," Kit said.

"That's what Ralph said." Dianna pulled out a filter-tip cigarette and lit it with a large gold lighter. "Anyway, I spent three nights with Ralph while he waited for Suzanne to call. He was mad—furious—but not depressed. The third night she called. She wanted Ralph to tell her who the men were. She was calm—sedated, I suppose—but insistent. It took Ralph a while to get enough of the story out of her to figure out what had happened."

"She wanted *Schuster* to tell her who the men who raped her—"

"That's right. It seems that they kept telling her that Ralph would explain. That Ralph had sent them."

"I see," Kit said. And he did. "And she blamed Schuster?"

"No, not at all. She knew it was some sort of horrible mistake and Ralph would explain. She apologized to him."

Kit felt ill. "That's incredible."

"That's the last time I saw Ralph," Dianna told him. "And I have to know whether he—whether he did it to himself or had help. I don't think that if he had help they would have left that note. But I have to know. Either way, I'll feel just as guilty, but I have to know which it was."

"Suicide," Kit said. "I'm no expert myself, but the police sergeant who handled the case is, and he explained the findings to me carefully. Schuster typed the note himself. The shot was heard, and people were on the stairs and in his room within a minute. And it's not your fault."

"I had just decided to quit and come into the open when I heard the news. I was going to call him that day and tell him."

"And now?" Kit asked.

"Now I'll keep boring from within. Gather the facts and try to find people on the outside who aren't afraid to use them."

"Be careful," Kit said. "What you're doing could be dangerous—even lethal." As he said it he realized, for the first time, that it was only too true.

"Someone has to do something," Dianna said.

"You can't fight the whole executive branch," Kit told her.

"Oh, you can fight them," she said. "You just can't win."

Late that night Kit drove to Aaron Adams' house, taking a roundabout way and doubling back several times to make sure he wasn't followed. "I have to talk to you," he told Adams.

• CHAPTER THIRTEEN

TRANSCRIPT: AMERICA WANTS TO KNOW (*excerpt*)

Sunday, February 24, 1974

Today's interview is with United States Senator Kevin P. Ryan, a New York Democrat, very much in the news today because of the serious charges he has leveled against the administration.

Interviewers:

Daniel Gores of the *Baltimore Sun*

Roberta Gondolphe of the United Broadcasting Company

Morris Feffer of the *New York Post*

Moderated by George Brownworthy

BROWNWORTHY: Welcome to *America Wants to Know*, Senator Ryan. You startled America at a news conference Thursday with a series of broad-based charges against the administration and its policies, particularly in regard to specific allegations of wrongdoing in several government agencies. Do you intend to further document these charges with hard evidence, and do you intend to have the Senate Judiciary Committee, of which you are a member, launch an investigation?

RYAN: Let me, ah, state my position once again, Mr. Brownworthy. These were not specific charges of wrongdoing, for I named no individual and cited no specific acts. There have been serious allegations made to my office, and I felt that the American public has a right to know what is going on in its government.

BROWNWORTHY: Mr. Gores.

GORES: Don't you feel, Senator, that such charges should be investigated and their veracity determined before you make them public and, perhaps, frighten a lot of people?

RYAN: As I said in my press conference, Mr. Gores, a list of the specific charges, with as much detail as was consonant with preserving the anonymity of the informants, was turned over to the Justice Department for action some two weeks ago. They have informed me that there is no basis for action, which I do not believe. As I do not have the facilities myself to conduct the necessary investigation, my only recourse was to go to the people. As to frightening the public, if an express train is racing down the track out of control and about to hit you, telling you about it might scare the heck out of you, but it will probably save your life.

BROWNWORTHY: Miss Gondolphe.

GONDOLPHE: As you know, Senator, the President's press secretary, Robert Fuller, was questioned about these changes at a White House briefing on Friday, and he denied the truth of any of them. He was quoted as saying, "Senator Ryan is a Democrat and it's an election year. I wouldn't be surprised to hear even wilder charges coming from his office before November."

How would you reply to this?

RYAN: Over national television I will refrain from using the first phrase that comes to mind. But just let me say this: The information has been coming into our office for some time from a wide variety of sources. How Mr. Fuller—or his boss—can completely refute it overnight is something I would like explained. Such efficiency should be shared with the other branches of government.

BROWNWORTHY: Mr. Feffer.

FEFFER: Let us go over some of the charges we're talking about here. You said that the IRS was using its authority to investigate tax returns for political motives—

RYAN: In certain instances.

FEFFER: Yes, in certain instances. And that the FBI was engaging in political activities—

RYAN: That's right.

FEFFER: And that certain governmental regulatory agencies—like the FCC and the CAB—were using their power to harass the political enemies—you did say "enemies"—of the administration.

RYAN: You understand that these were not accusations. That is, not on my part. These allegations were made to me, and I couldn't ignore them. I tried to get confirmation or denial from the various agencies. What I got was a constant runaround. So I had no choice but to go to the people.

FEFFER: What do you think that this governmental interference indicates, Senator? Assuming that the charges are substantiated. What is it that's happening to the government?

RYAN: That's an interesting question, Mr. Feffer. I was about to reply that it wasn't the government but the executive branch, but that wouldn't be true. There are signs of a great malaise in this country, and it is the government, and the people, who are feeling it and who are causing it.

We live in a period of increasing polarization, between black and white, between young and old, between city and country, between political right and left. The government's role should be to minimize and try to eliminate this condition, but it seems to be doing everything possible to exacerbate it.

I think this must stop, and I think it must stop soon. If it doesn't, either the country will blow apart or we'll be living in a police state. And my Irish ancestors wouldn't like that.

Vandermeer leaned back in his Executive Swivel Rocker and laced his hands behind his head. For a couple of minutes he stared up at St. Yves, who stood in front of his desk, without saying anything. Then he leaned forward and the chair popped back up to work position. "You're sure?" he asked.

"Quite sure," St. Yves said. "Our routine checking was bound to pay off sooner or later. We've found the leak."

"The President will be pleased," Vandermeer said. "Hell,

136

he'll be overjoyed. You may get a pair of cufflinks for this."

"Right under our noses all the time," St. Yves said. "It was—"

Vandermeer raised a restraining hand. "I don't want to know," he said, removing his glasses and sighing wearily before he looked up at St. Yves. "Just get rid of the son of a bitch."

"Right," St. Yves said. He returned to his own office and picked up the phone.

FEDERAL COURTHOUSE BOMBED

BY BELINDA CHOMSKI
Special to The New York Times

SAN FRANCISCO, March 1—A bomb went off at eight o'clock Friday morning in a downstairs washroom of the Federal Courthouse at 450 Golden Gate Avenue in downtown San Francisco. Several people entering the building at the time suffered minor injuries and Mrs. Edith McCabe, a clerk of the court, was rushed to San Francisco General Hospital for treatment of a serious head wound.

A group calling itself the People's Revolutionary Brigade took credit for the blast in a phone call to the *Berkeley Barb*, a counter-culture weekly newspaper, which was received apparently only a minute or so after the bomb went off. The PRB called the blast an act of war against the "totalitarian pig fascist government."

• CHAPTER FOURTEEN

THERE WAS NOTHING in the world for George Warren but the car in front of him on the twisting road: the hunter and his prey. He goosed his engine and flicked his brights on. The car in front speeded up in response. Keeping his brights on, Warren edged up and fell back, edged up and fell back, closing the gap on the straightaways, and falling back on the curves.

The driver of the car ahead must have thought Warren some sort of idiot; only Warren knew that he was the hunter. He and those who had given him license. He edged forward, this time keeping the pace on the curve. The car ahead was handled well, but that didn't matter. The end would be the same.

Warren kept crowding, forcing the car ahead to speed up. Now Warren had to pay full attention to handling his Camarro through the curves. But the car ahead, pushed, was going even faster. Now a straightaway and Warren pushed harder, tailgating and forcing the car ahead up to seventy—seventy-five—eighty.

Now the curve.

The item in the *Washington News* was brief, and Kit,

idly skimming the pages over his morning coffee, almost missed it. He was turning the page when something made him turn back and read.

BETHESDA. A freak one-car accident at 10:15 P.M yesterday evening on the Little Falls Parkway killed the lone driver. The victim, Miss Dianna Babbington Holroyd, 49, of the Bethesda Garden Apartments, reportedly died instantly when her foreign sports car went out of control and plunged into one of the deep ravines beside the Potomac River.

The State Highway Patrol stated that a mechanical failure on a sharp curve had apparently caused the fatal accident.

Miss Holroyd was employed in the Office of Management and Budget.

Kit read it through slowly three times, expecting the words to somehow rearrange themselves between readings. They refused to do so. Carefully putting down his cup, he called up the White House switchboard and left word for his assistant that he wouldn't be in. He poured himself another cup of coffee, and read the brief news story three more times. Then he picked up the phone again and called Sergeant Veber at Second District Police Station. "I need a favor," he said.

"Who doesn't?" Veber asked. "Let's hear it."

"Do you have any connections in the Maryland State Police?"

"I could manage an introduction," Veber said cautiously. "What for?"

"I need to look at an accident report," Kit told him.

"That, ah, sounds arrangeable."

"I need to look like I'm coming from you," Kit said.

"You mean as opposed to—"

"You got it."

"I don't like it," Veber said. "But for a friend . . . You *are* a friend?"

"I do my best," Kit said.

"I'll call you back. Give me your number."

Two hours later Kit was at the Maryland State Police Headquarters for Montgomery County in Rockville introducing himself to a Sergeant Yost, a thin, graying man with a pencil mustache.

"Yes, sir," Yost said, shaking his hand. "Sergeant Veber said you were coming, Mr. Archer, and he said not to ask for any ID."

"I appreciate his calling," Kit said. "And I appreciate your taking the time to help."

Yost shrugged. "Luckily, I'm not a very curious man. Veber said to expect a Miles Archer, and here you are. He said you wanted details on the Holroyd case. I've pulled the file for you. We only have a prelim—ah, a preliminary workup—"

"I know the terminology, Sergeant," Kit said.

"Yes," Yost said, "I thought you might. We have the prelim: accident report, eyewitness account, coroner's prelim. No reason we can see to go further. Of course, we'll follow the routine, but right now it looks like a typical traffic accident."

"Anything to say it wasn't?" Kit asked.

"The fact that you're here."

Kit took the report folder, opened it, and leafed through the typed forms. "Who was the investigating officer?"

"As it happens," Yost said, "I was."

"Tell me about it."

"The victim was alone in her car, driving fast—but as far as we can tell, not abnormally fast—southbound on the Little Falls Parkway when the car failed to negotiate a sharp left curve and shot off into the ravine. This is the testimony of the two eyewitnesses, and it's substantiated by the tire marks, which start right before the edge of the pavement and continue straight off through the shoulder and over. The pavement was dry. There are no skid marks—that is, no breakaway marks to either side. The tire marks show locked brakes, so it was clearly not suicide. Car caught on fire, but it didn't burn too bad. We put it out with hand extinguishers when we showed up."

"Is that what killed her?" Kit asked.

"No, sir. The body was burned some, but the coroner says she broke her neck clean—died instantly."

"Badly burned? Any question of identity?"

"Oh, no. Thumbprints check with Motor Vehicle Bureau records. It's Miss Holroyd, all right."

"Um," Kit said, feeling sick.

"Witnesses were a couple in a parked car on a turnout above the curve. Had a clear view. Said the car just shot right off. They looked out when they heard the brakes squeal."

"Any other witnesses?"

"That's not clear. There was a car behind. Our couple saw it pass by a few seconds after. But it might not have been close enough to even know there had been an accident."

"The driver must have heard the brakes squeal if the people above did."

"You'd think so. Anyway, he didn't stop."

"Where's Miss Holroyd's car now?"

"In the police garage. Our mechanic will give it a going-over, probably this afternoon."

"Mind if I watch?"

"I don't, but he might," Yost said. He scribbled on a note pad, then ripped the page out and handed it to Kit. "Take this over with you."

"Thanks," Kit said, sticking out his hand.

Yost took it. "My pleasure, Mr. Archer," he said. "Stay out of alleys."

"What?"

"I read mysteries," Yost said. "Love them. Miles Archer was Sam Spade's partner. Died in an alley in San Francisco. Shot through the pump."

"Veber picked the name," Kit said. "I didn't know he had a sense of humor."

Dianna's Jag was up on the rack with two men going over it when Kit arrived at the garage. The body was burned paint and twisted metal, except, miraculously, for the front end; the sleek feline bonnet with its twin headlamps still gleamed British racing green. But from the windshield back, the car was junk.

"I'm sorry, sir," one of the mechanics said, as Kit walked past the row of police cruisers being serviced, toward the Jag, "but this area is off limits to civilians."

Kit handed him the note. "Yost sent me," he said. "I'd like to ask a few questions."

"Yes, Mr. Archer," the mechanic said after reading the note. "Always glad to help you government people. What can I do for you?"

The note said: *Jim—give Mr. Archer whatever assistance he requires.—Yost.* Kit wondered how and where it was encoded that he was a government man, but he knew better than to ask. "It's about the Jag," he said, pointing. "You been looking it over?"

"That's right, Mr. Archer. We just got started."

"Looking for anything special?"

Jim shrugged. "We've got to assign some cause to the accident," he said. "Have to rule out sabotage. It doesn't happen very often—but it does happen. If the brakes failed,

142

we check for rusty or rotted brake lines—or for cleanly cut or hacksawed ones. If it's a wheel lost, we check for stripped threads, or saw marks. If it's a gas fire or explosion, we check near hot spots for fresh-looking punctures or cuts in the tank or fuel lines. Once found a drilled tank directly above a drilled-through muffler. Never found out who did it, though."

"And if it's steering?" Kit asked.

"That's what it was with this one, okay," Jim said. "Faulty maintenance, probably, but an accident. The universal went. It does that sometimes."

"The what?"

"The rubber universal on the steering column. Here, I'll show you." He called over to his assistant. "Bill, lower the thing, will you?"

The assistant dropped the hydraulic lift, and Jim opened the hood, raising it onto its stand-bar. "There," he said, pointing to the disconnected joint halfway down the steering linkage.

"Got a flashlight?" Kit asked.

"I'll do better than that," the mechanic said, and he swung a powerful sodium light down from its stand and turned it on.

Kit focused the light on the broken piece. The hard rubber-metal bonded part had separated from its lower U-fitting, which now dangled uselessly from the lower arm.

"It just came apart," the mechanic said. "Old and brittle. Cracked. The heavy strain of a high-speed turn ripped it apart. It should have been replaced years ago."

"I want it," Kit said.

"Well," the mechanic licked his lips. "I dunno—"

"Call Yost if you want," Kit said, "but get that part out for me."

"I guess it's okay," the mechanic said. He went off for

143

his socket wrench set and in two minutes had the unit off. "You'll sign for it?"

"Sure," Miles Archer said.

Lowell MacDuffee of MacDuffee's English Motors, Silver Spring, Maryland, stared sadly down at the rotted rubber of the universal. "This piece of crud was not off Dianna's car," he said.

"I saw the police mechanic remove it," Kit told him.

"I don't care what you saw," MacDuffee said. "This is a standard maintenance item, and I've been maintaining Dianna's car for two years. For that matter, she bought it here. Wait a minute." He turned to the office file behind him and slid open one of the drawers, leafing through it until he found the right folder. "Here's a record of the work we've done on the car. And here—wait a minute—here is the part. We sold it to her a little over a year ago."

"You install it?"

"It doesn't say. She may have done it herself—she did all her own minor maintenance. Or I may have done it for her. She wasn't charged for labor, but for good customers we're careless about that."

"But you can't swear you installed it."

"No, I can't. But look"—he picked up the defective part —"this thing's at least five years old. Hell, it's probably ten. It's a routine replacement point on all circa 1960 Jaguars— the XK-150 sports cars, the three-point-four and three-point-eight sport saloons, even the big Mark IX mothers. It's a five-dollar part, takes five minutes to change. This isn't the one that was on her car. This is off a junker—or a junk pile." He pulled a jeweler's loupe from his top desk drawer and stuck it in his right eye. Then he carefully went over the part: the severed metal end-plate, the eight bolts, the eight nuts and washers.

"There's two overlapping sets of impressions where the

144

end pieces have been socked up against the holding flanges on the steering column arms. That means this piece of crud has been installed twice. And look at this rubber: most of it has torn across, but here where it started is a clean, even break. It was sliced about a quarter of an inch to get it started. I'm not a detective, but it sure looks to me like someone wanted that part to give at the next major strain."

"You're doing fine," Kit said. "Thank you."

• CHAPTER FIFTEEN

URIAH "BILLY" VANDERMEER inspected the front page of the *Washington Post* and slowly his thin lips arranged themselves in a tight, bloodless smile of satisfaction. "It's pretty," he said, "it's very pretty."

Charlie Ober nodded from where he stood, his ramrod-straight back to Vandermeer's closed office door. "They bought it," he said. "It took them three months, but they bought it."

"'Documents Link Kennedy to Diem Assassination' right across the front page. Do they mention anywhere where they got the documents?"

"They're, ah, reticent about that point," Ober said. He looked out the window and saw the roses blooming in the White House formal garden. "What's our move?"

"Sit down, Charlie, you make me nervous standing there like an usher. Our move? I suppose we must take some sort of official action. Against the *Post*. Against Coles. Of course we have to show that Coles is responsible first. Get the FBI in on that." He tapped a pencil against the desk and stared across at the framed picture of himself and the President getting off a helicopter at Camp David.

Ober perched on a chair in front of the desk, even now

retaining his military bearing but for the reflexive tapping of his foot. "I'll call the Director, see that he's pointed in the right direction. We don't want to lose momentum on this."

"Right. Hit the Democrats where it hurts—right in the Kennedy myth. We can keep this in the front pages until the election, and all the time we're the good guys, trying to suppress government leaks. Put Coles in prison for a few years. Get the *Post* shut down, or hit them with a big fine, or something."

Ober nodded. "We need a friendly judge on this one. I'll speak to the boys in Justice, see who they advise. The right handling of this might put someone on the Supreme Court."

Vandermeer put down the paper. "I saw the Old Man this morning," he said. "We had breakfast. He passed the word to okay that operation of St. Yves. The toned-down version."

"That code-word thing? Sibilant?"

"That's it. I'll never get used to these code words. But I suppose if we're going to use CIA types, we have to put up with their little idiosyncrasies. Sibilant. Use the Hoover blackmail file, or what we have of it. But that hiring a yacht full of whores is out—too expensive. After all, this is a mid-term election."

"But it's such a great image," Ober said, chuckling. "Those fat asses humping in the air"—he pantomimed with his hands—"with our little cameras going behind the glass. And the little girlies with vacant smiles on their faces and wireless mikes in their pillows. Or, better yet, little boys."

"You'll have to live with just the image for a while," Vandermeer said. "We've already got a few of our noble legislators pinned down."

"Senator Slater, Senator Chaymber, Congressman Pliney, and Congressman Korr."

"So far."

"When do we put it to them—and how?"

"That's up for discussion soon. The Old Man isn't sure whether to use the material to recruit them or to eliminate them. Slater's up for reelection, and Korr, of course, is too. Chaymber we could get recalled. With what we've got on him, we could get him lynched."

"I think we should use them—if they'll play."

Vandermeer laughed. "Playing is what's getting them in trouble."

Kit sat on the edge of Aaron Adams' pool and swished his long legs through the tepid water. "Twelve pages single-spaced," he told Adams. "I stuck them in a March *Time* on your desk. The one with the drawing of an African nation emerging on the cover."

Adams looked casually around to make sure none of his other guests was within earshot, then sat next to Kit on the cement. "Here," he said, handing Kit a tall glass. "A Tom Collins for your troubles. Give me the highlights. Anything good?"

"Barry's trial starts this week," Kit said.

"Not news," Adams said.

"You wonder how the FBI was able to track him down so fast when the *Post* refused to reveal their source?" Kit asked. "Ober told them who to look for."

"Told them? By name?"

"That's right. It was a setup. And I think those cables were phony."

"So," Adams said.

"A lot of trouble to go to just to get Barry Coles," Kit said.

"Coles was secondary," Adams said, "or even tertiary. The real objects were the *Post* and the Democrats and the Kennedy myth."

Kit sipped at his drink, feeling the ice-cold booze wash

down his throat. "It's incredible," he said. "What's going on in this government right now is—there's no other word for it—incredible. On the surface, as far as the people can see, everything's all right and business goes on as usual. The President goes to China. And we've all got to pull together now to end the dissension that's polarizing the country. The great silent majority is behind the President, and only a few nuts are going around the country bombing things. On the surface."

"That's right," Adams said. "On the surface this administration is no more troubled and no less responsible than any other."

Kit put his drink down and tipped himself into the pool, sliding down feet first until he reached the bottom. The water was up to his chest. "You don't suppose," he said, turning back to where Adams squatted on the concrete, "that all other administrations were actually like this one, except we never found out about them? You don't think that Roosevelt had his political enemies' phones tapped, or that Wilson knocked off his opponents?"

Adams shook his head. "There's one fundamental difference between this bunch of sweethearts and any previous administration. All the rest used public-relations techniques—to the extent that they used them at all—to put a good light on what they were doing. These people put up a public-relations front of what they *should* be doing—and it has no relation at all to what's happening or what they really intend."

"I still want out," Kit said. "Someone in room sixteen murdered Dianna Holroyd, and I have no way of finding out for sure who it was, and no chance in hell of proving it."

"What good will your quitting do," Adams asked, "except to cut me off from the best source of information I have?"

"I notice you don't say 'only,' " Kit observed. "I hope

149

you're feeding this stuff to the Old Boy Network. If you're a conduit to the Russians, or the French, or the Democrats, I'm going to be very disappointed."

Adams sighed. "It's a problem," he said. "Your friend the President is getting a tight grip on CIA, and pretty soon we won't know who to trust. It's a very effective technique."

"Well, at least he's on his last term," Kit said. "If we can keep him from doing too much damage for the next few years, maybe we can make some of the bastards accountable after the 'seventy-six election." He pulled himself out of the water and grabbed for a towel.

"I thought you wanted out," Adams said.

"More than anything in the world," Kit said. "I want to wake up tomorrow morning and find that this has all been a dream. But, barring that, I want the man who got Dianna Holroyd to swing from the nearest oak."

Adams nodded and appeared lost in thought for a minute. "We'd better work through a cutout from now on," he said. "You can keep coming here as my guest, of course, but never speak privately to me after today. And don't ever bring any documents, books, or papers in with you. It's too dangerous."

"Who are we going to use as a cutout?" Kit asked.

"Miriam."

Kit froze for a second and then, realizing where he was, resumed rubbing himself with the broad red towel. "You're crazy," he said. "I won't let her get involved in this."

Adams stood and wrapped a towel around his neck. They walked back toward the house. "I understand your feelings," Adams said. "But consider what an egotistical ass you'll sound like when you tell Miriam."

"I don't intend to tell her," Kit said.

"Great," Adams told him. "Then when St. Yves sends two thugs to her door she won't even know why they're there."

"You son of a bitch!" Kit said. They walked into Adams'

den and Kit dropped onto the massive couch, feeling the leather upholstery stick to his damp skin. "But you're right. Miriam is probably safer witting than unwitting. I'll talk to her."

"Not at your house," Adams said, "or hers."

"You know something?"

"I know how great minds think. We must treat these people very carefully. And remember that they are very dangerous."

"They killed Dianna Holroyd," Kit said. "There's no way I'll forget that."

"That's good," Adams said. "But go beyond anger and let the memory make you very cautious. Very."

"I'll do my best," Kit said.

Representative Clement W. Korr (D. Ohio) was a squat, dour, energetic man with a face like a petulant bulldog's. Chairman of the House Appropriations Committee, and one of the five most powerful men in the House, he was running for his fifteenth consecutive term as the elected representative of the people of Ohio's 27th congressional district. The Republicans, wasting neither time nor money in opposing him, were fielding a chiropractor with a seat on the local school board who saw Communists in the schools, in the churches, in the waterworks, and presumably under his bed. Korr was not worried.

Now, suddenly jerked out of the cocoon of prestige and power he had been thirty years weaving, Korr sat on a camp chair that was too small for his bottom and stared into the face of his doom. "Moving pictures?" he asked.

"Yes, sir," Warren said, allowing a smile to briefly flicker over his composed features. "I have a hand viewer with me with a few feet of film on an endless loop. Would you like to view it, sir?"

Korr shifted his weight and the canvas and wood frame

under him creaked alarmingly. He was sitting in front of a gaily colored tent, one of a row of similar tents along the edge of a meadow on the grounds of a state institution in Maryland. There was a medieval fair and tournament in progress on the meadow before him: three hundred or so people in costumes out of the King Arthur coloring book. At the entrance to the fair, Korr had been given a one-piece garment resembling a bath towel with a hole cut out for his head. His nemesis, who squatted on the ground facing him, was garbed in the rough olive robes of a mendicant monk. "Do I have a choice?" he asked. "Let's see it."

Warren produced a small plastic object shaped like a toy gun from under his robe. "Look into the muzzle," he told Representative Korr, "and pull the trigger."

Korr did so, hooking his thumb through a trigger guard obviously designed for hands somewhat smaller than his own. The gun muzzle flickered to life, and he was treated to a jerky, six-second loop of himself and Miss Tish Johnson, a secretary in his office, in an intimate embrace on the king-sized vibrator bed in room seven of the King's Park Motel. The camera was somewhat behind and above the action, and it made him look frenetic, undignified, and ridiculous; but there was no question that it was, indeed, he.

Korr handed the viewer back to Warren. "How much?" he asked quietly.

"Oh, a couple of hours' worth easy," Warren said. Behind him two men in mock armor started bashing each other with mock swords.

Korr stood up. "You mistake me, sir," he said. "Are you empowered to negotiate or must you consult with your principal? Tell him I will buy this material, but I must have the original and any copies that have been made. And I will not make the mistake of submitting to blackmail twice. The second time you come back I call the police, regardless of the consequences to me."

"It's you who are mistaken," Warren said.

"State your price," Korr demanded, the muscles tightening around his jaw.

"The material is not for sale," Warren said. "This is not a blackmail scheme. We'll safeguard the material and, with your cooperation, nobody else will ever see it."

"Cooperation?"

"I represent a political group," Warren said. "We believe that the only hope for the salvation of this country is in the program of the President of the United States. We'd like to see you support that program."

Korr sat down, his mouth open. "You must be kidding."

"We're very serious."

"You expect me to start voting Republican? You think maybe nobody will notice?"

Warren shook his head. "No, of course not. No more than four or five times a year. We'll call you, let you know."

"I—"

"Otherwise we use these pictures and your opponent gets elected. He is, after all, a Republican."

Korr stared at the two fighting knights without seeing them. "I was wondering," he said. "All my liberal colleagues are getting smeared. They're soft on communism, they're against law and order, they have sexual designs on small children; charges springing out of the woodwork in well-organized smear campaigns. A lot of money is out there somewhere. But nothing on me. I wondered about that. Thought maybe I was too powerful for you. That was foolish wasn't it? And all the time you had me with my pants down —as it were."

"It's your decision," Warren said.

"Yes. Well, I'll need some time to think about this."

"I'll call you tomorrow at two at your office," Warren said, standing up. "If you're not there, you can leave a message for me. Yes or no. No negotiating."

"No one will ever see that film?" Korr said, trying to sound firm and not succeeding. "That's understood. If I—no more than five times a year—if I—"

"That's the deal," Warren said. "You save your honor, your dignity, your office, and your marriage, and we get five votes a year for the President of the United States. It's not as if we were asking you to do anything subversive, just support your President." He turned and walked off across the field with the slow, measured steps appropriate to his costume.

"I'll be damned!" Korr said. "I'll be goddamned!" It was some minutes before he found the strength to push himself out of the chair and head down the hill toward the parking lot.

Malcolm Chaymber tossed his overnight bag on the floor and dropped into one of the chrome and canvas chairs that littered Sandy's living loft. "Well, I'm here," he said.

"Thank God you've come," Sandy said, closing and double-locking the loft door behind him.

"When you called I had to assume it was important," Chaymber said. "The fact that you know my real name and phone number came as quite a shock. I've felt guilty all these months, you understand, but it's very hard to change a lie back into the truth, and the longer you wait the harder it gets. I won't ask you now how you knew, since you should have known months ago if I'd had the courage to tell you. What do you need?"

"We're still—friends?"

"Yes, Sandy, even without the dramatic pause we're still friends. And I'm sure that you didn't get me on an early-morning plane from Washington just to show me that you know. Did you?"

"No. Of course not. Oh, Richard— Oh, shit! Now I don't

even know what to call you. It isn't Richard, it's Malcolm. Do I call you Malcolm?"

"Usually it's Mal."

"I've known for some time, Mal. Since the first time, as a matter of fact. I'm nosy. I looked in your wallet. So I knew that you're a United States senator. But I don't give a damn what you call yourself. Why should I? You could have stayed Richard Hatch forever as far as I was concerned."

"That's very nice, Sandy," Chaymber said dryly. "Now tell me what I'm doing here."

"I had a phone call yesterday."

"A phone call?"

Sandy looked up and Chaymber saw that his eyes were bloodshot. "A man called," he said. "He told me about—about you—us. His language was—obscene."

"What did he say?"

"He gave me to understand that he knew who you were. He has pictures of us together. Very together."

"Pictures?" Chaymber's brain refused to work. He felt suddenly as though someone were throwing buckets of warm shit on him and he were unable to move aside. "How could anyone have pictures?"

"Through the skylight over my bedroom," Sandy said. "I mean, you must understand, you must know that I had no *idea* that such a thing was even possible. I mean, how the hell anyone got up on the roof to take pictures I can't tell you."

"It's a bluff," Chaymber said. "It must be a bluff."

Sandy went over to the long wall where a stack of plastic boxes in primary colors were stacked to serve as a random-form bookcase. "Here," he said, taking an envelope from one of the shelves and tossing it over. "I said something like that over the phone, so these were slid under my door."

Chaymber looked at the four-by-five color prints of acts

155

of what the Marquess of Queensberry had called "somdomy" being performed on Sandy's oversized bed. They were good pictures and very clear.

"This is—most disconcerting," Chaymber said. The words came stiff and hollow from his mouth. "Did the man on the phone say what he intended to do with the pictures?"

"He said to tell you he had them. He said he'd be in touch."

"With me or you?"

"He didn't say. If it's blackmail it must be you he's after. Everyone knows I'm gay—even my mother."

Chaymber stared at Sandy without saying anything. He got up and walked into the kitchen and looked at the array of orange pots on the wall over the stove and didn't see them. After a few minutes he went back into the living area. "I have to think," he said. "This catches me off guard. I suppose it was inevitable. But I'm not prepared at all. I don't know what to do. Hell, I don't even know what they want."

"Money," Sandy said.

"Did he say that?"

"No."

"Well, I suppose it's possible."

"I could help," Sandy said earnestly. "I mean, if you decide to pay."

"Thank you, Sandy. Thank you for saying that. But I doubt if it will be that simple. Nobody bothers to get at a United States senator for money—even if he is a closet queen."

"What then?"

"Power, influence, votes. Somebody wants to buy me. I'm on the meat rack and it's a long jump down. I'm about to pay for my sins."

"It's not a sin!" Sandy said. "I don't care what it says in Leviticus; I don't care what the law is, what two adults do in the privacy of their own bedroom is not a sin!"

Chaymber smiled. "That's one hell of a private bedroom you've got there, fellow." Then the smile disappeared from his face and he shook his head. "That's not the sin, Sandy. In politics the only sin is getting caught. I'm too tired to think about anything now. I'm going to take a nap. Here, on the couch, I think. There's no skylight in here."

"I'm sorry," Sandy said.

"Don't be silly," Chaymber said. "It's not your fault." He stretched out on the amorphous softness that was Sandy's modern couch. "I'm glad they called you instead of me. If my wife hears about this, the shit will really splatter about."

"You told me your wife knew about you."

"About me she knows. But she doesn't know any, ah, details. And she doesn't want to. And, more to the point, she doesn't want anyone else to. What will it make her look like, her husband a faggot? And what will it do to the kids? Jesus. I don't want to think about it. I'm going to sleep. Don't wake me. Unless *he* calls back."

"Right," Sandy said. He padded quietly out of the room. Sometime later, when Chaymber's regular breathing showed him to be really and truly asleep, he cautiously picked up a phone in the bedroom and dialed.

"St. Yves," he said. "Tell him it's Sandy. . . ."

• CHAPTER SIXTEEN

"SAY, EXCUSE ME, but aren't you Senator Ryan?"

Kevin Ryan looked up from his *Time* magazine. An apple-cheeked stewardess with perfect teeth was standing over him, an ice-filled plastic cup poised expectantly in her left hand. "That's me," he admitted, smiling back up at her. "What, is it cocktail time already?"

"Oh," she said. "That's right." She gestured toward the drink cart in front of her. "A dollar a drink. What would you like?"

"A Bloody Mary would be comforting," he said, digging into his pocket for his wallet.

She poured the mix into the plastic glass, then, putting down Ryan's tray for him, set the napkin-wrapped glass on the tray, and put a tiny bottle of vodka next to it. He handed her a dollar.

"It's just that I'm surprised to see you here," she said, adding the dollar to the money tray on top of her cart. "I mean, in tourist class. I thought all you government people traveled up front in first class."

"Bureaucrats with expense accounts do," Kevin said. "We elected officials have to get by on our own salaries. Most of the time, anyway. Sometimes someone else pays and we travel first class, but we always wear false noses and dark glasses so none of our constituents will recognize us."

She laughed. "I don't vote," she said, "or I would have voted for you."

"I don't know what to say," he said. "Come back when you're done pushing that cart and we'll talk about it."

"Yes, sir," she said. "I'll do that." She maneuvered her drink cart on down the aisle and Kevin watched the slow undulation of her hips like a man hypnotized by beauty. Women had always been one of the great preoccupations of his life, at first because he couldn't get them, and then because he could.

All his adult life Kevin Ryan had gotten along well with women. Probably because he treated them like people. "It's amazing how many men treat women like another species," a lady friend had told him once, "and then can't understand when women respond in kind. You're not like that. You're interested in a woman's mind, not just in her vagina."

"The mind," Kevin remembered telling her, "is the sexiest part of the body."

Now, perhaps, Kevin Ryan was going to have to pay for his lifelong easy friendship with women. What he thought of as a casually intimate friendship could easily be blown up by an unfriendly press as a torrid, sleazy affair. Anything involving sex outside of marriage could be torrid and sleazy to the press.

And it was last Friday that a phone call had come to his private number and threatened to turn his private sex life into public scandal. A low, scratchy male voice had breathed the name "Nancy" and the address of a cabin in Vermont, and suggested that he had photographs the Senator might be interested in seeing.

"If you have them, publish them," Ryan had said

angrily into the phone before slamming it back down into its cradle. He had since then had second thoughts. Not that he'd even consider going along with any sort of blackmail; he'd see them—and himself—in hell first. But it would have been wiser to arrange a meeting with this man so he'd know who his adversary was and could handle him better. A counterthreat to prosecute for extortion might be an adequate way to handle a blackmail threat, if he knew whom to prosecute.

And then last night, another phone call. This one from Tom Clay, the Majority Leader of the Senate. "Kevin, boy, I've got to talk to you. It's important."

"Of course, Senator. What is it?"

"Not over the phone, Kevin. I hate to ask this of you, and I wouldn't if it weren't so damn important, but could you fly out here? The National Committee'll pay for your ticket."

"Fly out . . . to Minnesota? Are you in Minnesota?"

"That's right. I hate to bother a senator between sessions, especially in an election year. Even if you're not up at bat yourself. I know how it is. But I *need* to see you, boy. And I need to see you *now*."

"In Minneapolis."

"That's right. I've got you booked on a nine-thirty flight out of Kennedy Airport. Can you make it?"

"If you say it's that important . . ."

"I do."

"I'll be there."

"Fine, fine. I'll meet you at the airport. 'Bye now, Senator."

And so here he was drinking Bloody Marys at ten fifteen in the morning, ten miles over the state of (maybe) Ohio, waiting to find out what the Majority Leader wanted to see him about. Was he about to be shown some interesting photographs? The last time he had seen Tom Clay, the

Majority Leader had asked him to go easy on the administration. "We've got to live with them, Senator," Clay had said in his clipped, nasal voice, "just like they've got to live with us. We all get more done that way with less hassle, if you see what I mean."

Senator Clay was waiting for him at the exit gate. "Good to see you, Senator," he said, shaking hands with Kevin. "Come this way, please."

"What's this all about?" Kevin asked, following Senator Clay through the exiting throng.

"Patience," Senator Clay said. "All will be revealed in a minute. Thanks for coming on such short notice, by the way. Ah, here we are." He led the way through a door marked PRIVATE: AIRPORT PERSONNEL ONLY and up a flight of stairs. "The airport manager has loaned us a conference room," he said, stopping before a white door and pushing it open.

Kevin recognized the three men seated around the oval table in the small conference room. The large, florid-faced man was Senator Horace Slater, the Democratic whip. The small man in the rumpled suit, whose face looked as though each feature had been chiseled in unyielding stone, was David M. Wittling, who had given up his seat in the Senate to run for Vice-President of the United States, against his better judgment, and had lost. The third man, slender, aging, wearing the black suit some said he had been born in, was Laurence Harris, Democratic leader of the House, who'd been on the Hill since before Kevin was born. *One hell of a star chamber*, Kevin thought, now more curious than ever.

"You all know each other," Senator Clay said. He ushered Kevin through the door and closed it carefully behind him. "Let's get down to business. Senator Ryan doesn't know why he's here. Senator Wittling, would you like to inform him, please?"

Wittling smiled, his craggy features rearranging themselves into a rugged ugliness that surpassed good looks. He was what Lincoln would have looked like, one political caricaturist had remarked, if Lincoln had been a Democrat. "We've never actually met, Senator Ryan," he said, extending his hand across the table. "It's a pleasure, I assure you."

Kevin shook the offered hand firmly and then sat down. "I've admired you since—"

Wittling held up his hand. "Please," he said. "Don't tell me how, as a babe suckling at your mother's breast, you listened to my speeches over your primitive crystal set. It makes me feel like even more of a troglodyte than usual."

"I shall restrain my, ah, youthful enthusiasm," Kevin said.

"Good. You have no idea how inflating it is to one's ego and deflating it is to one's morale to read about oneself in a high school history text. At one with the pharaohs and not even decently laid to rest and out of sight yet."

"Get on with it, David," Harris said, staring across the table with unblinking eyes.

"Yes," Wittling said. "Of course." He leaned back and laced his fingers together over his chest. "You have, of course, been following the campaign, even though you, yourself, are not up for reelection?"

"Of course," Kevin said.

"You're aware of the tenor the campaign has taken on of recent weeks? All over the country, in many individual, unrelated districts—or, I should say, districts related only in having incumbents antagonistic to the President—sudden, vicious smear attacks have been made through anonymous front organizations against these incumbents."

"I've been reading the newspapers," Kevin said nodding.

"Bah!" Senator Slater said. "Not ten percent of it has gotten into the papers. Not ten percent."

"True," Senator Clay said. "Most of it's unprintable.

"We have a file here," Congressman Harris said. "Well, file is perhaps too formal a word. A compilation of documents collected from various sources around the country." He slid a cardboard file box about the size of the Manhattan phone book across the table toward Kevin. "Take a look through it," he said.

Kevin opened the box and sorted through the collection of papers, letters, telegrams, handbills, booklets, and other scurrilous material inside. Most of it was the common sort of indirect political slander—a handbill that appears to be from the candidate's own committee, for example, which makes him a supporter of gay rights, or black activism. There were news stories: MARINGER DENIES BLACK PANTHER SUPPORT was one headline, CONGRESSMAN DEVOE ASSERTS HE AND WIFE NOT SEPARATED was another.

"That was all the early stuff," Wittling said. "In the past couple of weeks the tactics have shifted. Now it's all sex, law and order, communism, perverts, and a lot of stuff designed to incite the hidden racism of that silent majority the President keeps talking about."

Senator Clay nodded. "And that rash of bombings that's going on isn't helping either. Every time a terrorist bomb goes off the President's team gets another ten thousand votes."

Kevin shifted his gaze from the papers to Senator Clay. "You think all this is being orchestrated from the White House?" he asked.

"I didn't say that," Clay said. "Which reminds me, did you know that your phone is tapped?"

"What?"

"Truth."

Kevin shook his head. "I hate to disagree with you, Senator," he said. "But I'm paranoid enough to have that

163

out once a month. The office phones and my home ⟨ ⟩ I pay a private detective firm to do the checking."

"They can check all year," Clay said, "but if the tap is put on at the central switching gizmo in the phone company office, there's no way in hell to detect it."

"Then how do you know?"

"A loyal—or maybe a disloyal, depends on how you look at it—American who works for the phone company thought I ought to know. Gave me a list."

"Who'd he say is doing the tapping? And how do you know he's not putting you on?"

"It seems like an elaborate joke for an earnest man with twenty years working for the central switching office to suddenly spring. He says that they say they're CIA, but he says they're not."

"How does he know?"

"He says the CIA taps phones out of that office all the time and they have an established procedure. And this group doesn't know anything about it."

"The CIA taps phones all the time? I thought their charter says they can't work within the United States."

"It does. Let's handle one problem at a time. It isn't the CIA who's tapping you, it's these other people."

"What do we do?"

"I'd suggest you be a little discreet in your telecommunications for a while. Nothing much else we can do at this time."

Kevin leaned back and wiped his mouth with the back of his hand. "You're saying that the administration is smearing candidates, frightening voters, tapping congressmen's phones, and there's nothing we can do about it?"

"That's the American political system," Wittling said. "You run for office and accuse your opponent of whatever you think the public will believe, and a few things they

164

won't, and he does the same for you. It's called democracy. What we're seeing now is the democratic process being manipulated by a man with a lot of money, an insatiable lust for power, and no scruples."

"It's the goddamn best political media manipulation I've seen in thirty-five years in the game," Congressman Harris said. "By God, you've got to respect the son of a bitch for that. Every time anything bad about the administration comes out, it's the Eastern Establishment Press gunning for the President. It must be obvious to every political reporter covering the election that these unrelated events are being manipulated from above, but they're scared to death to open their mouths."

"That's why we called you here," Wittling said, leaning forward and fixing Kevin with his deep-set eyes.

"You've lost me," Kevin said.

"We've bought half an hour of prime time on all the networks for the evening of November Fourth. We want you to speak to the American people on behalf of the Democratic party. We want you to reassure them."

"The only thing we have to fear," Congressman Harris intoned, "is that son of a bitch in the White House."

"We want you to calm down an overheated silent majority," Senator Slater said. "Tell them that the Democrats aren't trying to take their jobs or rape their daughters."

"You want me to do a Muskie," Kevin said.

"You could put it that way," Harris said.

"Yes," Wittling said, "that's it."

"Why me?"

"You have exactly the right image," Wittling said. "Our first thought was to use some old and honored statesman of the party—I speak in this roundabout manner of myself—but it was wisely decided that I possess insufficient relevance to today's young people. Or, to put it another way, most of them don't know who I am. Anything that happened more than a month ago is prehistory to modern Americans."

"We commissioned a special poll," Senator Clay said. "People trust you as much as any Democratic politician, and more than most. You have astounding name recognition."

"What about the way I picked on the administration last year?" Kevin asked.

"Very courageous and with the highest motives, the poll says," Clay said. "It must be your smile."

"The administration isn't going to be very pleased with me," Kevin said.

"They don't exactly weep for joy when your name is mentioned now," Harris told him.

"That's true. I get to write my own speech?"

"Of course."

Kevin looked slowly around the table at each of the four men. Senator Slater was staring at the tops of his own hands. The other three looked back at Kevin with unreadable expressions.

"I may be vulnerable," Kevin said slowly, one of the hardest things he had ever had to say in his life.

"How's that?" David Wittling asked.

"I recently received a phone call. The caller claimed to have certain photographs which could embarrass me politically. It didn't occur to me at the time, but the caller might represent the White House."

"How embarrass you?" Clay asked sharply. "What do they show? And for God's sake, be straight with us!"

"I haven't seen them," Kevin said. "But they purport to show me and another person engaged in acts of sexual congress."

"May I ask the sex of this other person?" Clay asked.

"Female," Kevin said, looking slightly surprised.

166

"And the age?" Wittling added.

Kevin smiled. "Well over the age of consent," he said. "And single."

"What did you tell this person on the phone?" Congressman Harris asked.

"I told him to go to hell," Kevin said.

"You'll do," Senator Clay said.

Wittling smiled. "I look forward to hearing your speech," he said. "Now let's break this little gathering up and get back to work."

San Francisco, 1200 noon

And now it's twelve noon here at KCGB and time for the news. Well, the People's Revolutionary Brigade have had a busy night of it. In Chicago, the early-morning hours were marked by the bright red flames of the Federal Welfare Building as the entire second-floor records section was gutted by a two-alarm fire supposedly set off by a bomb. The Brigade claimed credit in a phone call to the Chicago *Tribune* just as the bomb was going off. A spokesman for the government said that this shouldn't hold up welfare payments to the recipients since the city makes those directly, but it might delay for an indefinite time the federal grants to the city.

And in New York City this morning a bomb threat kept worshipers out of twelve of the city's major places of worship. The bomb was finally located in world-famous St. Patrick's Cathedral and removed by the police bomb squad. The bomb went off in the bomb wagon before it reached the disposal site, injuring one of the officers accompanying the device. The officer was taken to New York's Bellevue Hospital, where he is said to be in stable condition following emergency surgery. A written communiqué from the PRB said that the PRB was prepared to blow up a church a week until the religious leaders showed "serious commitment to aiding the poor."

Closer to home, Representative Quintan Pliney, the Democratic congressman from San Lorenzo, was found dead in his

167

car late this morning. An apparent suicide, Congressman Pliney was sitting in his car, in his garage, with the motor running, and was apparently overcome by the carbon monoxide fumes. A note found beside his body apologizes to his wife and children for the act, but gives no reason. The police are still investigating the case, and have not yet officially called it suicide. But, police chief Grossman says, there is little reason to suspect anything else.

Milton Notide, the Republican challenger for Representative Pliney's seat in the House, has issued a formal statement of regret, and says he has talked to Congressman Pliney's wife Hilda on the phone to express his great sorrow at her loss.

• CHAPTER
SEVENTEEN

IT WAS EIGHT THIRTY Monday evening in Washington, D.C. The President of the United States sat in the small room off the Oval Office with his two chief aides, Vandermeer and Ober. Hunched forward in his chair, the President stared intently at the small screen of the color television set perched on the Wilson bureau across from him.

FADE IN

EXTERIOR. STOCK FOOTAGE

of the rolling hills of America. As the MUSIC overplays *America the Beautiful* we see the sun setting behind the snow-covered Rocky Mountains. Then we cut to a distant shot of a steel mill. And fade through to an interior shot of a car-assembly line showing American workers making America work. Then the title roll:

AMERICA THE BEAUTIFUL

and the credits over shots of wheat fields, dams, soldiers at parade with the American flag passing in review. Some high-flying jets do precision maneuvers. And, over this:

Welcome to "America the Beautiful," a half-hour message being brought to you by the Democratic National Committee. We want to speak to you, the people of America, tonight, on election eve, to remind you that America *does* work. That our system of government, with its separation of powers, has brought to the people of this country greater security, more personal freedom, and a higher standard of living per capita than anywhere else in the world.

EXTERIOR. SHOT OF MOUNT RUSHMORE.

A distant shot, which pans by all the faces of the presidents and then, very slowly, closes in on George Washington.

ANNOUNCER

The founding fathers of this country were perhaps the most brilliant political minds ever assembled to do a practical job—to set up a brand-new government on a system never tried before. And it has worked—for almost two hundred years now.

EXTERIOR. CROWD FOOTAGE.

News footage of angry crowd of students being held back by police.

ANNOUNCER

But there is unrest in this country today, as there has always been. There are some who want to see the political and social system changed; and there are others who think it has already been changed too much.

INTERIOR. AUDITORIUM. SENATOR KEVIN RYAN IS ONSTAGE.

Senator Ryan is seated on a high stool, like the narrator in *Our*

Town, in a rumpled gray suit, looking relaxed and at ease. The camera pans over the audience, showing it to be mixed ethnically, culturally, and socially.

ANNOUNCER

And, as usual, some unscrupulous people would use this unrest for their own gain. They would pit segments of our society against each other for their own political advantage. We cannot allow that. That is why the Democratic National Committee, as a nonpartisan gesture in the name of all America, has asked Senator Kevin Ryan, Democrat from New York, to speak with you tonight. Senator Ryan.

CAMERA CLOSES IN TO A MEDIUM SHOT OF SENATOR RYAN.

SENATOR RYAN

Good evening. It is always a pleasure to speak to the people of this great country even when, as tonight, some of the things I have to say are not pleasant.

I know you will evaluate and judge what I tell you, and I know that you will act in a calm, rational manner to do what's best for you—and best for your country.

Some people believe that you are easily swayed, that you will believe innuendo without demanding proof, that you will follow the man who yells the loudest or tells the biggest lie.

I do not believe that.

Some people have been going around this country telling smutty, obscene stories about fine men who have served you loyally and honestly for many years. They expect you to believe these stories and vote against these fine men when you go to the polls tomorrow.

I don't believe you'll do that.

171

There has never been a man, no matter how fine, no matter how honest, no matter how ethical, no matter how intelligent, that someone has not reached up from the slime and tried to drag down. And the weapon used is the most powerful, the most deadly, the most indefensible that the human mind has ever discovered: the word.

A word cannot be guarded against; it cannot be blocked; once uttered, it cannot be destroyed. The only defense against words is an open, inquiring mind. A mind that can weigh truth and falsehood, and reject the false.

If a democracy is to succeed, its citizens must have open, inquiring minds. And our democracy has succeeded for almost two hundred years now, so it looks as if we've learned the trick. . . .

As Senator Ryan continued to speak over the television set, the President of the United States rose. His shoulders were hunched, his mouth was tightly closed, his head was down. Walking slowly, almost mechanically, he left the room. Ober and Vandermeer continued listening.

TRANSCRIPT OF TAPE RECORDINGS FROM THE OVAL OFFICE

THE WHITE HOUSE *Wednesday, November 6, 1974* (1:26–1:52 A.M.)

MEETING: The President, Vandermeer, and Ober (Background noise identified as television set obscuring some conversation)

P. There's another one.

O. Five seats. I make that five seats we've picked up.

P. They'll still have a majority.

V. Yeah. But we're cutting it down. We're whittling it down.

O. We may get a few more before this evening is out.

P. I want a majority in the House and Senate. Especially in the House. That's where the money is.

O. I thought we had it. I really thought—

P. Something went wrong.

V. Not entirely, sir. We have a few people in our pockets now. We have more control than what shows up on the tallies.

O. There's another one final. They're posting it now. That check mark. That's one of ours.

P. Keegle. He's been one of ours for twenty-five years. They keep voting him back in. He's senile, you know. Used to be just a drunk, but now he's senile, too.

V. There's Korr. He's final now.

P. We've got him, don't we? I mean, we've really got him.

V. Damn right. And a few others. Chaymber. Senator Chaymber.

P. That pervert. That filthy pervert.

V. Yes, sir. But now he's our pervert. (unintelligible) and expense. Still have to handle him with kid gloves. But he's bought and paid for.

O. It was that speech. That son of a bitch Ryan.

P. A good speaker. Very effective. Knows how to do it. Like me. A natural speaker. I want you to get him.

V. We almost had him, you know. Photographs. Our operative called and told him about the pictures. Made them sound bad— you know.

P. And?

V. And he told him to go to hell.

P. Gutsy. We've got to nail him.

V. We'll work on it.

P. Have to do something now. Get the people's minds off the election. Something strong, statesmanlike.

O. And we've got to get this Coles thing cleared up. Coles and the *Washington Post*.

V. I've talked to the judge. Judge Peadman.

P. There's a slot open on the Supreme Court. I've got to nominate someone.

O. Peadman's mediocre. I got a report on him.

V. We promised him the seat.

P. Let's see how this trial comes out. If he nails Cole.

O. Right. After all, the mediocre deserve to be represented too.

V. That's good.

P. Right. That's the ticket. And what about some real upheavals in the country. Bombings or riots?

V. Bombings and riots.

P. Right.

O. Race riots. Call out the National Guard. Show how the country needs you.

V. Need to give them something to riot about. I'll work on it.

P. Let Artie handle them. Do something presidential. We're probably going to have to run him in '76.

V. I don't know, sir. Arnold makes a good Vice-President.

P. Unless we can find some loophole in the Twenty-second Amendment, he's it. Don't worry, we'll pull his strings.

V. We have to make him look presidential if we're going to get him elected.

P. Got to stop making those speeches. Damn shame. He sure gives good speeches. What was that? "The lambent Lucinas of libertine liberalism?" He certainly said that with feeling. I doubt if he understood one word. The man has the brain of a pigeon. His wife dresses him in the morning.

• CHAPTER
EIGHTEEN

It was the third Thursday in February and TEPACS met. The card players gathered around Aaron Adams' table were, as they had become more and more of late, a glum and self-centered group. They spoke seldom, tersely, and only of poker. All of the group were there except Ian Faulkes, who was on a story in the Midwest. It was the first meeting in two months that had the rest of them assembled.

Colonel Baker, the last to arrive, mixed his drink and settled into his chair. They cut for deal. Grier Laporte won the cut and the game began.

"Well!" Obie Porfritt said from across the room where he was watching television and awaiting his turn at the table. "Our Father who art in the White House has added Moscow to the European itinerary for his April trip. I wonder what he's up to."

"God knows," Adams said.

"International peace and good will," Laporte said.

"Can you open, Aaron?" Masters said.

"What? No, no."

"You sound a bit bitter," Colonel Baker said to Obie Porfritt. "After all, the gentleman is from your own party."

"*I* am not the one who has forgotten it," Porfritt said.

"Just between you and me and the mike in Aaron's potted palm over there, there are several of my colleagues who do not feel indebted to the incumbent President for their recent reelection."

"How's that?" Colonel Baker asked.

"I have heard allegations," Porfritt said, "from gentlemen who would just as soon not be quoted, that the Republican campaign funds were not distributed with anything approaching an even hand."

"I'm not overly surprised," Sanderman Jones said dryly.

"Those on the President's Boy Scout list received an abundance of largesse, these allegations say. While those on Our Leader's shit list received no help. Those toward the top of the shit list, as a matter of fact, noticed a tendency for their opponents to come up with an unusual supply of ready cash. And such is life in Washington in this, the Year of the Rat."

"How did your campaign go, Obie?" Adams asked.

"You think you detect sour grapes?" Porfritt said. "No, not so. My campaign went, as my campaign always goes, with my own hard-raised funds. I don't ask anything from the National Committee, and they don't send me anyth:-

"Nothing?"

"Well, they did ask if I'd like the Vice-President to co᷄ down to Ogallala to talk. Seeing as how he'd be passing ᴸ that way anyhow."

"And?"

"And I told them that Artie Arnold and his 'blustering bards of Bowdlerized balderdash' was much too deep for my innocent farmers, and he'd best go on by. And so he did, at forty thousand feet."

"You didn't want Arnold to appear with you?" Jones asked. "Wouldn't he have at least drawn a crowd?"

"I don't need a crowd. Those people know me. They would have been coming to see *him*. And his set speech on

176

law and order, crime in the streets, race problems, drugs, and immorality isn't what Nebraska farmers need to hear. One of them was bound to ask him what he thought about parity and then we'd watch the stupid expression cross his face while he tried to figure out what it was and whether he was for it or agin it."

With this Obie Porfritt returned his attention to the national news, and the poker game continued. After a while Porfritt turned off the television and came over to the table to kibitz.

Admiral Bush, after folding a seven-card-stud hand with a snort of disgust on the third card, looked over to Porfritt and shook his head. "You've got it easy," he said, "over there on the Hill. If you had to deal with the executive branch from the inside, like I do, your bitching would be raised to a new level. Things have changed in the hallowed halls of the Pentagon since the last election. There's no describing it."

"Yes, there is," Colonel Baker said. "FUBAR: Fucked Up Beyond All Recognition. It's taken over from FUBB: Fucked Up Beyond Belief."

"That's what I've always admired about you military people," Sanderman Jones said, raising his eyes from his cards, "your natural poetry."

"Are we going to play cards," George Masters demanded, "or are we going to talk?"

"Let's talk," Adams said. "I could use a short break." He got up and stretched. Masters stared at him as though he'd just lost his mind.

"What's with this FUBAR business?" Porfritt asked. "What sort of interaction are we getting between the Executive and the military?"

"Remember that the Executive is the Commander-in-Chief of the military," Admiral Bush said. "Well, our President is taking command."

177

"Those who do what the President wants get promoted and get the good slots," Colonel Baker said. "Those who don't see the light get some interesting duty assignments. And the Army has some pretty awful places to send you if you don't play the game."

"It's not just the Army," Masters said.

"Yes, George?" Adams prompted.

Masters shook his head. "Never mind. I didn't say anything."

"Look," Adams said. "This is ridiculous. Here we are, a bunch of old friends, and George is afraid to open his mouth."

"Not exactly afraid," Masters said.

"Okay, I'll grant you. Fear is not the word. But there's something wrong when old friends won't talk to each other. Look—let's broaden the TEPACS Constitution"—he pointed with his thumb to the document hanging on the wall—"and include an oath of—what?—fealty?—silence? Maybe brotherhood."

Grier Laporte nodded. "Right," he said. "An oath of inviolable confidentiality between the group. Nobody talks to anybody outside the group about what we say here. Code word Top Secret TEPACS. Goes no further."

Sanderman Jones stood up and sauntered over to the bar. "Like a bunch of twelve-year-olds," he said. "Shall we prick our thumbs and sign it in blood?"

"Whatever form of oath you feel is most binding, Sandy," Adams said. "Blood it is, if you want blood."

"You're serious," Jones said as though it were an accusation. "You really are serious."

"Nevermore, as a famous blackbird is supposed to have said."

"Why?"

"How's life in the State Department, Sandy? How are

things going in State Department Intelligence? I haven't heard you talking about such things recently."

"Come on, Aaron," Jones protested. "You know my work is classified."

"And you know that there isn't a man in this room who isn't cleared for Top Secret. And you know that for the past five years we've been doing our private bitching over the card table. There's this thing we political science types call an acquaintanceship network that spreads classified information outside the need-to-know boundaries. It's an ancient, respectable, and useful way of communicating as long as it's used carefully. And when it stops being used—when, to put it bluntly, good friends stop talking to one another about anything except trivialities, this is a very bad sign. And, except for Obie, who's outside of the bureaucratic rat race, we're not talking about anything except trivialities."

"Frank and David have just been doing some pretty heavy badmouthing of presidential influence in the Pentagon," Sanderman Jones said, waving an unlit cigarette in their direction before he stuck it in his mouth.

"You know, Sandy, Aaron's right," Admiral Bush said. "Frank and I have been making a lot of noise, without saying anything that could really get us in trouble. Staying out of trouble is becoming a way of life at the Pentagon. I'd like to be able to talk to someone, and if I can't trust you six, who can I trust?"

"I hope you never need an answer to that question, David," Adams said.

"That oath," Bush said, "Whatever form you want—I'll take it."

"I don't think we need an oath," Adams said. "Let's just call it Secret TEPACS. Nothing said inside this room is to be repeated outside this room. The only thing you need say is, 'I agree.'"

179

"I agree," Colonel Baker said.

"Let's call it 'Top Secret TEPACS,' " Admiral Bush said. "Just to follow the form. Do it right."

"Okay. I agree," Adams said.

"I agree," Bush echoed.

Sanderman Jones looked around the room, at the faces of his friends. "I agree, too," he said. "But only if I hear all the rest of you say it. And you know, come to think of it, the fact that I just felt impelled to say *that* proves you're right, Aaron. I had to hear myself say it to believe it."

George Masters of the FBI grinned without humor. "If the Old Man were still alive," he said, "I'd report all this to him and he'd start one of his secret files. Then I'd be the inside man in this clandestine organization and every time we met to play poker I could draw overtime. As it is, I think I can honestly see the use of our being able to talk freely and pool information. Divide and conquer, as the man once said. I agree."

Grier Laporte nodded. "Information is my business," he said. "But I don't give it out, I just take it. I agree."

Representative Obediah Porfritt was silent, a thoughtful look on his face. Slowly the gazes of the six other men in the room fixed on him. "Now look, fellows," he said. "I think I'm in a different position from the rest of you. I wouldn't want to agree to this unless I meant it. You can see that. And I'm not sure I should. After all, I have a responsibility to the people of the United States. I'm their elected representative. And if I know anything that affects their interests, it's my job to act on that knowledge."

"You have a responsibility to the people in one section of Nebraska," Laporte said. "Not that I'm putting that down. It's important. But it isn't exactly the whole United States. You're making a federal case out of this, Obie."

Porfritt shook his head. "That's not how I see it," he said, speaking slowly and thoughtfully. "As a member of the House of Representatives, I'm not just asked to vote on bills that affect Nebraska. And I'm bound by an oath to the Constitution of the United States. The same oath the President takes."

"We won't ask you to break that oath, Obie," Adams said. "As a matter of fact, someday we may hold you to it."

Porfritt thought about that for a long moment. "Okay," he said. "I agree."

FROM THE PRIVATE JOURNAL OF AARON B. ADAMS

FRIDAY. TEPACS here last night. Finally got the group talking again. Broke down the wall of conversational reticence by creating our own classification—Top Secret TEPACS, Bush insists we call it. It has long puzzled me, the importance humans place on symbols. We couldn't just mutually agree to keep our conversations private—we had to have a name—a symbol—for the process. So TST it is.

The President—or, more likely, somebody under the President —really knows and understands the principle of divide and conquer. More like divide and control in this case, I suppose. Ober? Vandermeer? Gildruss?

Am I getting paranoid? We are not yet a police state, but I wonder how far from it we are.

Two more years. How much more damage can he do? I'll have to start giving K. specific assignments—which will make it more dangerous for him, but he's a big boy now. Assemble a dossier of the evils of the Executive. The TEPACS papers.

And do what with them? Nothing, I hope. But thinking the unthinkable is necessary, if unpopular. I pray it doesn't lead to doing the impossible.

AS MUCH THE PROVINCE OF THE WRITER AS OF THE DIRECTOR, MR. BIRD DECLARED. THE EMPHASIS GIVEN

OVER THE PAST THIRTY YEARS TO THE DIRECTOR OF A
MOVIE, WHICH HAS RESULTED

                                                      BUST

BUST
BUST
16MPS
      B U L L E T I N
FIRST LEAD HANOI BOMBING
WASHINGTON, 23 MARCH AM 3:40 (MPS)—AN UNIDENTIFIED
SOURCE HAS STATED THIS MORNING THAT A MASSIVE
BOMBING RAID IS EVEN NOW IN PROGRESS OVER THE CITY
OF HANOI AND THE PORT CITY OF HAIPHONG IN NORTH
VIETNAM. FLIGHTS OF B-52 BOMBERS, APPARENTLY IN
VIOLATION OF THE PEACE TREATY SIGNED BETWEEN THE
UNITED STATES AND NORTH VIETNAM, ARE SAID TO BE
DROPPING TONS OF CONVENTIONAL BOMBS.

      PHONE CALLS IN TO THE CITY OF HANOI HAVE
CONFIRMED THAT SOME SORT OF RAID IS IN PROGRESS.

      THE PENTAGON REFUSES TO EITHER CONFIRM OR DENY
THE REPORT. THE WHITE HOUSE PRESS OFFICE IS CLOSED.
                  (MORE)

TO THE DIRECTOR OF A MOVIE, WHICH HAS RESULTED

                                                      BUST

      BUST
SECOND LEAD HANOI BOMBING COMING
      W A I T   W A I T

**********_____

SECOND LEAD HANOI BOMBING
      WASHINGTON 23 MARCH AM 4:00 (MPS)—WHITE HOUSE
PRESS SECRETARY ROBERT FULLER APPEARED BRIEFLY TO
THE MASS OF REPORTERS WHO WERE GATHERED OUTSIDE
THE EAST GATE AWAITING SOME WORD ON THE REPORTED
BOMBING OF HANOI AND HANDED OUT A PREPARED
STATEMENT. EXACT TEXT FOLLOWS:

      182

"THE PRESIDENT OF THE UNITED STATES, ACTING IN HIS CAPACITY AS COMMANDER IN CHIEF OF THE ARMED FORCES, HAS ORDERED THE UNITED STATES AIR FORCE TO COMMENCE THE RETALIATORY BOMBING OF THE NORTH VIETNAMESE CITIES OF HANOI AND HAIPHONG. THIS ACTION HAS BEEN TAKEN REGRETFULLY, AND AFTER CAREFUL DELIBERATION, IN RESPONSE TO THE CONTINUOUS AND REPEATED VIOLATIONS OF THE PARIS PEACE ACCORDS THAT THE TWO COUNTRIES OF THE UNITED STATES AND NORTH VIETNAM AGREED TO AND SIGNED IN 1973.

"OTHER COUNTRIES MUST LEARN THAT THE UNITED STATES WILL KEEP ITS COMMITMENTS AND WILL LIVE UP TO ITS WORD."

(MORE)

Major Donaldson, the pilot of the Air Force 707, appeared in the cabin doorway. "Excuse me, gentlemen, but we'll be landing in about twenty minutes at Travis," he said. "We're starting our descent now, so please put your seat belts on." He gave a brief, habitual salute, then disappeared back into the pilot's cabin.

Kit tightened his seat belt and turned to stare out the window. Six miles below, under a layer of scattered cumulus clouds, lay a dry, mountainous countryside that looked like the gateway to hell: very beautiful but bleak, barren, and inhospitable to human beings.

St. Yves rested his 16-millimeter Bolex on the seat beside him and fastened a seat belt around it before tightening his own. "I'll have to pick up some more film for this baby," he said for the fourth or fifth time. His eyes were unnaturally bright.

"Calm down, Ed," Vandermeer said.

"I can't help it," St. Yves told him. "It's confrontation.

183

It always gets to me. Being on the front line of life. Pow!"
He smacked his right fist into his left palm.

Kit, looking around the passenger compartment of the
large jet, empty except for himself, Vandermeer, St. Yves, a
communications sergeant, and four Secret Service men, felt
himself to be now very firmly in the center of power. But
as it was a power he could neither wield nor influence, it
was like being in the eye of a hurricane. He was safe while
he stayed where he was, but motion in any direction could
get him picked up and dashed to pieces without warning.

The plane banked to the left and descended below the
cloud cover as they headed in toward Travis Air Force Base
across the flat farmland of California's Central Valley.

"What's the word from Berkeley?" Vandermeer suddenly
asked the communications sergeant. "Anything happening?"

"I'll check, sir." The communications sergeant turned to
his little console and moved his fingers over the keyboard.

Vandermeer turned to St. Yves. "My daughter almost
went there, you know," he said.

"Kathy?"

"That's right. Then she got the appointment as a Senate
aide. Now she's all hot about government and politics."

"Berkeley has a good political science department," Kit
said.

Vandermeer looked at him as though he had just taken
his pants off in public. "Bullshit," he said. "Marcuse, Marx,
and moral turpitude—that's what they teach at Berkeley!"

"You sound like Artie Arnold," St. Yves said, steering the
conversation away from the shoals. "What's Kathy doing
now? It must be a year since I've seen her."

The plane lowered its flaps with a sudden roar.

"Georgetown," Vandermeer said. "In her spare time she's
on Senator Jensen's public-relations staff. Quite a busy little
girl." Vandermeer smiled with paternal satisfaction.

Kit was once again amazed by St. Yves' ability to handle people. If he weren't so fanatically dedicated to the concept of being completely dedicated, St. Yves would be one of the most awesome men Kit had ever known. As it was, he was probably the most dangerous.

The communications sergeant ripped a sheet off the teletype and handed it to Vandermeer.

"Getting worse," Vandermeer said, quickly reading the communiqué. The satisfaction showed in his voice.

"Any casualties yet?" St. Yves asked.

"It doesn't say."

"There must be a dozen news services there," Kit said.

"Right," Vandermeer agreed. "Want to have complete coverage. Complete. Every thrown rock or smashed window is a thousand votes."

"Every bloody head is ten thousand," St. Yves added.

"Right," Vandermeer said.

An Air Force helicopter was waiting for them when they landed. Vandermeer sat up next to the pilot and watched critically as the chopper lifted off and headed west. "You do that well," he told the pilot.

"Thank you, sir," the pilot said.

"You know, I used to drive one of these things."

"Is that right, sir?"

"I didn't know that, Billy," St. Yves said, his voice a controlled scream under the roar of the chopper blades.

"That's right," Vandermeer called into the back seat. "I was a chopper pilot in Korea. Warrant officer. Closest thing to hell I've ever seen."

In a few minutes they came to a low range of hills and followed a freeway through it. On the other side San Francisco Bay came into view in the distance and, across the water, the skyline of San Francisco peeked dimly through the smog.

"That's the Golden Gate Bridge," the pilot said, pointing into the haze. "That's Alcatraz. Off to the right here"—he pointed down—"is Berkeley."

The air was haze-free on this side of the bay, and the streets below showed clearly, except for an occasional obscuring puff of smoke billowing along one street to their right. At first Kit thought it was an outbreak of arson, and then he realized that it must be tear-gas bombs going off. The drone of the copter obscured any possible sound that might be coming from below, but clearly the riot was still in progress.

"There's the field," the pilot said, nodding toward a cleared area fronted by tennis courts between the campus and the Berkeley Hills. He dropped cleanly down, raising a cloud of dust that turned the sky brown around them for a few seconds until the sharp west wind carried it away.

St. Yves slung his Bolex over his arm and trotted off to the tennis courts, where the Army had set up tents, to collect his extra film. Vandermeer and Kit went over to a police command car, where Vandermeer identified himself to an impressed inspector of police in a powder-blue uniform. "What's happening?" he demanded.

"We've managed to confine the rioting to the campus area and the streets around Telegraph Avenue up to Ashby," the inspector said. "Of course, inside that area the whole thing is still out of control."

"Oh," Vandermeer said. "Still pretty bad on campus, is it?"

"Yes sir. Right now we're just trying to keep them bottled up and prevent them from trashing the rest of Berkeley. But I sure wouldn't want to own a store on Telegraph Avenue now."

"Is there any way to get close to the action without interfering with the police?" Kit asked. If he'd come all this way to see a riot, then he damn well wanted to see the thing.

186

The police inspector looked at him curiously, and Kit realized he had no idea who he was. "Christopher Young," he identified himself. "Intelligence liaison for the White House."

"Right," the inspector said, clearly having no idea what an intelligence liaison was. "I don't recommend your trying to get close. You're bound to get a dose of tear gas at least, and somebody's liable to take a shot at you, if they see you wandering around the cleared zone."

"The students have guns?"

"No, but the officers do."

St. Yves came over, the Bolex under his arm. "Army copter's going to drop me on campus, behind the lines," he said. "Get some pictures from the inside. See you later." He ran back to the little Army helicopter and climbed in. A few seconds later he was headed toward the campus.

Vandermeer turned back to the police inspector. "I want to get a closer look at what's happening," he said. "The President is going to want a report."

"Okay," the inspector said. "Let's see what I can do." He studied a map on the aluminum table in front of him. Then he looked over at a group of policemen standing a few yards away and yelled, "Dietz!"

One of the group took a few last gulps from a paper cup, then crumpled it and tossed it into a waste can. "Yeah?"

"This is Mr. Vandermeer and Mr. Young." He turned to Vandermeer. "Sergeant Dietz will take you around to University Avenue. There should be enough action there to show you what's going on, and the wind is blowing in the right direction to keep you comparatively clear of the tear gas."

"Yes, sir," Sergeant Dietz said. "If you gentlemen will come with me." They set off in a police car and circled the back of the Berkeley campus.

Dietz parked the car on University Avenue, a couple of

blocks from the campus. From somewhere ahead of them, they could hear the shrill bleating of a bullhorn as one of the student leaders exhorted his young masses to action.

Vandermeer and Kit walked together up the street toward the line of police at the campus end. "Not much to see," Vandermeer said sourly.

"I expect the inspector sent us around to the safe end of things," Kit said.

A line of students appeared at the edge of campus and quickly became a crowd. More of the hard-helmeted policemen ran forward to join the line separating the students from the street.

One of the bullhorn-equipped student leaders came to the front of the group. "All right, let's hear it!" he screamed through his horn. The shrill words echoed off the buildings until they seemed to have been torn from some inhuman throat.

"Baby butchers!" the crowd yelled. "Baby butchers! Baby butchers! BABY BUTCHERS! BABY BUTCHERS!"

"It looks like we'll get some action over here after all," Vandermeer told Kit.

"I'd say so," Kit agreed. "You want to stay?"

"Of course. Where the hell are those cameramen? They should be getting this. This is just what we need."

""Need?" Kit asked.

"Sure," Vandermeer said. "You can mold public opinion without tools. This rioting gives us a handle."

"BABY BOMBERS! BABY BOMBERS! BABY BOMB-ERS!" chanted the students.

"What good does this do?" Kit asked, gesturing toward the screaming youths. "How do they fit into your plan?"

"Middle America," Vandermeer said, "that great silent majority, is not altogether sure that we did the right thing in bombing Hanoi."

"And this will convince them?" Kit asked.

"Of course. Middle America does not understand or like the young sex-crazed, drug-freak, rock-and-rollies that they brought into the world. If you want them to be for something, just tell them that the college students are against it. Particularly in Berkeley or New York."

Some people from the back of the student mass were throwing rocks and bottles at the police, and now the police responded by lobbing tear-gas cannisters into the crowd. The students scattered to avoid the tear gas. Some of them picked up the hot cannisters and tossed them back down the street.

The police tried to keep the crowd confined, but the students broke free and raced down University Avenue, a disorganized mob, with police after them and among them dragging down who they could. Kit saw one slim blond boy clubbed down by two policemen, who then stood over him and kept hitting him in the chest and body with their batons. A girl stepped in to try to stop it and got clubbed across the side of the head by one of the cops. She collapsed on top of the boy and they were both dragged to the side of the street.

A squad of police in powder-blue uniforms came trotting around a corner carrying shotguns and headed down the street.

Four Secret Service men, who had followed them to the campus, came up to surround Vandermeer and Kit. "Come this way, please," the agent in charge said, "It's time for you to leave."

• CHAPTER NINETEEN

THE PRESIDENT'S SPEECH to the nation was scheduled for
6 P.M. Sunday. At five minutes before the hour Aaron B.
Adams went into his study and turned on the small color
television built into his bookcase. Settling into his brown-
leather reclining chair, he flipped channels around to each
of the three network stations. Each shared the same video
pickup: a view of the leather chair behind the great oak
desk in the Oval Office. Framing the scene on the left was
the American flag, on the right the presidential flag, both
carefully furled behind the desk. Then the President appeared on the screen left, and Adams settled back to watch
the show.

ANNOUNCER

Ladies and gentlemen, the President of the United
States.

PRESIDENT

*(Smiling, giving characteristic salute, and easing him-
self into his seat)*

Good evening, my fellow Americans. I have much
to talk to you about tonight. Some of my news is good

190

and—I would not try to fool you—some is bad.

But before I delve into matters of national and international interest, I have a brief announcement to make. One that gives me a great deal of personal pleasure.

As you know, I have submitted the name of District Judge Cecil Peadman to fill the vacancy now existing in the Supreme Court. Well, word has just come to me that the Senate approved the appointment. As many of you know, Judge Peadman presided over the case of the *United States* versus *Barry Coles and the Washington Post*. He did a fine job on that prolonged and difficult case, and he will make a fine Supreme Court justice.

Now to more substantive matters.

I have not spoken to you, the people, since I, in my capacity of Commander in Chief, ordered our Air Force to bomb the North Vietnamese capital of Hanoi.

Now let me make one thing perfectly clear: I took this drastic step only after repeated and continuous violations of the peace accords by the leaders of North Vietnam, and after many diplomatic attempts to get them to honor those accords. But those enemies of the United States, both abroad and at home, must know as clearly, as our friends must know, that we will honor our commitments and that we will protect our friends.

And let me say that the Hanoi government can stop these raids anytime they want to. They know our representative in Paris will talk to them at any time of the day or night. But until they make some effort to show good faith, we cannot abandon our allies in the South. I would not be able to sleep at nights if I knew that my name would be coupled to such an action.

The President paused and stared into the camera, which slowly closed in on him.

Which brings me to the final thing that I would like

191

to talk to you about, and certainly the most serious.

Although most of you out there, most citizens of this great country, support your government and your President in this important decision, there are those dissenters who do not. Individuals, many of them, unfortunately, young, and groups who have chosen to take the law into their own hands. Who have decided that the decision-making power in this country should rest not in the Executive Branch, but in the mob; not in the halls of Congress, but in the streets of Berkeley; not in the chamber of the Supreme Court, but in the barrel of a gun.

And we cannot allow this.

These groups, aided in many cases by money and training from abroad, are undermining the freedoms—the traditional freedoms—of this country. And they must be stopped.

The scene cut away from the President and to a montage of shots of rioting on the Berkeley campus, of rioting and looting in downtown Chicago, of thousands of students milling around the White House in a peace demonstration. Then Adams was shown empty streets in the aftermath of the riots: burned-out and gutted buildings, looted stores, close-up shots of the wounded and the dead. Over all of this played an artistically created sound track of police sirens, explosions, gunshots, screams, moans, and an undercurrent of intense police radio chatter which blended into emergency-room professionalism. The film ran for two minutes and was designed to shock. Then it cut back to the President.

PRESIDENT

What you have just seen, my friends, is newsreel footage of what has been going on in America over the past few weeks. The very fabric of our society is

192

threatened by these acts of vandalism, of mob violence, of moral outrage. This has gone beyond dissent, my fellow Americans. This mob action, directed by forces from outside these United States, tears at the very vitals of everything we hold sacred.

What we see here has a name. A name that the framers of our Constitution were well aware of when they drew up that great document. As great a threat to this country as any external enemy is the threat of internal sedition.

When I became the Chief Executive of this great land I swore a mighty oath—an oath to protect this country, and its constitution, from any enemies, both external and domestic. And I mean to do that. I will not be the first President to turn away from this great trust.

Therefore, in my capacity as President of the United States and Commander in Chief of the Armed Forces, I have ordered the following steps be taken:

First: All those who have been actively disrupting the legal and legitimate activities of their fellow citizens, or who conduct such disruption in the future, are to be arrested and confined, subject to trial for sedition or—if their actions warrant—treason, under the authority of the Emergency Powers Act.

Second: Six of the internal confinement camps set up around the country under executive order by previous administrations are to be activated, so that such persons as are confined will not put a sudden burden upon the jails or prisons of any locality, and so that the individual's civil rights can be maintained until his trial.

Third: Two hundred special federal marshals are going to be sworn in immediately to expedite the arrest and confinement of these individuals.

Fourth: The foreign governments who have aided and abetted internal sedition in the United States either directly or indirectly are hereby put on notice that such activity will no longer be tolerated.

Now some of you, who have not been near these centers of violence and disturbance during the past few weeks, may feel that these measures are excessive, that these dissenters can be handled by ordinary police measures. But it is my judgment that the time has come to take sterner measures to protect the decent, law-abiding majority of this country from fear, from crime, and from unreasoned acts of violence.

I put all of those young people who think the way to dissent is to destroy, on notice; from now on, acts of internal sedition will not be tolerated.

This country must be kept safe for its citizens to walk the public streets in safety and honor.

I thank you.

Adams got up and shook his head sadly. As the scene cut away from the President to the network anchorman, Adams turned off his set and poured himself a double shot of scotch. Raising the glass to the empty air, he muttered: "My friends, I give you Thomas Jefferson! He would have known what to do." Then he sat down and slowly drank the scotch.

The young man from the presidential Office of Emergency Preparedness stood quietly at the lectern and looked out at the assembled officers of Fort Ord. His face showed a studied vacancy behind the dark glasses as Brigadier General Ames, the post commandant, introduced him and then sat down. *Cocky bastard,* Ames thought, taking an instant dislike to the young man from his razor-cut hair to his alligator shoes. *Probably thinks he's got the world by the tail.* And he probably did too, Ames was honest enough to admit. And that was certainly a good part of the instinctive dislike.

"Good afternoon," the young man said, taking off his dark wire-rims and placing them carefully on the lectern in front of him. "What I have to say to you this afternoon is top secret, and is to be treated as such." He paused to clear his throat. "As General Ames told you, I speak directly for your Commander in Chief, the President of the United States."

Bullshit, Ames thought, *that wasn't what I told them. But never mind.* It was close enough to make no difference, except semantically.

The young man looked around the room. "What I tell you now must not leave this room until the orders are implemented. I hold each and every one of you separately and individually responsible for seeing that complete secrecy is maintained."

He paused dramatically.

"As of oh-one-hundred hours tomorrow morning, Operation Garden Plot will be brought into effect. . . ."

Garden Plot? Ames racked his memory.

"As you know," the young man continued, "since the President's speech of June twenty-second, implementing the detention of terrorists and rioters, only about four hundred persons have been arrested and detained nationwide. This despite the continued, even the increased incidence of destructive rioting and acts of terrorism throughout the country.

"Meanwhile the administration has been biding its time, allowing the shrieking protests of the East Coast liberal press to die down, and preparing to act. The carefully planned implementation of Garden Plot is the first phase of that action.

"As some of you will know, Garden Plot is the Pentagon's standing contingency plan—formulated under President Lyndon Johnson's nineteen sixty-seven order—to suppress civil disorder in time of internal crisis."

Clever, Ames thought, *innocence by association.*

"At oh-one-hundred hours this morning the President's

order initiating Garden Plot will be effectuated. This will formally initiate a limited application of martial law. Immediately, Army personnel—mostly military police—from five locations around the country will join federal marshals in rounding up some two thousand terrorists and dissidents and bringing them to the internal confinement camps which have been made ready to receive them.

"Fort Ord, as you have probably guessed, is one of the five military bases, and you officers will be participating in this action.

"Now I should stress that the names on the lists you will be given are all suspected or known dissidents or terrorists. The civil rights of those who are rounded up will be observed. They are not to be manhandled or mistreated in any way—unless, of course, they attempt to resist arrest or otherwise threaten or endanger the arresting troops."

The young man paused and turned to deliver a stern glance to General Ames. *I wonder if this young gentleman has any clear idea of what he's saying,* Ames thought. He pictured Army troops in battle fatigues rounding up and arresting hundreds of college students. It was not an image that went with General Ames's idea of life in the United States of America. Some banana republic, maybe, but not the streets of San Francisco—or even Berkeley. Ames had not fought in three foreign wars to end up arresting—maybe even killing a few—teenage Americans. At the same time, he had not spent twenty-eight years in the Army without developing a respect approaching religious conviction in the chain of command, and the necessity of obeying the lawful orders of your superiors.

"A direct link," the young man told his audience, "has been set up between your message center here and the Situation Room in the White House. As the operation continues you will be reporting directly to the Situation Room, and any changes or amendments to your orders will come directly from the President himself."

He looked around and smiled at the assembled officers—smile number 7A, groups, for use in—carefully letting his gaze include them all, from left to right, front to back. "This is our chance to clean up America," he said. "To make it safe for democracy, for our children, and for our posterity. I know you won't let your President down. Thank you."

He left the stage. General Ames stood up and an aide called the room to attention. "Effective immediately this is a closed post," Ames said. "All leaves and passes canceled until further notice. You may have the pleasure of telling your men. I'll see that each of you knows the part you are to play in Garden Plot as soon as the word comes down. Dismissed."

Ames returned to his office and sat down heavily behind his desk. He wasn't sure of the full meaning of the activation of Garden Plot, but he didn't like it. It wasn't merely the arresting of civilians he objected to, although he didn't really think the Army should be involved with that—they had a bad enough image already—but the obvious flouting of the chain of command in the President's implementation of the plan. It should have come through the Pentagon, not from the President's Office of Emergency Preparedness. But the Pentagon could stall, could bitch effectively if they disagreed, could leak the plan to the Congress or the press if they felt strongly enough about it. The President didn't own the Pentagon yet, although he was working on it.

But a brigadier general at a California post, given a direct order from the President and not too much time to consider it, could be depended on not to think of any option except to obey orders.

Yes, General Ames was willing to bet that Garden Plot would be as big a surprise to Army Chief of Staff Tank

MacGregor as it would be to the dissenters who were scheduled to be rousted out of bed in the wee hours of the morning.

Ames pulled a yellow pad over to him and stared down at it for a minute. Then he took an ancient ink pen from a desk stand carved out of a German PAC 38 antitank shell and printed a brief message in block letters. He pushed his comm button down. "Get a code clerk in here," he barked, "I have something to send."

• CHAPTER
  TWENTY

ELEVEN O'CLOCK the next morning Tank MacGregor, in answer to a presidential summons, appeared at the side gate to the White House and was immediately escorted to the West Wing. The President awaited him in the Oval Office, pacing the floor in front of his desk in short, furious steps. As MacGregor entered, the President retreated behind his desk and sat down, lacing his fingers together and breathing deeply.

MacGregor marched to the President's desk, came to a position of attention, saluted, then stood at ease. He wasn't going to let the President forget for one second who was the career soldier and who was the civilian—no matter what rank his political office gave him. Three rows of ribbons gleamed from the breast of General Tank MacGregor's dress-green jacket, topped by the ribbon for the Congressional Medal of Honor.

Three presidential advisers sat in leather-backed chairs at—for some reason—the far end of the long office. Sprawled across one chair, his long legs hooked over its low arms, was Uriah Vandermeer. Charles Ober was perched on the edge of another chair, his hands resting on the arms, elbows out, as though waiting for the order to stand. In a third chair,

David Steward, the President's counsel, sat neatly, arms folded, back straight, head erect, staring straight ahead. The three of them were frozen in position, as though afraid to make any motion or sound that might distract the President's attention from the Army Chief of Staff standing in front of him.

"You sent for me, sir?" MacGregor said, calmly.

"You're goddamn right I sent for you," the President exploded. His face twitched as he tried to regain control of himself. His fingers unlaced and he made little chopping motions with his right hand that did not relate in any way to what he was saying. "General MacGregor," he said, his thin lips freezing in what might have been meant for a smile, "we seem to have been acting at cross purposes for the last few hours, you and I."

"Yes, sir," MacGregor said.

"You, ah, realize what I'm talking about then?"

"Yes, sir."

"Why then, can you explain—is there any possible way in hell—would you please tell me what it is you think you've been doing?"

"Yes, sir," MacGregor said. "At oh-three-thirty hours this morning I sent a general order to every commandant of every Army base in the United States. That's Eastern Daylight Savings Time, sir, which would have made it, for example, zero-zero-thirty hours local time in California."

"Get on with it," the President said.

"Yes, sir. In my order I canceled Operation Garden Plot, and gave specific instructions that no orders emanating from the presidential Office of Emergency Preparedness, or through any other channel outside the normal chain of command, were to be obeyed, and that any such orders were to be immediately forwarded to my office."

"You did."

200

"Yes, sir. I have a copy of the order here, if you'd like to examine—"

"No, thank you, General!" the President said, waving a teletype flimsy in his hand. "I have my own copy, thank you. I'm not totally without resources." He stared up through his heavy eyebrows at MacGregor. "You didn't think you could get away with this, did you?"

"That's a matter of interpretation, sir," MacGregor said.

Vandermeer sat up. "How's that?" he said, sounding interested.

"It might seem to some of the interested parties in this, ah, misunderstanding," MacGregor said steadily, "that it was not the Pentagon that was trying to get away with anything, but the Executive Office of the President."

"Ah!" Vandermeer said, nodding his head judicially. "Good point."

"Are you trying to tell me," the President said, still making unrelated chopping gestures with his hands, "that there are more people involved in this conspiracy than yourself? That I have more disloyal high-ranking officers?"

"No, sir."

"I will not have this, General MacGregor," the President said. "I will not tolerate disloyalty in any government official, whether he's in the Department of Agriculture or the United States Army."

"Yes, sir."

"Is that all you're going to say, 'No, sir' and 'Yes, sir'?"

"Do you want me to comment, sir?"

"You're goddamn right I want you to comment. I want to know how the hell you found out about Garden Plot, and by what right you canceled a direct presidential order. Don't just stand there in your goddamn greens with your goddamn Medal of Honor and the goddamn knife-edge crease in your trousers and that goddamn smug, superior look on your face and smirk at me. Tell me what the goddamn hell you thought you were doing. And how many of your fellow goddamn West Point career boobs are in it with you. You know, you're not the only son of a bitch who was in the service. I was in the Navy during World War Two. On a destroyer escort. Just like that son of a bitch Kennedy, but they made a movie about him. Expendable. I'd say the son of a bitch was expendable."

The President paused and looked up at MacGregor expectantly. MacGregor had no idea how to respond to the outburst, which had been mumbled in a low, almost expressionless monotone.

Charles Ober spoke up from his seat at the far end of the Oval Office. "Let me ask you a few specific questions, if I may, General MacGregor," he said. "Make sure we're all talking about the same thing."

The President glanced back and forth between Ober and MacGregor as though weighing the two of them on some mental balance beam, and then nodded. "Yes," he said, "good."

MacGregor turned a quarter turn, so he could face Ober without turning his back on the President. "Go ahead," he said.

"Please sit down, General," Ober said.

MacGregor folded himself into a green-leather chair by the side of the President's massive desk. "Right," he said. "What are your questions?"

The President leaned forward across the desk, his head shaking slightly from side to side. "I could fire you," he said. "You know I could fire you. For insubordination. I could probably have you court-martialed, when it comes to that." He looked up. "Isn't that right, David, couldn't I have him court-martialed?"

"Yes, sir, Mr. President," the President's counsel said quietly from his chair. "You could certainly do that, sir."

"So don't you think that I'm without authority in this matter," the President said. "I am the Commander in Chief."

"A couple of questions, General MacGregor," Ober said. "I don't want you to in any way think of this as an inquisitorial proceeding. You can understand that the President feels that you have exceeded your authority and abused his trust in you. But you're not a schoolchild and we're not here to reprimand you. I'm sure you had a good reason or thought you had a good reason, for your actions. We'd like to know what that reason was. As you see, there's no stenographer present and no recording equipment being used. This is a private discussion, and will go no further."

"I understand that," MacGregor said. For all their outward calm, Ober's tapping foot and Vandermeer's eyes, darting from speaker to speaker behind his glasses, betrayed their inner turmoil. The President and his men were more nervous and upset about this confrontation than he was. *They have entered unknown territory*, he thought. *There is unfamiliar handwriting on the wall and they want me to interpret it. MENE, MENE, TEKEL, UPHARSIN. They are weighed in the balance and found wanting*. He thought he knew what the problem was: They didn't know whether they were facing a private action by a stubborn Chief of Staff or a full-fledged revolt of the generals. They had attempted to use the military for what was essentially a civilian action by circumventing the chain of command, and the attempt had blown up in their faces.

Now they couldn't afford to get tough with him—give him a direct order to commence Garden Plot, or just fire him outright—until they had probed the extent of the damage. And he was just the man to keep them guessing. It would certainly cost him his job, but he had been reconciled to that since he sent last night's order. He didn't think they'd dare try to pull his stars and, what the hell, he was ready to retire anyway, and spend the rest of his life stomping around the country as Tank MacGregor the legend. Spend his time speaking before any group that would listen. Reminding them that in order to stay free—and keep this great country free—they'd better keep one eye on the military and both eyes on the politicians.

"Our first question is, how did you find out that Garden Plot had been activated?" Ober asked.

You're kidding! MacGregor thought. Aloud he said, "I received five separate messages."

"Five?" Vandermeer sat forward. "Five?"

"Yes, sir. I think you'll find it a common feeling among career officers that, ah, that the General Staff should have a good idea of everything that's going on in the Army."

"The second question," Vandermeer said, taking over the questioning, "is on what basis did you decide to countermand Garden Plot?"

"It was my decision," MacGregor said firmly. "Whatever advice I received from others, I made the decision and I alone am responsible for its consequences." *That should keep them guessing.*

Vandermeer looked at Ober and shook his head slightly. Then he turned back to MacGregor. "Yes," he said, "but why? You must have had powerful reasons, strong enough to override, ah, personal considerations."

MacGregor smiled. "What you mean is, I knew I was laying my job on the line, so why did I do it? Is that right?"

"Something like that," Vandermeer said.

"I am the President," the President said.

"We did not anticipate an action like this on your part," Vandermeer said. "Or, quite frankly, that it would be so effective. As far as we can tell, not one of our designated units has moved against its targets."

"I'll tell you why I did it," MacGregor said. "Operation Garden Plot, carried out at this time in this way, would have politicized the Army. Using the military against a defined group of civilians—American citizens—who were not at the time actively engaged in rioting or guerrilla warfare, whatever their intentions might be for the future, would be bringing the Army into activities that every commander since George Washington has done his best to keep it out of.

"It's an unacceptable precedent to use the Army against American civilians, either to round them up for arrest or to guard them in concentration camps."

"Internment camps," Ober corrected.

"Whatever. It's not my job to comment on police policies within the United States, whatever I may think of them. But it is my job, as I see it, to prevent the use of the military for such functions."

"Even to the point of disobeying your Commander in Chief?" Ober asked.

"Yes, sir. That precedent was established at Nuremberg in nineteen forty-six."

"Well," Vandermeer said. "You've clearly given the matter a lot of thought."

"That's right," MacGregor said.

Vandermeer stood up and stretched, then shook his head as though clearing it. "Here are the options as I see them, sir," he said to the President. "We could fire General Mac-Gregor here for disobeying a presidential order."

"I could court-martial him," the President said. He turned to stare at MacGregor. "I could court-martial you."

"That's certainly an option," Vandermeer said.

"What else?" Ober asked Vandermeer. "What other options?" There was a slight artificial quality to the question, and MacGregor realized that he was seeing how the President's top two advisers manipulated the President.

"We could ask General MacGregor under what conditions he'll permit his Commander in Chief to continue carrying out his function as Chief Executive Officer of this country."

Nicely loaded, MacGregor thought, admiringly.

Ober nodded. "Compromise is the art of good government," he said. "Of course he will have to resign."

MacGregor was not used to being discussed in the third person and he found it disconcerting. "I'm prepared to resign," he said. "Are you prepared to give me your assurance that the Army will be kept out of the concentration-camp business?"

"Internment camps," Ober said.

"You will resign for reasons of health?" Vandermeer asked.

"I'll retire," MacGregor said. "I've been in the Army long enough."

"I think we should accept that, sir," Vandermeer told the President.

The President leaned back in his chair and closed his eyes. When he opened them again his whole face had changed; the nervous tic gone, the anger lines disappeared. His lips creased into a genuine smile and his eyes lit up as though he were seeing MacGregor for the first time. "We made a mistake in judgment," he told MacGregor. "You won't hold that against us, will you?"

"No, sir," MacGregor said.

"You know," the President said, his voice firm and clear with no trace of the petulant anger in it, "all the men who have sat behind this desk have had great plans. There's not one of them—I'm sure of it—who didn't have a vision of what this country could become under his leadership.

"And we've all made mistakes and gone perhaps too far in pursuit of his goal or that goal or the other goal, but even the mediocre presidents have, on balance, helped this country more than they've hurt it. And the great presidents, the few truly great presidents, have brought this country through trying crises and made it richer, stronger, and greater than it was before."

"That's so, sir," Ober said.

"You know," the President told MacGregor, "General Eisenhower once said that he would rather have won the Congressional Medal of Honor than have been President of the United States. Out of respect for that, and out of respect for your fine—your outstanding—career as a soldier . . ." He stood up. By reflex the other four men in the room stood with him.

"Good-bye, General MacGregor," the President said, extending his hand. "I'm glad we've had this little talk." He shook hands, three quick up-and-down motions, bending from the elbow. "I shall regret losing you, but your wish to retire shall certainly be honored. I'll make the announcement at my next press conference."

"Good-bye, sir," MacGregor said.

"I will speak to Congress about awarding you your fifth star upon retirement. You'll be one of America's few living five-star generals. Sweeten the pot."

"Yes, sir," MacGregor said. "Thank you, sir." He saluted and left the room.

"Son of a bitch!" the President said as the door closed. "I didn't dare fire him, the son of a bitch is too popular. Think he'll keep his mouth closed?"

"It's a good bet," Ober said, crossing the room.

"What's the game plan?" the President asked. "We've had a foul called on us, lost a few yards, but it's still our ball."

Vandermeer dropped into the chair that MacGregor had just vacated. "We run it through the line," he said. "Right down the middle."

The President nodded. "Sounds good," he said. "Call the play."

"We'll have to hire about a hundred more federal marshals," Vandermeer said. "Recruit them from police forces, give them six weeks' quick training, then use them as a strike force. Another few hundred—call them deputy marshals—to start manning the camps until we can bring them up to strength."

"How long?" the President asked.

"Say two months."

"Go with that."

• CHAPTER TWENTY-ONE

Two MONTHS LATER, at three o'clock on a Thursday morning in New York, an attorney named Tom Varmer staggered out of bed and groggily crossed the room in response to the urgent knocking at his door. "Whazzit?" he called through the door.

"Police! Open up!"

"Wha? Sure thing." What the hell would the police want with him? Maybe they thought one of the antiwar protesters he defended was hiding under his bed. He threw back the two bolts and unlatched the door, pulling it open. "Come on in," he said. "What's up?"

It took a moment for him to focus on the two men outside and realize that, whatever they were, they were not policemen. They were dressed in Marine fatigue uniforms, with odd-looking insignia on the lapels. One of them had a sidearm strapped to his waist, while the other carried a short-barreled carbine. Tom Varmer was quickly waking up.

"Thomas H. Varmer?" the one with the sidearm demanded.

"That's right. Who the hell are you?"

"We're federal marshals. We have here a warrant for your arrest and detainment."

Varmer shook his head to make sure he was really awake, and this wasn't just another in the series of bad dreams he'd been having lately. "What kind of warrant?" he said. "What are you guys talking about?"

"Here," the talker said, holding a folded document under Varmer's nose. "Take a look."

Varmer unfolded the paper, which proved to be quite long, and turned on his desk lamp to study it. It was a multiple arrest warrant, issued under the Emergency Powers Act, to detain "the below listed individuals." Varmer's name was number fourteen out of about two hundred.

"Okay, Varmer," the talker said. "Let's get going. What are you trying to do, memorize it?"

"I'm not altogether sure this is legal," Varmer said. "You know I'm a lawyer."

"That's not our affair," the talker said. The other man just stood there mute, clutching his carbine.

"I'm going to make one phone call," Varmer said.

He reached for the phone, only to have it slapped out of his hand by the talker.

"None of that!" the talker said.

"You son of a bitch!" Varmer swung his fist wildly toward the man's face.

The other marshal took one step and brought the butt of his carbine down smartly across the back of Varmer's head. Varmer crumpled to the floor, a red haze in front of his eyes. An incredibly brilliant pain cascaded from the back of his head to the front. He lay where he had fallen, trying to allow this throbbing pain to become a part of his reality. Nothing like this had ever happened to him before.

One of them kicked him sharply in the ribs. "Get up," the talker said, "you ain't out. Grab your bathrobe and come along. We got a lot more stops to make tonight."

It was two o'clock in the morning in Chicago when a

squad of marshals quickly broke into a Hanscomb Street building and herded twenty-one blacks into a waiting bus. Their action warrants had specified merely "the occupants of 347 Hanscomb Street," and so everyone in residence at the time of the raid was arrested—men, women, and children. Tom Varmer would have been glad to offer his opinion that this was an illegal proceeding, based on a fraudulent warrant. But he wasn't asked.

It was four thirty in the morning, Pacific States Time, when the first buses arrived at the gates of John Muir Camp and began offloading groups of frightened prisoners. The guards, deputy marshals in the President's new expanded corps, herded the prisoners through the gate to a large compound in front of the rows of detention barracks. There the prisoners were left to examine their surroundings and one another in the early-morning chill.

Few of the prisoners were dressed for the occasion. Most of them were in pajamas, bathrobes, or nightgowns. Some wore only their underwear, and one man had nothing but a blanket clutched around his portly body. They looked scared, or numb, or tired, or angry. One man began screaming about his rights and tried to run back out through the gate, but two of the guards clubbed him to the ground. After that there was little commotion.

By five thirty, there were at least eight hundred people grouped together in the compound. A small, neat man in civilian clothes climbed onto a wooden platform to the left of the gate and picked up a microphone. "Good morning," he said cheerfully, his words reverberating off the barracks across the compound.

A muttering rose from the crowd in front of him, which he ignored. The powerful public address system easily carried over the noise. "My name is Davies," he said, "and I am executive officer of Internal Confinement Camp Number

211

Five, the John Muir Camp. You are all my guests, and I would like to define the terms of our relationship for you right now.

"You have been arrested, from points all over northern California, and are being held here by authority of Presidential Order Fourteen, under the Emergency Powers Act of 1941.

"Lists of your names will be made public as soon as they can be drawn up, so there can be no question of 'secret confinement' or any other police state procedures. Forms will be distributed for you to fill out, and we will attempt to notify two persons of your choosing about your confinement. I assure you, despite what you may think, there is nothing arbitrary or illegal about this procedure.

"Special magistrates are now being appointed so that each of you can have his or her day in court. Unfortunately, I can't say how long it will take to process all of you through the courts, but it will be as speedy as possible, of that I can assure you.

"There is no bail procedure set up, so each of you will have to bear with us—and remain with us—until your hearing. We'll try to make it as pleasant as possible for you all. We realize that, as of yet, you are guilty of no crime and are merely being held in protective custody. After you are assigned to a barracks, you'll be on your own. Those of you who wish to work can go to the mess hall or the laundry or volunteer for camp assignments.

"How well we get along is entirely up to you. Anyone attempting to escape from this camp will be shot. That is all."

THREE THOUSAND MILES AWAY
AND TWO WEEKS LATER
The helicopter circled the camp twice before sitting down on a patch of dirt by the main gate. St. Yves hopped

212

off first, his Bolex slung over his shoulder like an assault rifle, and Kit clambered down behind him. They hurried through the downdraft of the rotor blades to the small welcoming committee of camp officers who were clumped together on the far side of the field, trying to look informal. This was, after all, an informal visit.

"St. Yves," St. Yves said, indicating himself. "Young," he added, pointing to Kit.

"Welcome to Camp Washington Irving," a chubby man in the almost-Marine uniform of the Federal Internal Confinement Camp Command said, giving them an offhand salute. Kit studied the uniform with interest; it was the first time he had seen one up close. It had been personally designed by the President, and showed clearly the President's tendency toward unconscious parody. Maroon piping sewn along every seam of a Marine Corps class A uniform, and maroon detail added to the shoulders, pockets, cuffs, and lapels. Gleaming gold insignia had been designed for the lapels: the executive eagle for the left, and the inch-high letters FICCC in a semicircle for the right. The military insignia of rank was reserved for the shoulders. The service caps were heavy with gold braid and sported a large eagle carrying the letters FICCC. The motto "We Serve" was stitched in gold across the breast pocket. With the addition of a dress sword, Kit decided, the uniform would not have looked out of place as a costume for *The Merry Widow*.

"You must be Nickerson, the camp commandant," St. Yves said, eyeing the highly polished birds on the shoulders of the man's crisply starched uniform.

"That's right," Commandant Nickerson said. "I thought Mr. Vandermeer was coming with you." He was trying not to sound disappointed, but it was clear that in his eyes a St. Yves and a Young were not a Vandermeer. Kit had a clear image of the hundreds of man-hours the staff of Camp Washington Irving must have put in polishing boots and brass and starching and pressing uniforms preparing for a visit from the second most powerful man in Washington.

"Mr. Vandermeer is still in the helicopter," St. Yves said. "He's having the pilot check him out on the controls. He used to fly one of these during the Korean War, you know."

"I didn't," Nickerson said. "Do you suppose he'll be long? I have a schedule—"

Vandermeer appeared in the doorway of the copter and jumped down with the easy grace of a man who spent an hour in the White House handball court three days a week. The clump of camp officers came to attention as he approached, and Nickerson saluted. "Welcome to Camp Washington Irving, Mr. Vandermeer," he said, holding the salute for four beats and then bringing it smartly down. "I'm Commandant Nickerson, and this is my aide, Captain Peters. This is the adjutant, Captain Reager . . ." He continued down the line, introducing all twelve members of the welcoming group.

Vandermeer shook all the hands. "You know why we're here," he said. "We want to see everything. Everything. The President wants a direct report on the status of the internment camps at this point in time."

"We understand, sir," Nickerson said.

"How's it going?" Vandermeer asked. "Any complaints? Any problems? It looked pretty good from the air—neatly laid out, peaceful."

"No troubles, sir," Nickerson said, falling into step alongside Vandermeer, who was striding toward the administration building. "No troubles at all. That is, beyond what you'd expect."

"Yes, but what do you expect, Commandant? That's what I'm here to find out. We're so new at this we don't really know what to expect."

St. Yves raced ahead and got into position to photograph the group entering the building. He crouched by the door, his Bolex whirring, and then leaped between two startled members of the camp staff to get a close-up of Vandermeer's face as he talked to the commandant. Vandermeer, a camera sophisticate, ignored St. Yves' antics, but the commandant started and took an involuntary step backward, crashing into an aide and almost knocking him down.

Kit resisted an impulse to take off his hat and hold it in front of his face like a gangster entering a courtroom. He would just as soon not have had a 16-millimeter record of his visit. With a conscience newly prodded awake by the death of Dianna Holroyd, Kit thought that these internment camps were the most visible, most egregious excess of a power-mad White House. He wanted to quit, but, as Aaron kept pointing out, Kit was his best pipeline to the White House. So he tagged along on trips like this, since St. Yves seemed to like having him along, and reported to Aaron whatever he saw.

"Some of the prisoners are troublesome," Nickerson said, "but nothing we can't handle. Most have settled down pretty quickly to their new status, with the help of the tranquilizers we add to their food. But a few of them insist on being troublesome."

"Troublesome?" Vandermeer said. "How troublesome? Trying to escape? Fighting with the guards?"

"No, sir," Nickerson said. "Not much of that. A couple of men tried to make it over the fence about a week ago, but a guard on the tower spotted them and let go a burst with his gun. Killed one of them outright. The other's still in the hospital. It was in the report last week. Haven't had any incidents like that since."

St. Yves tucked his camera under his arm and fell into step with the group. "That's surprising," he said. "I wouldn't expect any of the internees to try to escape yet. It's too soon. They should be exhausting all the legal procedures first. That should keep them busy for another couple of months anyway. Those two must have had a heavy date."

Nickerson shrugged. "That's one of the things they keep bitching about," he said. "Come this way, let me show you the main mess hall."

"What's one of the things they keep bitching about?"

"The legal procedures," Nickerson said. "Or, to be more precise, the fact that there aren't any legal procedures."

"You mean they're getting tired of waiting for trials and that sort of thing?"

"The prisoners demand the right to see their lawyers," Nickerson said. "Also to write letters."

"Internees," St. Yves said. "They're not prisoners, they're internees."

"Internees," Nickerson said.

They entered the mess hall, a 1940s paradigm of institutional efficiency. Camp Washington Irving, as it was now called, had been constructed during World War II but not needed, and had been waiting for use ever since. The mess hall, cleaned to antiseptic purity in anticipation of Vandermeer's visit, was all chrome and white linoleum and bleached wood. Only the food looked out of place; it wasn't symmetrical, and it wasn't neat. It wasn't, Kit noted as they walked by the steam table, very appetizing either.

Vandermeer allowed himself to be seated at a table and brought a cup of coffee. Kit, at Nickerson's insistence, took a tin tray and went through the chow line behind St. Yves, who was helping himself to the watery canned corn and unidentifiable creamed meat with unlikely enthusiasm.

St. Yves slid onto the bench next to Vandermeer and dropped his tray in front of him. "I want to get a shot of the internees going through this line," he told Vandermeer. "And some close-ups of them eating. Good, healthy food. Nothing spared to make the lives of these unfortunate men

216

comfortable until they can take their rightful places in society again."

"This is one of two mess halls at the camp," Commandant Nickerson said. "We can chow fifteen hundred prisoners through this hall in an hour."

"Internees," St. Yves said.

Vandermeer turned to stare at Nickerson. "You must not make the mistake again," he said. "These men and women are internees. Federal prisoners have certain rights: the right to a speedy trial, the right to be accused of something specific, the right of habeas corpus, the right to see their lawyer. If these men were prisoners, why then we'd be violating their constitutional rights. You see that, don't you?"

Nickerson stared at Vandermeer, his eyes wide. He seemed to have lost the power of speech.

"These people are being interned for the good of the state," Vandermeer said. "Think of the Japanese during World War Two. No trials, no habeas corpus, no lawyers, no mess, no fuss. We do likewise. But you must learn, Commandant Nickerson, that terminology is very important."

St. Yves put down his fork and nodded. "A spade is not always a spade," he told Nickerson, who was sitting opposite him at the table. "Sometimes it is a shovel. Sometimes it is a digging implement. Do you understand?"

Nickerson nodded his understanding. Kit, at the far end of the table, wondered just what it was that the commandant understood.

Captain Reager trotted over to the table. "The, ah, internees are lining up outside for lunch," he said. "You wanted to get pictures?"

"Right!" St. Yves said, swinging his Bolex up to his shoulder.

"You want them all in at once, or just a few at a time?" Reager asked. "I'll have to call in more guards if you want them all in. Just as a precaution."

"A few of them," St. Yves said. "Thirty or forty—no more. We don't want the joint to look crowded, do we?"

"Ah, no," Reager said. "Right." He trotted back to the door.

"We haven't found the necessity of isolating the internees from the guards," Nickerson told Vandermeer. "These aren't really violent people, it seems."

"How would you characterize them, Commandant?" Kit asked.

Nickerson looked down the table at him, as though trying to remember who he was. "Confused," he said finally. "I would say, mostly, that they're confused."

"That's wonderful," Vandermeer said. "The President locks up several thousand people as being 'an immediate and present danger to this country,' and the commandant of one of the lockups says they're not really violent, they're only confused. I can only hope that the commandant does not give interviews to the press. Or to anyone else, for that matter." His tone was bantering, but Nickerson would have had to be a damn fool not to see that he was dead serious.

"Between us, Mr. Vandermeer," Nickerson said eagerly, "I don't give interviews to the press in any case. You have my word." Kit noticed that fear made Nickerson's brow bead with sweat.

St. Yves positioned himself by the steam table, the Bolex balanced on his shoulder. A guard opened the front door and counted out the first forty internees from the line outside, waggling a finger at each one as he entered, and then promptly closed the door.

The internees who came in were as widely assorted a group of men as Kit had ever seen. About half of them had been standardized by a common uniform—denims and a white T-shirt—but the others still wore whatever they had been wearing when they were removed from society. One man was in rumpled evening clothes, a second in an airline flight officer's uniform, a third didn't seem to have anything on under a tweed overcoat. Several of them looked like college students, some like college dropouts, and many of the others like perfectly respectable professional men who had no business being incarcerated and knew that it was all some horrible mistake. As Nickerson had said, they did not look dangerous, only confused.

They walked dully along the line to the steam table. Except for two of the college-student types, who were having an intense, low-pitched conversation, they were mute and seemed uninterested in their surroundings.

St. Yves, camera grinding, followed them along the steam table, closing up on an occasional face, or tray, or hand. He moved among them like a fish in the water, and they parted for him without really noticing his presence.

One of the men in the line, a neat-looking man with close-cropped hair, already in internee denim, had been staring at Vandermeer as he walked along. Suddenly he stepped out of line and pointed a finger. "You're Vandermeer," he said.

A guard moved toward the man, but Vandermeer waved him back. "That's right," he said.

"Son of a—" the internee said. A light came into his eyes. "Listen," he said. "Do something for me, will you? You can do it. Listen, it's not much to ask. Will you do something for me?"

"What do you need?" Vandermeer asked.

"Listen, nobody knows I'm here," the man said. "That's all I want is for somebody to know I'm here. My name is Jacob Stein, and I live in Brooklyn, Bensonhurst. Call up my wife and tell her I'm here. She doesn't know where I am. She must be worried sick about me. I've got two kids. Please, for the love of God, do that for me!"

219

"I'll see what I can do," Vandermeer said. He pointed to Kit. "You give this man your phone number. He'll take care of it. You take care of it, Young."

Kit took out his pen and a small pocket notebook, and suddenly the other internees, who had been watching silently, started to babble. They pressed forward, but were discouraged by two guards with short clubs, so they stood in line and shouted names and phone numbers at Kit.

"Wait a second!" Vandermeer yelled, holding up his hand. When they had quieted down, he stood up and shook his head. "I can't address the problem of why you're here," he said. "In an operation of this size, there are bound to be a few screw-ups, and you, any of you, may be one of them. We'll get that sorted out as quickly as possible. But if you people say you haven't been allowed to write home, I say that's wrong. And I can do something about that." He turned to the commandant. "Is this true?"

"What's that?"

"Have these people been deprived of the chance to write home?"

"Well—yes," Nickerson said, sounding puzzled.

"I want that rectified immediately!" Vandermeer said. He turned back to the internees. "Pencils, paper, and envelopes," he told them. "As soon as possible. I promise you." He stood up. "You people will not be forgotten," he said.

One of the college students, who had taken a seat with his back to Vandermeer, suddenly twisted around in his seat. "You've got to be shitting me!" he said loudly, in a high-pitched, nervous voice.

"What's that?" Vandermeer asked, maintaining his bland neutrality.

"I said you've got to be shitting me, you pig!" the college student yelled. "What's this 'We will not be forgotten' bullshit? It's you motherfuckers who put us in here in the first place. You arbitrary, motherfucking, high-handed fascist pig!" The student stood up as his voice rose and two of the guards moved in closer to him.

His buddy, sitting across from him, put a hand on his shoulder. "Watch it, Marve," he said softly.

"Watch it, hell," Marve said and, picking up his tin tray, he flung it across the room at Vandermeer. The tray skimmed by Vandermeer's left ear, and a great glob of the creamed meat splatted Vandermeer squarely across his face. The two guards leaped for the youth.

Commandant Nickerson jumped to his feet and stood protectively in front of Vandermeer. "We'd better get you out of here, sir," he said.

Vandermeer, his body rigid with fury, clawed the creamed crap out of his eyes. "Just get me a goddamn napkin!" he snapped. Kit grabbed a handful of paper napkins from the table and helped Vandermeer clean his face.

As two guards clubbed the youth to the floor, St. Yves moved his camera in for a close-up of the clubbing, a look of unholy joy on his face. Then he stared mournfully at his camera for a second and strode back to the table. "Shit!" he said. "I'm out of film."

Vandermeer stared disgustedly down at his jacket. "Let's get the hell out of here," he said. "My suit is ruined."

"What about this letting them write letters?" Nickerson asked, trotting alongside Vandermeer as they left the building. "It was your instruction not to let them write, sir."

"Let them write," Vandermeer said. "Get them pencils and paper. Just don't mail the fucking letters. We'll set up a unit to read the mail. Can't tell what we might get." He took his jacket off and rolled it into a tight ball. "Let the bastards write."

• CHAPTER TWENTY-TWO

AT A TABLE in the bar of Bigg's Bavarian Chophouse in Silver Spring, Maryland, Senator Kevin Ryan sat nursing a draft lager. He'd been sitting there for fifteen minutes when the door opened, admitting a blast of cold air along with Tom Clay, the Senate Majority Leader. Right behind him was David Wittling. An ex-Senator, and one of the most respected, influential men in the party. They took their heavy overcoats off and stamped their feet clear of snow before coming over to join Ryan.

Ryan smiled as they sat down opposite him. "We have to stop meeting like this," he said.

"I think the Senate is bugged," Clay said, rubbing his hands together.

"I know," Ryan said, "you told me."

"My office is bugged," Clay continued. "My home is bugged, my car is probably bugged." He shook his head. "Have you ever stopped to consider the size of the staff necessary to conduct an operation like this? The amount of tax money that must be going to support it? That degenerate paranoid is costing this country a fortune."

"I, ah, don't think you could support either of those pejoratives, Senator," Ryan said.

"Not to mention what he's doing to the Constitution," Clay added.

Wittling signaled the waitress for a pair of lagers and then turned back to the table. "It's good to see you again, Kevin," he said. "I haven't had a chance to congratulate you on that speech you made before the 'seventy-four election. Damn good. I don't get to Washington much anymore. Not so much as I'd like."

"We'd like to see more of you, Senator," Ryan said. "We could use the benefit of your advice."

"Sure," Wittling snorted. "Nothing you young pols need more than an old man like me hanging around and telling you how we used to do it back in my day. Now Tom here," he added, patting Clay on the shoulder, "he's different. He was around in my day. He was the bright young Senator back then. And now look at him. Never made it. Poor Tom."

Clay grinned and slapped Wittling fondly on the shoulder. "He flew in last night," he told Ryan. "Staying at my house. And he's been nagging me since he arrived about how I 'never made it.' I think the old man's getting senile."

"What do you mean, 'never made it'?" Ryan asked. "Senator Clay is the Majority Leader—most important job in the Senate."

"That's as it may be," Wittling said, "but he had the fever in his eyes back in the old days. The presidential fever. I could always spot it."

"What about our present incumbent?" Ryan asked. "He was in the Senate with you. Did he have it?"

"I could never read his eyes," Wittling said. "Narrow and close together, and he'd never look you in the eye, but always off behind you. And have you ever noticed the way he moves when he talks? His gestures have nothing to do

223

with what he's saying. It's as though his mouth and his body were under the control of two separate people—like a badly handled marionette."

"That's so," Clay said, nodding. "But the man has a brilliant political mind, you have to give him that. He can find the lowest common denominator of any given group of voters faster and more surely than any man since Huey Long."

They paused while the waitress, in a short skirt and blouse that looked like the deMille version of Bavarian peasant garb, brought over the two lagers. She walked away again with a very nice hip swing. When she reached the bar Ryan, with a sigh, raised his gaze from her legs. "I suppose you two brought me down here for something beyond discussions of the President as a politician," he said.

Clay smiled. "Not exactly," he said.

Wittling leaned forward. "We want you to run," he said. Clay nodded.

Ryan looked slowly from one to the other. "Me?" he said. "You want *me* to run?"

"Surely you've given it some thought," Clay said.

Ryan nodded. "I have," he said. "A lot of thought. I was thinking of giving it a try in four years. Nineteen-eighty sounds good to me." He looked up at Clay. "Hell, I'm not even fifty yet. What's the idea? Why me?"

"Here's our thinking," Clay said. "The President's going to get behind Artie Arnold this year and run him as a figurehead. Eight more years of the same."

"I guess that's obvious to all of us."

"Yes. Well, with the country so badly polarized, he's got a good, solid hold on the great mass of middle Americans. Law and order sounds damn good to them now, and he's appropriated that motto to himself and his people. And the opposition is fragmented into so many pieces that, unless we do some strong pulling together now, by the time the campaign starts we'll have a dozen contenders fighting each other for the nomination."

"And he's got the money and the office to get almost unlimited access to the voters," Wittling said. "And you can bet your ass he's not going to let a little thing like the fact that it's improper and illegal stop him from using his office to wring every last vote out of every last voter."

"And that brings me in?" Ryan said.

"A group of us old boys got together and had us a little talk," Clay said. "And we decided on a strategy to beat the son of—ah—to ensure victory for the righteous and defeat for the ungodly. And you're it."

"I see," Ryan said. "You fed a list of the requirements into a computer and a card popped out with my name on it."

Wittling stabbed a finger out at him. "You've decided not to run this year because you have it figured the same way we do. This is the President's year, and Artie Arnold is his man. Give Artie four years to sit in the White House and be shown up for the idiot that he is, and he'll be ripe for replacement."

"Well—"

"Only this country can't *take* four more years of what it's been getting. The Constitution has been punched so full of holes that it's sinking bow first. And the country is being ripped apart to the point where in a couple of years there's going to be no way to put it together again."

Wittling stopped talking and he and Clay drank beer and stared at Ryan.

"What do you want me to do?" Ryan asked.

"Run for President," Clay said.

"And get chewed apart in the primaries?" Ryan said. "Our party has too many potential candidates and nobody who looks like a front runner—certainly not me."

"You underrate yourself," Clay said. "The polls show you right up there in popularity with the other potential candidates, and you got there a lot faster. You have momentum going for you."

"But I don't have the political base," Ryan said. "Not nationwide."

"We do," Clay said.

Ryan looked at him, his eyebrows lifted. "Oh," he said.

"Do you understand what you're being offered?" Clay asked.

"Yes," Ryan said, "I think I do."

"You run," Clay said. "We'll see that there's enough opposition to you to keep you in the media, and we'll see that it drops out at the proper time."

"Of course you'll still have a fight on your hands," Wittling said. "We don't control the whole damned party. Remember what Will Rogers said: 'I'm not a member of any organized political party; I'm a Democrat.'"

"What you're saying is that you'll make it possible, but not easy, for me to get the nomination," Ryan said.

"Something like that," Clay agreed.

"We'll keep the momentum going for you," Wittling said. "And we'll do our best to see that the party doesn't get fragmented. And our best is pretty good. Tom and I have a lot of chips to call in."

"You understand that if I do this, and if I get elected, I am going to be the President. Neither of you is going to serve for me or through me, and I owe no favors outside of what you would normally expect from a president of your party."

"We're quits when you get elected," Clay said. "Just serve in the best interests of the country and within the limits of the Constitution, and you owe us nothing."

Ryan was quiet for a minute, his thoughts deep and distant from his surroundings. Then he shuddered very slightly and looked up. "You want my decision now?"

"Preferably," Clay said.

"Yes. My decision is yes."

"Congratulations," Wittling said. "I was going to say you won't regret it, but that's ridiculous. Of course you'll regret it."

THE WHITE HOUSE

THE OVAL OFFICE, Friday, April 23, 1976 (10:02–10:27 A.M.)

MEETING: The President, Vandermeer, and Ober

AUTHORIZED TRANSCRIPTION FROM THE EXECUTIVE ARCHIVES

The President and Vandermeer are discussing household matters. At 10:02 Ober enters.

P. Charlie.

O. Good morning, Mr. President. Morning, Billy.

V. You're up late this morning, Charlie.

O. Don't you believe it. I've been here since six thirty. I've been working.

P. Good. Good. At what?

O. I've been correlating the reports on Ryan's Wednesday speech. The public's reaction, what they got out of it, what they agreed with, what they disagreed with, what they thought was important, what bored them. That sort of thing. One of our press people came up with a great idea: we're putting together a personality profile of Senator Ryan's public personality. Not of Ryan, you see, but of who people see when they look at Ryan. Sort of the personality he projects.

P. I don't see how that mick son of a bitch is getting all that media time recently. It's like the Democrats are handing him the nomination.

V. What do we do with this profile of the media Ryan when we've got it?

O. It tells us who we're fighting. Can I have some coffee? It tells us what image the public sees as against the image we project. Then we can manipulate both images and distort them into whatever shapes we want. Thanks.

P. You know, I wouldn't put it past them.

V. How's that, sir?

P. A conspiracy by the, you know, Democrats, to run Ryan against Arnold.

O. We picked him as the front runner months ago.

P. Yeah, the front runner. But there's no pack.

V. I see what you mean.

O. We have a couple of bugs in the DNC headquarters. But I don't know how heavy the surveillance is. I'll put someone on it.

P. That's the sort of thing. No surprises, if you see what I mean. We want to keep the ball—keep making goals. We don't want the other side to run with it.

O. Right.

V. Right.

P. How's that ACLU thing going? Anything on that?

O. It looks like the Emergency Powers Act is going to hold. The courts are throwing it right back at Congress. And we sure as hell don't have to sweat Congress on that. The IC camps are going to be with us for a while.

V. What's the latest count?

O. Count?

V. How many internees?

O. At last count, nine thousand.

V. There's some votes Arnie isn't going to get.

P. I spoke to Arnie's mother on the phone yesterday. She isn't going to vote for him. His wife is going to vote for him, but he's got something on her. Boys, I tell you, I don't know how we're going to pull this off.

V. We could still ditch him. It isn't too late to ditch him.

P. For who?

O. That's the question.

P. Arnold, the poor stupid son of a bitch, is my man—body and soul. We make him President and we keep the reins for another eight years. Have to move out of the White House, of course, but we keep the country. Who else can we trust?

O. That damned Roosevelt and his four terms.

228

P. I've got some big things going for this country. A big game plan. But I need Arnold in. Then he appoints me Secretary of State, and puts you two in the Cabinet, and goes back to his comic books.

(About a minute of conversation was lost here while the tape was changed)

V. . . . him. So we'd better either get someone else or develop another game plan.

O. Or get rid of Ryan.

P. That's another game plan.

V. It wouldn't do any good. Not in the long run.

P. We're only interested in the run that ends in November at the polls.

V. Yes, sir. That's what I'm talking about. The Democrats have several people to replace Ryan. And we're still stuck with Arnold.

O. It sounds like we have to replace both Ryan and Arnold.

P. Yes. The perfect play. But at just the right time. Not too soon for them or too late for us. But we'd have to have a replacement ready.

V. Not necessarily.

P. No? Let me hear your thinking on that. . . .

● CHAPTER TWENTY-THREE

STRETCHING LIKE A thin green arm through Washington, Rock Creek Park separates governmental Washington from the maze of bedroom communities to the north and northwest. In part clipped and manicured, and in part as wild and unmanaged as when the Algonquin Indians fished the now-polluted waters of Rock Creek and hunted through the present volleyball courts and bicycle paths of the park itself, Rock Creek Park is a favorite with those outdoors-lovers who can't get further out of town.

Kit Young and Miriam Kassel tramped along one of the park's hiking trails, a knapsack over Kit's shoulder and a blanket roll over Miriam's, looking for the perfect place to picnic.

"This is it, I think," Kit said, indicating a smooth hump of rock to the right surrounded by boxwoods and thick brush. "If there's a clearing around on the other side of that rock, it's the place."

"It certainly is secluded," Miriam said dubiously, staring at the thick bushes. "Are you sure that's not poison ivy?"

"Ask me in about six hours," Kit said. "That's the only way I can tell."

"Don't you know what poison ivy looks like?"

"Sure, it's got waxy green leaves—or is that poison sumac? And sometimes it has red berries which you're not supposed to eat." He fought his way into the bushes on the far side of the rock. "Look—here's a path."

"If this is a path," Miriam said, pushing in behind him, "I'm a camel. And I won't mention what you are."

"Well, a track," Kit said. He carefully held the branches aside as he moved so they wouldn't snap back in Miriam's face. After a minute's hard work, the track became an honest path, leading to a small, semihidden clearing surrounded by bushes and rocks, all of fifty feet off the hiking trail.

"Well," Miriam said, brushing herself off and looking around. "I certainly hope this is the place. If it isn't, Aaron will never find us."

"If so, it's his fault and none of my own," Kit said. "We followed his instructions and ended up here, and so should he."

"I hope so," Miriam said, spreading the blanket over an offending bit of brown earth that poked its way through the grass cover. "Would you eliminate those, ah, artifacts over there? They offend my esthetic sense of picnic."

Kit picked up the empty beer cans that littered one side of the clearing and chucked them deeper into the surrounding bush. Then he handed Miriam the knapsack and helped her get the food out and into some semblance of order in one corner of the blanket.

A few minutes later, Aaron Adams appeared over the top of a rock and slid down to join them. "Hi, all," he said.

"Welcome," Miriam told him.

He handed her a brown paper bag. "My contribution," he said.

Miriam opened the bag and removed a pair of plastic wrapped globs. "Chopped liver," she said. "And—what's this?—deviled eggs! How nice."

231

"I won't tell George that you called his pâté chopped liver," Adams said, smiling. He dropped cross-legged to the grass next to the blanket. "Did you know you were being followed?"

"What?" Kit said. He glanced back at the brush they had pushed through. "You're kidding!"

"Nope. I happened to come along a bit behind you, and I was just in position to catch two gentlemen in gray suits tippy-toeing through the underbrush after you, trying to look casual."

"Where are they now?" Miriam said, making an effort not to look around.

"If you look over those rocks to your right," Adams said, shifting his eyes toward the indicated direction, "you'll see a higher, kind of shoe-shaped rock behind. One of them is, even now, precariously perched atop the shoe."

"Watching us?" Miriam asked.

"I should assume so, certainly."

"What should we do?"

Adams turned to Kit and allowed the corners of his mouth to turn up. "What would you suggest?" he asked.

"Eat lunch," Kit said. "I'm hungry."

"But they're watching us," Miriam said. Her voice rose slightly. "There are two men out there in business suits watching us!"

"And they'll see three friends eating a picnic lunch and talking," Kit said. "Nothing to get alarmed about. Nothing subversive. Nothing to report." He took Miriam's hand, trying to give some empathetic force to the gesture while still letting it look casual to a distant observer. *It does get to you,* he thought wryly. "It's probably just a routine check," he told Miriam. "Everyone's always having their security clearance updated. The President's a bug on stopping leaks before they start. So room sixteen follows people around at random whenever they have a couple of spare men. They're hoping to catch someone walking into the Russian Embassy. Or, even worse, the editorial offices of the *New York Times*. It's meaningless."

"What are they going to think, seeing us together?" Miriam demanded.

"You have a guilty conscience," Kit told her. "You and I know why we're meeting Aaron here, but they don't."

"What is this country coming to," Adams said, "when three old friends are nervous about meeting openly in a public park? I ask only metaphorically. What this country is coming to is one of the things we're here to discuss."

"Here," Miriam said. "Rolls and cold cuts, cheese, butter, knife, um, potato salad, coffee, paper cups, salt and pepper, wine, plastic glasses. Make and pour your own."

Kit wrapped some assorted cold cuts around a hunk of cheese and thrust the mass into the heart of a roll. He twisted around to face Adams. "Think they can hear us?"

"Not unless they have the lunch bugged," Adams said. He poured himself a glass of wine. "Excellent idea, this. Decent wine, too."

"Let's talk," Kit said.

"That's what I'm here for," Adams agreed. "But keep it casual, or at least keep it looking casual. Three old friends enjoying each other's company and sliced salami."

"I've been feeding you information for months now," Kit said, leaning back on his elbows and not looking directly at Adams. "I want to know what you're doing with it. It's dangerous for me, and Miriam, and probably for you to keep this up, so I want to make sure it's worthwhile."

Adams regarded him steadily through his gray-tinted steel-rimmed glasses. "You know what I do with the information you supply," he said. "Or you have a damn good idea."

"There's a leak at the White House," Kit said. "Someone is funneling information through to Kevin Ryan's organization. I just want to make sure that it isn't me."

"It isn't," Adams said. "You know damn well that I'm a conduit back into the Company. We both feel that they have to know what's going on inside the White House if they're to make sane policy decisions. Especially since this administration doesn't seem interested in doing anything about foreign policy beyond racing around and grandstanding for home consumption. Your friends are very PR-conscious, but they're not so concerned with substance."

"I've been feeling all this time," Kit said, "that CIA is hearing what I'm telling you. And I agree: it's necessary. But I draw the line at feeding information to Ryan."

"Why?" Miriam said.

"Why?" Kit looked surprised. "Because that's political, and I want to keep this above the political level. That should be clear."

"It isn't, and that's nonsense," Miriam said. "It's incredible to me that anyone in government can say with a straight face that he's above politics. And I think it's unfair and immoral to consider it proper to feed information to the CIA, which is a government agency, but improper to keep a member of the Senate informed of what's happening to the government and the country. After all, the Senate is elected by the people, and who the hell made the CIA God?"

"You're excited," Kit said. "Calm down. Unclench your fists. Look like you're on a picnic, for Christ's sake!"

Adams meditatively refilled his wineglass from the thermos. "It was you, wasn't it?" he asked Miriam.

"Me what?"

"You what's been feeding information to the Ryan people."

Miriam unclenched her fists and took several deep breaths. "Don't look at me like that," she told Kit. "Yes, that's right, it was me. And it will continue to be me unless you boys find yourselves another cutout. I'm not just a dead-letter drop, you know; I'm a person. And I have a right to have some control over my destiny."

"But why Ryan?" Kit demanded.

"Calm down," Miriam said. "Your eyes are starting to bulge. We don't want our little snoops on the hill to have anything to write down in their little notebooks, do we?"

Kit took a deep breath, and then nodded. "You're right," he said. "You're using your judgment just as I'm using mine. I have no right to unilaterally decide that mine's better."

"Incredible!" Miriam said. "Did you say that?"

"But why Ryan?" Kit repeated.

"Well, it's either Ryan or Arnold. And if it's Arnold, it's eight more years of the same."

"There are other Democrats in the race," Kit said.

"But Ryan's going to get the nomination; anybody can see that."

"True," Adams said.

"That's what the President thinks," Kit said. "And he's not fond of the idea."

"Well," Adams said, smiling, "Miriam may be doing more good than we are with our more cautious approach. If Ryan gets elected we can unravel this whole mess at our leisure and present it to the proper authorities; presumably there will again be proper authorities. And if Arnold opens his mouth wide enough to insert his shoe a couple of more times he'll have blown the election for sure."

"The President isn't allowing Arnold any more press conferences," Kit said. "From now on he only speaks from a prepared script. They hope to stop the image erosion. That's what Ober calls it: Arnold's steady image erosion."

"Too late," Adams said.

"And they've got a big, secret master plan," Kit said. "Vandermeer and St. Yves have worked it out."

"What is it?"

"I have no idea," Kit said. "This is *the* secret, and nobody has the need to know except those in on it."

"A big deal, eh?" Adams said thoughtfully. "Any ideas? They've got to be dropping hints, people always do. What direction do the hints point in?"

"All I know is that it happens after the conventions. They expect Ryan to get the nomination. And they think they're ready for it."

"Some dirt, maybe," Adams said. "Something to smear him with."

Kit shook his head. "I don't know," he said.

"Ah, well," Adams said. "Let's eat our lunch. Let those boys on the rock get some good pictures for the archives."

"Oh!" Miriam said. "I'd forgotten—would you believe?—I'd forgotten about them."

"Never forget," Adams said. "From now on always assume that they're lurking around somewhere, just out of sight, and conduct yourself accordingly."

"It's one hell of a way to live," Miriam said.

"Consider the alternative," said Adams.

EXCERPT FROM THE SPEECH GIVEN BY GENERAL OF THE ARMY HIRAM T. MacGREGOR TO THE GRADUATING CLASS OF THE UNITED STATES MILITARY ACADEMY

Wednesday, June 2, 1976

Someday, probably, one of you will stand up here, facing some future West Point graduating class, and you will give them the benefit of your thirty years' experience distilled down into half an hour, much as I am expected to give you. If the statistics hold in the future as they have in the past, when one among you faces this not-yet-born class of apple-cheeked second lieutenants, half of you will have died violent deaths. Most of you still living will have long since retired and gone into some field where you can keep regular hours and have a home that stays put for more than two years at a time.

The service will turn some of you into drunks, some of you into drug addicts, some of you into martinets who abuse the power of your rank, some of you into toadies, some of you into politicians, and some few of you into soldiers.

It is to these last few that I address my remarks.

I want to tell you what none of your instructors or professors have told you in the four years you've been here, what none of your brother officers or commandants or DA civilians or congressional committees or reserve or retired officer groups or secretaries of the Army, or of defense, or presidents of the United States, will tell you during the twenty-plus years you spend on active duty. I want to tell you what you're doing here. And I want you to remember it all the days you wear the uniform of the United States Army.

You are here with that stripe around your sleeve and those little gold bars on your shoulders to preserve, protect, and defend the Constitution of the United States.

"Oh, that," you say, leaning back in those uncomfortable chairs, "I've heard that before. That's nothing new."

But now let me tell you what these words mean. They mean that outside of the chain of command, as the final arbiter of every order that is issued to you and of your every official act, is a two-hundred-year-old piece of parchment. And every time you receive or give an order, or contemplate a course of action, you have to ask yourself, "Is there anything in the Constitution that would affect what I am going to do?"

You cannot be relieved of this responsibility by any commanding officer. Indeed, it may happen that the desires—or even the direct orders—of your commanding officer may come into conflict with what you believe the Constitution tells you to do. You may be court-martialed and dismissed in disgrace, or even imprisoned, by your brother officers, who honestly believe that they are right and you are wrong. And it is easier to stand up to the fire of the enemy than to the scorn of your brother officers.

But these are times when your belief in and adherence to the principles of that great experiment known as the Constitution of the United States may be tried early and often. Hopefully, these times shall pass, and peace and accord shall again prevail in this great nation of ours—but only if honorable men like yourselves see to it, at whatever the cost, that it does.

But now off my hobby horse and on to cheerier topics. . . .

END OF EXCERPT

RYAN ON FIRST BALLOT

LEADING DEMOCRATS PLEDGE SUPPORT;
WILL CHOOSE RUNNING MATE TODAY

> —Headline, the *New York Post*
> Friday, July 9, 1976

ARNOLD CHOICE OF CONVENTION

NO SURPRISES IN KANSAS CITY

> —Headline, the *New York Times*
> Wednesday, August 18, 1976

• CHAPTER TWENTY-FOUR

On Thursday, September 30, at a quarter past seven in the morning, limousines began arriving at the North Entrance to the White House to discharge people attending the President's prayer breakfast. The various senators, representatives, and important lobbyists were shown by the White House staff into the State Dining Room as they arrived.

At seven thirty, the President, flanked by Ober, Vandermeer, and Gildruss, entered the State Dining Room from the side door leading to the Family Dining Room and took his place at the head of the long table. His chiefs of staff took their seats at the foot, Ober and Gildruss on the left and Vandermeer on the right. Congressman Obediah Porfritt (R., Neb.), seated at the middle of the table, his back to the Healy portrait of a brooding Lincoln, kept his hands folded in his lap and wondered what he was doing there. Not that he was entirely *persona non grata* at the White House, but there were so many *personae* far more *gratissimae* than himself that the list seldom reached down as far as his name.

The President seemed in splendid sorts this morning as he looked out at his assembled guests and nodded somberly. He raised his hands to the level of his chin and clasped them together in a washing gesture to be sure he had everyone's attention. "Good morning, Senators, Congressman, gentlemen," he said.

"Good morning, Mr. President," the table replied in ragged unison.

"As most of you know," the President said, "I've had these prayer breakfasts for members of my Cabinet and members of Congress several times during my years in this office. They have been smaller gatherings, held in the Family Dining Room. I think of them as attempts to commune with our Maker, whatever religion you may happen to be, and, in a very real sense, as opportunities to communicate with each other.

"During my few remaining months in office I'm going to hold these larger gatherings on a regular basis. I think you—especially those of you who have not been to a previous breakfast—will agree that the increased sense of community, of togetherness, and of spiritual values makes the time spent well worthwhile.

"And now let us pray. For that purpose, I have asked the Reverend Dr. Hake Smith to lead us."

The President nodded, and a tall man with silver hair, whom Porfritt recognized as a popular television evangelist, stood up at the President's right hand and sunk his chin deeply into the sharp knot of his fifty-dollar Baroness Silva tie. "O Lord!" he cried.

Not seeing the face of the Lord in the polished maple table, he lifted his eyes to the gold chandelier hanging above. "O Lord our Father, hear us poor sinners as we beseech your forgiveness," he intoned. "Help us to make the right decisions in these troubled times. Guide us through the valley of darkness. . . ."

While Dr. Smith continued his sonorous instructions to the Lord, Vandermeer left his seat and quietly made his way around the table to the only empty place, a chair between Senator Jensen and Congressman Porfritt. "Where's Kathy?" he whispered to Jensen. He removed his horn-rimmed glasses and squinted at Jensen in great concern. "I thought she was coming with you."

"I asked her to pick up some papers for me," Jensen replied in an undertone. "She'll be here shortly."

Vandermeer nodded. "You understand," he said. "I expected to see her come in with you."

"I know," Jensen said. "I'm a father myself. She's a fine little lady, your daughter. If she wants to come to work for me full time when she gets out of school, she has a job. I've told her so."

"I'm very proud of her," Vandermeer said. "Thank you." He went back to his seat.

At eight o'clock, just as the scrambled eggs and bacon were being served in the State Dining Room, Kevin Ryan took the subway from the Dirksen Office Building to the Capitol basement. "It's a bunch of bullshit, Tom," he told Senator Clay, who was waiting for him in the Senate snack bar.

"You know that," Clay said, pausing between bites of his sweet roll, "and I know that, but the Great American Public, he don't know that."

"You think the Great American Public is waiting to see Arnold and me shake hands and come out fighting, like a pair of plump middleweights? I wonder what put this bug up Artie's ass?"

"I think he just got trapped by his own rhetoric," Clay said. "He found himself telling some reporter that the two candidates should heal this country's ills by appearing together to slap each other on the back and declare that the good of the nation is more important than any campaign."

"I'll bet this was the President's maneuver," Ryan said, gulping down a cup of black coffee.

"Not this time," Clay said. "He's scheduled a big prayer breakfast for this morning. You know he'd never go into competition with himself."

They went upstairs to the Majority Leader's office, and Ryan carefully closed the door behind him. "This smells wrong," he insisted. "Up till now Artie's theme has been that I'm a crypto-Communist, a child molester, and have secret plans to fluoridate the country's water supply. Suddenly he wants to shake hands with me."

"Perhaps it's occurred to him that you're going to win," Clay said. "Perhaps he wants an ambassadorship in your administration. In about ten minutes we'll know."

There was a knock on the door and Ryan opened it. A young girl with long blond hair stood outside. "Hi," she said. "I'm Kathy Vandermeer, Senator Jensen's assistant."

"We've met," Ryan said, smiling. "Once, briefly, at Senator Jensen's house."

"I wasn't sure you'd remember," Kathy said. She turned to Senator Clay. "Senator Jensen asked me to pick up his workup on S-47. Mrs. Modell says you borrowed it to have a copy made."

"That's right," Clay said. "Let's see, it should be here somewhere—"

"No hurry," Kathy said.

At twenty past eight, a white, unmarked panel truck pulled to the curb on Delaware Avenue, a block away from the Capitol. Calvin Middler slid from the passenger's seat and into the back of the truck. "You sure you're over that mark?" he asked, licking his lips nervously.

"Sure," Zonya told him. "Right where we're supposed to be."

"Right," Middler said. He stared out of the truck's back window. There before him was the Senate wing of the

Capitol and, looming over it, the great Capitol dome. No question, he was going to make a name for himself today.

At twenty-five past eight, the White House stewards began clearing away the remains of the scrambled eggs. Vandermeer rose and walked stiffly down the table to the empty seat his daughter should have been sitting in. "Kathy hasn't arrived?"

Senator Jensen looked at his watch. "I don't understand it," he said. "She just had to stop at my office to pick up a document. Of course, she may have had to go over to the Senate Chamber to get it; that might have delayed her a bit. Still—"

"The Senate Chamber?" Vandermeer clutched the side of Jensen's chair and his face went white.

"Yes. Is something wrong?"

"No, no. I'm just—it must be—indigestion. Something I just ate. If you'll excuse me—"

"Do you need help?" Jensen asked.

"No. I'll be all right. I'd just better go and take something." Vandermeer, looking dazed, walked out into the hall. Once the door was closed behind him he dashed down a flight of stairs and entered the Map Room, where he dropped into a chair and picked up an extension phone. "This is Vandermeer," he said. "Get me the sergeant-at-arms's office at the Senate. Quick!" He took his watch off and stared at the face. It was now twenty-seven minutes past eight.

At twenty-nine past eight Ryan sighed. "Might as well get it over with," he said. "Just think, twenty television cameras on the floor of the Senate just to catch my expression when I shake hands with Artie Arnold."

"They're ready to record your inane remarks, too," Clay

said. "And for God's sake, don't say anything intelligent. You want the Vice-President of the United States to look bad?"

"You shouldn't make fun of poor Mr. Arnold," Kathy Vandermeer said. "He's really a nice old man."

Clay laughed. "Don't ever tell him that," he said. "It would hurt him worse than losing this election. He thinks he's hot stuff with the ladies. Calling him a nice old man would be more unkind than all the nasty things we've been saying about him."

A Senate page caught sight of them as they left Clay's office. "Oh, Miss Vandermeer," he said, running over to the group. "Would you please go over to the Sergeant-at-Arms' office? Your father is on the phone."

At exactly eight thirty, Calvin Middler pulled the arming pin from the bulbous gold nose of the ATX-3 antitank rocket and took one last squint through the sighting reticle. This is it, baby," he said. "We're in the history books!" And he kicked open the rear doors to the panel truck and squeezed the trigger.

For a second nothing happened. Then the rocket rose slowly into the air, the brilliant white flame of its exhaust searing the inside of the truck for a long moment as it pulled away from its launcher. Calvin felt the blast scorching his exposed hands and face, and he saw a universe of pure white that instantly etched through to a red afterimage and faded to black as his retinas burned out.

"Zonya!" he screamed. "Zonya, get us out of here. I can't see! I can't—"

"Calvin!" Zonya yelled from the front seat. "You're on fire!" Grabbing an army blanket from behind the seat, she scrambled over the transmission hump to wrap it around him.

The rocket ascended slowly and deliberately, disappearing from sight over the roof of the Senate wing of the Capitol. Then, with a crumping sound that seemed to be wrenched from the bowels of the earth, the roof and top floors of the Senate wing disappeared in a ball of smoke and flame. Debris exploded outward through the upper-floor windows, parts of the marble façade were thrust out with such force that they landed half a mile away. Several of the outer columns collapsed as the explosion reached them. Sections of the Capitol dome were lofted high into the air. Then the remaining mass of the Capitol dome collapsed, and jagged sections of the facing sloughed off onto the lawn.

Calvin Middler's face was black, mottled with angry red patches. Zonya sobbed and beat at what was left of his hair with the blanket, but Calvin just stared sightlessly out the open back door of the truck and muttered, "That son of a bitch! That dirty son of a bitch," over and over like an obscene mantra.

"We've got to get out of here," Zonya screamed at him. "Do you understand? We've got to get away from here! I've never seen anything like this. Christ, Calvin, what have we done?"

"I can't see," Calvin said. "I can't see. That son of a bitch! He knew. He must have."

Across the street from them a fire hydrant suddenly burst, sending a torrent of water in an arcing path in front of the truck.

"I've got to get us out of here," Zonya said. "Wrap the blanket around you and hold on to something. I'll get the doors."

"I can't," Calvin said plaintively, holding his hands up before his sightless eyes. "There's no feeling in my fingers."

"Oh, my God!" Zonya said, putting her fist in her mouth to choke back a scream. Calvin's hands were burned black, and large blisters were forming under the scabs. The tips of his fingers were gone.

George Warren appeared at the back door of the truck. There was a revolver in his white-gloved hand. "You two did very well," he said.

Calvin Middler turned his head from side to side like a bird. "George?" he said. "You fucking son of a bitch, is it you?"

"Can you get us out of here?" Zonya demanded. She held up her own hands, which were blistering from wrapping the blanket around Middler. "I don't think I can drive."

"Very brave," Warren said. He lifted the gun.

"It *is* you, you son of a bitch!" Calvin cried. Warren shot him through the chest. Zonya turned and dived for the driver's seat. Warren aimed carefully. His bullet caught her in the back of the head and came out the left eye.

Warren gingerly tossed the gun into the truck. " 'Bye now," he said.

PRESIDENT CANCELS ELECTION
VOWS THAT "TERROR WILL NEVER RULE THIS COUNTRY"

Special to The New York Times

WASHINGTON, Oct. 4—In a televised press conference today the President announced that he has sent to Congress an executive order announcing the suspension of the upcoming presidential elections and asking for a vote of confidence from both houses for this action.

"Both political parties must have time to bind their wounds and bury their dead," the President said, referring to the atomic missile that was fired on the Senate last Thursday, claiming the lives of Vice-President Arthur Arnold and Senator Kevin Ryan, the presidential nominees of the two major parties.

"New nominating conventions must be held and new candidates picked. But before this happens, the reign of terror must be ended. Terror will never rule this country," the President vowed.

Among victims positively identified, in addition to Senator Ryan and Vice-President Arnold, is Katherine Vandermeer, 21-year-old daughter of the President's domestic policy chief, who was working as a public-relations aide to Senator Jensen. The death toll now stands at 213.

ATOMIC MISSILE VERIFIED

THE PENTAGON, Oct. 4 (UPI)—The Army verified today that the weapon found in the back of the truck manned by two young terrorists was an experimental model ATX-3 rocket launcher, which fires a tactical rocket with a nuclear warhead.

"These weapons are in limited production for testing purposes," an Army spokesman said. "They are a battlefield weapon, with a range of about one thousand yards, designed to allow one infantry man to have enough firepower to neutralize a company of tanks."

He said that, to the best of the Army's knowledge, all of these weapons are accounted for, and there are none missing.

• CHAPTER
TWENTY-FIVE

DRESSED IN THE faded black corduroys and sweat shirt that were his evening jogging costume, Aaron Adams loped around the corner and proceeded at a steady, rhythmic pace down the tree-lined Chevy Chase street. He was well into the second mile of his three-mile ritual and was pleased to note that he wasn't even slightly out of breath. The street was empty and quiet, and fairly dark except for the occasional streetlight and the sporadic spill of brightness from a picture window in one of the big houses.

This early-evening quiet was not normal for the bureaucrats of official Washington, but it had grown common in the past few months. People stayed home more now, minded their own business. You didn't want to go to a party and say the wrong things to the wrong man after one too many drinks. Far better not to go.

As Aaron approached the next corner he saw a car with its hood up and a man in sports clothes fiddling with the engine. "Need a hand?" he called, jogging closer.

The man looked up from his fiddling. "Good evening, Aaron," he said, wiping his hands on a piece of paper toweling draped over the fender.

Aaron stopped, and for a second he felt a touch of fear. Then he recognized the speaker. "Tank!" he said. "Tank MacGregor." He smiled. "A better evening than I'd thought."

MacGregor slammed down the hood of his car. "I hope you don't mind my interrupting your evening run," he said. "I'd like to talk with you. Get into the car."

As they drove off down the street, Aaron leaned back and examined the general's profile. "You have the makings of a born conspirator," he said. "I hope it's nothing trivial."

"I don't want to seem melodramatic," MacGregor said. "I wanted to make sure that we were neither observed nor overheard."

"The car—" Aaron said.

"I had a couple of techs from Fort Meade come out and check it for bugs this afternoon," MacGregor said.

Aaron pursed his lips. "I see," he said. "What are we going to talk about?"

General MacGregor stared through the windshield and concentrated on his driving for a few minutes. Aaron waited silently for him to speak. "The President of the United States," he said finally, "has no intention of leaving office and holding a general election anytime in the near future. In order to preserve constitutional democracy, or whatever shreds of it we can salvage, he must be removed."

Aaron was silent for some unmeasurable length of time. "Removed," he said. His voice sounded weak, and he coughed and repeated, "Removed."

"Yes."

"Well," Aaron said. "I'm certainly glad it was nothing trivial. Can you prove your, ah, contention?"

"Yes. Certainly to your satisfaction."

"What do you intend to do about it?"

MacGregor pulled the car over to the side of the road and stopped, keeping the motor running. "I'm not in a position to do too much about it," he said, turning and staring intently at Aaron. "I will, of course, give you whatever help I can."

"I see," Aaron said quietly. "I'm the expert at running coups, so it's on my head."

MacGregor seemed to shrink a little in his seat, and there was a strange, almost frightened expression on his face. "Aaron," he said, "I can't run a coup myself. Don't you see what it would mean if I succeeded? Our country would never survive the precedent. The next time a MacArthur disagreed with a Truman, would he let himself be fired—or would he ride down Pennsylvania Avenue on his white horse and pound on the gates of the White House to let him in?"

Aaron nodded. "I see what you mean," he said. "I hadn't thought it out."

"Besides," MacGregor said, "I'm no good at intrigue."

"About your theory that the President doesn't intend to leave office," Aaron said. "I know that he's stalling, but that's not the same as saying he's usurped the office."

"I'm afraid that, for a change, I have some information that you lack," General MacGregor said, shifting back into gear and moving the car slowly down the almost empty road.

"Yes?"

"That ATX-3 missile that blew out the North Wing of the Capitol and precipitated this constitutional crisis—do you know where it came from?"

"I know what the Bowker committee came up with," Aaron said.

"Forget about the so-called heist of the missile by the People's Revolutionary Brigade. It's a cover story. The truth is much more complex. Let me trace it out for you," MacGregor said. "A colonel name of Diton was in charge of the Special Weapons Depot at Fort Dix. The man is a rabid anti-Communist, and he was suckered with a plan to save— I think it was Argentina—from the Red Rabble. He released two ATX-3s to his buddy General Netherby of the White

Sands Proving Ground for 'training and practice,' of course removing the atomic warheads and returning them to storage. Except that it was two dummies that were returned to storage. General Netherby made out the paperwork stating that the two missiles—fitted with dummy warheads—were test-fired. Then he took them off base in his camper.

"The missiles and their atomic warheads were reunited in New Jersey, and then turned over to a Carlos Muentis of New York and Buenos Aires. At this point a lot of money changed hands, proving that it can be profitable to be patriotic. Señor Muentis, however, did not ship the weapons south. Instead he almost immediately handed them over to one Edward St. Yves of the Executive Office of the President."

"Then the Oakland Army Terminal—"

"I don't know what they got at the Oakland Army Terminal, but it wasn't the ATX-3."

"St. Yves?"

"That's right."

"You're sure?"

"Yes."

Aaron shifted in his seat and stared out at Burning Tree Golf Course as they drove slowly by. "I've got an in—you know—to the White House. I have a dossier on this administration that you wouldn't believe. Murder, rape, arson, forgery; you name it, they've done it or condoned it. But this—"

"I know."

"I guess I didn't want to believe it. Hell, I didn't even want to think it."

"I know."

"You're right, of course. The man *must* be removed."

"Not assassinated," MacGregor said quickly.

"No, not assassinated. Removed from office and brought to trial. All this must come out. What happened over the last four years, or however long it turns out to have been happening, must be analyzed and understood so that it can never happen again."

"Unfortunately, there's nothing that can never happen again," MacGregor said dryly. "After every war the generals and politicians get together and analyze it and write books about it so it can never happen again. But it hardly matters what they conclude. It'll still happen again. It always does, bigger and better."

"Don't give me that existential crap, Tank," Aaron said. "The human race does improve, slowly and painfully. And governments and political systems do work better now than they did in the past. We've gotten two hundred years out of this one already; maybe with a retread we can go another couple of hundred."

"We won't go another year if that man isn't stopped. You'd better go to it," MacGregor said. "Bring the Jubilee."

"I may need you," Aaron said.

"Name it," MacGregor said.

"I'll have to think about it," Aaron told him. "I'll be in touch."

Uriah Vandermeer sat behind his desk, his feet planted squarely on the floor, his fingers laced together over the glass desktop. There was a pensive, somewhat distant expression on his face. He was staring at—or possibly through—the John Pelow oil portrait of his daughter Kathy on the wall to his right. Pelow had captured the youthful coltish look, perhaps in the flow of the long blond hair, or the hands frozen in mid-gesture. Underneath, for Pelow was a master, the quick intelligence shone through, and something of the curiosity, the innocence, of the child-woman: the child she had been, and the woman she now would never become.

"You blame me," Vandermeer said. "I know you do."

Did the girl in the portrait shake her head slightly—or

was it merely a trick of the light? Pelow was good with light.

Vandermeer took off his glasses and rested his head on his arms. "It seemed like—" he paused and thought, then peered back up at the picture. "You get carried along by events. One thing leads to another and you never stop to reexamine your basic premises. Things polarize. Good is what you do for the President. Bad is what's done by those against you and the President. Can you understand that?"

Kathy stared silently down at him.

"I should have done it long ago," he said. "I will try. You'll see. I didn't permit myself to think about what was happening. That man led me, step by step, inch by inch, and I— What's that?" He cocked his head and listened closely, for a minute, to the picture.

"I don't know how yet, but I will," he told it. "Trust me."

There was a polite knock on the door, and Vandermeer turned away from the portrait as Mrs. Fleischer, his private secretary, entered the room.

Aaron Adams leaned back in the leather armchair and looked slowly around his study, surveying his six companions. Each of them had been quietly and separately approached, and each had agreed, with differing degrees of fervor, that Something Must Be Done. But now, together, they were slowly pulling themselves toward the only conclusion, forcing themselves to face what it was that had to be done, and what their parts in the doing would have to be. Adams had shepherded them along through the discussion, explaining carefully what the options were and keeping the discussion headed in some loose way from the premise to the inevitable conclusion.

And now it was done. The words were said, the thought was spoken, and the vast chasm was suddenly open before them.

"Here we are then, gentlemen," Adams said. "We are now, each of us, guilty of conspiracy to commit treason. Within the next two months we'll have succeeded in unseating the President of the United States and forcing a new election, or we'll all be in prison or dead. I think we can pull this off, but it is, at best, a long shot. If any of you have not faced the possibility of your death in the past, you will have the chance to do so now."

"Hell, Aaron," Grier Laporte said, stirring the ice in his bourbon around with his finger, "you can get killed crossing the street. You can go to prison for a lot less than that. Especially these days."

Adams smiled grimly. "I just wanted to make sure that none of you could say he wasn't warned."

"Don't play with words," Admiral Bush said. "We've got to get that crazy son of a bitch before he turns this nation into a dictatorship."

"Something I don't understand, Aaron," Grier Laporte said.

"What's that?"

"Why us? I mean why TEPACS? How does it happen that the group of people you play poker with are the ones you choose to form a cabal?"

"Not the whole group, Grier. Just you six. Principally because of what we sociopolitical scientists call your acquaintanceship network. Each of you is in a position, because of your current job or the professional friendships you've built up over the years, to fill one of the slots I need filled."

"Don't waste time on the lecture, Aaron," Colonel Baker said. "You're conducting this orchestra. Just lay it out for us."

"Now, I think we should discuss this fully," Obie Porfritt said. "And I still maintain that, if the President announces a date on which the election will be held, we should abandon the scheme."

254

"Until we see how he weasels out of it? Come on," Sanderman Jones said, "you know that the longer this cabal is in existence without *having* a coup, the greater the risk of it blowing up in our faces. If we're going to do this at all, we follow through."

"A couple of things," George Masters said.

"What?"

"We're not going to assassinate the son of a bitch."

"That's understood. We have to bring him to account, to put him and his people on trial."

"Right. And if we succeed, we hold elections as soon as possible after."

"Of course."

"If we're going to do this," Admiral Bush said, "let's get with it. What's the plan, Aaron? I assume you have a plan.

"I have a few notions," Adams admitted. "But before I go into my ideas, I'd like a little input from you people. Just how do we overthrow the government?"

"Well, to start with, of course," Sanderman Jones said from his corner, "we don't actually overthrow the government. We merely displace the Chief Executive and immediately proclaim loudly that we have restored the government to the people. As, indeed, we shall have. Then we hold an election as soon as possible."

"What do you mean, 'displace the Chief Executive'?" Grier Laporte asked. "Just march into the White House and kick him out? That can't be all it takes."

"Well," Adams said, "in a sense we do just kick him out. We impeach him in the House, if possible, at the same time as we arrest him. This makes us quasi-legal. Then we put him on trial in the Senate right after the election."

"We'd need to establish military control of the District," Colonel Baker said. "The Eighty-second Airborne is the obvious unit for that."

"Too obvious, I'm afraid," Aaron said. "If I were the President—certainly if I were *this* President—I'd make sure the command of the Eighty-second was in safe hands. As the major ready unit in the Washington area, it's too tempting a target. But I don't know the commander, and haven't made any attempt to sound him out."

"We don't need the whole division, you know," Baker said. "Just a couple of regiments, and a way to immobilize the rest. The regimental commanders aren't picked for their political purity, that's too far down the totem pole."

"A good point, Francis. We have to determine what the minimum number of troops we need to control the area is."

"To do that," Jones pointed out, "we have to determine first what the area we need to control is. Can we get away with just grabbing the White House, or do we need to hold a perimeter including say, the Capitol and the Pentagon?"

"My feeling is that we don't have to physically take much beyond the White House itself," Aaron said. "And effectively neutralize a few other key areas, like the Pentagon, for some limited time."

"There's another consideration," Admiral Bush said. "The United States is the linchpin of free world defense. We don't want our adversaries to get the wrong idea of what our internal situation is while this is going on. The men with the go codes will still have their hands on the buttons."

"There's another side to that, David," Sanderman Jones said. "We can't take any chances that the President, in his last seconds, will start a global war."

"He wouldn't—" Laporte said, looking startled. "I mean, not even—"

"We can't take the chance," Jones insisted. "It has to be covered."

"I see what you mean about acquaintanceship nets, Aaron," Bush said. "I think I know the man who knows the man to take care of that. And I think he'll go along."

"That puts us halfway there," Aaron said.

"Media!" Laporte said suddenly.

"Excuse me?"

"Media. That's the way. Immediate live television coverage of the whole thing."

"What good will that do?" Masters demanded.

Laporte bit off the tip of a cigar and spat it into the ashtray, and then busied himself puffing it to life before he answered. "As I see it," he said, "the problem is credibility. Right? I mean, if we're going to do this thing, then we have to make people believe as quickly as possible that it's done. That it's over. That we've won. And we do a couple of highly visible acts that will get the people behind us. Then no military unit, no matter how loyal they are to the President, will try to move in and re-coup—or countercoup—or whatever."

"What kind of highly visible acts?" Porfritt asked.

"There's one great obvious problem with that," Jones said. "If we have TV coverage there and it looks like we're losing instead of winning, that's likely to encourage the opposition. But it might be worth the risk. For one thing, the cameras will be on our side of the lines."

"Why isn't Ian Faulkes here?" Masters asked. "He could help plan this media thing if we do it."

"I didn't ask him because he's British," Aaron said. "I thought we should have an all-American coup. But I suppose we could clue him in enough so that he could have cameras at the right places at the right time. I'll sound him out."

"Say," Jones said. "Has anyone kept up with the count on those internal confinement camps of the President's? How many are there now, and what's the population?"

"I believe there are somewhere around eight of them now," Masters said. "With about twenty-five hundred inmates per camp."

"That's incredible!" Obie Porfritt said. "Are you sure? Twenty thousand people?"

"It is incredible," Masters said. "I have a notion that the American people—that great silent majority—would be very upset if they realized the extent of this thing. But it's been kept very low profile. Burying twenty thousand people in a country this size is easy, if you're the government. The public does *not* know."

"*I* didn't know," Obie said. "A few camps, I thought. A few hundred dissenters. Even that disturbed me, but that I could live with. I had no idea—"

"What's the point, Sandy?" Aaron asked.

"There's one of our 'highly visible acts,'" Jones explained. "Like Lincoln freeing the slaves. As soon as we have anything like a toehold, we announce the immediate closing of all the IC camps and the release of the prisoners. And we announce the total number of camps and their population—with lists, if possible."

"Good!" Aaron said. "Very good."

"How long, do you estimate, before D-Day?" Baker asked.

"Soon," Aaron said. "So we'll all have to get on the stick, there's a lot to do. I don't think I have to tell everyone here to keep their mouths shut, do I?"

"We need an operational code word," Sanderman Jones said. "A nice, innocuous, operational code word."

Everyone in the room turned to look at Aaron Adams.

"Jubilee," Aaron said. He looked at each of them in turn—thin, elegant Sanderman Jones; tall, plump Grier Laporte; Colonel Baker, who took things too seriously; Obediah Porfritt, who wasn't sure; Rear Admiral David Bush, who could do what he had to do; George Masters, the consummate professional—and he wondered which of them would come through and which of them would fail. And he wondered what they would think of him six months from now—if any of them were still alive.

"Jubilee," Obie Porfritt said. "Let's drink to that. Might not get another chance." And he bustled around handing out glasses and opening a bottle of champagne that had been sitting in Aaron's refrigerator since New Year's Eve.

When Obie had finished pouring, Aaron raised his glass to the group. "Gentlemen," he said, "bring the Jubilee."

They drank.

• CHAPTER
TWENTY-SIX

HEADQUARTERS

MARINE CORPS EDUCATIONAL CENTER

QUANTICO, VIRGINIA

TO: All Officers and Enlisted Personnel
SUBJECT: Post Lecture

On Saturday, 6 November, 1976, at 1330 hours, General of the Army Hiram MacGregor will deliver the Post Lecture at the O'Bannon Theater.

— Lieutenant General Moor is pleased to welcome General MacGregor to Quantico, and wishes all off-duty officers to attend the lecture. Enlisted personnel are encouraged to attend.

General MacGregor's topic will be "The Chain of Command."

> T. R. Roseau, COLONEL, USMC
> OIC   TRAINING AND PLANS

The lecture attracted a standing-room-only crowd, which the commanding officer, Lieutenant General Clement C. Moor, assured Tank was unique in the history of the post lecture series. "You're still a hero, Tank. Maybe even, by now, a legend."

The lecture had been followed by the usual VIP show: a tour of the base, a cocktail reception at the Officers' Club, and a formal dress dinner for the senior officers and their wives at Quarters Number One, the residence of the base commander, General Moor.

Now, as the last guest left, Generals MacGregor and Moor settled down in the living room to talk over old times. They spoke of Uijonbu and Yudam-ni, of Humhung and Yongdok, and they toasted fallen comrades, MacGregor with his bourbon over ice, and General Moor with a tall glass of ginger ale. "You're not drinking," MacGregor said, gesturing with his glass. "I mean, you know, drinking."

"I was drinking," Moor told him. "Believe it, I was drinking. Then one morning I woke up in a strange bed, staring at a white ceiling, with no feeling from my shoulders down. And a man with a white smock and a stethoscope came in and told me what my gut looked like from the inside, and gave me a choice." Moor lifted his glass, and grinned. "I chose ginger ale."

"A good choice," MacGregor said.

"My wife and kids think so," Moor said. "And I'm of more use to the Corps as a teetotaler than as a dead drunk— with the emphasis on 'dead.'"

MacGregor looked at the stocky, broad-shouldered Marine sitting opposite him and weighed the words he had come to say, and wondered how best to say them, and his glass felt heavy in his hands. "I'm glad you're alive, Clem," he said. "I'd rather have a Marine next to me in a fight than anyone else. And I'd rather it be you than any other Marine."

"Go on," Moor said, grinning broadly. "At my age!"

"There are fights, and there are fights," MacGregor said. "I've got a good ten years on you, Clem, and the kind of fights a man my age gets into aren't won with your fists."

General Moor leaned forward in his chair. "Speaking of fights," he said, "that was an important bit of business you did, Tank, in keeping the Army out of the prison-camp business."

"You heard about that?"

"It was the worst-kept secret since 'He is risen,'" Moor said. "I don't know what you told our C-in-C, but you must have made it strong. We were trying to figure out how to keep the Corps's skirts clean if he asked us, but he never did. We did get involved in that riot."

"What riot?"

"Down in Florida, in one of those camps. The prisoners— or internees, or whatever we're supposed to call them—went on a hunger strike that turned into a riot. I understand the guards threw the food at them, or something. Anyhow, they trashed their barracks and grabbed a few guards as hostages. The warden, or whatever he calls himself, called in the Marines. One company was dispatched. By the time they got there there were cameramen all over the place. Almost had to trample them down to get to the riot. And they weren't from any of the networks, either; they were government. The whole thing was hushed up, and the pictures were never used, as far as I know."

General Moor lit a new cigarette from the stub of his last one, and smiled at MacGregor's disapproving expression. "I couldn't give up everything, Tank," he said. "Now, do you want to tell me what you're here for, or do we have to stall around some more until you're good and ready?"

"What do you mean?" MacGregor asked.

"When Jerry Rosen called up and suggested that you come give our post lecture this month, I was delighted. But I got the feeling that it was your idea. Which is fine. But if you'd wanted to come visit, you would have just come visit. You wanted to be invited. Which means you have some reason for wanting to be here without seeming to want to be here. If you follow that."

"I follow, Clem. I hope I'm not that transparent to the rest of the world."

"Tell me what you want to when you want to," Moor said. "You can trust me."

"I believe you," MacGregor said. "Give me one of your cigarettes, Clem. I'm trying to stop smoking, but it can wait." He took the cigarette and lit it and took one deep drag from it. "I hear you're going back on the *Guam*, Clem; is that right?"

"Right. Next week. We're going on a training cruise."

"Before you go I'd like you to take a run up to Washington," MacGregor said. "Meet a friend of mine. His name is Adams, Professor Aaron B. Adams. He lives in Chevy Chase. Give him a call."

"I will, Tank. What sort of thing is he interested in?"

"I think you'd better let him ask the questions," Tank said. "Now, if you don't mind, I'd better get to bed." Mac-Gregor got up and left the room. General Moor heard his steps going up the stairs toward the guest room.

Moor lit a new cigarette and stared into the smoke for some time before turning the lights off and heading up the stairs himself.

Brigadier General Landau, Commandant of the Eighty-second Airborne Division, leaned back in his swivel chair and laced his fingers behind his head. "Just what do you mean, Captain?" he demanded. "Can you be more precise?"

"No, sir," Captain Willits said. "I mean, it's hard, sir." He shifted uneasily from foot to foot. "Maybe I shouldn't have come, sir, only I felt it was my duty."

"No, no; you did right, Captain. Sit down and try to give me something more specific. When you say Colonel

Green is talking treason, what, precisely, do you mean?"

"Well, he's sort of sounding out the officers under him in the regiment, sir. Very subtly, sir. Determining their loyalty to the President, sir. Like what we think of the IC camps, and whether we think he had a right to suspend the elections."

"Have you mentioned your suspicions to anyone else?"

"No, sir. I thought I should come directly to you."

"Very good. I need honest, reliable officers like you, uh, Willits, to keep tabs on what's going on in my command. You just keep your eye on your CO, and make up a weekly report for me on what he says. If it begins to sound like he, uh, has anything in mind, notify me right away."

"Yes, sir!"

"It's our job, Willits, to keep the Army out of politics. The President is our commanding officer, and we must obey his commands, whatever we think of them."

"Yes, sir."

The room, buried deep in the bowels of CIA's Langley, Virginia, headquarters, was furnished like a model living room out of *Architectural Digest*. From the Remington reproduction on the far wall, balanced by an antique bric-a-brac cabinet opposite a French-tile-framed fireplace, the room smelled of conservative good taste. Closed curtains at one end of the room, with just a hint of light glowing through, suggested the obligatory picture window. Pleasant, innocuous classical music drowned out the ever-present hum of the air conditioning. It was designed to make you quickly forget that you were two stories underground, surrounded by rooms full of computers, code machines, analysts, area experts, photo interpreters, psychological warfare experts, interrogation experts, armed guards, and locked doors.

The man in the impeccable gray suit sat on one corner of the sectional tan couch, his yellow pad across his knees. "You realize," he told Aaron Adams, "that you're not here and we aren't having this conversation."

"Who was logged in?" Adams asked, amused.

"A house name," the man said. "Usually used for Eastern European contacts. That's why you're down here in the debriefing area. Also because, by the nature of the process, you're automatically escorted in and out without anyone else seeing you or knowing you're here."

The man facing Adams was Robert Sims, a CIA career professional who occupied a position in the hierarchy that in private industry would have been called middle management, or in regular government service, entrenched bureaucracy. He was one of the men who had been on the outside feeding information in, and was now on the inside shuffling papers to see that the information was somehow utilized. An earnest, self-important man who had years ago forgotten how to smile, he nonetheless did his work well, and honestly felt that what he did was worth doing.

Sims was a member of the Policy Coordinating Committee, which took the directives handed down by the Director and his top aides and turned them into working orders that could be implemented by the various semiautonomous directorates of the Agency. In practical terms the committee acted as a buffer between the political demands instigated at the top and the pragmatic operations conducted by those who did the work.

"All right, Bob," Adams said. "Let it be that I'm not here." He dropped into an armchair opposite the couch and pulled his pipe from a side pocket of his tweed jacket. "What aren't we talking about while I'm not here?"

"You're laughing," Sims said. "I'm trying to save your hide, and you're laughing."

"I wasn't aware that my hide required saving, Bob."

"Come off it, Aaron. I've know you for twenty-odd years. Let's not play games about this."

"No game, Bob," Adams said. "Don't try to lead me on, because I won't be led. If you know something, spit it out. If you're on a fishing expedition, at least dangle some bait in front of me. Don't just tell me 'all is discovered,' and expect me to drop my pants." Adams tamped a plug of tobacco into his pipe.

"I really am trying to help you," Sims said. "The Company can't do anything, you understand. Not with people hand-picked by the President in the fourteen top slots. You've no idea how much time is wasted in keeping their hands out of the works."

"I know the system," Adams said, slightly impatiently.

"The recording devices for this room are turned off, Aaron," Sims said. "We know you're planning a coup."

"What—"

"We got onto it through one of those chains of circumstances that nobody can control, so don't waste time denying it—or looking for the traitor in your organization. One of your people deposited a large sum of money in a Swiss bank, and we found out and wondered why. So we started watching him. He led us, in a tortuous route, to you."

Aaron nodded. "No point denying it if you're convinced," he said.

"The word is Jubilee, Aaron," Sims said. "Like with cherries."

Aaron lit his pipe with the Zippo lighter he'd been carrying since the Battle of the Bulge. His hands were steady. "What do you intend to do with this theory of yours?"

"We intend to do our best to see that it doesn't get out," Sims said. "Not that we're going to aid you in any way, you understand."

"I understand."

"But we want to know the time and date of execution."

266

Aaron smiled. "I wasn't intending to be executed," he said.

"Everything we've got about Jubilee is in a protected file," Sims said. "If you guys blow it, the file gets shredded and dumped."

"You're not helping or hindering, you're just ignoring it and covering your ass. Is that it?"

Sims leaned forward. "Several of our mutual friends in this organization are very interested in your, ah, project and its outcome. But they won't take a chance on being seen with you. I'm instructed to inform you that, after this meet, you're to avoid coming to this building or contacting any CIA personnel in any way. If any Company people are in this with you—and I'm not asking—they are to withdraw. Now."

"So that's it," Adams said.

"On the other hand," Sims said, "we can't neglect our obligation to the government—to this country, if you like."

"Very patriotic," Adams said dryly.

"That's why we're asking you to give us the date and time of your operation."

"As you should very well know," Adams said, "I've no idea of the date and time of my operation. There are a thousand things that could delay it—or advance it. When the stars are in their right conjunction and the entrail readings are favorable, then we march on Rome. But not before."

"I understand," Sims said. "That's why we're giving you a special phone number to call in when you know."

"And a reason," Adams said. "You still haven't given me a reason. Just for old times' sake isn't good enough."

"There are certain foreign governments that are sensitive to the internal, ah, politics of the United States government. They must be warned, or in some cases reassured, that this is purely an internal matter which doesn't concern them."

"That has occurred to me," Adams admitted. "Are you saying that the Company will undertake to perform that function?"

"It's our job," Sims said. "That's what I've been trying to tell you."

"You realize that if we blow it, it's bound to come out that someone in the Company knew something about it. One of those foreign governments is bound to mention it to someone."

"It seems probable. Do your best not to blow it."

Adams puffed on his pipe and watched the little clouds of gray smoke get sucked up by the air conditioning. "What's the number?" he asked.

"Here," Sims said, handing him a piece of paper. "Memorize it and burn it in this ashtray. Your code word is Kingfisher. Say it, followed by a date and time. Try to give us at least five hours' warning. Cancel code will be just "Kingfisher Off,' I guess."

"Kingfisher?"

"Taken from a random list," Sims said.

"Sure." Adams lit a match to the phone number. "Be talking to you."

• CHAPTER
TWENTY-SEVEN

Mrs. Fleischer, Uriah Vandermeer's private secretary, put her ear to the door of his office and listened intently, "You'd better wait a minute," she told St. Yves, "I don't want to disturb him now."

St. Yves chuckled an ingratiating chuckle. "Don't tell me, Mrs. Fleischer, that Billy has a young lady in his office at this hour."

"Mr. St. Yves!" Mrs. Fleischer did her best to sound shocked, although the halls of power had few surprises left for her. Then she dropped the pretense and shook her head. "A young lady," she said. "Maybe that's what he needs. He's in there by himself, he is. Talking."

St. Yves' eyes widened slightly. "Talking? You mean he's on the phone?"

"No, sir. It started when his daughter was killed in that awful bombing. He walks around the room talking to himself."

"What does he talk about?"

"I couldn't say," Mrs. Fleischer said, and her mouth closed to a thin line. Whether or not she could say, it was clear that no power on earth would make her.

"Has he seen anyone about this? I mean, a doctor?"

"No, sir. When it started I was very worried and I talked to my daughter's brother-in-law, who's a psychiatrist in Baltimore. He said it was nothing to worry about, just a standard grief reaction. He said it would disappear with time."

"I see." St. Yves nodded thoughtfully. "Thank you for trusting me, Mrs. Fleischer. Let me think on this and see if I can come up with something helpful. I'd better go in now."

"Thank you, Mr. St. Yves. I had to tell someone. You won't say anything, will you—I mean, to him?"

"Of course not."

Mrs. Fleischer buzzed the inner office and announced St. Yves, who winked at her and went through. As the office door closed behind him, he relegated Mrs. Fleischer's concern to his mind's inactive file. If Billy Vandermeer wanted to spend his spare time arguing with himself, that was his business and none of St. Yves'. But it was St. Yves' concern to see that the office staff was reassured, which he had done. *A pity about Kathy*, St. Yves thought fleetingly, *she was a lovely girl.*

"Good morning, Ed," Vandermeer said, nodding a greeting from behind his desk.

"Good morning, Mr. Vandermeer."

"What have you got for me?"

"A plot, Mr. Vandermeer. "We've uncovered a plot."

"What sort of a plot?" Vandermeer hitched forward in his chair. "Against whom?"

"Against the government, sir. Against the President."

Vandermeer nodded. "Tell me," he said.

St. Yves lowered himself into the chair opposite the desk with great care, as though he were afraid it might explode under him. "We ran across it during a routine congressional surveillance. Just a passing reference in a phone conversation. So we sat on the phone, built up a dossier. I didn't want to bring it to you until we were sure we had something."

"And now you're sure?"

"Right. Representative Obediah Porfritt of Nebraska. He's evidently on the periphery of some group that's plotting to overthrow the government. He's trying to drum up support with other members of the House to set up some kind of parliamentary cabinet to run the country until elections can be held."

"That's what they all say, you know," Vandermeer said, drumming his fingers on the desk top. "They just want to take over until elections can be held. But elections never are held."

"That's the pattern," St. Yves agreed.

"Porfritt. I remember him. Little man. Probably has a Napoleon complex. Most little politicians do, I've noticed. I'll have to get into the President with his plan so we can set up the best counter to it. Not that I think there's anything to worry about. What is his plan? How does he intend to take over?"

"We're not sure yet," St. Yves said.

"What!" Vandermeer stood up. "That's a hell of a report. What do you mean, you're not sure? God damn it, you're supposed to be sure. A lot of money gets funneled through your office for you to use making sure of things like this."

"Well, sir, actually we don't think Porfritt is sure yet himself. There are others involved, but we haven't been able to determine who yet. The code name for the operation is Jubilee."

Vandermeer walked around the desk. "Jubilee, you say? Son of a bitch—there may be something here bigger than you thought." He paced back and forth on the Shirvan rug.

"How's that, sir?"

"We have a report from General Landau of the Eighty-second Airborne. He suspects one of his regimental commanders of attempting to subvert the others in some kind of coup. The word 'Jubilee' was mentioned in the report."

ighty-second is the logical outfit to try to subject," Yves said. "A crack ready-response division, right the city. More firepower than anything else around."

/e need a report, a study," Vandermeer said. "Find out what anyone planning a coup would need to do, and head them off at the pass. Get inside the Jubilee and use it for our own purposes. Let them try to grab power, and snooker them in the ass after they've made their move. Get good TV coverage."

"Isn't that high-risk?" St. Yves asked. "Wouldn't it be better to grab them before they do anything?"

"It's a calculated risk," Vandermeer said. "But since we're onto them from the beginning, we can cut the risk factor way down. And a conspiracy to commit treason isn't nearly as showy as treason itself. We're heading to get the Twenty-second Amendment repealed so the President can run again. We can't keep this 'between elections' crap up very long."

"We could stage a coup," St. Yves said. "It would be safer."

"You going to stage a trial and execution?" Vandermeer asked, pausing in mid-pace to shake his fist at the air. "No, by God—a real-life coup, that's what we need! The smell of blood! Let it look like they've come dangerously close to snuffing out American Democracy, then step on them!" He resumed his pacing. "We need control, that's what. Can't let the thing get out of hand. And have to time it right. Lots of top-flight PR beforehand."

"I think it's dangerous," St. Yves said.

"You're the man who scoffs at danger," Vandermeer said. "Come on, Ed, don't blow your image."

"Physical danger is one thing," St. Yves said. "But the danger I see here is different. How do you know which side the public will be on in a thing like this? Holding up the elections isn't very popular, no matter how many excuses we keep coming up with."

"But that's it, don't you see?" Vandermeer said. "We can schedule the elections now. Say, the primaries for April. Then, when the coup attempt is made, cancel them again and focus public attention on the trial while we ram the repeal through the state legislatures."

"Supposing they cancel the coup attempt when we schedule the elections?"

"Not a chance. They won't believe us. Would you?"

"Guess not. But what if they do?"

Vandermeer considered it for a minute. "Then we grab them for conspiracy."

"I'll get the boys right on it."

"No," Vandermeer said. "We've got to keep this operation clean. We'll start up a special unit. Bring in outside people."

"What about the FBI?"

"The last thing we want is the FBI sticking its nose into political stuff. Same goes for the Secret Service. Let them guard the body of the President—throw themselves in front of him when some nut tries to shoot him—that business. We need a new group for political action. A separate group controlled by the President."

"I see," St. Yves said. "You're thinking in broader terms than just suppressing this coup attempt, then."

"Right. There'll be other attempts. We have to stay on top of it. Set up an undercover police unit. Use them as the nucleus of a national police force. I'll speak to the President. Who can we get for it?"

"What about some ex-servicemen, back from Vietnam? That would be good publicity, wouldn't it?"

"Right, good thinking. Not just soldiers, though—Special Forces, maybe. They're good, loyal men, aren't they?"

"Yes, sir. They're trained and indoctrinated for that."

"See if you can line some up. I'll give you the word. Meantime, keep an eye on this Jubilee business. Try to get a date. Let me know if it hots up."

"I'll stay on top of it," St. Yves said. He headed for the door. Vandermeer might talk to himself, St. Yves thought as he left the office, but he still had a sharp, incisive mind and stayed right on top of business. The President was lucky to have such a man at his right hand.

• CHAPTER
TWENTY-EIGHT

AARON ADAMS drove cautiously down Dumbarton Street to Wisconsin Avenue and made a left, pulling his car to the curb right past the corner. There had been five cars behind him and none of them made the turn. He waited two minutes and pulled out and went halfway up the block to a garage and turned in. It was three thirty in the afternoon of Tuesday, the twenty-first of December: three shopping days until Christmas. Even an unimportant shopping area like the middle of downtown Georgetown was crowded with shoppers.

Adams guided his car up the circular ramp to the fourth floor, where he paused briefly. When he came back down Kit Young was in the seat next to him.

The bored attendant at the exit glanced at the time on the ticket and at his clock. "Not here long," he remarked.

Adams nodded. "So it goes," he said, handing the attendant a dollar. He turned right on Wisconsin and headed out toward Montrose Park.

Neither he nor Kit spoke to each other until he had found a place to park. They got out of the car and strolled past the snow-dusted tennis courts.

"We should be reasonably safe now," Adams said. "Unless they've got your overcoat bugged. Which, come to think of it, I wouldn't put past them."

"I have some news," Kit said, tugging the collar of his tweed overcoat up around his ears.

"I hope so," Adams said.

"You know, I can't even talk about things when I get home, for fear the damned Plumbers have put a bug in my light switch and a TV camera behind the mirror over my dresser. Miriam's starting to show the strain, and I think I'm developing a twitch on the right side of my face."

"The waiting is the rough part," Adams agreed. "But hang on, we're almost there."

"So are they," Kit said.

Adams looked at him sharply. "What the hell do you mean?"

"They're wise. They've found out."

"Who's found out *what?*" Adams demanded. "Come on, man, be precise."

"I'll be as precise as I can," Kit said. "They—and by 'they' I mean Vandermeer and St. Yves, and presumably the President—know about the coup." He stopped walking and smiled a bitter smile. "How does that grab you?"

"Keep walking," Adams said. "How do you know?"

"St. Yves told me we have to be prepared for a coup attempt. 'We' meaning them, you understand."

"What did you say?" Adams asked. "When did this conversation take place?"

"The funny thing is," Kit continued, "that for a minute I had no idea he was talking about us. I mean I thought, well, I don't know what I thought, but the possibility that he knew about Jubilee never entered my mind. 'What coup?' I said. 'Who's attempting a coup? Left wing or right wing?'

"'A congressman named Porfritt doesn't think we're holding the new elections fast enough,' he told me.

" 'Porfritt,' I said to him, trying to figure out where I'd heard the name before. Aaron, I was really trying to figure out if I'd ever heard of this guy Porfritt. Talk about induced schizophrenia. The 'me' that works for the White House is a different person. I mean, there's a lot of psychological suppression going on while I'm there. Then as soon as I get off, I become this other person, convinced that St. Yves is having me followed."

"Yes," Adams said.

"Does any of this make sense?"

"Of course," Adams said. "You're under strain, and you're not used to it. Not this sort of strain. Tell me exactly what St. Yves said."

"We'll have to give it up," Kit said. "They're not onto the rest of us, yet. At least half the time I think they're not, and the other half I think St. Yves is being subtle."

"What did he say?" Adams asked patiently.

Kit concentrated. "He said that Representative Porfritt was part of a coup attempt. That they were having him followed to find out who else was in on it. That they didn't think it had gotten very far. No—he said that *Vandermeer* didn't think it had gotten very far but that *he* wasn't sure. And that Jubilee was an identity code or a go code, he didn't know which."

Adams seemed to have regained his cool. "That's it?" he said.

"What do you mean, 'That's it'? Isn't that enough?"

"Not enough to cancel the mission."

"What will it take, the sound of fists pounding on your door at midnight?"

Adams shrugged. "Try not to worry about it."

Kit looked at him. Adams managed a smile. "I'm not insane," he said. "I expected the operation to be partly blown at some stage. It was bound to happen, just by the laws of chance. As few as we are, we're still too many to keep a secret for long. Remember, the German High Command knew the date and location of D-Day. Now, we're lucky enough to know when and how we've been blown. If we're smart, we can cause their interest in Obie to lead them away from us."

"I see what you mean," Kit said, thoughtfully. "Will Porfritt go along?"

"We can't tell him," Adams said. "It would make him too nervous."

"He's going to be pissed when he finds out."

"I'll apologize."

A flurry of snowflakes, blown from nearby trees, filled the air around them. Kit suddenly had the impression that everything had become incredibly clear and unbelievably three-dimensional around them. "I keep thinking that a coup can't work—not in the United States."

"It can, Kit. What we must do is become a legitimate government as quickly as possible."

"How do we do this?" Kit asked.

"That's where our friend Congressman Obediah Porfritt comes in," Adams said. "We're going to have the House vote a bill of impeachment against the President and rush it over to the Senate for trial. Once the bill is voted, the removal of the President from his seat of power attains an air of pseudo legitimacy. Then his house of cards comes tumbling down, and we all live happily ever after. If we're still around."

"Then the military personnel we're lining up is just a smoke screen," Kit said.

"By no means," Adams told him. "We have to go in and grab the President. We have to fight off the White House guards and the Secret Service men and get him away and under arrest for this to work. And we have to hold the White House and the surrounding area for long enough so that any 'loyal' troops who come in to rescue him are convinced and lay down their arms. Unfortunately, unless we're damn lucky, a lot of those innocent soldiers are liable to end up shooting at each other, as well as at you and me. I plan to be lucky, you understand, but there is an imponderable element of—luck—involved."

"It's going to be harder than you think," Kit said.

"How's that?"

"St. Yves told me they've decided to recruit a new presidential force to deal with that sort of thing. An elite corps based around a nucleus of newly released Special Forces people. They're going to start recruiting for this group in the next few days."

"Fascinating," Adams said. "Who's doing the recruiting?"

'St. Yves," Kit said. "He asked me to send along any likely-looking prospects."

"And indeed you will," Adams said.

THE WHITE HOUSE

THE OVAL OFFICE, Tuesday, December 28, 1976 (2:14–2:30 P.M.)

MEETING: The President, Vandermeer, and Ober

AUTHORIZED TRANSCRIPTION FROM THE EXECUTIVE ARCHIVES

Vandermeer and Ober are in the Oval Office. The President enters.

P. Billy. Charlie. Have you heard? That makes eighteen.

V. Congratulations, sir.

O. Eighteen what?

P. States. Eighteen states tied up to pass the repeal of the Twenty-second Amendment.

O. Eighteen already. We've got those citizens' groups in every state now, don't we?

V. Citizens for the Repeal. Yes. A spontaneous show of support for the President and the administration. Can't have this lawless element taking over our society.

P. Damn right.

O. Speaking of the lawless element, how's the coup coming?

V. It makes progress. Thanks to the indiscretion of Congressman Porfritt, a few more of the pieces have dropped into place.

O. I still think it's dangerous.

V. Not at all. It can be controlled. Jubilee will be our creature, not theirs.

P. Did you find out who their leader is?

V. No. But we're closing in. And his identity doesn't matter now. It will all come out at the trial.

O. I still think that we should announce a date for new elections, sir. Then it would make the coup attempt seem even more dastardly.

P. No elections. Not yet. I haven't heard any popular groundswell in favor of elections. I have a very sensitive ear on such things. The people don't want elections, they want safety. Law and order. The people are afraid. And a frightened people need a strong leader. Not that there shouldn't be elections—at the right time. After all, this is a democracy.

O. That's right, sir. The American people aren't ready for elections yet. After the coup attempt, we'll be able to get the repeal through in jig time. Then an election. When there's no question that you can run.

P. The country needs me.

V. The ground is still radioactive at the Capitol.

P. How's that?

V. They can't begin rebuilding yet. It will be another couple of years before they begin rebuilding.

P. What's that? The Capitol?

O. The Capitol architect has come up with a really fine plan for the rebuilding. In the meantime, the Senate can continue to deliberate in Ford's Theater. Wait until you see the model!

P. We'll set up a command center in the bomb shelter in the basement. Get the media in on this. It will be quite a show. They have any military units besides the Eighty-second?

V. We doubt it. If so, they have to be very small. When they find out that they don't really have the Eighty-second, that should break the back of the operation. But, of course, by then it will be too late to back out.

P. How are those new boys working out? The Special Forces group?

O. The first unit is set up. Twelve men. They'll be the corps commanders of the group as we expand.

P. I think, "Special Federal Police Force." How does that sound?

V. Too formal. What about "Executive Police"?

O. Maybe.

P. It has to have the right sound. The name is all. And the dress uniform. Very important. A really impressive dress uniform. I like the feel of the, you know, the coup thing. Let them carry the ball through the defense—almost to the goal line. Then smash! Hit them with everything we've got. Cream them. And mop them up on national television.

V. The greatest show of the season.

O. We just have to make damn sure we don't get hit by a surprise end-around play. Or something. I still worry.

V. We're secure on this one.

P. Maybe Charlie has something. We should go for protection in depth. Some group ready to slide in and provide defense when we need it. Some outfit standing by, ready to move. And when the morning comes, we attack with the sword in our right hand, the marshals, and defend with the shield in our left hand—this group. Whoever.

V. I'll get on that. I wouldn't want anything to go wrong on this. There's too much at stake.

P. Damn right.

• CHAPTER TWENTY-NINE

MAJOR CONNOR FITZPATRICK was a short, stocky man with a round, swarthy face, thick black hair, and shrewd eyes. He peered about suspiciously as he entered the downstairs bar of E. J. O'Reilly's Alley Pub and walked toward the rear. At first he didn't see Colonel Baker, or perhaps didn't recognize him in civilian clothes, so he strode up to the bar and ordered a draft beer.

Baker stayed quietly in his shadowed corner, nursing his scotch and water, and took this opportunity to observe Fitzpatrick, who had leaned back against the bar and was facing the door, obviously under the impression that the colonel hadn't yet arrived.

On the surface, Connor Fitzpatrick was a calm, self-possessed man with the restrained air of command that the Army looks for—and so seldom finds—in its officers. Colonel Baker, who had spent years training himself to read below the surface, felt that a man revealed himself most clearly when he thought himself unobserved. So for five minutes he sat and watched Major Connor Fitzpatrick, commanding officer of the 404th Military Police Battalion, as he fidgeted, adjusted his tie, checked his watch, and worked at suppressing a growing impatience and irritation.

Major Fitzpatrick, Baker was pleased to observe, handled growing impatience well. One of the traits necessary to a good officer, or a good conspirator, is the ability to wait.

Just as Colonel Baker was beginning to think about attracting Major Fitzpatrick's attention in some unobtrusive manner, the major spotted Baker at his corner table. For a second he wasn't sure it was Baker. Then a look of annoyance passed over his face. He casually sat down.

"Glad you could make it," Colonel Baker said. "Good to see you."

"I could have made it a few minutes earlier," Fitzpatrick pointed out, "if I'd known you were back here."

Baker shrugged. "It gave me a chance to see whether anyone followed you in here," he said.

The thought seemed to startle Major Fitzpatrick.

"People follow people these days," Baker added. "It's in the air."

Fitzpatrick looked around. The bar had a few other patrons, but none close enough to catch the conversation, and none who seemed to be paying the least bit of attention to the corner table. "About what we were discussing the last time we met—I'd like you to be more specific."

"Specific?"

"About my part, I mean. Just exactly what do you want me to do, and what will it accomplish?" He finished his beer and signaled the bartender for another one. "I'm the commander of a battalion of MPs. Three companies of men armed with sidearms. An armory full of carbines, except for a few M-1 rifles with their stocks painted white for parades. This isn't exactly my idea of the invincible strike force in the coming revolution."

Colonel Baker leaned forward, his arms on the table, and stared off somewhere to Fitzpatrick's right, in the general direction of the front door. "You can be of great assistance," he said in an intense, low voice, "take my word for that. But before I get into it in any greater detail, I'd like to know—we'd like to know—how you feel about the project."

Fitzpatrick leaned back. "When asked by the judge whether he advocated the overthrow of the government of the United States by force or violence," he said in a conversational tone, "the little man admitted that he rather preferred force, if it was all the same to the judge." He paused, brooding into an empty glass of beer, and appeared to be slightly startled when the waitress suddenly appeared and replaced it with a full one.

"I'm a career officer in the United States Army," Fitzpatrick continued. "It's all I ever wanted to be, and I'm satisfied with it. For the last eight years I was in Counterintelligence. It's not a great, glamorous job—you know that—but I enjoyed the work and I was good at it. Very good. I speak eight languages. I knew more about the Soviet intelligence networks in Indochina than they did."

Fitzpatrick made an indecipherable gesture involving both hands. "And here I am," he said. "A spit-and-polish major in charge of a spit-and-polish MP battalion right in the middle of goddamn Washington goddamn D. of C. And all because I wrote a position paper—my job, you see, writing position papers—that said we ought to zig when the politicos really wanted to zag. So, as you might guess, we zagged and got our asses handed to us. This did not please the President. So I got pegged for disloyalty, relieved of my job, and shipped back to the States."

"I see," said Baker, who had heard the story before from another source.

"It's not that I'm pissed about losing my job," Fitzpatrick said, "although I am. I'm frightened of a man with ultimate power who fires anyone around him who tells him he's wrong. By now I'm sure there isn't anyone who works within a square mile of the White House who's prepared to disagree with the President. I think this fellow should be stopped. But I'm not going to stand up there with you and try to stop him unless I've got a pretty good idea of what you'd expect from me and my three companies of men in white gloves. If you have us scheduled to assault the Executive Office Building, or neutralize the Pentagon, we may have nothing further to discuss."

"Can you control your men?" Baker asked.

"If I can control my officers," Fitzpatrick said, "I can control my men. And I can handle the officers.

Colonel Baker leaned forward. "If you had to create a traffic jam—a real monster of a traffic jam—do you think you could do it?"

"I haven't been at this job for so very long, but some of my sergeants directed the Normandy landing—according to them. We're trained to clear up traffic jams, of course, but if they can clear it up, I'm sure they can fuck it up.

"You might want to practice that a bit," Colonel Baker said. "I'll be in touch."

"I feel an unwilled speeding up of my pulse," Major Fitzpatrick said. "We do live in exciting times."

• CHAPTER THIRTY

VANDERMEER FLEW the helicopter himself. He had spent two hours an afternoon, three afternoons a week, for the past few months recapturing the necessary skills, and he was as proud as Hermann Goering at the stick of an ME-109. Ober and St. Yves were his passengers. St. Yves seemed to be enjoying himself, but Charlie Ober would clearly rather have been almost anywhere else. He sat rigidly in the fold-out back seat with his hands on his lap and refused to look anywhere but straight ahead.

"There it is, I think," St. Yves said, pointing ahead of them and to the right. They were flying over low hills covered by a thin forest of evergreens. Yesterday's mid-January snowfall had blanketed everything below, creating the illusion of picture-postcard clarity, but making it hard to pick out any detail.

Vandermeer expertly sideslipped the helicopter over to the right, a maneuver that made Ober stare even more rigidly straight ahead. "You're right," he said, "that's the highway. Good. It shouldn't be more than a couple of miles now. We wouldn't want Colonel Hanes to get impatient."

A few miles ahead of them Colonel Jonathan "Johnny-on-the Spot" Hanes, commanding officer of the Fifth Army

Brigade, stood on top of a snow-covered hill in Fort Meade's backwoods bivouac area and surveyed the surrounding neat rows and files of pup tents with satisfaction. Three days before, Colonel Hanes and his outfit, one of three "quick-response" brigades stationed on the East Coast, had been snug in their home barracks, in Fort Dix, New Jersey. The men were just buckling down to their rigorous training schedule after holiday leave. Then, two hours after receiving their movement orders, they were in their vehicles and rolling. And now the whole brigade—men, gear, food, ammunition, jeeps, trucks, APCs, artillery, and tanks—were on alert in Fort Meade, only seventeen miles north of Washington.

After satisfying himself as to the geometric precision of the matrix of pup tents, Colonel Hanes peered around, searching the sky for the first sign of Vandermeer's helicopter. He checked his watch and then peered around again, his impatience growing with every ten seconds. It was already almost a full two minutes past the fourteen hundred hours that Vandermeer and his party were scheduled to land.

With still no sign of the executive helicopter. Colonel Hanes pulled off his right glove and reached inside his overcoat for his copy of the order that had brought him and his boys out into the snow. He read it over again, searching once more for whatever hidden meaning might lie between the lines of the formally phrased deployment order.

After spending several hours in the morning thinking it out while the men had breakfast from the spotlessly clean field kitchen, Hanes had reached a conclusion he didn't even like thinking about. His instructions seemed to indicate that the President feared an armed insurrection in which other military units might play a part. But clearly the President didn't doubt Hanes's loyalty, or that of the men of the Fifth. And he would not waver if the call came. He wouldn't like fighting his brother soldiers, but the President of the United

States was the Commander in Chief of the Armed Forces, and orders were to be obeyed.

The helicopter was in sight now, coming over the crest of the hill, and soon he would know what it was all about. Whatever must be done, Colonel Hanes resolved as the whirlybird settled onto the hastily-scraped-clear landing pad, would be done quickly, efficiently, and with distinction. The Fifth Army Brigade, and its commander, would not be dishonored.

• CHAPTER THIRTY-ONE

AFTER CIRCLING the block three times looking for a place to park, Representative Obediah Porfritt slammed his old Buick into a dollar-bill-sized space in front of a fire hydrant. The House of Representatives medallion on the rear license plate would save him from a ticket, and he would somehow live with the guilt.

A black Ford stopped about three car lengths back, and two men in gray suits got out and separated, one crossing the street and the other falling into step behind Porfritt. The third man, the driver, stayed with the car.

Obie, clutching a large paper bag to his stomach as though it contained all the world's woes, scurried around the corner to J Street. Sticking out of the bag was the top of a brightly colored box, of the sort toys for small children come in.

The man behind Porfritt watched him enter a non-descript red-brick building and start climbing its worn wooden staircase. The man waited until his partner was in sight across the street and Porfritt was out of sight around the first landing, and then went in after him.

Obie climbed to the third floor. The only door on the landing was a steel fire door which had once been painted tan. A sign pointing to it read B & J TOY WHOLESALERS—RECEIVING. After a moment's hesitation, Obie pushed open the door and went in.

The gray man rounded the lower landing just in time to see the door closing on Porfritt's back. He went on up the stairs, past the landing to the floor above, and then pulled a miniature transceiver from his belt and said a few brief words into it in a low monotone.

Behind the door was a small bare room suitable only for meditation. Across the room a wooden office door with an inset glass window provided the only light: a yellow glow that came through the frosted glass of the window. There was a small bell screwed into the side of the window, and, Scotch-taped to the glass, a hand-printed sign that advised: RING BELL FOR SERVICE.

Obie rang the bell. Nothing happened. He heard footsteps outside the fire door. They paused for a moment on the landing before continuing upstairs. Obie didn't want to think about that. For some time now he had had the nagging feeling that someone was following him, and it was doing bad things to his digestion.

Obie gave up on the bell and pounded on the glass. After a moment it slid up. A bulky woman with short gray hair and round steel-rimmed glasses stuck her face through the opening. "Whyn't ch'a ring the bell?" she demanded.

"I did," Obie said.

"What ch'a want?" she asked, not mollified.

Obie pulled the box halfway out of the paper bag so the woman could read the legend on the front. BILD-A-MAN, the box said, with appropriate illustrations of the snap-together parts of a plastic body. "This is defective," he said. "I got it for my son for Christmas, and it's defective."

"What's a madder widdit?"

"I want to see Mr. Biddle," Obie explained.

"Oh," the woman said. "Why'n cha say so?" She slammed the window closed and, after a couple of preparatory clicks and thumps, pulled the door open. "Dat way," she told him, pointing down a narrow corridor. "To de end and toin left. Name's onna door."

Obie scurried down the corridor like a man pursued by invisible demons. At its end he turned left, to find another corridor. The name Biddle was on the glass panel of the third door down, on the right.

Obie knocked.

"Come in!"

Obie entered. The room was filled with unboxed toys and games, and an undifferentiated rubble of thousands of toy and game parts. At the rear a small man crouched behind a large desk was assembling a three-foot plastic dinosaur. "Welcome," the small man said without looking up. "What can I do for you?"

"My name is Porfritt," Obie said. "I got a note; it said to ask for you."

The small man looked up and examined Obie intently for a second. "Next door," he said, turning back to his dinosaur. "One office down." He carefully glued one saurian arm into place.

Obie backed out and closed the door. A feeling of annoyance was beginning to overtake his underlying feeling of fright. The two sat uncomfortably in his stomach. He took two chewable antacid tablets from his breast pocket and popped them into his mouth before knocking on the next, unmarked, door. A voice urged him to enter, which he did.

This room was small, and packed to the ceiling with banded cartons of posters that celebrated the toys of Christmas Past. There were two chairs in a narrow aisle between the stacked cartons. Aaron Adams sat in the first chair, with his feet up on the second. "Hi, Obie," he said.

"Aaron!"

"Close the door, Obie," Adams said, taking his feet off the chair. "Sit down."

Obie closed the door and lowered himself into the folding chair. "Aaron," he breathed, "do you know what you've just put me through?" He dropped the Bild-A-Man kit heavily onto the floor. "This kid slips a message to me in the goddamn men's room: 'Bring a toy to the B and J Toy Company. Destroy this note.' What am I doing here, Aaron?"

"I have to talk to you," Adams said.

"Sure," Obie said. "But why the toy? Why the back room? Why all the secrecy? I feel like I'm in a grade C spy movie. Why the hell couldn't you just come up to my office, Aaron, if you want to talk to me?"

"I didn't think that would be wise, Obie. You and I are conspiring against the President of the United States, which is, to put it mildly, against the law. Treason is, I believe, a capital offense."

Obie shook his head. "I feel like such an idiot. Why, I actually convinced myself that someone was following me around as I came up here. It's enough to make me paranoid."

"Don't let it get to you, Obie," Adams said, keeping his own voice calm and level. "You're just not a born conspirator, that's all. You're going to have to be careful; take a few precautions. There's nothing to worry about. From now on, we're not going to have time to be worried."

Porfritt simply stared at him.

"Jubilee," Adams continued, "is called for the day after tomorrow." He leaned back in his chair until it was balanced on the two back legs. "Two days, Obie. Can you hold out for two days?"

"Sunday?" Obie fell silent. Crossing his arms, he hugged them against his chest and stared at the gray wooden floor.

Adams watched Obie, but kept silent, leaving him alone

with his thoughts. Obie deserved to spend his declining years in honorable retirement, with a small law practice in Ogallala, telling stories about the big bills that got away. Instead, by an accident of relationship and time, he was thrust into the middle of desperate events.

But there was no going back now. They must all, as Franklin had said at an earlier insurrection, hang together, or they would most assuredly, all hang—separately.

Obie looked up. He had come to a decision and the worry lines had disappeared from his face. "It's going to be hairy," he said. "Congress is just back from Christmas recess. At least, I assume enough of my fellow congressmen are back to call a quorum. But Sunday—"

"How many of your comrades have you discussed this with?" Adams asked.

"A few," Obie said. "But I wish you wouldn't use the term 'comrades.' It has unfortunate connotations in my business."

"You have a point," Adams admitted. "Call them Sunday morning. Use a pay phone. I assume each of them is primed to call others."

"Right," Obie affirmed. "Each of my colleagues said he could contact at least five others, and the chain will grow from there, but I can't promise that there will be any senators on it."

"Let me worry about the Senate, Obie. Are you ready with the bill?"

"The bill of impeachment? I've been working on it as a labor of love for these past weeks. You should see the list of high crimes and misdemeanors in the statement of particulars. It's a beaut!"

"Nothing petty, I hope?"

"There are a few minor, petty items on the list," Obie said. "I had to put a few items in for my colleagues to knock out. Even at a time like this, you don't think they'd pass a bill the way it was written without deletions or amendments, do you?"

"Okay," Adams said. "You know your business." He reached behind him and produced a box labeled TINKER-TOT with a picture on the cover of a four-year-old child standing next to a three-tower suspension bridge made entirely out of small snap-together plastic pieces. "Take this home with you," he said. "Inside is a beefed-up CB radio with a strap so you can wear it over your shoulder. Keep it turned on and tuned to channel four. There's a little earpiece, if you want to listen privately. Pick a code name. So I can call you something besides 'Congressman Porfritt' over the radio. Something that has a meaning to you, so you'll be sure to catch it. Something short."

"What about 'Omaha'?"

"Fine," Adams said. "Capital of Nebraska."

"No, it isn't," Obie said. "It's the largest city, but Lincoln's the capital. I was thinking of Omaha Beach. On June sixth, nineteen hundred and forty-four, I was a corporal in a combat assault team. We hit the beach in the first wave. By the end of the day, I was the highest-ranking man still alive in my company. On June eighth I got a battlefield commission. Not because I was brave or clever, but because there were only two officers alive in the battalion. It was then I decided that, if I got out of that alive, I was going to go into politics."

"Oh," Adams said.

"I don't follow it either," Obie said, "not anymore. But it made perfect sense at the time. Anyway, if it wasn't for the Normandy invasion, I wouldn't be here today. So, if you don't mind—Omaha."

"Omaha it is, Obie," Adams said. "When you hear 'Omaha Go!' over your little radio, you get that bill of impeachment passed by whoever you've got there—I don't care if it's only three of you—and over to the Senate. Any senator you can find will serve as 'the Senate' for our purposes. The regular channels of government aren't exactly going to be in order, but I'll have a couple of senators over in that hall waiting for you."

"That's good, Aaron."

"Okay," Adams said. "Take your new toy and go home."

Obie stood up. "It's going to be hard not to keep looking over my shoulder, but I'll do my best."

"Very good, Obie." Adams rose and shook his hand. "Good luck."

"A hell of a thing," Obie said. He turned and left the office.

Adams stayed where he was for about ten minutes; then he left the building by an exit that led to an alley on the side street where he had parked his car. When he was halfway home he noticed that a black Ford with two men in it was staying a steady half-block behind him. Just to be sure, he stopped at a grocery store and a liquor store and made some unnecessary purchases. The car picked him up when he left and fell in behind him again.

Whistling softly to himself, Adams drove home.

• CHAPTER
THIRTY-TWO

MIRIAM CAME HOME to find Kit sprawled on top of her velour bedspread, fast asleep. His jacket was hooked over a chair, and his shoes and tie were on the floor by the bed. One sock was off, but that was where he had run out of energy. He hadn't even unbuttoned his shirt.

She sat down on the bed beside him, silent and motionless so as not to wake him. For a long time she sat looking at him. The tension and anger that had become a part of him while he was awake, lining his face beyond its years, were washed away by sleep. She hated to disturb him, to bring him from his peaceful sleep to the nightmare that reality had become.

After a time he rolled over, and his hand fell on her knee. He groaned slightly and opened one eye. "Huh," he said, closing the eye and wrapping his arm around her leg.

In a little while the eye opened again. "Hello, love," he said, slurring the words. "You home already?"

"It's after eleven," she told him. "Not that I object to finding you in my bed, but what are you doing here?"

"Waiting for you," he said. "Taking a nap." He sat up and rubbed his eyes. "Had a hard day."

"It's good to see you," she said.

He kissed her. "It's good to be seen," he said. "Hungry?"

"No," she said, "but I'll fix you something."

"Don't bother." He started putting his shoes on, looked surprised to find one sock missing, and fished around by the side of the bed for it. "Let's go to that coffee shop on K Street. My treat."

"I don't mind fixing you something," Miriam said.

"Apple pie," he told her. "À la mode. I crave apple pie à la mode."

"You win," she said. "I'll get my coat."

It was cold outside, and Miriam shivered and clutched Kit's right arm as they crossed to his car. "I'm sorry," she said.

"What?" He focused his attention on her. It had clearly been a long way off.

"I'm sorry I didn't pick up your cue faster," she said. "You want to tell me something."

"That's right."

"I can't get used to living in a house that might be bugged," she said. "I think that's the worst part: not knowing for sure whether it is or not. Wondering every time I say anything whether or not someone else is listening. . . . Speaking of which, you're not exactly listening yourself, are you? To me, I mean."

He opened the car door for her. "We can talk in here," he said. "I had it checked out this afternoon."

She slid into the freezing car and unlocked his side while he went around. When he got into the car he sat hunched over the steering wheel, staring off in some private world of his own.

"Start the engine," Miriam said, "and turn on the heater. It's freezing in here. What are we going to talk about? Hadn't we better drive to that coffee shop, in case anyone's checking?"

"It's tomorrow," Kit told her.

"What?"

"It's tomorrow. Jubilee is tomorrow."

"You mean—" she sat there staring at him, unable to say anything and feeling like an idiot because the words wouldn't come.

"I spent the afternoon with Laszlo setting things up," Kit said.

"Laszlo?" Did they know anyone named Laszlo? Perhaps she'd misunderstood him. Perhaps they were talking about something else. Tomorrow couldn't be the tomorrow they'd been planning for months, the tomorrow she'd prayed deep in her heart would never really come. If they failed she'd probably stand trial, and God knew what they'd do to her. She didn't care so much about that. But if Jubilee had come, then win or fail, Christopher Young, her Kit, whom she loved more than breath, would most probably be dead before the long tomorrow was over. She held her breath and felt the air from the car's heater, still cold, whip under her skirt.

Kit turned the car's headlights on and pulled away from the curb. "We're conspicuous sitting in a parked car," he said. "Might as well head toward the coffee shop."

"Who's Laszlo?"

"Colonel Laszlo Kovacs," Kit said. "The Special Forces man."

Miriam remembered Laszlo now. "The Special Executive Police," she said. "St. Yves' men."

"That's what he thinks," Kit said.

"Damn, Kit," Miriam said, "this whole thing's insane!" She wanted to grab Kit, and hold him, and shake him; but instead she hugged herself tightly and stared through the windshield. They were approaching the traffic light on Wisconsin Avenue. "I love you," she said, irrelevantly.

"I love you, Miriam," Kit said. "I've been thinking about that. After this—"

"After this?" she started laughing. "What do you mean, 'after this'? You're going to be killed, you idiot. Don't you know that? The Secret Service isn't going to let you get anywhere near the President. They don't care what kind of a bastard the man is, their job is to guard him. And that's exactly what they're going to do."

"I think we can get closer than they expect," Kit said, mildly. "Believe me, Miriam, I have no intention of getting killed tomorrow. It will take luck, but if things go right, not an awful lot of luck. And it's time we had a little luck."

Miriam took a deep breath and her hand sought Kit's arm. "I'm sorry," she said.

They drove around for a while, neither of them saying anything, and then stopped at the all-night coffee shop. Miriam went to the pay phone and called the two women she had recruited to help, an associate professor of linguistics and a graduate student in the political science department who was completing a thesis on Roosevelt and the city bosses. Tomorrow the three of them would become telephone operators for the day at the risk of life and liberty. If Jubilee succeeded, their minor but essential jobs would receive at most a footnote in the histories of the coup; if it failed, they would stand in the dock with the rest.

Miriam and Kit drank coffee. Kit ordered a piece of apple pie and pushed it around the plate before giving up.

"Let's go home," Miriam said after a while.

"I don't think I can sleep," Kit said.

"I'll hold you," Miriam said. "Maybe you'll sleep. I don't think I can do anything else tonight, but I want to hold you."

Kit paid the check, and they left.

General Tank MacGregor turned off the eleven-o'clock news and stared bleakly at the television set. It had been a long time since he had heard anything on the news to bring him pleasure, but he found himself watching compulsively. Some deep-seated masochistic impulse, he surmised, or a trace of the childhood belief that the good guys always win in the end.

He got up and walked slowly around his den, touching and examining the memorabilia of his long career. The walls were flocked with framed photographs that formed a bridge to the past—his past: a youthful Captain MacGregor standing at attention in front of his battle-worn Sherman tank while Generals Eisenhower and Bradley strolled by: a cigar-chomping two-star general shaking hands with Major MacGregor outside a demolished Wehrmacht command post, inscribed "To the only sonofabitch I ever had to tell to slow down—from his CO, George S. Patton"; a picture of his wife, Maggie, standing in front of the gray fieldstone cottage in Scotland that had been their honeymoon cottage—if a three-day pass the week before D-day could be called a honeymoon. And then she hadn't seen him for eight months, and had twice been told that he was taken prisoner and once that he was dead.

There was a photograph of Lieutenant General Tank MacGregor pointing what looked like an accusing finger at Colonel Clement Moor, USMC. It had been taken by an alert war photographer outside of Inchon, and had been published in *Stars and Stripes* over the caption "Tank tells it to the Marines."

He stopped before the flag standing in the corner by the door: a tattered American flag with a field of thirty-three stars. His grandfather, legend had it, had three horses shot from under him carrying that flag from Atlanta to the sea. Attached to the tip of the staff were a pair of battle streamers that had once been stiff gold brocade, but were now limp with age. He held them out and could still make out the faded motto embroidered thereon:

> *Harrah! Harrah! We bring the Jubilee!*
> *Harrah! Harrah! The flag that makes you free!*

MacGregor smiled to himself and turned to go upstairs to join his always patient, very dear wife. But as his foot touched the first step, the phone rang. He turned back to answer it.

Harrah! Harrah! We bring the Jubilee!

It was a quarter to midnight and the President of the United States still sat behind his great desk in the Oval Office. He was signing papers. He took great pride in his often-quoted claim that he served the people of this great country "sixteen hours a day, seven days a week." And he meant to keep to that schedule. It was an inspiration to the Youth of America, an example to his staff—which he fully expected them to emulate—and a prod to the lazy career bureaucrats that still cluttered the lower levels of government.

A soft chiming noise startled the President, and he looked up to see that the red phone on one side of his desk was blinking a subdued red bulb at him. He snatched the handpiece from the cradle and glared at it for a long moment before putting it to his ear. "Yes?"

"Mr. President?"

"Yes?" Who the hell did that idiot think it would be?

"This is Beadle, sir, in the Special Situations Room."

"Yes?"

"Jubilee has been activated, sir. The Comint staff intercepted the go parole on two separate nets in the past half hour, sir. We've put the Special Situations Room onto full alert status, as per standing orders, sir. Do you wish us to notify the Pentagon, or the Special Executive Police, or the FBI, sir?"

"Jubilee?"

"Yes, sir. We've notified Mr. Vandermeer, sir. He said to call you immediately. Standby procedure Bull Run has

301

been called up, sir, but we need your okay to continue."

"You're sure?"

"What's that, sir? You mean about Jubilee? Yes, sir. We're sure, sir."

"Okay," the President said. "Vandermeer's in charge. You do whatever he tells you."

"Yes, sir."

The President hung up the phone and stared down at the mass of papers on his desk. Suddenly he found them all very offensive, and with the back of his hand he pushed them off the side of his desk and onto the floor. It was beginning. The biggest crisis of them all. And he was ready, by God, he was ready for it! Only why hadn't Vandermeer called himself instead of letting some flunky do it? It was very bad for staff discipline to have the chain of command broken like that. Besides, Vandermeer knew how he depended on him, how he needed him to make the crucial decisions that had to be made. Not that he wasn't fully capable of handling the job by himself; not that he didn't have the breadth of intellect, the decisiveness, the almost instinctive grasp of world and national affairs that made a truly great president. Gildruss might get the credit; Gildruss might get the peace prizes; but if Gildruss was the quarterback, he was damn well the coach. And in the long run it was the coach who was remembered. And as for national affairs, well, another chapter in that book would be written tomorrow. And they'd see whether he could handle himself in a crisis or not.

Only where the hell was Vandermeer? Tomorrow they were going to try to take it all away from him. It was those shitty Eastern Jew intellectuals. They always had hated him. But it would all come out right in the end. He would triumph, as he always had—in the end. Vandermeer had it completely under control. But—

The corridor door opened and Vandermeer came in. "I'm here, Mr. President," he said.

"Damn good thing," the President said. He looked at his watch. It was two minutes past twelve. His sixteen-hour work day was over. "I'm going to bed now, unless you need me for anything."

"No, sir," Vandermeer said, taking his accustomed seat to the right of the desk. "The activation of Bull Run is right on schedule. I'm holding off calling in the camera crews. We don't want to let this peak prematurely. With any luck we'll hit prime time tomorrow night."

The President shook his head. "Be careful," he said. "We don't want to preempt a football game. You know how the people hate it when we preempt a football game."

"This is big enough," Vandermeer assured the President. "We won't have any backlash on this."

"Good, good," the President said. "Do you think there's any chance of these Jubilee people starting anything tonight?"

"Highly unlikely, sir," Vandermeer said. "The troops we believe them to be depending on are not on ready status. Our experts estimate it will take them at least six to eight hours after the go code is sent to be ready to move. That means the coup attempt can't begin before six tomorrow morning at the earliest."

"Okay," the President said. "Stay on top of it."

"I have a cot in the bomb shelter right next to the Special Situations Room," Vandermeer told him.

"Very good," the President said. "Call me if anything breaks." He put his jacket on, buttoned it, and left the office. He walked past the Secret Service guards without acknowledging their "Good evening, Mr. President." That was one thing about being president; you didn't have to say a damn thing to a damn person if you didn't feel like it.

303

Upstairs in the family quarters, the President paused at the door to his bedroom and looked over to the door to his wife's bedroom. He felt a no longer familiar urge. Perhaps it was the excitement. He went into his bedroom and took off his clothes, hanging the suit carefully over the clothes horse and folding the rest of his garments neatly on a chair. Then he went to the connecting door between his bedroom and his wife's and opened it. His wife was asleep. He went over and climbed on top of her. She stirred but, as usual, she did not fully awaken.

Vandermeer stood up as the President left the office. When the door had closed behind the President, Vandermeer sat back down and looked around the room at the great oval of the walls as though he expected to find someone hiding in one of the shadows. He stared down at the great presidential seal woven into the rug at the foot of the President's desk as though he had never seen the device before. "You'll see," he told the empty air. "It will all work out, just as I promised you it would."

Vandermeer got up and went outside through one of the French windows. Off to one side of the Rose Garden a small two-seat helicopter was parked on the White House lawn. He went over to it and methodically began checking it out, detail after detail, working from a complex preflight check list.

When he returned to the Oval Office, St. Yves had just entered. "They told me you were in here," St. Yves said. "I have something for you."

"What?" Vandermeer asked.

"I understand Jubilee is go," St. Yves said.

"That's right. For the morning, presumably."

"Then I'll sack out in the guard room," St. Yves said. "If you want me, I'll be there."

"Right," Vandermeer said. "See you bright and early. I think I can promise you that it's going to be quite a day!"

Senator Malcolm Chaymber rolled over irritably and switched on his night light to peer at the clock. It was ten past one. Who the hell would be calling him now? He picked the handset off the receiver to stop the ringing and then paused a minute to wake up before putting it to his ear. "What?" he demanded.

"Malcolm? Adams here."

"Yes?" He was fully awake now; his heart was pounding.

"I hope you're ready for the Jubilee, Senator. We're bringing it tomorrow morning."

"Yes," Chaymber said. "I'll be ready."

"If you could contact some of your colleagues on this, Senator, we'd be grateful. And, by the way, I'm calling from a pay phone. You might want to do the same."

"Yes," Chaymber said. "I see. Of course. I'll do what I can."

"Very good, Senator," Adams said. "Thank you."

"No, Aaron, thank you," Chaymber said. He hung up the phone. Tomorrow he and a handful of his fellow senators would vote to accept a bill of impeachment against the President of the United States—and his own career would be over. The President would not be one to give up without a prolonged and vicious fight, and even as he went down kicking and screaming he would drag Chaymber down with him. The country was not ready for a senator who was a faggot.

At least he'd be able to pay the President back for the long months of wearing the mantle of a senator while doing the work of a toady. He put his robe on and hunted for his slippers. He was going to have to get dressed and go out hunting for a pay phone, but first it occurred to him that it would be good to go into the other bedroom. It had been a long time since he'd talked with his wife.

It was after two in the morning when George Warren reached the Mini-Stor Private Storage Company outside of Charlottesville, Virginia, and roused the night watchman to let him into his locker. The bulky package he took out wouldn't fit in the trunk of his Chevy, but with a little maneuvering and an extra fiver for the watchman, the two of them managed to cram it into the back seat.

He stopped for coffee at an all-night diner before heading back to Washington. It had been a long day and promised to be a long night, and he wanted to be fully alert while handling his cargo. He would take the return drive slowly and carefully. It's no time to have an accident when you're traveling with a missile with an atomic warhead in the back seat of your car.

Ian Faulkes staggered into his New York hotel room at three in the morning to find his phone ringing. He stared at it suspiciously for a minute and then picked it up. "Evening," he said, holding the handpiece like a microphone and shouting into it. "Evening, America. This is your British consh—cons—this is Ian Faulkes speaking to all of you out there, and I'm just the tiniest bit smashed at the moment."

He heard a tinny sound coming from somewhere. After a while he realized that it was coming from the earpiece, which was upside down in his hand. He turned it around and put it to his ear. "Sorry about that," he said. "You still there, whoever you are?"

"Ian, you bastard, this is Aaron Adams. You're drunk!"

"I didn't know I wasn't supposed to be," Ian said. "I've had a most wonderful evening, Aaron. I'd still be with the lady if there wasn't some question of her husband arriving before dawn casts its rosy lips o'er the billowing watchama-callit. What do you need, Aaron?"

"I need you, Ian. I need you now, and I need you sober."

At that moment an operator came on the line and told Adams to "signal when through."

"You're calling from a pay phone, Aaron," Ian said.

"Yes."

"You in New York?"

"No, Washington."

"And you need me now? In Washington?"

"Right again, Ian. And if you don't want to miss the biggest news story of this or any other century, you'll hustle your ass down here."

"Why? What's happening?"

"Your ass and a camera crew and a helicopter. We won't let you play unless you bring a helicopter."

Faulkes shook his head. "Aaron, what the fuck are you talking about? Hold on a minute!" He put the phone down and went into the bathroom. Sliding open the glass door to the shower, he turned on the cold water and stuck his head under the showerhead. In seconds the cold had permeated from the top of his head to the base of his spine, and he turned the water off.

"I think I'm sober enough to talk with you now," he told Adams. "But you're sure as hell going to pay my hospital bill if I catch pneumonia. Now what the devil is going on?"

Adams talked to him for about twenty minutes, at the end of which he was completely sober and extremely awake. "You can count on me, Aaron," he said. "Isn't this a hell of a thing? See you later, old man."

The duty officer of the U.S.S. *Guam* knocked on the door to General Moor's cabin and entered. "Excuse me, sir," he said.

Moor was instantly awake. A lifetime in the Marines had given him the ability, but he had never learned to like it. "What is it?" he asked, turning on the lamp over his head.

"A priority message, sir. It came in from Atlantic Command about half an hour ago, addressed to you. The communications officer thinks it's some sort of action code, sir, but he can't find it in the book. I'm sorry to bother you, sir, but we thought it might be important."

"Let me see it," General Moor said, swinging his legs over the side of the bunk. He took the flimsy and stared at it.

```
FROM NAVATCOM WASHINGTON
TO GENERAL CLEMENT MOOR USMC
USS GUAM
TEXT:
    JUBILEE REPEAT JUBILEE 16 JANUARY
```

Moor reached for his shirt. "This ship is now on full alert," he said. "Tell the captain."

• CHAPTER
THIRTY-THREE

It was six o'clock in the morning, barely an hour before sunrise, and the first hint of color was creeping into the cloudless eastern sky. To the west the sky was still black and star-studded, with Leo just preparing to drop below the horizon. Tommy Green, his eleven-year-old body well padded against the predawn chill, hurried down the street of identical two-story houses that made up this part of Fort Bragg's officers' row. Already the lights were on behind a good many of the bedroom and kitchen windows.

Tommy paused for a second to make sure he had the right house and then went up and rang the doorbell.

The blond woman who answered the door was in a housedress with her hair up in curlers. She looked surprised to see him. "Why, good morning, Tommy. What are you doing here at this hour?"

"I have a message for Captain Beddow, ma'am. Is he up?"

"Yes. He's in the kitchen," she said, now thoroughly puzzled. "Come on through." She closed the door and took Tommy through the living room and into the kitchen. "You have a visitor, Frank," she called.

"Well," Captain Beddow said, as his young visitor came

to something approximating a position of attention in front of him. "Hello, Tommy. What can I do for you? Does your father need something?"

"My father sends his respects, sir," Tommy Green said. "He asked me to tell you that this is Jubilee morning, sir."

"Oh!" Beddow said. "I see. Well, thank you very much, Tommy. Tell Colonel Green that I understand."

"Right, sir," Tommy said. "Thank you, sir." And with that he turned and raced out toward the front door.

"What was all that about?" Mrs. Beddow asked her husband as he poured himself a second cup of coffee. "Why didn't the colonel just call if he had a message for you?"

"That was a classified message, Betty, my love," Beddow told her, smiling broadly. "Not to be transmitted by unsecure channels." He climbed up on a kitchen chair and began fishing for his .45 in the overhead cabinet where they kept it to be sure it was out of reach of their five-year-old.

"Oh, no," Betty Beddow groaned. "Not another one of your war games! You'll be gone for two weeks."

Beddow stepped down off the chair and buckled the holstered .45 around his waist. "Probably not that long," he said. "But I might be away for a few days. Why don't you take the boy and go over to your mother's until this is over. I'll give you a call." He took the automatic from his holster, pulled the clip, then worked the slide a few times. "I love you, Betty. Remember that."

Betty Beddow looked at her husband intently for a long moment, and then reached out almost shyly to touch his shoulder. "I'll pack a bag," she said.

At 0630 General Moor was on the flight deck of the U.S.S. *Guam* with the ship's captain, Commander Halberstrom. All around them men in fatigue jackets and men in dungaree jackets were busy fueling up and checking out the

310

big Chinook helicopters of the Forty-first Marine Helo Squadron, Reinforced, that filled the *Guam*'s flight deck. The air was full of the sounds of engines and pumps, and the smells of oil and AVGAS mixed with the smell of the sea.

"We'll be ready to start feeding your men in less than ten minutes," Halberstrom said. "Should have the last shift out by seven thirty. By which time we'll be just off Assateague Island, right where you wanted."

"Very good, Captain," General Moor said. "If you'd be good enough to call all NCOs and officers of the battalion to the briefing room, I'd appreciate it. And have your armory crew break open the magazine and begin bringing the ammo up to the distribution area on deck. We should be out of your hair by oh-eight-hundred."

"I'll see to it, sir," Halberstrom said. He stuck his hand out. "Good luck," he said.

General Moor took the hand. "Right," he said. Behind him one of the Chinooks roared into life, as the mechanic continued his preflight checkout on the big copter.

Major Connor Fitzpatrick strode out to the front of the assembled three companies that made up the 404th MP Battalion. "Good morning, men," he yelled.

Close to six hundred men yelled back something incoherent, but probably obscene.

"I thank you all for responding so promptly to the alert," Fitzpatrick bellowed, "and apologize for making you give up your Sunday.

"I think you'll all appreciate this more when I tell you this is not a drill. We're about to hop into our vehicles and drive off to downtown Washington. In fifteen minutes sharp, at oh-seven-hundred, our little caravan will start.

"Remember, this is very serious. Strange gentlemen in various uniforms may come up to you and request you to cease what you're doing. Some of them may be driving tanks. You will not listen to them. This will anger them, but as long as you do your jobs as we've practiced, they can't get at you, so don't worry about it.

"This could be your moment of glory, boys. I'm counting on you. Don't fuck up." He saluted his men, and then turned and strode back into his office.

His adjutant turned to the men. "All officers into the squad room," he called. "NCOs take over your companies!"

At a few minutes past eight on Sunday morning, Grier Laporte parked his panel truck on Seventeenth Street off Constitution Avenue, right across the Ellipse from the White House. Aaron Adams, sitting in the back of the truck, flipped on the illegal linear amplifier that would boost the signal on their CB rig from the legal five watts to a highly illegal kilowatt.

A traffic cop pulled alongside them in his car, and was about to tell them to move on when he noticed the neat lettering on the door panel of the white truck: ATOMIC ENERGY COMMISSION— NUCLEAR EMISSIONS TEST TRUCK, and caught a glimpse of Grier and Aaron in their white smocks surrounded by apparatus. He looked over at the broken dome of the Capitol across the Mall, still off limits after all these months, and nodded at the two. "Going to be long?" he asked.

"I hope not," Grier told him.

"This is Jubilee," Adams said into his microphone. "This is a go, repeat, go! This is Jubilee to Omaha—go, Omaha. Jubilee to Green Leader—go, Green Leader. All units are go."

"Jubilee, this is Eire," came a distant voice over the loudspeaker. "We're going, even as we speak."

Grier half turned to the inside of the truck. "Air?" he asked.

"Eire," Adams told him. "That would be Major Fitzpatrick. I didn't expect any of them to answer me, but it's good to know someone's listening."

"Everyone's listening," Grier grumbled. "Hell, I'll bet even money that the President's listening. This isn't exactly a secure channel."

"Of course he is, Grier," Adams said. "That's part of the game."

The President reached his office at eight o'clock to find Vandermeer waiting for him. "Morning, Billy," he greeted his Chief of Staff. "You haven't been up all night, have you?"

"Good morning, Mr. President," Vandermeer said. "I arrived here about ten minutes ago. I've been down in the Special Situations Room for the past hour, sir. Everything's ready for Bull Run, and we're proceeding as planned. The roundup of traitors will begin in about fifteen minutes."

"Is the media stuff—the coverage—ready?"

"I have all three networks standing by," Vandermeer said. "They're curious as to what's going on, but they know better by now than to ask questions before we're ready to tell them anything."

"That's right," the President said. "That's good."

"When do you want them notified?" Vandermeer asked. "We should give them some time to set up. They have to have some warning to get their cameras positioned."

"Wait till the thing's under way," the President decided. "We don't want it to fall flat at the last minute. Think how stupid we'd look if we show Cronkite how well prepared we are for a coup, and then there's no coup."

"Right," Vandermeer said. "Although there's little chance of them backing out now. They're committed and we're committed. Colonel Hanes should be on his way in with his tanks by now. There'd better be someone here for him to shoot at, or we're not going to look too good."

The red phone rang, and Vandermeer picked it up.

"Vandermeer," he said. "What's that? I see. Okay, thanks. Keep it up. Increase the coverage, if you can. We'll be right down."

"What was that?" the President asked.

"The Comint people in the Special Situations Room have just picked up what they call the go parole for Jubilee. That's the official go-ahead. They're using CB stuff and their signal is very loud. Probably from somewhere around here. Our boys are trying to get a triangulation on it now."

"That's good," the President said. "Isn't it?"

"Yes. Very good, sir. Everything's going according to plan. I think we'd better get down to the Special Situations Room now. There may be some Jubilee people with access to the White House."

"You mean someone who works here is plotting against me?" the President said. "Who? Who in the White House is disloyal?"

"It's just a precaution, sir," Vandermeer said soothingly. "We mustn't take any chances until we're sure Jubilee has bought it."

"Right," the President said. "Good thinking. Sock it to 'em. Let's go to the basement."

At 0800 Rear Admiral David Bush entered the Fleet Communications Office at the Pentagon. "You're holding a ready-coded message under the code name Widowmaker," he told the duty officer. "See that it goes out to all ships as soon as you can get it on the net. That includes the VLF sub net."

"Aye, aye, sir," the officer said. "On what authority?"

"Here's my authority," Admiral Bush said, taking a sealed letter from his breast pocket. "It's signed by the Deputy Chief of Staff for Intelligence."

"Yes, sir." The lieutenant glanced at the letter and then turned to the CPO at the desk behind him. "Pull Widowmaker and put it on global and subcom," he said.

Within minutes the doubly encrypted message was going out to all ships' captains. It was short and simple, and probably puzzling to most of those who read it. It was a precaution against insanity, against the fear that the Supreme Commander, in his last moments, might start pushing buttons.

TO ALL CAPTAINS
FROM CHIEF OF STAFF, NAVY
TEXT:
  REMAIN ON STATION OR CONTINUE SCHEDULED MISSION DESPITE POSSIBLE MESSAGE TO THE CONTRARY FROM ANY SOURCE. ACCEPT NEW ORDERS ONLY DIRECTLY FROM CINCAT OR CINCPAC OR COSN. IGNORE HIGHER AUTHORITY UNTIL THIS MESSAGE IS SPECIFICALLY COUNTERMANDED BY COSN. END.

It was pushing eight thirty when Charles Ober arrived at his office in the Executive Office Building. There might be an attempted coup going on, but after all *somebody* had to run the government. Let Billy Vandermeer and the President get all the glory, as usual. He was content to stay behind the scenes and see that everything ran in as orderly and correct a fashion as was ever possible to get out of a bureaucracy. That was what government was all about.

Three men were waiting in his office when he came in: George Masters of the FBI and two other gray-suited men who looked to Ober's trained eye like field agents. "Good morning, Masters," Ober said, smiling grimly. "What can I do for you?" It probably had something to do with the coup, Ober thought.

Masters pulled his badge case from his jacket pocket. "Good morning, Mr. Ober," he said. "I'm George Masters of the Federal Bureau of Investigation, and these are special agents Garber and Wilcox."

"For Christ's sake, Masters," Ober said, annoyed, "what's all this formal bull? I know who the hell you are. Now what's this all about?"

"We have a warrant for your arrest, Mr. Ober, signed by Judge Bryan Bellows of the Ninth Court of Appeals," Masters said. "Here it is, if you'd like to look it over. Will you please come with us."

Ober crossed over to his desk and sat behind it, acting on some kind of primitive bureaucratic instinct, as though once behind his desk he were safe and couldn't be dislodged or removed. "Is this a joke?" he demanded. "I'll see you busted down to flatfoot, you stupid son of a bitch! Who the hell put you up to this? I'm going to launch an immediate investigation. You just stand there, while I call the Attorney General. We'll get to the bottom of this right quick!"

"The Attorney General was named on the same indictment," Masters said. "He's been relieved of his job and placed under arrest, also."

"I'm calling the President!" Ober snapped. "I'm calling Billy Vandermeer!"

"I have a warrant for Mr. Vandermeer, also," Masters said. "I don't expect to get to serve it—at least right now—but I have it. The indictment also names the President as an unindicted co-conspirator. There was some legal question as to whether he could be indicted, so we compromised."

"You people are part of the coup!" Ober said, waving a finger in sudden realization.

"What coup is that, Mr. Ober?" Masters asked politely.

"You can't do this!" Ober snapped. "It's against the Constitution!"

"That's very amusing, coming from you," Masters said. "Come along, Mr. Ober."

• CHAPTER
THIRTY-FOUR

COLONEL DEWITT GREEN stood at the front of the small briefing room, facing the assembled officers and noncoms of the Fourth Regiment, Eighty-second Airborne Division. "Our task is very simple," he said. "We're going to get into the APCs assembled in the company street and hightail it into the capital. When we arrive at the White House, we're going to deploy around it and not allow anyone in or out."

He sat down on the desk and dropped the pointer he had been holding to his side. "Now here's the situation as I know it," he said. "The House of Representatives is going to vote out a bill of impeachment against the President. The Senate is going to vote to accept the bill. The President will be held under house arrest—not by us—until his trial. Our major function there is to see that nobody gets hurt. Our secondary function, but the one that may cause the greatest bloodshed, is to see that no forces inimical to the orderly process of democratic government break through to release the President.

"Now, some of you may think that this is disloyal, that we are staging a *coup d'état*. It could be looked at that way, but in a larger sense it's not true. We're aiding in restoring free elections, and seeing that the continuity of power in

317

the government proceeds as it has since General Washington assumed office in seventeen eighty-nine. Are there any questions?"

Colonel Green looked around at the sea of clean-shaven faces, and they looked back with varying degrees of interest and intelligence. A few of them had already been briefed; some of them had only a vague idea of what was going on, but would have followed him if he'd suggested three-legged races down Interstate 95; and some of them were trying to figure out how it would look in their service records.

Finally one hand went up. A young second lieutenant named Grice. "Yes, Lieutenant?" Green said.

"Ah, it's about the rest of the division, sir," Grice said, rising. "Are they involved in this, and what are they going to be doing, sir?"

"They're not involved," Green said. "As far as I know, the division will spend a normal Sunday polishing boots and cleaning rifles. We, Lieutenant, are the lucky ones."

"Yes, sir," the lieutenant said, sitting down.

"Okay," Colonel Green said. "Just follow orders, and see that your men follow orders, and let me do the worrying. If any of you have any doubts about this politically, remember it's my ass, not yours. You're doing what soldiers are supposed to do: following the direct orders of your superior officer. You may get shot at, but that's what your government has been paying you for all these years. Worse, you may have to shoot back at soldiers in uniforms similar to your own. If you must do so, then don't hesitate; but for the love of God, don't use your weapons unless you absolutely have to."

Green looked around. "Is that clear?" When nobody responded, he nodded. "Okay. I assume that means it's clear. If any of you, for whatever reason, feel strongly about not accompanying us on this jaunt, speak up now."

An audible silence followed this remark. "Okay," Green

said. "Assemble the regiment, gentlemen; form on the Head-quarters Company street and load into the vehicles. Good luck!"

Captain Beddow, Colonel Green's adjutant, approached him as the group filed out of the briefing room. "There's something I don't like, sir," he said in a low voice.

"What's that, Frank?"

"Outside this door, Colonel, in two long rows stretching from HQ Company to Con Mess Three, are all the regimental vehicles, all gassed up and ready to go. Climbing into them at this very moment are all the men of our regiment in full battle dress."

"That's right, Frank. So—"

"So, Colonel, why isn't anyone from Division, or from another regiment, or from anywhere else on this goddamn post even curious about what's going on here on a Sunday morning, when they must know damn well there are no field exercises or maneuvers scheduled?"

Green scratched his jaw. "When you put it that way, Frank, it does seem rather odd."

"Yes, sir. I think we've been set up."

"Great!" Green turned around and stared thoughtfully at the big map of Fort Bragg posted on the wall behind him. "I think what we'd better do," he said, "is get out of here quick, and get out of here in an unexpected manner."

"Yes, sir," Captain Beddow agreed.

"Okay," Colonel Green said. "Let's get going. Pass the word down the line that there may be trouble on the way out; but make sure the men don't even load their weapons until someone fires on us first."

"Right, sir," Beddow said, stepping back and saluting. "How are we going?"

"Right through the main gate!" Green said. He patted Beddow on the shoulder. "Move it, Frank," he said. "I'll take the lead APC. Give me about a seventy-yard lead, then bring the column on behind me."

They went out together and Colonel Green climbed up into the command turret of his APC. "You fellows ready?" he called down.

"Yes, sir," his driver said cheerfully. "Just waiting for you, sir."

Green's APC was fitted out as a communications vehicle, and contained an Army command radio specially modified to use the citizens band frequency Jubilee was sitting on. "Plug me in," Green told the radio man as his driver brought the APC into lumbering motion. "Jubilee Control, this is Green Leader."

"*We read you, Green Leader.*" It sounded as though it were coming from next door, Green noted. That must be one hell of a transmitter Adams had rigged out.

"Jubilee Control, we're operational. See you soon, we hope."

"*We hope so too. Good luck, Green Leader.*"

Colonel Green gave his driver instructions and then, as the huge APC turned onto C Company Street, he flipped to the command frequency. "Onward!" he said, and then thumbed the switch off.

The APC rounded the next corner and headed toward the main gate, about a quarter of a mile away. There was nobody on the street as they passed the post exchange and the church, Green noted—not a good sign. He watched expectantly as they rounded an ancient grove of pine trees that shielded them from the main gate.

When the firing started, Colonel Green took one look at what was facing them and slammed down the hatch cover. "Put her in reverse," he yelled at his driver. "Get us the hell away from here!"

Thumbing the radio back on, he took a deep breath. "This is the boss," he said. "Turn in your tracks, men, and head back where you've been."

"What's happening?" the voice of Captain Beddow sounded in his earphones.

"Two M-60 tanks bracketing the main gate," Green said, as a pine tree exploded somewhere to his left. "And what looks like the rest of the division behind them. You were right, son, we've been set up. Fall back and re-form at the C Company street."

When they turned back on the company street, Green popped the hatch and jumped out of his vehicle. A double row of vehicles jammed the street in front of him. The firing had stopped, and there was no sound of pursuit.

Captain Beddow raced over to him from somewhere in the column. "What now, sir?" he asked.

"I'm not sure yet," Green said. "They don't seem to be in a hurry to follow us in. We can hold these brick buildings at C Company. We'll use the APCs as a bridge to connect them."

"We'll be trapped in there with no way out if they come after us," Beddow said.

"There's no practical way out now," Green told him. "If I were General Landau, I'd take my time in closing this little trap, knowing the mouse has no place to hide. But I think we can hold out for five or six hours, and that may be helpful."

"If it's just a question of holding out, sir," Beddow said, "we could probably hold out for a week."

"I think five hours will be long enough to decide the issue. They can keep us here, Frank, but only by staying here themselves. We can effectively keep the division pinned while others decide the, ah, main issues. The trick now will be to see that as few men as possible get killed."

"Yes, sir," Beddow said.

"Get that CB rig turned on and inform Jubilee what's happening here," Colonel Green ordered.

"Yes, sir," Beddow said.

• CHAPTER THIRTY-FIVE

CONGRESSMAN OBEDIAH PORFRITT left his house at 8:35 A.M., headed for the clandestine meeting of the House Impeachment Committee. He had spent the early morning at an outdoor pay phone by a gas station. As a result he had only had three hours' sleep, and may have caught pneumonia to boot. His nose was stuffed, the four aspirin he had taken were doing nothing for his headache, and he couldn't seem to shake off the morning grogginess and awaken fully. And for this day he would have to be fully awake.

In the briefcase he carried were the detailed particulars of the charges they were going to bring against the President of the United States. And, while his colleagues knew in general what those charges were, some of the details would shock and horrify even those hardened cynics. Political chicanery, no matter how gross, was something they understood. But the indictment against the President charged him with ordering, directing, or condoning acts, for his personal or political gain, that were so far outside the political process as to make a mockery of it.

Porfritt hurried toward his car, clutching his briefcase and hoping that the aspirin would take effect before he had to talk. He was so preoccupied that he didn't notice the two men who scrambled out of a black sedan at the curb until they had almost reached him. He looked up to find them only a few steps away. They wore dark suits, and had badges of some sort pinned to their jacket pockets. "Congressman Porfritt?" one of them asked as Porfritt looked up.

"Yes?" Porfritt's heart was suddenly beating very fast.

"We're federal marshals, sir. We have orders to place you in protective custody. Please come along with us."

Porfritt dropped the briefcase and ran around the side of his car. One of the marshals cursed and lumbered after him. The other headed around the car from the other side to cut him off.

Seeing that he could never make the driver's door before they had him, Porfritt raced for the six-foot wooden fence that separated his driveway from his neighbor's. With a strength born of desperation, he pulled himself over the fence and dropped to the other side. His feet tangled up in the bicycle that was resting on the far side of the fence, and he fell heavily on the concrete driveway. The two marshals, proceeding more gingerly, pulled themselves over the fence after him.

Porfritt grabbed the bicycle and ran out into the street with it. Then he mounted it and began pedaling for his life. It had been more years than he liked to think since he had been on a bicycle, but he was relieved to discover that he could still make the machine go in a straight line without falling over.

The two marshals were back on the street now, staring after him. He was about half a block away, and getting farther with every second. In a few seconds he'd be at the corner. Two blocks to the right was a school that took up three blocks. The streets between had been blocked off for cars, but a bike could get through without any trouble. If he could make it that far, he had a chance.

One of the marshals pulled a revolver and, holding it

in both hands, leveled it at Porfritt's wobbling back. A moment later, Porfritt heard the shot and felt a sudden searing pain along his lower thigh, running into his left leg. Then the pain disappeared, but his leg wouldn't work the pedals anymore. He tried to stay erect, so he could glide around the corner and out of sight, but a haze came before his eyes and the bicycle slowly tipped over.

When they reached him on the ground, his face was white and bright arterial blood was spurting from his leg onto the black asphalt. "You do know," he said, holding his leg with both hands to try and staunch the flow, "that what you two are doing is illegal." He took a breath and almost passed out, but it seemed important to him to finish what he was saying. He shook his head to clear it and stared up at the marshals. "It is specifically forbidden by the Constitution," he said clearly, "to arrest or detain a Member of Congress while Congress is in session."

"You should have thought of that," one of them told him, "before you committed treason."

Porfritt passed out.

Kit pulled his car into the Executive Office Building garage entrance and slid his ID card into the slot to open the gate. Two EPS policemen were loitering inside the gate, and one of them peered through the windshield at Kit and Miriam and then waved them on.

Kit pulled alongside the officer and rolled down his window. "What's up?" he asked.

"Checking everyone who comes in, Mr. Young," the officer told him. "Orders. Something's happening, but they never tell us anything."

"Don't feel left out," Kit said with a weak smile. "They never tell me anything, either." He drove down the ramp and parked his car on the second level. "Typical, isn't it?" he said to Miriam. "They put out the guard, but don't bother telling them what to guard against." He took the key out of the ignition, dropped it into his jacket pocket, and stared at the whitewashed wall in front of him. "This is it," he said.

"I keep feeling that there's been some mistake," Miriam said, taking his hand. "That any second we're going to wake up and find that this is a particularly nasty dream. Or that Adams is going to pop out from behind a post and say, 'Okay, boys and girls, I was just kidding, you can go home now.' But he isn't."

Kit squeezed her hand. "Are you going to be all right?" he asked, peering into her eyes as though he could read the future in their depths.

"No, of course I'm not going to be all right," Miriam said. "And you're not going to be all right, and nothing's ever going to be all right again. But life will go on—for those of us around to live it. Don't look at me like that. I'll do fine. I just won't feel fine."

"I'd like to say something helpful," Kit said, "but I have no idea what that would be. We must do this."

"Of course," Miriam said. "It is a far, far better thing we do— I love you, Kit. No, don't say anything. I'd better go now. Take care."

"I will." Kit kissed her and watched her cross the car-studded room to the stairway. Then, checking his watch, he locked the car and started in the other direction.

The two women who had volunteered to help Miriam were waiting for her in the Executive Office Building lobby. Their passes, supplied by Adams from some secret cache, had gotten them into the building without problem. The door guard had taken one look at their skirts and blouses and heels and pastel-colored sweaters, and would have passed them in if they had held up bus passes. There were hundreds of women in the building who dressed that way, and it was hard to imagine any of them as a potential security threat.

Miriam led the way, following directions she had learned from Kit. There was supposed to be a man waiting for them, one of Colonel Kovacs' Special Forces recruits; if he wasn't there, they were in trouble. She found the stairway and the three women headed downstairs, their high heels clacking on the cement steps.

At the end of the underground corridor two levels down, there was a door marked WHITE HOUSE SWITCHBOARD. A burly man in an ill-fitting blue suit was lounging just outside the door. He looked at them questioningly as they approached.

Miriam smiled at him. "You're looking jubilant this morning," she said.

"Right on, lady," he answered. He gave her the thumbs-up sign, then pushed the door buzzer.

A tinny voice came out of the speaker over the door. "Who is it?"

The man held up a badge to the small peephole in the door. "McKay," he said. "Special Executive Police."

The door opened a crack. "What do you need?" a voice asked from inside.

McKay hit the door with his shoulder, springing it open, and then he was inside. The three women were right behind him. There were two men in the room, one sprawled on the floor where McKay's door-opening technique had thrown him and the other still sitting on a stool in the far corner. They both looked startled, but they moved very carefully since McKay had them both covered with a Mauser machine pistol which had appeared from somewhere under his suit jacket.

The room was a long narrow one with one entire wall taken up with a great series of switchboards, in front of which sat twelve operators who were all frozen in different attitudes of surprise and astonishment.

McKay removed the guns from the two guards, and then herded them and the operators into a large supply closet connected to the switchboard room. He locked the door.

Miriam and her two companions sat at the switchboard and began clearing up the blinking lights.

"White House . . . I'm sorry, he cannot be reached."

"White House . . . I'm sorry, I cannot complete that call."

"White House . . . I'm sorry, the information officer is not in at the moment. You wish to verify what rumor, sir? Yes, sir, that is perfectly true. The President has been placed under arrest, and is being held for impeachment. What? No, I'm sorry, but that information is not available at this time. No—he is perfectly all right. Yes—everything is under control. Thank you."

"White House."

"Jubilee."

"Hello, Jubilee. You're cutting it close. We just, ah, came on shift here."

"How did it go?"

"No problems, Jubilee."

"I'm calling you from a pay phone on the Mall. The number is four-two-four-nine-five-four-six. If anything erupts, try to call and let us know."

"Will do, Jubilee."

"Good luck."

"You, too, Jubilee. White House, good morning . . ."

New York and Massachusetts Avenue come together at Mount Vernon Place. To add to the confusion, Seventh, Eighth, Ninth, and K streets also feed into this narrow oval.

Major Fitzpatrick had decided that this was the perfect place to set up the command post of his MP brigade. From the north side of the oval he directed his jeeps into the streets and avenues to set up a network of roadblocks. They would create a river of stopped cars flooding back along the twelve streets and stopping traffic in all directions. When added to the fourteen other carefully selected sites, these roadblocks should succeed in freezing traffic all over downtown Washington.

Fitzpatrick's first concern was to open a landline between his command post and Jubilee Leader. There was a pay phone near his jeep from which he called a pay phone next to Aaron Adams' truck; he kept the line open by charging it on a government credit card. "All systems go," he told Adams. "I sure hope you know what you're doing."

"I share that hope," Adams said. "Keep me informed."

The Special Situations Room, created out of the conference room in the White House bomb shelter, was crowded with communications equipment and the people working it. Every few minutes one of the operators would wave and a runner would take a sheet of paper from him and run it over to an analyst's desk, where it would join the flood of papers already there. Occasionally, one of the analysts would wave and a runner would take a paper from him to the command desk, where a summary would be prepared to be sent to the President.

At the moment the President was down in the Special Situations Room reviewing his troops. "We're taking a gamble," he told Vandermeer as they walked through the underground room together. He smiled his strained smile. "But that's nothing new for me."

"That's right, sir," Vandermeer said. "Everything's under control. We're going to come out of this in good shape—in better shape than we went in. We'll have the whole country behind us by tonight."

"All three networks," the President agreed. "This is prime-time action; they can't pass it up."

"That's right, sir," Vandermeer said. "What happens here today is going to be seen by everyone in the country."

The President stopped by a bank of teletype machines. "What's this?" he demanded.

"We're surveilling the news services," Vandermeer explained. "To see if they come up with anything on the coup we don't have."

"The bastards," the President said. "Let's go upstairs."

Vandermeer stared at the paper that was just handed to him. "Here's some good news, sir," he said. "The protective detention of Congress is going very well."

"Good," the President said. "There's no way those bastards can legalize this thing without Congress. Even if those bastards win, they lose."

"They can't win," Vandermeer said. "I have it all planned. Everything is planned."

The President stared at Vandermeer, who had a strange expression on his face. He was about to say something when they were interrupted by another message. Vandermeer read it, squinting thoughtfully. "This is it," he said, waving the yellow sheet in the air. "We've broken their back!"

"What? What are you talking about?" The President snatched the paper from Vandermeer's hand and read it himself.

TOP SECRET BULL RUN
INTERCEPT REPORT, SPEECH
SSR/47/0843
CITIZENS BAND CHANNEL 14
1) JUBILEE COME IN JUBILEE THIS IS GREEN LEADER

2) GREEN LEADER THIS IS JUBILEE

1) JUBILEE IT LOOKS LIKE WE'RE GOING TO HAVE TO ABORT AT THIS END. WE HAVE BEEN SURPRISED BY A LARGER FORCE. DO YOU READ? WE ARE STILL INTACT BUT COMPLETELY SURROUNDED. (GARBLE) HOLD OUT FOR A WHILE, BUT NO CHANCE REPEAT NO CHANCE OF BREAKING OUT. DO YOU UNDERSTAND, JUBILEE?

2) WE UNDERSTAND. DO WHAT YOU CAN.

1) SORRY ABOUT THIS JUBILEE.

2) HOLD OUT AS LONG AS YOU CAN, GREEN LEADER, OR UNTIL YOU HEAR THAT THERE IS NO NEED. GOOD LUCK.

1) THANK YOU JUBILEE. GOOD LUCK TO YOU. GREEN LEADER OUT

END

TOP SECRET BULL RUN

"What does it mean?" the President asked. "Who's 'Green Leader'?"

"The coup forces—the troops at the Eighty-second Airborne—are headed by a Colonel Green," Vandermeer said. "I assume the message means that our surprise was complete and we've grabbed them all. I'll get a message through official channels to Fort Bragg right away and verify, but I'm sure that's it."

"Then it's all over," the President said.

"Not quite over," Vandermeer said. "There's still some mopping up to do."

"Right," the President said. "And that's what we want on every newscast tonight. Get the camera crews out here now, Vandermeer, and start the mop-up now. With any luck we might even make the noon news. Is that Johnny-on-the-Spot Hanes on his way?"

"The Fifth Brigade is proceeding toward the White

House," Vandermeer said. "Hanes estimates another hour, last I heard."

"Good, good," the President said. "Let's go back upstairs to the Oval Office. I have work to do. See that the photographer gets pictures of me working behind my desk."

"Yes, sir," Vandermeer said.

Colonel Hanes stared at the street map laid out on the hood of his jeep. "New York Avenue is jammed for blocks," he said. "Any of our scouts find a way around yet?"

"Reports are coming in now, sir," Captain Fargo, his adjutant, said from the back seat of the jeep. "A pattern is emerging."

"How's that, Captain?"

"All the streets into the downtown area seem to be jammed. One of our scouts who surveyed the jam on foot reports that there's a roadblock on Pennsylvania Avenue."

"Police? Construction?"

"No, sir. MPs, he says."

"MPs?"

"Yes, sir. I have the other scouts checking their streets now, but I'll give four to one that they find the same thing."

During the next few minutes two more reports came in confirming the adjutant's bet. "This," the colonel said, "is a whole new ball game!"

"Yes, sir."

"Notify the senior officers to get their collective asses up here on the double."

"Yes, sir."

Colonel Hanes paced in front of his jeep while waiting for his officers, hands locked behind his back, shoulders up, jaws thrust forward—the way he had once seen Omar Bradley pacing in some World War II film footage. When his officers were gathered around the hood of his jeep he stood

331

in front of them and jabbed at the street map with his right forefinger. "New York Avenue is jammed for ten blocks," he said. "Roadblocks set up by some MP unit. Half a mile of civilian vehicles piled up and no way to get around them." He turned to his officers gathered around him. "You know our mission, gentlemen," he said. "What do you suggest? We have an appointment with the President in front of the White House in approximately twenty minutes. I intend to keep that appointment—with your help."

"What about sending some infantry forward to eliminate the blockage?" This from Major Morgan, the commander of one of the three heavily armed battalions that made up the Fifth Brigade.

"I don't think so, Morgan," Hanes replied. "A firefight would get all the civilians out of their cars and scattered from here to Baltimore. We'd never get the mess cleared up."

"What do we do, then, sir?" one of his captains asked respectfully.

"We divide the brigade up into three elements," Hanes said. "Major Morgan will take the first element along the B and O Railroad tracks, cutting off somewhere this side of Union Station and heading in toward the White House on interior streets. Captain Fargo will take the second and backtrack to Montana and around, coming in on Rhode Island. If it's blocked at any point, jog to the left." His finger stabbed down on the map. "If you make it to here," he said, "where you intersect Massachusetts and Sixteenth, go in on Sixteenth, if it's clear. If not, keep heading west until you find a clear street. They can't have the whole city cut off."

Colonel Hanes folded up the map. "I'll take the third element and head in through Mount Olivet and over to Maryland," he told them. "We'll keep in close radio contact. Remember, the important thing is to get through to the

White House as fast as possible and set up a defensive perimeter. If you find a thin spot, with only a few cars between you and a clear street, remember a tank will go over a car. It won't leave much of the car, but that's just a goddamn shame. Try to get the civilians out first before going over their vehicles."

"What about the use of weapons, sir?"

"If those damn MPs get in your way, blast them. When you reach the White House, defend it. Remember, don't take orders from anyone but the President himself, Mr. Vandermeer, one of their direct representatives, or me. I intend to beat you there, but in case I don't, remember who's in charge."

"Yes, sir," Major Morgan said.

"What about civilian casualties?" Captain Fargo asked.

"Try not to shoot civilians, but if any get in your way and refuse to move, you may assume they're enemy force and treat them accordingly." Colonel Hanes waved his hand. "Back to your vehicles. Let's get out of this mess and go do our jobs."

The scene was deceptively peaceful. There was a roadblock visible about ten blocks down Constitution Avenue, and the cars were backed up past the White House. But most of the drivers were being very phlegmatic about it. For whatever reason, there was surprisingly little fuss.

The Executive Protection Service guards behind the White House fence paced stolidly by in their parody uniforms and pretended to be unaware that anything unusual was happening.

Grier Laporte was slumped against one wall of the phone booth across from the van, the handset cradled between his shoulder and his ear, making notes with his oversized black pen on a yellow pad. He looked like nothing so much, Adams thought, as an anxious bookie.

The plan was proceeding much as Adams had expected it to. Colonel Green and his regiment from the Eighty-second Airborne were not going to make it. Adams had never expected them to. In the world he was trained to operate in, the surface plan was what you fooled the enemy with. You might also have to fool a couple of friends, but those were the breaks of the game. Colonel Green's regiment would keep the remaining two thirds of the Eighty-second holed up in Fort Bragg, and that's all Adams had ever really hoped for.

A coup is a largely mystical process, Adams thought, involving the transfer of an intangible godhead of power from one group to another. If the transfer occurs, regardless of the size of the force involved, then the coup is legitimatized and the fighting stops. And if everyone thinks that power has been transferred, then it indeed has been.

The trick, then, is to convince those who make the decisions—the great majority of noninvolved military, judicial, bureaucratic, and political personnel—as well as the television-viewing public, that, for good or evil, the deed has been accomplished. Even in a country as vast as the United States, the number of people required for success is astonishingly small, if the other factors are right. Within the next couple of hours Aaron Adams would discover whether the United States of America was prepared to remove a sitting president.

Laporte dropped the phone, leaving the handset dangling, and stomped across to Adams. "A couple of bad breaks. The President's troops are on their way," he told Adams morosely.

"Which troops?" Adams demanded.

"At least two companies of mixed armor coming in from the north. Fitzpatrick says he figures it's a reinforced brigade—probably the Fifth."

"Can he hold them?"

"As long as they can't get at him, he can hold them. He says that when it occurs to them to use infantry to knock out the roadblocks, he won't be able to stop them."

"But even after that, it will take better than an hour to clear out traffic so the tanks can get through."

"Fitzpatrick says that, too. He says they'll probably try to go around."

"Well, that will take an hour, anyway."

"Have you heard the news on the radio?"

"What news?"

"Federal marshals picked up most of the members of Congress this morning."

"Shit!" Adams said. "Not that it's unexpected—but shit!"

"You expected it?" Laporte asked. "Doesn't this blow the whole thing? Don't we need the impeachment business? I thought that was the heart of the plan."

"It's like playing chess, Grier," Adams said. "There are layers within layers. You hope the outer one will work, but you're always prepared to play a deeper game."

"Are we prepared?" Grier Laporte asked.

A faint droning noise came from the south like a distant swarm of bees, and a phalanx of troop-carrying helicopters dotted the southern sky and came steadily on.

"What you see before you," Adams said, waving his hand toward the southern sky with the air of a smug magician, "is phase two of the master plan, otherwise known as the unexpected jab to the solar plexus."

"They're on *our* side?" Laporte demanded.

"I do believe," Adams said.

Adams watched the approaching Marines. It was like watching a textbook exercise. The twenty-two helicopters from the U.S.S. *Guam* spread out into their prearranged pattern and began touching down, rapidly, one after another. They landed inside the White House fence, as well as in Lafayette Square in front of the White House and the Ellipse behind it. Battle-dressed Marines leaped from the great cargo doors of the Chinook copters and immediately began setting up a defense perimeter surrounding the Executive Mansion. Within minutes the full complement of Marines and their air-portable equipment was off-loaded, and the copters then lifted off and settled, in neat rows, along the far side of the Mall.

Sporadic shooting broke out as some members of the Executive Protection Service and Some Secret Service men fired on the Marines. But General Moor's training held; the firing was answered and stopped by the specific troops fired upon, and did not spread. Within a few minutes the shooting had stopped. Most of the EPS officers, unsure as to which side the Marines were on, and lacking specific instructions, retreated to the inside of the White House or the small guardhouses by the White House gates and awaited instructions. The Marines left them alone.

Five minutes after the first copter had put down, the tranquil scene had transformed into an armed camp, ready for battle. Squads of Marines covered each entrance to the grounds and the White House itself, and antitank squads and sharpshooters settled behind the statues in Lafayette Square. General Moor, in plain battle fatigues with no sign of rank visible beyond an almost palpable air of command, ignored Adams and set up a command post to the side of the statue of Rochambeau.

A contingent of four Secret Service agents came out into the West Wing garden to try to find out who was in command of the Marines, and just what they thought they were doing there. The discussion quickly grew heated, and one of the Secret Service men pulled out a pistol and waved it at the corporal he was arguing with. The corporal, a credit to his training, merely gestured toward his squad of men, whose automatic weapons were all more or less loosely pointed in the general direction of the Secret Service agent. The agent cursed, holstered his revolver, and stalked back inside the White House with his companions.

Meanwhile a squad of Marines trotted across the street to the Treasury Building to block off the far end of the so-called secret tunnel which ran from the White House to the Treasury Building cellar.

Adams checked his watch and nodded. Those things that could be controlled had been controlled. The game was well under way. It was time to put the last counters into play. From this moment on, as George Washington had said so many years before, the event was in the hands of God. He lifted the microphone of his CB radio and spoke softly into it.

George Warren found himself stuck in traffic on Connecticut Avenue, unable to approach any closer to downtown Washington. It took the better part of half an hour for him to work his Chevy onto a side street. He would have made better time on foot, and many around him seemed to have deserted their cars to do just that. But Warren could not leave his precious cargo.

With many backs and cuts, occasionally driving along the sidewalk, he tacked his way toward the White House.

Suddenly, turning a corner, he found his way blocked by four deserted cars with flat tires—one of a series of improvised unmanned roadblocks that the MPs were creating as fast as they could between the oncoming tanks and their goal.

And then Warren found himself between the tanks and *their* goal, as two medium tanks came around the corner, blocking his retreat. "What the hell are you guys doing here?" he yelled. "This street's blocked. Back up so I can get out of here!"

The tank commander in the lead tank waved a leather-gloved hand at him. "Get out of the way, mister," he said. "We're coming through."

"What the hell are you talking about?" Warren demanded. "I got to get out of here. Come on, back up."

"Move it, mister!" the commander ordered.

This was too much. After the hours of fighting traffic, Warren had had it. He would simply have to go through on foot, lugging that mother of a missile on his back. He climbed into the back seat to pry the missile out.

The tank commander watched Warren climb into the back seat of his car, and then through the back window he saw the bulbous nose of the missile appear, and could just make out the shape of the firing tube behind it. "The son of a bitch has an antitank weapon in the back seat!" he announced over his intercom. "Move it before he gets it lined up. Hit that car!"

The tank lurched forward and crunched into the Chevy. The right track climbed the side of the car, ripping the door off and lifting the thirty tons of tank up onto the car. After a few seconds the tank leveled off, with the car collapsing under it. By the time the tank spat the car out from under its massive treads there was nothing recognizably human inside the mangled wreck. The ATX-3 missile was crushed and broken in half. The atomic warhead, safely nestled in a concussion- and radiation-proof shell, escaped major damage.

The second tank followed in the path of the first.

• CHAPTER THIRTY-SIX

CHRISTOPHER YOUNG went to the Map Room on the ground floor of the White House and joined Colonel Kovacs and four of his Special Forces volunteers. They had entered the building early that morning and had settled in the Map Room, the room from which FDR had plotted the daily changing course of World War II. They had variously spent the time playing solitaire, reading paperback novels, smoking, dozing on the couch, drinking coffee—and waiting. There wasn't much conversation in the room during the waiting hours; there wasn't much to say. But there was a lot for each of them to think about in the mutually respected privacy of these last moments. These men were the hit squad —the enemy within—Aaron Adams' secret weapon. Their mission was to arrest the President of the United States.

It was Adams' theory that the longer they waited the more the President's men would focus on the growing external dangers, and the less prepared they would be to handle a sudden internal threat.

And so they waited. The Eighty-second Airborne came in and out of action, the 404th MPs moved about the chessboard of downtown Washington, the Fifth Brigade smashed

339

through toward the White House, Miriam and her friends occupied the White House switchboard, the Marines landed on the White House lawn, and still they waited.

The CB transceiver next to Kit's leg squawked into life. "Good morning again," Adams' tinny voice sounded. "This is Jubilee to Trojan Horse. Time for you Greeks to move out. Good luck."

Kit got up and went to the door. Colonel Kovacs and his men came up silently behind him. As the one most familiar with the White House, and least likely to cause suspicion, Kit was the natural point man for the group. He opened the door to the corridor and stepped out.

There was nobody else in the West Wing corridor. Kit hurried along it, taking the most direct path to the Oval Office. Colonel Kovacs and his men stayed a constant ten yards behind.

Through one of the corridor windows Kit could see out to the L of the Rose Garden and past it to the great French windows of the Oval Office. There was someone in the Oval Office, but Kit could not make out whether it was the President. Here was the unavoidable weak point in the plan: they could not control the President's actions. There was an overwhelming probability that he would remain in the Oval Office, which he seemed to regard almost mystically as the seat of his power. But if Vandermeer had talked him into going anywhere else, they had a problem.

Kit wet his lips and started forward. The door to his left was the Cabinet Room, and past that the short corridor to the Oval Office. Kit strode forward confidently, as though he belonged there, and turned the corner.

The President sat behind his desk in the Oval Office watching a squad of Marines digging in behind the Darlington Oak. "These men," he said almost plaintively to Vandermeer, "they're not on our team?"

"That's right, Mr. President," Vandermeer said. "But they won't try to come in here."

The ranking agent of the six Secret Service men in the room shook his head. "I beg your pardon, sir," he said, "but we don't know that. I'd feel much better, sir, if you'd come back downstairs to the command post in the presidential bomb shelter."

The phone rang and Vandermeer turned to pick it up. The President looked at Vandermeer and then back at the Secret Service agent. Then he shook his head. "No," he said. "Fifth Brigade will be here any moment now. Those helicopter Marines won't be able to stand up to an armored brigade. And the television people are due. It would be bad for my image to be anywhere but the Oval Office in this time of crisis."

Vandermeer hung up the phone. "It will be your finest hour, Mr. President." He went to the hall door and opened it. "St. Yves!" he called .

St. Yves appeared in the doorway.

"I have a new name for you," Vandermeer said. "Just picked it up downstairs in an intercept. It will interest you." He wrote something on a slip of paper and handed it to St. Yves. "Keep an eye out."

St. Yves looked at the paper. "Son of a bitch," he said.

"What is it?" the President asked.

"Administrative, sir," Vandermeer said. "Detail. Have the television crews arrived yet?"

"I don't see them," the President said, peering out the window.

"Any second now," Vandermeer said. This crisis will be resolved on national television. As I said, your finest hour."

"Yes, it will be, won't it? The President of the United States directing an armored brigade against a bunch of traitors. It will be living proof that I've been right all along. That they've been plotting against me. That I was right in postponing the elections." He slapped Vandermeer on the back. "You planned it this way, didn't you? A real crisis. You've always—" He broke off as gunfire sounded in the outside hall. "What was that?" he demanded.

St. Yves was standing by the door to the Oval office with four Secret Service men when Kit rounded the corner. "Morning, St. Yves," Kit said, nodding. "Is the President in?"

St. Yves eyed him for a moment, and then extended his right arm rigidly, pointing an accusing finger at Kit. "You're a traitor," he said. "You're one of the enemy."

"What are you talking about?" Kit demanded, his heart pounding even faster.

"We just found out," St. Yves said. "You're one of the bastards—*get him!*"

The Secret Service agents reached in unison for their guns, and Kit dove back around the bend of the corridor. Four shots boomed through the narrow hall. Four slugs passed through the space Kit had just vacated and buried themselves in the pastel-blue wall, gouging out craters of white plaster to mark their entrance.

Cursing St. Yves, Kit backed up into the protection of the Cabinet Room doorframe and drew his gun. What, he wondered, had gone wrong? How much did St. Yves know? Colonel Kovacs and his men silently scattered into other doorways or behind pieces of furniture in the long corridor.

After a few seconds, a Secret Service man, his head at baseboard level, peered around the corner. Two quick shots from Kovacs' men caused him to withdraw hastily. Kovacs darted from doorway to doorway until he reached Kit. "We'll have to rush them to get by," he whispered. "And the longer we wait, the readier they'll get."

"You're right," Kit agreed. "We seem to have lost the element of surprise."

• • •

"What are you waiting for?" Vandermeer barked at the Secret Service agents in the Oval Office. "Get out there and help the men in the corridor!"

"Our job is to stay with the President," the senior agent protested.

"Your job is to protect the President," Vandermeer said, tightly controlled rage sounding in his voice. "And the threat to the President is out there, not in here. Having a divided force will just make it easier for them to take you in two batches."

"Vandermeer is right," the President screamed. "Get out there and stop them!"

The senior agent looked from the President to the door, and then made up his mind. "I'll go out," he said. "Hoskins, Malzberg, Pronzini; you come with me. Lynn, you and Randall stay in here." And he headed for the door, beyond which a suspicious quiet awaited.

"You think I'll be safe here, Vandermeer?" the President asked. "I'm not concerned with my personal safety, you understand, but for the good of the country the President must be kept safe."

"I've been preparing for this moment," Vandermeer said. "I made ready."

"How's that?" the President asked. The staccato cough of a rapid-fire gun riveted their attention to the door for a second.

Vandermeer turned to the two remaining Secret Service agents. "Cover the door from the inside," he told them. Reaching under his jacket, he pulled out a small revolver that had been stuck in his waistband. "It's time to make our move," he said, turning back to his chief.

"Move?" the President asked. He was standing behind his great desk, looking uncertain.

"The most dramatic move, Mr. President," Vandermeer told him. "The best PR. This will do it."

"What will it do?"

"There's a small two-seat helicopter sitting out in the Rose Garden, right on the other side of the French doors," he said. "I'm going to get you out of here in it."

"Running away?" the President said. "Wouldn't that be running away?"

"No, sir," Vandermeer said. "I'll land you in the middle of the Fifth Brigade, and you'll take command of the troops and smash the coup. Yourself. Personally. On national television."

The President thought it over. "I like it," he said.

"I was sure you would."

"Let's go!" the President said.

In the corridor, St. Yves and the Secret Service agents tipped over a heavy desk that sat to the right of the Oval Office door. Most of them crouched behind it, while St. Yves and one of the agents flattened themselves against the door to the Roosevelt Room across the hall.

Colonel Kovacs cocked his Mauser machine pistol and nodded at two of his men. They began a heavy covering fire and, under its protection, Kovacs and then Kit dived across the T of the corridor and rolled to their feet on the other side. Kit felt clumsy and exposed, but he made it across.

They waited exactly thirty seconds by Kovacs' watch, and then they rushed the hall from both sides, setting up a continuous barrage of fire as they came. The Secret Service agents fired back, resting their revolvers on top of the overturned desk, and St. Yves snapped off shot after shot with the calm imperturbability of a sailor in a shooting gallery.

The firefight lasted less than a minute, at the end of which the small corridor was strewn with bodies. The superior firepower of the Mauser machine pistols that Kit had smuggled in in the trunk of his car had made the difference. As the last shot was fired, Colonel Kovacs and two of his men were down, along with four of the Secret Service men. Another Secret Service man, with a bullet in his shoulder, was desperately trying to reload his revolver with one hand until Kit knocked the weapon aside. St. Yves and the agent who was with him had disappeared inside the Roosevelt Room and closed the door behind them.

Kit had no time to consider St. Yves: his job was to get into the Oval Office. With the two standing Special Forces men behind him, he kicked the door open and dived into the room.

The two Secret Service men in the room were flanking the door, and they fired simultaneously at Kit as he burst through. Then the Special Forces men shoved machine pistols in their ribs, and they reluctantly dropped their guns.

Kit got to his feet. The President and Vandermeer were by the French windows. Vandermeer was trying to open one with one hand while he kept a small pistol in the other.

"Hold it right there," Kit said. He raised his pistol, trying for the two-handed, FBI stance. When his left arm wouldn't obey his instructions to raise, he realized he had been hit. No time to think about it now. "Mr. President, in the name of the Congress and the people of the United States, I am placing you under house arrest."

"You son of a bitch!" Vandermeer screamed. "You're not going to stop me now!" He raised his pistol; but he was pointing it at the President, not at Kit.

"What's this?" the President said, in a choked voice.

"This is for Kathy," Vandermeer said.

Two shots sounded together. The President spun and fell on his face. Vandermeer dropped his gun, clutching his shoulder where Kit's bullet had entered, and staggered out the French window.

Everyone in the office, weapons and antagonisms forgotten, rushed over to the fallen President.

One of the Secret Service men rolled him over and propped him up. He opened one eye and looked down at his chest, covered with a spreading red blotch.

St. Yves went out through the window of the Roosevelt Room in time to see Vandermeer dashing for the helicopter.

"What's happened?" he demanded, intercepting Vandermeer by the copter door. "Where's the Chief?"

"Dead," Vandermeer said. "Get in."

"Jesus!" St. Yves exclaimed. He climbed into the helicopter. "You sure you can fly this thing?" he asked. "Looks like you've been hit."

"Minor," Vandermeer said. "Flesh wound. I'll make it for long enough."

As the small helicopter climbed into the air over the White House, St. Yves transferred his interest to the scene below. "There's a column of tanks arriving," he said. "Right down F Street. About goddamn time. Johnny-on-the-spot-Hanes sure as hell didn't make it this time. Who got the Chief?"

"Me," Vandermeer said.

"Who?"

"Me," Vandermeer repeated.

St. Yves stared at him. His mouth opened but no words came out.

The copter hovered over the Ellipse as the tanks moved up South Executive Place and continued around until they had partially surrounded the White House. A second column of tanks came into view, heading up Fourteenth Street to join them. Now there was a battalion of Marines dug in around the White House facing an armored brigade, which surrounded them around the outside. Neither side seemed to have any idea of what to do next.

"Some kind of joke?" St. Yves demanded, staring at Vandermeer. "You offed the President?"

"I've known for a long time," Vandermeer said, "what I had to do. I wanted him up here with me, but perhaps this is better. You and I together, St. Yves; the right and left hand—after the head."

"I don't follow," St. Yves said, his voice very calm, as if he were talking to a child. "Perhaps you'd better land this thing so you can explain it to me."

"I wanted to get him alone up here," Vandermeer said, "to talk about the past."

"Past?"

"The whole thing," Vandermeer said. "The way it grew, step by step. Until we—all of us—ended up somewhere that none of us were ever headed for. Did you ever get that feeling, St. Yves?"

"I don't know what you're talking about," St. Yves said, staring across at Vandermeer. He noticed that Vandermeer's left sleeve was saturated with blood, but it didn't seem to affect his handling of the craft.

"Responsibility," Vandermeer said. "I'm talking about responsibility." The little helicopter dipped back over the White House. Below, more and more tiny white and black faces, framed by olive-green helmets, stared up at them as they passed.

"I think you need help," St. Yves said. "You've been under strain. You wouldn't really shoot the President."

" 'Some say the world will end in fire,' " Vandermeer quoted softly, " 'some say in ice.' Our world, Edward, is ending in fire. Don't you feel that?"

"I don't think so, Billy," St. Yves said as calmly as he could. "Land this thing and then let's talk about it."

"Look down," Vandermeer said. "That used to be the Capitol. Where Kathy died. The President has joined her. And now we shall."

"You're crazy!" St. Yves said, thoroughly alarmed. "What do you think you're doing?"

"The Washington Monument, I think," Vandermeer said. "That would be appropriate."

St. Yves grabbed for the control rod, but Vandermeer pushed him aside and steered the tiny craft toward the tall spire of the Washington Monument a few thousand feet away. "It's no use," he said. "You can't fly this anyway."

Down below, the zoom lenses of the television cameras focused on the scene as the two men fought for control of the helicopter. The machine wavered and dipped across the sky as they struggled; one fighting desperately for his life, the other fighting calmly for their death.

Slowly but inevitably the copter headed back across the Mall toward the observers. Then, as those below watched in horror, the little craft darted toward the five-hundred-and-fifty-five-foot spire of the Washington Monument. It crashed two thirds of the way up and bounced off the rough stone side. A human figure was flung away from the spiraling copter like a rag doll and plummeted to earth. The copter followed, weaving and bucking like a wounded bird, finally falling into the reflecting pool and bursting into flame.

• CHAPTER THIRTY-SEVEN

OVER THIRTY THOUSAND PEOPLE stood and watched the small helicopter crash into the side of the Washington Monument. Millions more saw it on television. The event was bloody and horrible. The only question was, Who was in the helicopter? One of the network anchormen announced that it seemed to be Vandermeer and the President. But no word had come from inside the White House, and nobody on the outside knew.

Colonel Hanes, feeling that he should do something, switched on the giant loudspeaker mounted above the 155-millimeter gun on his tank. "All Marines in this immediate area," he yelled, "will lay down their arms and come forward with their hands above their heads. This is a direct order."

A Marine corporal, leaning behind the statue of Rochambeau in Lafayette Square, took casual aim with his rifle and plinked two harmless rounds off the tank. Colonel Hanes immediately dropped down into the tank and slammed the hatch shut. A few seconds later the air was full of small-arms fire.

Within minutes the firing spread, completely surrounding the White House and sending the television camera

349

crews scurrying for cover. Two Marines and three soldiers were killed in the first exchange, and somehow the nose was clipped off the statue of General Sherman in Treasury Place.

The sound of a helicopter once again came from overhead, and the firing lessened while both sides craned their necks to see who was coming in. As the machine landed in the middle of Pennsylvania Avenue, the MacPherson News Syndicate logo could be made out on the door.

Two television cameramen raced out, oblivious to the continuing gunfire, to get close-ups of it as it came down. Ian Faulkes must have primed them for this, Adams thought.

An Army officer jumped out of the helicopter, brass gleaming, ribbons sparkling, and an unlit cigar clamped firmly between his teeth. As he strode away from the copter, it lifted off and moved to the far side of Lafayette Square.

Slowly and deliberately the officer walked forward, surrounded and protected by the innate majesty and assurance of command. He marched steadily down the clear space between the opposing forces.

Yea, though I walk through the valley of the shadow of death, Adams intoned as he watched Tank MacGregor's progress, *I shall fear no evil.* Then he held his breath as one lone rifle barked and one bullet splatted off the pavement a yard in front of MacGregor.

Tank paused and glared in the direction of the shot, and then, firmly, he continued his walk.

When he was directly in front of the White House, MacGregor stopped and looked around. He took in the surrounding scene with an unhurried sweep of his gaze. The firing had stopped as everyone watched this American legend—this hero—and tried to figure out what he was going to do.

MacGregor pointed to the vehicle nearest to him, Colonel

Hanes's command tank, and gestured like a man calling his dog. Nothing happened. He gestured again.

The M-60 rumbled into life and slowly came forward until it reached MacGregor, who climbed up onto the turret and pounded on the hatch. After a few seconds it opened and Colonel Hanes stuck out his head cautiously. MacGregor grabbed the loudspeaker microphone from him and stood up on top of the turret, staring around him.

"Can you all see me?" he demanded. "I am General of the Army Hiram MacGregor," he spoke slowly and distinctly. "And I hereby take command of all United States military units within the sound of my voice!" The words echoed off the buildings and rolled on down the avenues. "All officers will report to me, here, immediately! Let me repeat that. *All* military officers, of whatever service, within the sound of my voice, will report to me immediately. All enlisted men, of whatever service, will immediately ground their weapons and stay in place."

The troops on both sides stared at him. Nobody moved.

"I want this clearly understood," MacGregor said, enunciating carefully, "if any of you fire any of those weapons you're waving around I personally will come over and bend it over your head. Put them down *now!* All commissioned officers report here *now!* This has gone far enough."

The television cameramen had gathered on Pennsylvania Avenue in front of MacGregor while he was talking, and now seven cameras were aimed up at him, catching the expression on his face as he chewed savagely on his cigar. Army and Marine officers were climbing out of their tanks and trenches and heading toward him from all around the disputed area. The cameras slowly panned around to catch the moment, and then turned back to MacGregor.

Tank looked down at the cameras and stared into the soul of America. "It is over," he said, discarding the loud-

351

speaker mike. "Whatever has been happening here is over."

"Will you speak to the American people now, General?" the reporter asked. "They're watching and listening."

MacGregor looked around at the officers who were gathered around the tank. "Let me speak to my officers now," he said. "Please."

"But the American people?"

"I shall speak to the people this evening," MacGregor said. "For now, just let me say that the time of hate and division is over. We shall return to a constitutional government with all deliberate speed. As a first step in achieving this," he added, "let us immediately open the gates to all the internment camps. Thousands of Americans are, right now, locked up behind barbed-wire fences without due process. They have been deprived of their basic civil rights. I hereby order all camp commanders to open their gates."

"By what authority do you order this, General?" the reporter asked.

MacGregor glared at him. "Justice," he said. "And the Constitution of the United States—the final authority. Now go away, son, and let me do my job."

All around, soldiers and Marines, their guns grounded, were standing up, stretching, and looking relieved. Tank MacGregor had arrived. Tank could be trusted. It was in his hands now.

• CHAPTER THIRTY-EIGHT

AARON ADAMS put the phone down and turned to stare across the room to where Kit and Miriam were sitting on the ancient leather couch. Kit's left arm itched where the bullet had torn through, but he couldn't get under the plastic splint and bandage contraption to scratch it, so he kept twisting around uncomfortably on his side of the couch.

"Obie is dead," Adams said.

"Obie?" Kit repeated.

"That's right," Adams said. "Congressman Obediah Porfritt. He died on the operating table about an hour ago. He caught a bullet 'resisting arrest.' They didn't think it was serious, but he died on the table. Son of a bitch!"

"I'm sorry," Kit said.

"So am I," Adams said. "Are you sure you're up to wandering around with that arm?"

"I'm not wandering around," Kit said. "I'm sitting quietly on my corner of the couch waiting for ten o'clock."

Adams looked at his watch. "In fifteen minutes," he said, "General MacGregor will address the nation, and we shall discover our fates."

"Our fates?" Miriam looked surprised. "What do you think he's going to say?"

"I have no idea what Tank will say, but he can't ignore what happened today. And he certainly can't ignore those who made it happen."

"Us," Kit said.

"Us. Indeed."

The front-door chime sounded the opening bars of "Yankee Doodle," and then they heard the solid footsteps of George on his way to open the door. Kit had a momentary frightening vision of who George might find outside, and he put his good arm around Miriam and held her close until Ian Faulkes came through the study door and waved at them.

"Greetings, my friends," he said. "Thought I'd drop in, if you don't mind."

"Hello, Ian," Adams said. "Take a chair. I thought you'd be where the action is."

"I am where the action is when I'm with you," Faulkes said. "Which may sound like the first line of a love ballad, but nonetheless—"

"We're just sitting here quietly, waiting for the general to tell us what's happening next," Adams said. "Why aren't you by MacGregor's side, waiting to ask him a few selected incisive and pertinent questions after his speech?"

"I've already filed my story," Faulkes said, "having taken advantage of my providential closeness to the great man earlier. I can learn nothing more than we shall all see on the telly shortly, so I've come to watch the proceedings with you, and perhaps catch the expression on your faces when Tank throws you to the wolves."

"You think that's going to happen?" Adams asked.

Faulkes shrugged. "It wouldn't be entirely without precedent," he said. "And what are friends for, but to provide me with good copy?"

"I've often asked myself that very question," Adams said. He reached over and turned on his television set. A bearded news commentator appeared on the screen. Then the scene switched to tape, and they saw Vandermeer pilot the helicopter into the side of the Washington Monument in slow motion.

As they watched silently, a figure seemed to float out the door of the craft and fall slowly away from it. Then, with the magic of television, the figure froze in midair and the camera closed in on it until the falling body filled the screen. It was St. Yves. Kit thought he could see a look of rage on St. Yves' face as he fell to his death.

The program cut away to the commentator for a moment, and then switched again. The scene was now the exterior of the main gate of an internment camp. Kit thought it was Camp Washington Irving, the one he had visited, but he couldn't be sure. The camp gates were wide open, and a steady stream of internees were making their way down the asphalt road to freedom. One full bus pulled out as they watched, and an empty one swung in to fill up. But most of the prisoners didn't wait for the buses; they were walking. Some were crying.

"That," Adams said, "is a good sign."

"That's a beautiful sight," Miriam said. "I thought that was one of the reasons we did all this."

"Yes," Adams agreed. "But the fact that it's actually happening shows that they're taking Tank seriously where it counts. The mantle of authority is a delicate thing, but Tank seems to have assumed it successfully."

"What do you suppose he's going to do about the President?" Kit asked.

Adams eyed Kit sourly. "That son of a bitch had better live," he said. "Nobody's ever going to believe that Vandermeer shot him. I'm not sure I believe it myself."

"The doctor at Bethesda said the bullet penetrated a lung, but the operation was clean and he's in no real danger," Kit said. "He'll be in the hospital a few weeks at most."

355

"If I were Tank," Adams said, "I'd keep him in the hospital until the impeachment starts. Nice and safe and out of the way. I'm glad I'm not."

The picture on the screen switched to an overview of the blocked streets of Washington as they had been a few hours earlier. "It will take a strong hand to hold this country together until we can hold elections," Adams said. "Tank has that. But did you ever consider that a hand strong enough to do that is also strong enough to take over the elections if he so chooses?"

"I thought you trusted MacGregor," Kit said. "You think he could be tempted?"

"I think *I* could be tempted," Adams said. "The most powerful temptation in the world: the knowledge that you know what is good for the people, that you alone can bring it all about in the way that you know is best."

Miriam wrapped her arms around her knees. "Here he comes," she said. "We'll know in a minute."

Tank MacGregor came on the screen. He was seated behind a large desk with the Great Seal of the United States on the wall behind him. Adams turned up the volume.

"My fellow Americans—" MacGregor said. He paused and looked directly into the camera. "My fellow Americans," he repeated, "this talk will be very brief. We have just been through a grave national trauma. But one which has shown the strength of our nation and our constitution. I have three announcements to make.

"The first is that a special election will be held ninety days from today to elect a new president and a full House of Representatives, as well as to replace those senators whose terms have expired.

"The second is that the man who, until today, was occupying the White House as President, will be brought to trial in a federal court for various crimes against the United States and against many of its citizens. I have been informed by the Justice Department that impeachment proceedings are redundant, as he was illegally holding office and is now removed.

"The third is that I will not be a candidate for the presidency of the United States under any conditions whatsoever.

"Thank you."

Adams looked at Faulkes and broke into a broad smile. Kit and Miriam looked at each other. Kit grinned and squeezed her so hard with his good arm that it hurt her shoulder, but she didn't wince. She just took his head in both hands and kissed him harder than she had ever done before.

CRITIC'S CHOICE
Espionage and Suspense Thrillers

THE FORTRESS AT ONE DALLAS CENTER
by Ron Lawrence $3.50
FATAL MEMORY by Bruce Forester $3.95
A FIST FULL OF EGO by Bruce Topol $3.75
THE PALACE OF ENCHANTMENTS
by Hurd & Lamport $3.95
THE PANAMA PARADOX by Michael Wolfe $3.50
THE CHINESE FIRE DRILL by Michael Wolfe $2.95
THE VON KESSEL DOSSIER by Leon LeGrande $3.95
CARTER'S CASTLE by Wilbur Wright $3.95
DANGEROUS GAMES by Louis Schreiber $3.95
SHADOW CABINET by W.T. Tyler $3.95
DOUBLE TAKE by Gregory Dowling $2.95
STRYKER'S KINGDOM by W.A. Harbinson $3.95
THE HAWTHORN CONSPIRACY by Stephen Hesla $3.95
THE CORSICAN by Bill Ballinger $3.95
AMBLER by Fred Halliday $3.50
BLUE FLAME by Joseph Gilmore $3.75
THE DEVIL'S VOYAGE by Jack Chalker $3.75

Please send your check or money order (no cash) to:

Critic's Choice Paperbacks
31 East 28th Street
New York, N. Y. 10016

Please include $1.00 for the first book and 50¢ for each additional book to cover the cost of postage and handling.

Name _____

Street Address _____

City _____ State _____ Zip Code _____

Write for a free catalog at the above address.